Together for the first time in this delightful[...] these beloved holiday stories are from four bestse[...] and award-winning Regency authors.

Sandra Heath is the ever-popular author of numerous Regencies, historical romances, novellas, and short stories. Among other honors, she has won the *Romantic Times* Reviewers' Choice Awards for Best Regency Author and for Best Regency Romance. She lives in Gloucester, England, and can be contacted at sandraheath@blueyonder.co.uk.

Emma Jensen has won numerous awards, including two RITAs and the *Romantic Times* Reviewers' Choice Award. She grew up in San Francisco and is a graduate of the University of Pennsylvania, with degrees in nineteenth-century literature, sociology, and public policy.

Carla Kelly has written more than a dozen novels and won two RITAs for Best Regency. She lives in Valley City, North Dakota, where she has done historical research for the North Dakota State Historical Society, writes for various publications, edits the Confluence News, and formerly worked for the National Park Service on the North Dakota–Montana border.

Amanda McCabe lives in Oklahoma with two very spoiled cats. When not reading or writing romances, she loves doing needlework, taking dancing lessons, and digging through antiques stores. A RITA and *Romantic Times* Award finalist and a Booksellers Best Award winner, she loves to hear from her readers via e-mail at Amccabe7551@yahoo.com.

A
Homespun Regency
Christmas

FOUR STORIES BY

Carla Kelly

Emma Jensen

Sandra Heath

Amanda McCabe

A SIGNET BOOK

SIGNET
Published by New American Library, a division of
Penguin Group (USA) Inc., 375 Hudson Street,
New York, New York 10014, USA
Penguin Group (Canada), 90 Eglinton Avenue East, Suite 700, Toronto,
Ontario M4P 2Y3, Canada (a division of Pearson Penguin Canada Inc.)
Penguin Books Ltd., 80 Strand, London WC2R 0RL, England
Penguin Ireland, 25 St. Stephen's Green, Dublin 2,
Ireland (a division of Penguin Books Ltd.)
Penguin Group (Australia), 250 Camberwell Road, Camberwell, Victoria 3124,
Australia (a division of Pearson Australia Group Pty. Ltd.)
Penguin Books India Pvt. Ltd., 11 Community Centre, Panchsheel Park,
New Delhi - 110 017, India
Penguin Group (NZ), 67 Apollo Drive, Rosedale, North Shore 0632,
New Zealand (a division of Pearson New Zealand Ltd.)
Penguin Books (South Africa) (Pty.) Ltd., 24 Sturdee Avenue,
Rosebank, Johannesburg 2196, South Africa

Penguin Books Ltd., Registered Offices:
80 Strand, London WC2R 0RL, England

First published by Signet, an imprint of New American Library,
a division of Penguin Group (USA) Inc.

First Printing, October 2008
10 9 8 7 6 5 4 3 2 1

CONTENTS

An Object of Charity

Carla Kelly

Captain Michael Lynch never made a practice of leaning on the quarterdeck railing of the *Admirable,* but it hardly seemed to matter now. The crew— what was left of them—eyed him from a respectful distance, but he knew with a lift to his trounced-upon heart, that not one of them would give less than his utmost, even as he had.

His glance shifted to that spot on the deck that had glared so brightly only last month with the blood of David Partlow, his first mate. One of his crew, when not patching oakum here and there to keep the *Admirable* afloat, or manning the pumps, had scrubbed that spot white again until all trace was gone. Still he stared at the spot, because now it was whiter than the rest of the deck.

Damn the luck, he thought again. Damn the French who had sailed to meet the *Admirable* and other frigates of the blockade fleet, gun ports open and blazing a challenge rare in them, but brought about by an unexpected shift in the wind. Most of all, damn the luck that fired the *Celerity,* next frigate, and sent her lurching out of control into the *Admirable.*

And maybe even damn Partlow for rushing to the rail with a grappling hook just in time for the *Celerity*'s deck carronade, heated by the flames, to burst all over him. Another *Celerity* gun belched fire then, and another, point blank at his own beautiful *Admirable,* one ball carrying off his sailing master, and the other shat-

3

tering the mainmast at its juncture with the deck. "And they call that friendly fire," he murmured, leaning on the railing still as the *Admirable* inched past able ships in Portsmouth harbor.

There would be an inquiry, a matter of course when one ship had nearly destroyed another. He knew the Lords of the Admiralty would listen to all the testimony and exonerate him, but this time there would be no *Admirable* to return to. It would be in dry dock for three months at least, and he was sentenced to the shore on half pay. The lords might offer him another ship, but he didn't want any ship but the *Admirable*.

Lynch was mindful of the wind roaring from the north, wavering a point or two and then settling into a steady blow. He couldn't fathom three months without the wind in his face, even this raw December wind.

At some exclamation of dismay from one of the crew, he looked up to see the dry dock dead ahead. Oh, Lord, he thought, I can't stand it. He didn't mind the half pay. Even now as he leaned so melancholy on the rail, his prize money from years and years of capture and salvage was compounding itself on 'Change. If he chose, he could retire to a country estate and live in comfort on the interest alone; his wants were few.

The scow towing his ship backed its sails and slowed as it approached the dry dock. In another minute a launch nestled itself alongside. His bosun, arm in a sling but defying anyone but himself to do this duty, stood ready to pipe him off the *Admirable*. His trunk, hat case, and parcel of books were already being transferred to the launch. The bosun even forgot himself enough to lower the pipe and suggest that it was "better to leave now, sor."

"Damn your impertinence, Mays!" he growled in protest. "It's not really like leaving a grave before the dirt is piled on, now, is it?"

But it was. He could see the sympathy in his bosun's

eyes, and all the understandings they had shared through the years without actually calling attention to them.

"You'll be back, Captain," the bosun said, as if to nudge him along. "The *Admirable* will be as good as new."

And maybe it will be a young man's ship then as it once was mine, he thought, stirring himself from the rail. I have conned the *Admirable* for fifteen years, from the India Wars to Boney's Milan and Berlin Decrees that blockade Europe. I am not above thirty-six, but I feel sixty, at least, and an infirm sixty at that. With a nod to his bosun, he allowed himself to be piped over the side.

Determined not to look back at the wounded *Admirable,* he followed his few belongings to Mrs. Brattle's rooming house, where he always stayed between voyages. He handed a coin to the one-armed tar who earned his daily mattress and sausages by trundling goods about town in his rented cart. It was almost Christmas, so he added another coin, enough to give the man a day off, but not enough to embarrass him; he knew these old sailors.

And there was Mrs. Brattle, welcoming him as always. He could see the sympathy in her eyes—amazing how fast bad news circulated around Portsmouth. He dared her to say anything, and to his relief, she did not, beyond the communication that his extra trunk was stowed in the storeroom and he could have his usual quarters.

"Do you know how long you will be staying this time, sir?" she asked, motioning to the 'tween-stairs maid behind them to lay a fire.

He could have told her three months, until the *Admirable* was refitted, but he didn't. "I'm not entirely sure, Mrs. Brattle," he heard himself saying, for some unaccountable reason.

She stood where she was, watching the maid with a

critical but not unkindly eye. When the girl finished, she nodded her approval and looked at him. "It'll be stew then, Captain," she said as she handed him his key.

He didn't want stew; he didn't want anything but to lie down and turn his face to the wall. He hadn't cried since India, so it didn't enter his mind, but he was amazed at his own discomposure. "Fine, Mrs. Brattle," he told her. He supposed he would have to eat so she would not fret.

He knew the rooms well, the sitting room large enough for sofa, chairs, and table, the walls decorated here and there with improving samplers done by Mrs. Brattle's dutiful daughters, all of them now long-married. His eyes always went first to the popular "England expects every man to do his duty," that since Trafalgar had sprouted on more walls than he cared to think about. I have done my duty, he told himself.

He stared a long while at the stew, delivered steaming hot an hour later and accompanied by brown bread and tea sugared the way he liked it. Through the years and various changes in his rank, he had thought of seeking more exalted lodgings, but the fact was, he did not take much notice of his surroundings on land. Nor did he wish to abandon a place where the landlady knew how he liked his tea.

Even to placate Mrs. Brattle, he could not eat that evening. He was prepared for a fight when she returned for his tray, but he must have looked forbidding enough, or tired enough, so that she made no more comment than that she hoped he would sleep better than he ate. Personally, he did not hold out much confidence for her wish; he never slept well.

The level of his exhaustion must have been higher than he thought, because he slept finally as the day came. He had a vague recollection of Mrs. Brattle in his room, and then silence. He woke at noon with a fuzzy brain. Breakfast, and then a rambling walk in a direction that did not include the dry dock, cleared his head. He had the city to himself, possibly because Portsmouth did not lend itself much to touring visitors, but more likely because it was raining. He didn't care; it suited his mood.

When he came back to his lodgings, he felt better, and in a frame of mind to apologize to Mrs. Brattle for his mopes. He looked in the public sitting room and decided the matter would keep. She appeared to be engaged in earnest conversation with a boy and girl who looked even more travel weary than he had yesterday.

He thought they must be Scots. The girl—no, a second look suggested a young woman somewhere in her twenties rather than a girl—wore a plaid muffler draped around her head and neck over her traveling cloak. He listened to the soft murmur of her voice with its lilt and burr, not because he was prone to eavesdropping, but because he liked the cadence of Scottish conversation, and its inevitable reminder of his first mate.

As he watched, the boy moved closer to the woman, and she grasped his shoulder in a protective gesture. The boy's arm went around her waist and she held it there with her other hand. The intimacy of the gesture rendered him oddly uncomfortable, as though he intruded. This is silly, he scolded himself; I am in a public parlor in a lodging house.

Never mind, he thought, and went upstairs. He added coal to the fire, and put on his slippers, prepared for a late afternoon of reading the *Navy Chronicle* and dozing. Some of his fellow officers were getting up a whist table at the Spithead, and he would join them there after dinner.

He had read through the promotions list and started on the treatise debating the merits of the newest canister casing when Mrs. Brattle knocked on his door. She had a way of knocking and clearing her throat at the

same time that made her entrances obvious. "Come,
Mrs. Brattle," he said, laying aside the *Chronicle*
which was, he confessed, starting to bore him.

When she opened the door, he could see others
behind her, but she closed the door upon them and
hurried to his chair. "Sir, it is the saddest thing," she
began, her voice low with emotion. "The niece and
nephew of poor Mr. Partlow have come all the way
from Fort William in the Highlands to find him! The
harbormaster directed them here to you."

"Have you told them?" he asked quietly, as he rose.

She shook her head. "Oh, sir, I know you're far
better at that than I ever would be. I mean, haven't
you written letters to lots of sailors' families, sir?"

"Indeed, Mrs. Brattle. I am something of an expert
on the matter," he said, regretting the irony in his
voice, but knowing his landlady well enough to be sure
that she would not notice it. *What I do not relish are
these face-to-face interviews*, he thought, *especially
my Number One's relatives, curse the luck.*

"May I show them in, or should I send them back
to the harbormaster?" she asked, then leaned closer
and allowed herself the liberty of adding that while
they were genteel, they were Scots. "Foreigners," she
explained, noticing the mystified look that he knew
was on his face.

He knew that before she said it. David Partlow had
come from generations of hard-working Highlanders,
and he never minded admitting it. "Sturdy folk," he
had said once. "The best I know."

"Show them in, Mrs. Brattle," he said. She opened
the door and ushered in the two travelers, then shut
the door quickly behind her. He turned to his guests
and nodded. "I am Captain Lynch of the *Admirable*,"
he said.

The young woman dropped a graceful curtsey,
which had the odd effect of making him feel old. He

did not want to feel old, he decided, as he looked at her.

She held out her hand to him and he was rewarded with a firm handshake. "I am Sally Partlow, and this is my brother Thomas," she said.

"May I take your cloak?" he asked, not so much remembering his manners with women, because he had none, but eager to see what shape she possessed. I have been too long at sea, he thought, mildly amused with himself.

Silently, her eyes troubled, she unwound the long plaid shawl and pulled it from her hair. He had thought her hair was ordinary brown like his, but it was the deepest, darkest red he had ever seen, beautiful hair, worn prettily in a bun at the nape of her neck.

He indicated the chair he had vacated, and she sat down. "It is bad news, isn't it?" she asked without any preamble. "When we asked the harbormaster, he whispered to someone and gave me directions to this place, and the woman downstairs whispered with you. Tell me direct."

"Your uncle is dead," he told her, the bald words yanked right out of his mouth by her forthrightness. "We had a terrible accident on the blockade. He was killed, and my ship nearly destroyed."

She winced and briefly narrowed her eyes at his words, but she returned his gaze with no loss of composure, rather like a woman used to bad news.

"Your uncle didn't suffer," he added quickly, struck by the lameness of his words as soon as he spoke them. He was rewarded with more of the same measured regard.

"Do you write that to all the kin of your dead?" she asked, not accusing him, but more out of curiosity, or so it seemed to him. "All the kin of your dead," he thought, struck by the aptness of the phrase, and the grand way it rolled off her Scottish tongue.

"I suppose I do write it," he said, after a moment's thought. "In David's case, I believe it is true." He hesitated, then plunged ahead, encouraged by her level gaze. "He was attempting to push off the *Admirable* with a grappling hook and a carronade exploded directly in front of him. He . . . he couldn't have known what hit him."

To his surprise, Sally Partlow leaned forward and quickly touched his hand. She knows what he meant to me, he thought, grateful for her concern.

"I'm sorry for you," she said. "Uncle Partlow mentioned you often in his letters."

"He did?" It had never before occurred to him that he could be a subject in anyone's letters, or even that anyone on the planet thought him memorable.

"Certainly, sir," she replied. "He often said what a fair-minded commander you were, and how your crew—and he included himself—would follow you anywhere."

These must be sentiments that men do not confide in each other, he decided, as he listened to her. Of course, he had wondered why the same crew remained in his service year after year, but he had always put it down to their own fondness for the *Admirable*. Could it be there was more? The matter had never crossed his mind before.

"You are all kindness, Miss Partlow," he managed to say, but not without embarrassment. "I'm sorry to give you this news—and here you must have thought to bring him Christmas greetings and perhaps take him home with you."

The brother and sister looked at each other. "It is rather more than that, Captain," Thomas Partlow said.

"Oh, Tom, let us not concern him," Sally said. "We should leave now."

"What, Thomas?" he asked the young boy. "David Partlow will always be my concern."

"Uncle Partlow was named our guardian several years ago," he said.

"I do remember that, Thomas," Lynch said. "He showed me the letter. Something about in the event of your father's death, I believe. Ah yes, we were blockading the quadrant around La Nazaire then, same as now."

"Sir, our father died two weeks ago," Thomas explained. "Almost with his last breath, he told us that Uncle Partlow would look after us."

The room seemed to fill up with the silence. He could tell that Miss Partlow was embarrassed. He frowned. These were his lodgings; perhaps the Partlows expected him to speak first.

"I fear you are greatly disappointed," he said, at a loss. "I am sorry for your loss, and sorry that you must return to Scotland both empty-handed and bereft."

Sally Partlow stood up and extended her hand to him, while her brother retrieved her cloak and shawl from the end of the sofa. "We trust we did not take up too much of your time at this busy season," she said. "Come, Thomas." She curtseyed again and he bowed and opened the door for her. She hesitated a moment. "Sir, we are quite unfamiliar with Portsmouth. Do you know . . ."

". . . of a good hotel? I can recommend the Spithead on the High."

The Partlows looked at each other and smiled. "Oh, no!" she said, "nothing that fine. I had in mind an employment agency."

He shook his head. "I couldn't tell you. Never needed one." Did they want to hire a maid? he wondered. "Thanks to Boney, I've always had plenty of employment." He bade them good day and the best of the season, and retreated behind his paper again as Miss Partlow quietly shut the door.

Two hours later, when Mrs. Brattle and the maid

were serving his supper, he understood the enormity of his error. Mrs. Brattle had laid the table and set a generous slice of sirloin before him when she paused. "Do you know, Captain, I am uneasy about the Partlows. She asked me if I needed any help around the place."

Mystified, he shook his napkin into his lap. "That is odd. She asked me if I knew of an employment agency."

He sat a moment more in silence, staring down at the beef in front of him, brown and oozing pink juices. Shame turned him hot, and he put his napkin back on the table. "Mrs. Brattle, I think it entirely possible that the Partlows haven't a sixpence to scratch with."

She nodded, her eyes troubled. "She'll never find work here, so close to Christmas. Captain Lynch, Portsmouth may be my home, but it's not a place that I would advise a young woman to look for work."

He could only agree. With a speed that surprised him, considering how slowly he had dragged himself to the rooming house only yesterday, he soon found himself on the street, looking for the Partlows and hoping deep in his heart that their dead uncle would forgive his captain's stupidity. He stopped at the Spithead long enough to tell his brother officers that they would have to find another fourth to make up the whist table tonight, then began his excursion through town. It brought him no pleasure and he berated himself for not being more aware—or even aware at all— of the Partlows' difficulties. *Am I so dense?* he asked himself, and he knew the answer.

Christmas shoppers passed him, bearing packages wrapped in brown paper and twine. Sailors drunk and singing stumbled past. He thought he saw a press gang on the prowl, as well, and his blood chilled at the thought of Lieutenant Partlow's little nephew nabbed and hauled aboard a frigate to serve at the king's good pleasure. Granted he was young, but not too young to be a powder monkey. Oh God, not that, he thought, as he turned up his collar and hurried on, stopping to peer into restaurant kitchens over the protestations of proprietors and cooks.

He didn't even want to think about the brothels down on the waterfront where the women worked day and night on their backs when the fleet was in. She would never, he thought. Of course, who knew when they had even eaten last? He thought of the beef roast all for him and cursed himself again, his heart bleak.

When it was full dark and his cup of discouragement had long since run over, he spotted them on the fisherman's wharf, seated close together on a crate. Their arms were around each other and even as he realized how awful was their situation, he felt a tug of envy. There is not another soul in the world who would care if I dropped dead tomorrow, he thought, except possibly my landlady, and she's been half expecting such an event all these years of war.

He heard a sound to his left and saw, to his dismay, a press gang approaching, the ensign ready with his whistle, and the bosun with a cudgel, should Tom Partlow choose to resist impressment in the Royal Navy. As an ensign, he had done his own press gang duty, hating every minute of it and only getting through it by pretending that every hapless dockyard loiterer that he impressed was his brother.

"Hold on there," he called to the ensign, who was putting his whistle to his lips. "The boy's not for the fleet."

At his words, the Partlows turned around. Sally leaped down from the packing crate and stood between her brother and the press gang. Even in the gloom, he could see how white her face was, how fierce her eyes. There was something about the set of her jaw that told him she would never surrender Tom without a fight.

"Not this one," Lynch said, biting off each word.

He recognized the bosun from the *Formidable,* whose captain was even now playing whist at the Spithead.

To his irritation—he who was used to being obeyed—the young officer seemed not to regard him. "Stand aside," the man shouted to Sally Partlow.

"No," Sally said, and backed up.

Lynch put a firm hand on the ensign's arm. "No."

The ensign stared at him, then looked at his bosun, who stood with cudgel lowered. "Topkins, as you were!" he shouted.

The bosun shook his head. "Sorry, Captain Lynch!" he said. He turned to his ensign. "We made a mistake, sir."

The ensign was almost apoplectic with rage. He tried to grab Lynch by the front of his cloak, but in a moment's work, he was lying on the wharf, staring up.

"Touch me again, you pup, and I'll break you right down to able seaman. This boy is not your prey. Help him up, Topkins, and wipe that smile off your ugly phiz."

The bosun helped up his ensign, who flung off his assisting arm when he was on his feet, took a good look at Lynch, blanched, and stammered his apologies. "There's those in the *Formidable*'s fo'castle who'd have paid to see that, Captain Lynch," the bosun whispered. "Happy Christmas!"

Lynch stood where he was between the Partlows and the press gang until the wharf was deserted again. "There now," he said, more to himself than them. He turned around to see Sally still standing in front of her brother, shielding him. "They won't return, Miss Partlow, but there may be others. You need to get yourselves off the streets."

She shook her head, and he could see for the first time how really young she was. Her composure had deserted her and he was embarrassed to have to witness a proud woman pawn her pride in front of practically a stranger. He was at her side in a moment. "Will you forgive me for my misunderstanding of your situation?" he asked in a low voice, even though there was no one else around except Tom, who had tears on his face. Without a word, Lynch gave him his handkerchief. "You're safe now, lad," he said, then looked at the boy's sister again. "I do apologize, Miss Partlow."

"You didn't know because I didn't say anything," she told him, the words dragged out of her by pincers. "No need to apologize."

"Perhaps not," he agreed, "but I should have been beforehand enough not to have needed your situation spelled out for me."

Tom handed back the handkerchief, and he gave it to the boy's sister. "But why were you sitting here on the dock?"

She dabbed at her eyes then pointed to a faded sign reading FISH FOR SALE. "We thought perhaps in the morning we could find occupation," she told him.

"So you were prepared to wait here all night?" he asked, trying to keep the shock from his voice, but failing, which only increased the young woman's own embarrassment. "My God, have you no funds at all? When did you last eat?"

She looked away, biting her upper lip to keep the tears back, he was sure, and his insides writhed. "Never mind that," he said briskly. "Come back with me now and we can at least remedy one problem with a meal." When she still hesitated, he picked up her valise and motioned to Tom. "Smartly now," he ordered, not looking over his shoulder, but praying from somewhere inside him that never prayed, that the Partlows would follow.

The walk from the end of the dock to the street seemed the longest of his life, especially when he heard no footsteps behind him. He could have sunk to the earth in gratitude when he finally heard them, the boy's quicker steps first, and then his sister's steps, accompanied by the womanly rustle of skirt and cloak.

His lodgings were blessedly warm. Mrs. Brattle was watching for him from the front window, which filled him with some relief. He knew he needed an ally in such a respectable female as his landlady. Upstairs in his lodgings she had cleared away his uneaten dinner, but it was replaced in short order by the entire roast of sirloin this time, potatoes, popovers that she knew he liked, and pounds of gravy.

Without even a glance at his sister, Tom Partlow sat down and was soon deeply involved in dinner. Mrs. Brattle watched. "Now when did the little boy eat last?" she asked in round tones.

Sally blushed. "I . . . I think it was the day before yesterday," she admitted, not looking at either of them.

Mrs. Brattle let out a sigh of exasperation, and prodded Sally Partlow closer to the table. "Then it has probably been another day beyond that for you, missy, if you are like most women. Fed *him* the last meal, didn't you?"

Sally nodded. "Everything we owned was sold for debt. I thought we would have enough for coach fare and food, and we almost did." Her voice was so low that Lynch could hardly hear her.

Bless Mrs. Brattle again, he decided. His landlady gave Sally a quick squeeze around the waist. "You *almost* did, dearie!" she declared, turning the young woman's nearly palpable anguish into a victory of sorts. "Why don't you sit yourself down—Captain, remember your manners and pull out her chair!—and have a go before your brother eats it all."

She sat without protest, and spread a napkin in her lap, tears escaping down her cheeks. Mrs. Brattle distracted herself by admonishing the maid to go for more potatoes, and hurry up about it, giving Sally a chance to draw herself together. The landlady frowned at Lynch until he tore his gaze from the lovely woman struggling with pride and took his own seat next to Tom. He astounded himself by keeping up what seemed to him like a veritable avalanche of inconsequential chatter with the boy and removed all attention from his sister until out of the corner of his eye, he saw her eating.

Having eaten, Tom Partlow struggled valiantly to stay awake while his sister finished. He left the table for the sofa, and in a minute was breathing quietly and evenly. Sally set down her fork and Lynch wanted to put it back in her hand, but he did nothing, only watched her as she watched her brother. " 'Tis hard to sleep on a mail coach," she said in a low voice.

He didn't know why it should matter so much to him, but he felt only unspeakable relief when she picked up her fork again. She ate all that was before her like a dutiful child, but shook her head at a second helping of anything. Weariness had stamped itself upon all the lines of her body. She seemed to droop before his eyes, and he didn't know what to do for her.

Mrs. Brattle came to his aid again. After the maid had taken the dishes down the stairs in a tub, his landlady sat next to Sally Partlow and took her by the hand. "Dearie, I have an extra room downstairs and you're welcome to it tonight," she said. "Tom will be fine right here on the captain's sofa. Come along now."

Sally Partlow looked at him, distress on her face now, along with exhaustion. "We didn't mean to be so much trouble," she said. "Truly we didn't."

She was pleading with him, and it pained him that he could offer her so little comfort. "I know you didn't, Miss Partlow," he assured her, even as Mrs. Brattle helped her to her feet. "Things happen, don't they?"

It sounded so lame, but she nodded, grateful, apparently, for his ha'penny wisdom. "Surely I will think of something in the morning," she told him, and managed a smile. "I'm not usually at my wit's end."

"I don't imagine you are," he commented, intrigued by the way she seemed to dig deep within herself, even through her own weariness. It was a trait he had often admired in her uncle. "This will pass, too. If you have no objections, I'll think on the matter, myself. And don't look so wary! Call it the Christmas present I cannot give your uncle."

After she left, he removed Thomas's shoes, and covered the sleeping boy with a blanket, wondering all the while how someone could sleep so soundly. He sat by the boy, asking himself what on earth David Partlow would have done with a niece and nephew thrust upon him. Tom could be bought a midshipman's berth if there was money enough, but Sally? A husband was the obvious solution, but it would be difficult to procure one without a dowry.

He spent a long time staring into his shaving mirror the next morning. His Mediterranean tan had faded to a sallow color, and nothing that he knew, short of the guillotine, would have any effect on his premature wrinkles, caused by years of squinting at sun and sails and facing into the wind. And why should I ever worry, he considered, as he scraped away at his face.

He had waked early as usual, always wondering if he had slept at all, and moved quietly about his room. When he came into his sitting room, Tom Partlow was still asleep. Lynch eased into a chair, and gave himself over to the Partlows' dilemma. He knew she could not afford to purchase a berth for Tom, and oddly, that was a relief to him. *Life at sea is no life, laddie*, he thought, as he watched the boy. *After all, you might end up like me, a man of a certain age with no more possessions than would fit in two smallish trunks, and not a soul who cares whether I live or die.*

But I did have a mother once, he reminded himself, so I did. The idea hit him then, stuck, and grew. By the time Tom woke, and Sally Partlow knocked on the door and opened it for Mrs. Brattle and breakfast, he had a plan. Like some he had fallen back upon during years of toil at sea, it had holes a-plenty and would never stand up to much scrutiny, but it was a beginning.

"Miss Partlow," he announced over bacon and eggs, "I am taking you and Tom home to my mother's house for Christmas."

On his words, Mrs. Brattle performed an interesting juggling act with a teapot, recovering herself just before she dumped the contents all over the carpet. She stared at him, her eyes big in her face.

"We couldn't possibly intrude on your holiday like that," Sally Partlow said quietly, objecting as he had no doubt that she would.

Here I go, he thought. Why does this feel more dangerous than sailing close to a lee shore? "Miss Partlow, it is not in the nature of a suggestion. I have decided to visit my mother in Lincolnshire and would no more think of leaving you to the mercies of Portsmouth than, than . . . writing a letter of admiration to Napoleon, thanking him for keeping me employed for all these years!"

She opened her mouth to protest, but he trod on inexorably and felt himself on the firmer deck of command. "If you feel a burning desire to argue, I would not recommend it. I suspect that your uncle has funds on 'Change. Once the probate is done—and I will see that it is going forward—you should have funds to repay me, even with interest. Until that moment, I won't hear of anything else."

He returned to his eggs with what he hoped was the semblance of serenity. Miss Partlow blinked, favored him with a steady gaze, and then directed her

attention to the egg before her. "Captain Lynch, I
suppose we will be happy to accompany you to . . .
where was it? Lincolnshire?" she murmured.

"Lincolnshire," he said firmly. "Yes, indeed. Pass
the bacon, would you please?"

They finished breakfast in silence. He knew that
Mrs. Brattle was almost leaping about in her eagerness to have a word in private with him, so he directed Tom and Sally to make themselves useful by
taking the dishes belowstairs to the scullery. To his
amusement, the Partlows seemed subdued by his
plain-speaking, a natural product of years of nautical
command.

The door had scarcely closed behind them when
Mrs. Brattle began. "I never knew you had a mother,
Captain Lynch," she declared.

He looked at her in mock horror. "Mrs. B, everyone
has a mother. How, pray, do you think I got on the
planet?"

His landlady was not about to be vanquished by his
idle wit. "Captain, I am certain there are those of your
crew who think you were born fully grown and stalk-
ing a quarterdeck! I am not numbered among them.
I am not to be bamboozled. Captain, is this a good
idea?"

"I don't know," he was honest enough to admit.
"They have nowhere to go, and I have not visited my
mother in twenty-two years."

She gasped again and sat down. "You would take
two perfect strangers to visit a lady you have not seen
in twenty-two *years*? Captain . . ." She shook her
head. "Only last week I was saying to my daughter
that you are a most sensible, steady, and level-headed
boarder, and wasn't I the lucky woman!"

"Yes?" he asked, intrigued again that he would
come to anyone's notice. "Perhaps it is time for a
change."

"It's been so long, sir," Mrs. Brattle reminded him. "Twenty-two years! Is your mother still alive?"

"She was five years ago," he told her. "I have kept in touch with the vicar, at least until he died five years past and my annual letter was returned."

She looked at him with real sympathy. "A family falling out, then?"

"Yes, Mrs. Brattle, a falling out."

And that is putting too kind a face upon it, he decided, as he sat down after noon in the post chaise with the Partlows, and they started off, with a call to the horses and a crack of the coachman's whip. Even after all these years—and there had been so many— he could not recall the occasion without a wince. It was more a declaration of war than a falling out.

"Captain?"

He looked up from the contemplation of his hands to see Sally Partlow watching him, a frown between her fine eyes. "What is it?" he asked, clipping off his words the way he always did aboard ship. As he regarded the dismay on her face, Michael regretted the sharpness of his inquiry.

"I . . . I didn't mean any disrespect," she stammered. "I just noticed that you looked . . . distressed," she concluded, her voice trailing off. She made herself small in her corner of the chaise and drew her cloak more tightly about her.

"I am quite in command, Miss Partlow," he replied, the brisk tone creeping in, even though he did not wish it this time.

She directed her attention to the scenery outside the window, which amounted to nothing more than dingy warehouses. "I didn't mean to intrude."

And she did not intrude again, through the whole long afternoon. He heard her sniff once or twice, and observed from the corner of his eye that she pressed her fingers against her nose several times; there were no tears that he could see. She put her arm about her brother with that same firm clasp he had noticed yesterday. When Thomas drifted to sleep, secure in his sister's embrace, she closed her eyes as well, with a sigh that went directly to his heart.

I have crushed her with my grudging generosity, he realized, and the revelation caused him such a pang that he longed to stride back and forth on his quarterdeck until he wore off his own irritation. But he was trapped in a post chaise, where he could only chafe and wonder how men on land ever survived such confinement. I suppose they slam doors, kick small objects, and snap at well-meaning people, as I have done, he decided, his cup of contrition full. He couldn't think of a remedy except apology or explanation, and neither suited him. Thank God my father forced me to sea years ago, was the thought that consoled him. He found himself counting the days when he could be done with this obligation to the Partlows, which had forced him into a visit home that he knew he did not want.

The time passed somehow, and Sally Partlow was obliging enough to keep her eyes closed. Whether she slept, he had no idea. Darkness came even earlier than usual, thanks to the snow that began to fall as they drove north toward Lincolnshire. Inwardly he cursed the snow, because he knew he could not force the coachman to drive on through the night and end this uncomfortable journey. When after an hour of the slowest movement he saw lights ahead, he knew the driver would stop and insist that they spend the night.

The village was Firch, the shire Cambridge, one south of his own, but there was no budging the coachman, who looked so cold and bleak that Michael felt a sprinkling of sympathy settle on the crust of his irritation. It was an unfamiliar emotion; he almost didn't recognize it.

"We have to stop here," the coachman said, as Michael opened the carriage door. "No remedy for it, Captain."

"Very well." He joined the man outside the carriage, grateful for his boat cloak and boots. He noticed the other carriages in the yard, and made the wry observation that Christmas continued to be a challenge for innkeepers. "Can you find a place for yourself?" he asked the coachman.

"Aye, sir. I'll bed in the stables with t'others." The man scratched his chin. "You're the one who might not be so lucky, beggin' yer pardon."

He feared the man was right. With no allowance for argument, Lynch told the Partlows to move along smartly and follow him inside. He started across the yard, leaning against the snow and wind, and wondering as he had before on the Portsmouth docks if they would follow him. He slowed his steps, hoping they would catch up with him, but they did not, hanging back, not wishing—he was sure—to trouble him beyond what they were already doing.

Hoping for the best, even as he suspected the worst, he asked the innkeep for two rooms and a parlor. "Sorry, Captain," the man said, properly cowed by what Lynch suspected was the height of his fore and aft hat and gold braid, if not the look on his face. The keep glanced beyond him, and he felt some relief that the Partlows must have followed him inside.

His relief was momentary. The keep asked him, all hesitation and apology, "Can ye share a room just this once with your son and daughter?"

"She's not my daughter," he said before he thought.

"Sorry, sir," the keep apologized. "Then you and your lady'll have to have"—he hesitated, as if trying to determine the relationship—"the boy on a pallet in your room, I'm thinking. There's no parlor to be had. Once you take that room, there won't be another for anyone else, it's that full we are."

"Very well," Lynch said, disconcerted right down

to his stockings, but determined not to make it worse by saying more. "It seems we have no choice."

"None, sir," the keep replied.

Lynch was too embarrassed to look at Sally Partlow so he ignored her and followed the keep's wife up the narrow stairs to a room at the back of the inn. Again he listened for the Partlows behind him, because he knew that only the weather outside was keeping them tethered to his side.

The keep's wife apologized for the size of the room, but he could find no fault with the warmth from the fireplace and the general air of comfort in small places that he was used to, from life aboard a man o' war. When the woman left the three of them, Sally removed the plaid about her head, shook the flakes into the fireplace, and put the shawl on the narrow cot.

"I was thinking I should take that berth," he told her. "You and Tom can have the bed."

"Nonsense. I am fully a foot shorter than you, sir," she said, and nothing more; he had the wisdom not to argue.

He knew he would dread dinner in the common parlor, but he did not, even though the setting was not one he was accustomed to. No matter how rough his life at sea, his infrequent sojourns on land, in whatever port of the world, had always meant private parlors and deference. He sat at the long table next to Sally, and followed her lead, passing the common dishes around to the next diner, and engaging, eventually, in small talk with the farmer to his left, an act that would have astounded his late first mate. He decided to enjoy conversation about crop prices, and even yielded far enough to tell a sea story.

He never embellished tales, and he did not now, so he was amazed that anyone would care to listen to his paltry account of life at sea. Maybe he was trying to explain himself to the Partlows; he didn't understand either, beyond a sudden need to offer some accounting of himself.

When dinner concluded, he could beat no retreat to a private parlor; before he could say something about sitting for a while in the public room, Sally told him that she was going to settle Tom upstairs in bed. "It was a long day, sir," she murmured, and he realized with a start that it was only the second thing she had said to him since his unkindness at noon.

I suppose it was a long day, he thought as he watched her escort her brother upstairs, her hand upon his back, her motion on the stairs so graceful that he felt like a voyeur. He went into the public room, content to prop his booted feet by the fender and enjoy the warmth of the fire. He even leaned back in the chair and called it a luxury.

He had thought that his hearing was going after years of cannonading, but he knew her steps on the stairs when she came down later. Before he could say anything—had anything occurred to him—she was out the door and into the snow. He debated a moment whether to follow—surely she would never leave her brother behind—then rose, pulled his cloak around him, and head down, went into the snow after her.

He could barely see her in the dark, but he watched her pause at the fence beyond the high road. The wind swirled the snow, but she raised her face to it, as though she hated super-heated rooms as much as he did. He walked across the road to stand beside her.

"I was not running away, Captain," she said without looking at him.

"I know that. You would never leave Tom."

"It is just that I do not like being an object of charity, sir," she said.

The candor of her words startled him, until he recalled her uncle, who never feared to tell him anything. "Who does, Miss Partlow?" he asked. "May I remind you that you can repay me when your uncle's funds on 'Change are probated."

"There won't be any funds, sir."

She spoke so firmly that he did not doubt her. "How is this?" he asked. "He has always had his share of the salvage."

"Uncle Partlow sent his money home for my father to invest." She hesitated, then took a deep breath and forged on. "My father had no more notion of wise investments than a shoat in a piggery." He could hear the tears in her voice then. "He wrote such glowing letters to Uncle Partlow, and truly I think Da believed that he could recoup his losses. Year after year he thought so." She sighed and faced him for the first time. "We are objects of charity, Captain. What will you do with us?"

"I could leave you here and continue by myself in the morning," he said. "Every town of any size has a workhouse."

The look on her face told him that was exactly what she expected him to say, and her assessment of him bit deep. She did not flinch or try him with tears, but merely nodded and turned back to the fence to lean upon it again, accepting this news as though he told her that snow was cold and winter endless.

"But I won't leave you here," he assured her. He surprised himself and touched her arm. "I have a confession of my own, Miss Partlow."

"You have not been home in years and years," she said. "Mrs. Brattle told me."

He leaned on the fence, same as she, and stared into the snowy field. "I have not," he agreed, perfectly in charity with her as though they were of one mind. What happened just then between them he never could have explained, not even at a court of inquiry convened by the Lords Admiral themselves.

"I suppose I should hear the gory details," she said

at last, and he could not fail to note the amusement in her voice.

"Not out here in the snow. Your feet would freeze before I finished my tale of family discord, love unrequited, and blood in the orchard," he replied, turning toward the inn. He shuddered in mock terror and was rewarded with a small laugh.

Funny, he thought, as they ambled back together, but I have never made light of this before. Could I have made too much of it through the years? Surely not. He stopped her with one hand and held out the other one to her, which she took. "Let us be friends, Miss Partlow," he said, and shook her hand. "If you will help me keep my temper among my relatives, all of whom may wish me to the devil, I will figure out something for you and Thomas to do that won't involve the slave trade." It sounded so lame, but he had nothing else to offer that was remotely palatable. "Come, come, Miss Partlow, it is Christmas and we just shook on it. Have a little charity."

She laughed, and he knew he was backing off a lee shore. "This could be a Christmas of desperate proportions, sir," she joked in turn, and his relief increased. "Oh, very well, then!"

Once inside, he told her that he would remain in the parlor and give her time to prepare for bed. She thanked him with that dignity he was becoming accustomed to, and went upstairs. When he retired a half hour later, the room he shared with the Partlows was dark and quiet. By the light of glowing coals in the hearth, he undressed and lay down with a sigh, content to stare at the ceiling. His years at sea had conditioned him to brace himself against the ship's pitch and yaw, but the only movement was Tom sliding closer, seeking his warmth. He smiled and stretched out his arm and the boy curled up beside him. He slept.

Nightmare woke him an hour later or so, but that

was not unusual. He lay in bed, his heart pounding, his mind's eye filled with explosions and water rising and the ship—his first ship, well before the *Admirable*—slowly settling in the water: the usual dream, the usual time. After the moment of terror that never failed him, he closed his eyes again to let the dream fade, even though he knew he would not sleep again that night.

He opened his eyes in surprise. Miss Partlow had risen from her cot and was now perched on the side of his bed. Without a word, she wiped his face with her handkerchief, then pinched his nostrils gently with it until he blew his nose. His embarrassment was complete; not only had she seen his tears and wiped them away, she had made him blow his nose like a dutiful child.

"I would have been all right, Miss Partlow," he said in a whisper, unwilling to add Thomas to the audience. "Surely I did not cry out. I . . . I don't usually."

"You weren't loud, Captain," she whispered back. "I am a light sleeper, perhaps because I took care of Da for months before he died. Go back to sleep."

So he had cried out. The devil take her, he thought. He wanted to snap something rude at her, as he had done innumerable times to his steward, until the man never came into his quarters, no matter how intense the nightmare. But his steward was dead now, and he held his tongue in time.

"I thought your father was your ruin," he said without thinking.

She stared at him as if he had suddenly sprouted a dorsal fin. "And so why was I nice to him?" she whispered, after a moment in which she was obviously wondering what he was saying. "Captain, you mustn't throw out the bairn with the bathwater! He had his failings but he was my da." She rested her hand for too short a moment on his chest. "Have you never heard of forgiveness, this far south?"

"See here, Miss Partlow," he began, but she put her hand over his eyes and he had no choice but to close them.

"Good night, Captain."

He must have dreamed the whole matter, because in the morning, Miss Partlow made no mention by blush or averted eyes that he had roused her from her bed. She was seated by the window, Bible in her lap, when he and Tom trooped downstairs to the common washroom, leaving her to complete her morning toilet in the privacy of the chamber. When they returned, she was still seated there, but her marvelous hair was now captured in a bun and she wore a fresh dress. And she looked at him—he couldn't describe the look, except that it warmed his heart.

He waited until they were some hours into their journey, and Tom was dozing, before he explained himself. "You wanted the gory details, Miss Partlow," he began. "Let me lay the bare facts before you."

She looked down at her brother, whose head rested in her lap. "Say on, Captain Lynch."

He told his story for the first time in twenty-two years of avoiding any mention of it, astounded how easy it was to talk to this sweet-faced woman. "I was young and stupid and hot-headed, Miss Partlow, and quite in love with my brother Oliver's fiancée," he told her.

"How old?"

He almost smiled, because in the actual telling, it seemed almost ridiculous. "Fourteen, and—"

"Heavens, Captain Lynch," Sally interrupted.

"Yes, fourteen!" he retorted. "Miss Partlow, have you never been in love?"

She stared back at him, and then smiled. "Not at fourteen, sir!"

"Is it warm in here?"

"No, sir."

"Miss Partlow, you are a trial. Amelia was eighteen,

and I was a slave to her every glance. Did a boy ever fall so hard?"

"You were young," she said in agreement. "And did she . . . did she encourage you?"

"I thought she did, but I may have been wrong." He sighed, thinking of all the years he had hung on to that anguish, and wondering why now it felt so remote. "At any rate, Oliver found out and challenged me to a duel."

She looked up from her contemplation of her sleeping brother and frowned. "That does seem somewhat extreme, sir."

He nodded. "I can't say that Oliver and I ever loved each other overmuch before, and certainly not since. Twenty paces in the orchard with our father's dueling pistols. I shot him and ran away."

"Worse and worse," she murmured. When he said nothing more, she cleared her throat. "Possibly you could discard economy now, Captain, and fill in the narrative a little more?"

He could, but he didn't want to tell her about foggy days shivering on the Humberside docks at Hull, wondering if his brother was dead, wondering how soon his father would sic the Runners on him, and all the while eating potato peels and sour oats gleaned from ashcans in a city famous for its competitive beggars. He told her, and not even all his years, prizes, and honors could keep the distress from his voice.

As he spoke, Sally Partlow slipped out from beside her sleeping brother and came to sit next to him. She did not touch him, but her closeness eased the telling. "It's hard, not knowing what to do," she commented. "And to be alone." She looked at Tom and smiled. "I've been spared that."

And why do you seem unafraid? he wanted to ask her. Your future is even bleaker than mine was. "The magistrate nabbed me after a week of dockside living," he said instead.

"And returned you home?"

He shook his head. "Father would not have me. He wrote that Oliver was near death, and what did I think of that?"

"Was he?"

"No." He looked down at his hands where they dangled between his knees. "I learned that much later from the vicar, who also told me that Oliver from his bed of pain had assured my father that the duel was all my idea, and that I was a hell-born babe, impossible of correction." He clapped his hands together. "That ended my career as son and brother, and I was invited—nay, urged, at age fourteen—to seek a wider stage beyond Lincolnshire."

He could feel Sally's sigh. "The world can be a frightening place, eh, Miss Partlow?" he said. He hesitated, and she looked at him in that inquiring way. "Actually, I sometimes wonder if I even shot him."

"I don't understand."

"Well, when the smoke cleared, Oliver was on the ground. I just ran, and do you know, I heard a shot when I was on the edge of the orchard." He shifted in the seat, uncomfortable as though the event had just happened. "I sometimes wonder if he shot himself after I left. You know, just the veriest flesh wound to paint me blacker than I already was."

She stared at him with troubled eyes, and then did lean against him for the smallest moment. Or perhaps the chaise lurched in the slushy snow; he couldn't tell.

"My father—bless his nipfarthing heart—did buy me a midshipman's berth with Nelson's fleet, even though I was a little beyond the usual age." He couldn't help a laugh, but it must not have sounded too cheerful, since it made Sally put her hand on his arm. "In the first and only letter I ever received from him, he said he was in high hopes that I could not long survive an adventure with the Royal Navy." Another laugh, and the pressure of her hand increased.

"Deuce of it was, I did. I hope that knowledge blighted his life, Miss Partlow."

"Oh, dear, no," she whispered.

"He was a dreadful man!"

"He was your father."

On this we will never see eye to eye, he thought. He turned to face her then, sitting sideways. "I wrote to my mother every time we made landfall, but never a word in reply did she send, Miss Partlow! There is every likelihood that there will be no welcome for me, even at Christmas, even after all these years. And God knows I have wanted Oliver to suffer every single day of those twenty-two years." He wished he had not moved, because she had taken her hand from his arm. "If that is the case, then Miss Partlow, I've put you in an uncomfortable position."

"We can go to a workhouse and you can go back to sea, Captain," she said, as calmly as though they discussed whether to take tea in Barton or Fielding. She leaned toward him slightly. "But to harbor up such bitterness, Captain! Has your life been so horrible since that duel?"

What a strange question, he thought; of course it has. Under her steady gaze, he considered again, his thoughts directed down an avenue he had never explored before, much less even considered. "Well, no," he told her finally after he had thought through twenty-two years of war at sea, shipwreck, salvage prizes, foreign ports, exotic women, rum from tin cups, and the odd cat curled and warm at the end of his berth. He smiled. "I've actually rather enjoyed the Navy. Certainly I have done well." He lowered his voice when Tom stirred. "I doubt that Oliver's led such an exciting life."

"I daresay he has not," Sally agreed. "Uncle Partlow's letters were always interesting enough to share with the neighbors." She touched his arm again.

"Think what a nice time of year this would be to let it all go, sir, and forgive Oliver."

"You must be all about in your head," he blurted without thinking. "Never, Miss Partlow. Never." He made no effort to disguise the finality in his voice, which he knew sounded much like dismissal. She sat up straight again and directed her attention to something fascinating outside in the snow.

"It was just a thought," she said quietly, after some miles had come and gone, then said nothing else.

"Rather a totty-headed one," he growled back, then gave himself a mental slap. See here, he thought, irritated with himself, can you forget for half a minute that she is not a member of your crew and doesn't deserve the edge of your tongue?

Furious with himself, he looked at her, and noticed that her shoulders were shaking. And now I have made her cry, he thought, his mortification complete. His remorse grew, until he noticed her reflection in the glass. She was grinning, and for some odd reason—perhaps he could blame the season—that made all the difference. I see before me a managing woman, he thought, observing her reflection. We scarcely know each other, and I know I have not exactly been making myself charming. Indeed, I do not know how. She is a powerless woman of no consequence, and yet she is still going to make things as good as she can. I doubt there is another woman like her.

"Miss Partlow, what on earth are we to make of each other? And what is so deuced funny?" he asked, when he nerved himself for speech. She laughed out loud as though her mirth couldn't be kept inside another moment, her hand over her mouth to keep from waking her brother. She looked at him, her eyes merry, and he knew he had never seen a prettier woman. "I tell you a sad story—something that has been an ulcer all of my adult life—and all you can do is ask me if I really minded the Navy all that much! Drat your hide, I'm almost thinking now that going to sea was probably the best thing that happened! It's your fault! And you want me to give up my grudges, too? Whatever happened to the . . . the shy commentary of scarce acquaintance? Have you no manners?"

"None whatsoever, I suppose," she told him, when she could speak without laughing. "Do I remind you of my uncle?"

That was it, of course. "You do indeed," he replied. "David would twit me all the day long." He paused to remember, and the remembering hurt less than it had a week ago. "I don't know . . . what to think at the moment, Miss Partlow."

She was silent a long time. "We are both of us in an impossible situation, and I say at least one of us should make the best of it. I am determined that you at least will have a happy Christmas."

My stars, but you have a way about you, he marveled to himself. "If I must, I must," he said. "Can you think of any subterfuge that will explain your presence and that of your brother?"

"Not any," she said cheerfully. "Paint us how you will, there's no denying that while Tom and I are genteel, we are definitely at ebbtide in our fortunes at present. Just tell them the truth, because they will believe what they want anyway. We are objects of charity, sir."

Who of us is not, he thought suddenly, then dismissed the notion as stupid in the extreme. I am not an object of charity! I have position and wealth, and every right to be offended by my brother. She is lovely, but she is wrong.

Thomas was awake then, and Sally moved over to sit by him again. Captain Lynch envied the way the boy so matter-of-factly tucked himself under her arm.

He belongs there, Lynch thought, and could not stop the envy that rose in him.

"Do you know, Sally, I rather think I will give up the idea of the sea," Tom announced.

"That is probably best," she replied, "considering that I cannot buy you a midshipman's berth. What will you do then, sir?"

She spoke as though to someone her own age, and not to a little brother with wild ideas, and he knew she was serious. Lynch knew that this woman would never trample on a boy's heart and cause him pain. He watched them, and remembered a Benedictine convent, more of a hospital, in Tenerife where he had been brought during a terrible bout of fever. From his pallet he could see a carving in Latin over the door. He read it over and over, stupidly at first, while the fever still tore at him, and then gradually with understanding: "Care must be taken of the sick, as though they were Christ in person." That is how she treats people, he told himself, and was warmed in spite of himself.

"I think I will go into business in Fort William," Tom announced to Sally. "Wool. We can buy a large house and take in boarders and be merry as grigs."

"I think we should do that, too," Sally replied, and kissed the top of his head. "We'll serve them oatmeal twice a day at least and cut up stiff if anyone asks for hot water."

They both laughed, and Lynch wondered if that was their current lot. He wanted to ask them why they were not burdened down by their circumscribed life, or the bleakness of their future, but his manners weren't entirely gone. And besides, they didn't seem to be as unhappy as he was.

Sally Partlow was not a chatterbox, he knew, as they drew closer to Lynch Hall. She was content to be silent, and asked only one question as dusk arrived. "What is your mother like?"

He was irritated for a moment as she intruded on his own growing misgivings, then had the charity to consider her question. "I suppose you would call her a frippery lady," he said at last, "always flitting here and there, running up dressmaking bills, and spending more on shoes than you would ever dream of." He smiled. "I doubt my mother ever had two consecutive thoughts to rub against each other."

"But you loved her?"

"I did."

They arrived at Lynch Hall after dark. He wished the Partlows could have seen it in daylight. "I hope Oliver has not changed too much about the place," he murmured into the gloom. "Do you think anything will be as I remember?"

Sally leaned forward and touched his hand, and he had the good sense not to pull back, even though she startled him. "People change, Captain."

"I don't," he said quickly.

"Perhaps you should."

Cold comfort, he thought, and turned himself so he could pointedly ignore her.

"You never told me. Did your brother marry that young lady you loved?"

He sighed. How much does this woman need to know? "He did. I have this from the vicar. Apparently there have been no children who have survived even to birth."

"Seems a pity," Sally said, as the manor came into view. "What a large house, and no children."

He knew she was quick, and in another moment, she looked at him again. "Heavens, does this mean you will inherit someday?" she asked.

He nodded. "I suppose it does." He thought of the long nights standing watch and watch about on the *Admirable,* staring at the French coast and thinking about riding back to Lynch Hall in triumph. He never thought much beyond that, and the sour knowledge that Oliver would be dead then, and what was the point in triumph? "I suppose it does."

He was certain his voice had not changed, and he knew in the dark that Sally Partlow could not distinguish his features, but she leaned across the space separating them and touched his face, resting the palm of her hand against his cheek for a brief moment.

And then she was sitting up straight again, as though the gesture, the tenderest he could ever remember, had never happened. Her hand was grasping Thomas's shoulder as before, and she had returned her gaze to the window.

There were few lights burning inside Lynch Hall when the post chaise drew up at the door and stopped. He remembered nights with lights blazing in all the windows, and he wondered if there was some great shortage of beeswax this year, some wartime economy he had not heard of before.

"Does . . . does anyone live here?" Sally was asking.

"I believe so," he replied, no more sure than she.

The coachman said that he would wait there until he was "sartin, sor, that you'll not be needing me." Lynch helped Sally from the post chaise. He was prepared to let go of her hand, but she wouldn't turn loose of him. Or maybe he did not try hard enough. However it fell out, they walked hand in hand up the shallow front steps, Tom behind them. She did release his hand so he could knock.

After what seemed like an age, a butler he did not recognize opened the door, looked them over, informed them that the master and mistress were out for the evening, and prepared to shut the door. Lynch put his foot in the space. "I am his brother, and we will wait," he said. "Inside," he concluded, when the butler continued to apply the pressure of the door to his foot.

"I do not believe Sir Oliver has ever mentioned a brother," he said.

"I doubt he ever has," Lynch replied. "I am Captain Michael Lynch of the White Fleet, home for Christmas from the blockade."

The butler peered closer, as if to determine some family resemblance, then looked beyond him to Sally and Thomas, who were standing close together on a lower step. "Pray who, then, are these Young Persons?"

"They are my friends," Lynch said quietly, stung to his soul by the butler's condescension.

"Then may you rejoice in them, sir, at some other location." The butler pressed harder against the door.

"Where is my mother?" Lynch asked, his distress increasing as the Partlows left the steps and retreated to stand beside the coachman.

"If you are who you say you are, then she is in the dower house," the man replied. "And now, sir, if you would remove your foot, perhaps I can close this door before every particle of heat is gone."

Lynch did as the butler asked, but stood staring at the closed door, embarrassed to face the Partlows. He hurried down the steps and took Sally by the arm. "Miss Partlow, I do not believe there is a more top-lofty creature in all England than a butler! You must have formed such an opinion of this nation."

She leaned close to whisper, "I cannot think that Tom and I will further your cause with your mother, if the butler is so . . . so . . ."

She couldn't seem to think of anything to call the man, even though Lynch had half a hundred epithets springing to mind as he stood there in the snow. These two are babes, he thought. She is too kind even to think of a bad name, and Thomas, if I know that expression, is getting concerned. Look how closely he crowds his sister. He looked at the coachman. "Suffer us a little longer, sir, and drive around on the road I will show you."

No one spoke as the coachman followed his directions. They traveled through a smallish copse that he knew would be fragrant with lilacs in April. Somewhere there was a stream, the one where he sailed his first frigates years ago.

The dower house was even smaller than he remembered, and lit even less well than Lynch Hall. He took a deep breath, and another, until he felt light-headed. Be there, Mother, he thought; I need you.

The post chaise stopped again. He could see a pinpoint of light somewhere within, and he remembered the breakfast room at the back of the house. Silent, he helped down an equally subdued Sally Partlow. "I think I am home now," he told the coachman, walking around to stand by the box.

The man, his cloak flecked with snow, leaned down. "Sor," he whispered, "I know this trip has been on sufferance for you, wha' wi' your standin' an' all. No skin off me to take Sally and Tom wi' me. My missus'll find a situation for the girl wot won't be amiss, and Tom can 'elp me at stable."

Stables and Christmas, Lynch thought, and damn my eyes for acting so put upon because I have had to do a kindness. The man means well. "Thank you for the offer, but I will keep them with me," Lynch whispered back.

The coachman did not appear reassured, but after a moment of quieting his horses, he touched whip to hat and nodded. "Verra well, sor." With a goodbye to Tom and another touch of his hat to Sally, he was gone.

"Well, then, shall I knock on this door and hope for better?" he asked no one in particular.

"I think we are a great trouble," Sally said. "What will you do if no one answers, or if . . ." She stopped, and he could almost feel her embarrassment.

"Or if she will have nothing to do with me?" he continued. "Why then, Miss Partlow, I will marry you promptly, because I've compromised you past bearing already!"

He meant it to sound funny, to lighten what he knew was a painful situation for them both, but when the words left his mouth, he knew he meant them, as much, if not more, than he had ever meant anything. Say yes and then I will kiss you right here in front of Tom and all these trees, he thought, filled with wonder at himself.

To his disappointment, she smiled. Come, come, Michael, you know that was what you wanted her to do, he told himself. "You're being absurd, Captain," she said.

"So are you, my . . . Miss Partlow," he answered. "I think we are both deserving of good fortune at this very moment."

"I know I am," she said in such a droll way that his heart lightened, and then sank again when she added, "But please remember that you are under no real obligation to us, no matter how you felt about my uncle."

It was just as well that the door opened then, because he could think of no satisfactory reply; she was right, of course. He turned his attention to the door and the old man who opened it.

Simpson stood there, older certainly, but Simpson. "You have aged a little, my friend," Lynch said simply. "Do you remember me?"

After a long moment of observation, the butler smiled and bowed. "I did not expect this day," he said just as simply. "Your mother will be overjoyed. Do, do come in." He looked at the Partlows, and Lynch could see none of the suspicion of the other butler in the darkened house. "Come, come, all of you! Coal's dear. Let's close the door."

They stood silent and close together in the small entranceway while Simpson—dignified, and yet with a little spring to his step—hurried down the hall. He listened intently, shamelessly almost, for some sound of his mother, amazed at his own discomposure. For the first time in his life, he understood why so many of his men died with the word "Mother" on their lips. He felt a great longing that brought tears to his eyes. He could only be grateful that the hall was ill-lit. And then his mother was hurrying toward them from the back of the house, and then running with her arms outstretched. She threw herself at him and sobbed into his shoulder, murmuring something incomprehensible that eased his soul in an amazing way.

"Mother, I am so sorry for all those years," he managed, when her own tears had subsided, and she was standing back now to look at him.

Her eyes roamed him from hat to boot, assessing him, evaluating him. He smiled, familiar with that gaze from a time much earlier in his life. "I still have all my parts, Mum," he said finally, as he looked her over as well.

She was still pretty, in an older way now, a calmer way than he remembered, but her clothes were drab, shabby even, which caused his eyes to narrow in concern. She was no longer the first stare of fashion that he remembered, not the lady he never tired of watching when she would perch him on her bed while she prepared herself for a dinner party or evening out.

She must have known what he was thinking, because she touched her collar, which even to his inexpert eyes looked frayed. "La, son, things change. And so have you, my dear." She rose on her toes and he bent down obligingly so she could kiss his cheek. "Now introduce me to these charming people. Are you brother and sister?" she asked, turning to the Partlows.

"These are Tom and Miss Partlow," he said. "Next of kin to David Partlow."

"Your first mate?" she asked, as she smiled at the Partlows.

He stared at her. "How did you know that, Mama?" he asked. "We . . . you and I . . . have not communicated."

She tucked her arm in his and indicated the Partlows with a nod of her head. "Come along, my dears, to the breakfast room, where we will see if Simpson can find a little more coal, and possibly even another lamp. In fact, I will insist upon it."

This is odd, he thought, as they walked arm in arm. He remembered being a little taller than his mother when he left at age fourteen, but he fairly loomed over her now. The gray of her hair did not startle him, and then he remembered that the last time he saw her, she wore powder in her hair. It was another century, he thought in wonderment. How much had happened in that time!

As his mother sat them down in the breakfast room, he looked around in appreciation. Simpson was well ahead of the game. Even now he was bringing tea, and here was Cook, her sparse hair more sparse but her smile the same, following him with Christmas cakes. "One could almost think you have been expecting us, Mama," he said, taking a cup from the butler.

To his alarm, tears welled in her eyes. He held out his hand to her and she grasped it. "I have done this for twenty-two Christmases, son," she said, when she could manage. "Oliver and your father used to scoff, but I knew that someday . . ." She could not continue.

He sat back in amazement. "You astound me, my dear," he told her. "When I never heard anything, not one word from you, I knew that you must be of the same mind as Oliver and Father." He took a sip of the tea, then glanced at Sally, who was watching him with real interest. "After fifteen years, I quit writing to you."

His mother increased her grip on his arm until it

became almost painful. "You . . . you wrote to me?" she asked, her voice so low he could hardly hear it.

"Every time I reached a port where the natives didn't have bones through their noses, or cook Englishmen in pots," he replied with a smile. "Must've been two times a year at least."

He knew that he wouldn't have started to cry, if his mother hadn't leaned forward then and kissed his hand and rested her cheek on it. "Oh, son," was all she said, but it wore him down quicker than any lengthy dissertation ever could. After a moment he was glad to accept the handkerchief that Sally handed him, and had no objection when she rested her own hand on his shoulder.

"You never got them, I take it," he said, after he blew his nose. "And you wrote?"

"Every week." She said nothing more, but stared ahead with a stony look. "God help me, Simpson, I left those letters in the bookroom, along with my husband's correspondence. Did you never see them?"

"Madam, I never did," the butler said.

Lynch felt more than heard Sally's sharp intake of breath. She dropped her hand from his shoulder and sat down heavily in her chair. "Simpson, none of my letters ever arrived here?" he asked.

"Never, Captain."

No one said anything. It was so quiet in the breakfast room that Lynch could hear the clock tick in the sitting room. Then his mother sighed, and kissed his hand again. "Son, if the scriptures are true and we are held to a grand accounting some day, your father may find himself with more debt than even Christ chooses to cover."

She spoke quietly, but Lynch felt a ripple go down his back and then another, as in that long and awful moment before a battle began. He couldn't think of a thing to say, except to turn to Sally and say more sharply than he intended, "And weren't you just telling me about forgiveness, Miss Partlow?"

She stared right back. "Nothing has changed."

"All those years," his mother murmured. She touched his face. "You want to know how I am acquainted with your first mate?"

He nodded, relieved almost not to think of the hot tears he had shed—a man-child of fourteen—wanting her arms about him, when he lay swinging in his hammock over the guns. He thought of all the tears he had swallowed to protect himself from the laughter of the other midshipmen, some of them younger than he, and hardened already by war. "Mama, was it the vicar? I can think of no other."

"My dear son, Mr. Eccles was on his deathbed when he asked me to attend him. Oh, my, hadn't I known him above thirty years! He was too tired to talk, really, but he said he would not be easy if I did not know that for five years he had been hearing from you."

"It was never much, Mama, but I did want to know how you got on, even if you never wanted to speak to me . . . or at least, that was what I thought," he corrected himself.

She stood up, as if the telling required activity, and in her restless pacing, he did recognize the woman of years ago. I do much the same thing on a quarterdeck, Mama, he thought. To his gratification, she stopped behind his chair finally, and rested her arms upon his shoulders. He closed his eyes with the pleasure of it. "He woke and dozed all afternoon, but before he died that evening, he told me that you were well, and in command of a frigate of the line." She kissed his head. "He told me a story or two that included David Partlow, and ports from Botany Bay to Serendip." She sat beside him, taking his hands again. "He never would tell me if you wanted to hear from me or not; indeed, he feared that he was betraying your confidence."

"I didn't know what to think, Mama, when I never heard from you. All I had ever asked of him in letters was to let me know how you were." He squeezed her hands. "And that he did." He hesitated a moment. "He told me that Father died ten years ago."

"He did," she said, and he could detect no more remorse in her voice than he felt. "Since then, Oliver has had the managing of me."

"And a damned poor job he has done, Mama," Lynch said, unable to keep his voice from rising.

To his surprise, Lady Lynch only smiled. "I thought that at first, too, son." She looked at the Partlows. "Thomas—does your sister call you Tom? I shall then, too. Tom, you're drooping! I hope you will not object to sharing a chamber with my son. Miss Partlow . . ."

"Do call me Sally," she said. "It's what everyone calls me, even if the captain thinks I should be Miss Partlow."

"And here I thought he would know nothing of the niceties, after all those years at sea!" Mama exclaimed, with a smile in his direction. "Sally it is, then. My dear, there is the tiniest alcove of a bedroom next to my room, with scarcely a space for a cat to turn around. How fortunate that you are economical in size." She looked around the table, and Lynch could see nothing but delight in her face. "We will be as close as whelks in a basket, but I dare anyone in Lincolnshire to have a merrier Christmas."

She had directed her attention to the Partlows, but he followed them upstairs, leaning against the doorframe of the little chamber he was to share with Tom while Sally tucked her brother in. "I want my own bed," he heard the boy say to his sister as she bent over him for a good night kiss. "I want to be home." Don't we all? Lynch thought, remembering years and years of writing unanswered letters, letters where he pleaded with his parents to forgive him for being a younger son, for being stupid, for being a child who thought he was a man, until the day came when he could think of nothing that warranted an apology, and stopped writing, replacing remorse with bitterness. I was intemperate and wild, he thought, as he watched the Partlows, but these are forgivable offenses. Too bad my father never thought to forgive me, and Mama was never allowed the opportunity.

He thought his cup of bitterness, already full, should run over, but he was filled with great sadness instead. My parents have missed out on my life, he thought with regret, but no anger this time. He remained where he was in the doorway while Sally conferred with his mother in low whispers. He heard "nightmare" and "mustn't trouble you," and looked away while they discussed him. I am in the hands of managing women, he thought, and again, he was not irritated. It was as though someone had stretched out a wide net for him at last, one he could drop into without a qualm.

He said good night to Sally there in the hall, standing close because it was a small corridor, and then followed his mother downstairs, where she gave a few low-voiced orders to Cook, and bade Simpson goodnight. She took his hand and just looked into his face until he wanted to cry again. "Have I changed, Mama?" he asked at last.

She nodded, her eyes merry. "You're so tall now, and—"

"That's not what I mean," he interrupted. "You've changed in ways I never thought you would. Have I?"

"You have," she said quietly. "How much, I cannot say, because you have only returned."

"For better or worse?"

"We shall see, Michael," she replied. "Oh, why that look? Does no one ever call you Michael?"

No one ever did, he realized with a jolt, as he heard his Christian name on her lips. "No, Mama. I am Captain to everyone I know."

She stood on tiptoe to kiss his cheek. "Then we will have to enlarge your circle of acquaintance." She pulled him down to sit beside her. "And you must not look at me as an object of charity, son! I am nothing of the kind."

He knew he must only be pointing out the obvious, but he did it anyway. "Mama, there is little coal in this house, few candles, and I have never seen you in a dress so shabby!"

But she only smiled at him in a patient, serene way he had never seen before in his parent, and tucked her arm in the crook of his. "I don't know that any of it matters to me, son, now that you are home for Christmas."

"That is enough?"

"Why, yes," she replied, even sounding startled at his question. After a moment, she released his arm and stood up. "My dear, morning comes early, and we can be sure that Oliver will be over soon."

He stood up with her, more bemused now than agitated. "I don't understand, Mama."

She kissed his cheek again and stood up. "I don't know that things are ever quite as bad as we imagine they are, son. Good night."

Oliver was the last person he thought of when he finally slept, and the first person he saw when he woke hours later. He was dimly aware that at some point in the night someone came into his room and sat beside him, but he could not be sure who it was. He sank himself deep into the mattress and did not open his eyes again until much later, when he heard someone clearing his throat at the foot of the bed.

My, how you've changed, was his first thought as he stared—at first stupidly, and then with recognition—at the man gripping the footboards and glaring at him through narrowed eyes. "Oh, hullo, Oliver," he said with a yawn. "How are you?"

Comfortable in the way that only a warm bed and a venerable nightshirt allow, he gazed up at his older brother, and decided that if he had passed the man on the street, he would not have known him. He folded his hands across his stomach and observed his brother. So this was the object of my bitterness all these years, he thought, as he took in a man thin to the point of emaciation, but dressed in a style much too youthful for him. If I am thirty-six, then he is rising forty-four, Lynch thought, and there he is, dressed like a popinjay. Sir Oliver looked for all the world like a man denying age, with the result that he looked older than he was.

"Why did you think to come here now?"

To Lynch, it sounded more like a challenge than a question. "Well, Oliver, I have it on the best of authority that people who are related occasionally choose to spend certain calendar days together. I realize there's no accounting for it, but there you are," he replied. "And do you know, even though I am sure no one in the White Fleet believes me, I have a mother." He sat up then. "Is there some problem with the estate that she must dress like an old maid aunt no one cares about?"

Oliver smiled for the first time. "Economy, brother, economy! On his deathbed, our father made me swear to keep a tight rein on his widow, and so I did."

My word, two bastards in as many generations, Lynch thought. Vengeful even to death, was the old man? I imagine the next world was a jolt to his system.

"We have order and economy, and—"

"—tallow candles cut in half and coal doled out by the teaspoon!" He couldn't help himself; Lynch knew his voice was rising. "You won't object if I order more coal and beeswax candles for Mother, will you?"

"Not if you pay for them," his brother replied. "Through the years Amelia and I have been frugal with everything."

"You have indeed," Lynch agreed, remembering with some slight amusement that his brother had no progeny. "Last night we were even wondering if the manor was inhabited. Scarcely a light on in the place."

His brother shrugged, and sat down. "Why waste good candles when one is not home?" He leaned closer. "And when you speak of 'we,' brother, surely you are not married to that . . . that rather common person downstairs?"

Any manner of intemperate words bubbled to the surface but he stifled them all, determined for his mother's sake not to continue the fight where it had begun twenty-two years ago, over a woman. "No, I am not married to her. She and her brother were wards of my late first mate, with nowhere to go for Christmas."

To his further irritation, Oliver waggled a bony finger at him. "That's the sort of ill-natured charity that makes dupes of us all! I'll wager you don't even know them!"

Better than I ever knew you, he thought, *or wish to know you.* He got out of bed and pulled down his nightshirt at the same time that Sally Partlow entered the room with a tray and two cups of tea. He wasn't embarrassed because she seemed unconcerned. "Your mother thought you two would like some tea," she said, her glance flicking over him then coming to rest on the wall beyond his shoulder. Her face was only slightly pink, and dashed pretty, he considered. He took a cup from her and sat down again, remembering that this particular nightshirt—long a favorite—had been from Bombay to the Baltic and was thin of material. "And you, sir?" she said, indicating his brother. "Would you like some tea?"

Oliver shook his head. "Tea at midmorning smacks of waste and profligacy," he said, so smug that Lynch itched to smack him. "I ate my mush at daybreak, and will make it last until luncheon."

Over the rim of the cup, Lynch glanced at Sally and

knew without question precisely what she was thinking. He turned his head so Oliver would not see his smile. I do believe, my dear Sal, that it would not be beyond you to tell my prig of a brother just where to put his mush, he thought. You would probably even provide a funnel.

He feared that Oliver must be wondering at the expression on his face, but his brother was staring at the tray Sally carried. The color rose up from his scrawny neck in blotches. "I cannot imagine that Lady Lynch would ever permit someone she cannot know to be handling our silver!"

"Good Lord, Oliver, it's just that old teapot even I remember," Lynch said, stung into retort. "I hardly think Sally will . . . will stick it up her skirt and trot to the pawnshop!"

"That is precisely what I mean!" Oliver replied. "We have had years and years of order and serenity and now you are back one morning with . . . with— heaven knows who this woman is—and things are going to ruin! I am going downstairs directly to tell Mama to count her—my—silverware carefully!"

Sally gasped. Without a word she picked up the teacup on the tray and dumped it over his brother's head. Oliver leaped to his feet, his hand raised, but Lynch was on his feet as well, and grabbed his brother's arm. "I wouldn't," he said.

"But she poured tea on me!"

"I don't blame her," Lynch replied. "You're dashed lucky this isn't the Middle Ages and it wasn't hot tar! How dare you accuse her of having designs on the family silver?"

Oliver looked at them both, his eyebrows pulled close together, his face in a scowl. "I'm going to talk to Mother about the wisdom of houseguests at Christmas," he said primly as he left the room.

Sally stared after him, then looked down at the empty cup in her hand. Lynch smiled at her and sat down. "You should have a little charity, Miss Part-low," he said. "Didn't you tell me only yesterday that it was high time I forgave my brother?"

He decided that she must not have realized what she was doing, because she sank down beside him on the bed. "Perhaps I was hasty," she amended. "I hadn't met him yet." Lynch shouted with laughter. After a long moment, she smiled, if only briefly. She stood up then, as if aware of him in his nightshirt. "He may be right, Captain," she said as she replaced both cups on the tray and went to the door. "I really don't have much countenance, do I?"

"Probably not," he agreed, in perfect charity with her, although he was not certain that she appreciated the fact. "It doesn't follow that the matter is disagreeable." To his utter delight, she made a face at him as she left the room.

He lay back down, hands behind his head, content to think of Sally, when she stuck her head in the room again. "Your mother said most particularly that you are *not* to do what you are doing now! She wants your escort to the vicarage this afternoon."

"Shrew," he said mildly. "When am I to have the nap I so richly deserve, after nine months of watch and watch about on the blockade?"

Sally Partlow sighed and put her hand on her hip, which only made him want to grab her, toss her down beside him, and abandon naps forevermore. "Captain, I believe that one must rise, before one can consider the next rest as a nap."

To his relief, Oliver was gone when Lynch made his appearance in the breakfast room. The table was covered with material and dolls, dolls large and small, with baby-fine hair of silk thread, and abundant yarn hair. Sally was diligently embroidering a smile onto a blank face, and even Tom was occupied, pulling nankeen breeches onto a boy mannikin. Lips pursed, eyes narrowed in concentration, his mother—who to his

knowledge had never plied a needle in her life—
pushed the last bit of cotton wadding into a disembod-
ied leg.

He kissed her cheek, and cleared a little spot for
himself at the table, which only brought a protest from
Sally, and the quiet admonition of his mother to please
eat his breakfast standing up at the sideboard. He
didn't wish to spill eggs or tea on the dolls, did he?

Mystified at the doll factory on the table, he did as
he was told. "Is this one of Oliver's cottage indus-
tries?" he asked finally, when he had finished and sat
himself at the table.

"La, no," his mother said, as she attached a leg to
a comely doll with yarn ringlets. "Every year he com-
plains when I ask for a few shillings to make dolls for
the orphanage. He can be wearing, at times."

He leaned closer to her, wishing with all his heart
that he had come home sooner. "I can change things
for you now, Mother," he said.

If he expected to see relief in her eyes, he was
doomed to disappointment. With a few expert stitches,
she concluded the limb attachment and picked up another leg. "I suppose Oliver is onerous at times, son,
but do you know, his nipfarthing ways at my expense
have quite brought out a side of me I never knew."
She looked around the table and Lynch could see
nothing in her face but contentment. "When I think
how little I used to do with much, and now how much
I do with little, it fair amazes me!" She patted his
arm, and then handed him an empty leg and pushed
the stuffing closer. "And I owe Oliver this revelation
of character."

"I . . . I suppose I never thought of it that way,
Mother," he said, picking up the stuffing. He saw with
a frown that his fingers were too large to make any
headway on the leg. To his relief, Sally came to the
rescue, moving her chair closer until her glorious hair
touched his cheek as she expertly worked the stuffing

in place with her own slim fingers. I'm in love, he thought simply, as he breathed deep of her fragrance—probably nothing more than soap and water—and tried to think when any woman had stirred him as completely as this one. The deuce of it was, he didn't think she had the slightest idea of her effect on him.

The thought niggled at the back of his brain all morning as he sat at the table and brought his mother up to date on twenty-two years of his life. He had no need to enlarge upon his experiences, because they were vivid enough with war, shipwreck, illness—which set Sally to sniffling, even though she heatedly denied it when he teased her—salvages, and exotic ports as his topics. Before he brought his recitation to a close, even Simpson and Cook had joined them around the table.

"The blockade is the least pleasant duty of all, I believe," he temporized.

"We will have it, too, son, since you have told us everything else," his mother said.

"No!" he exclaimed, rather louder than he had intended. Sally looked at him in surprise. "It's . . . it's not worth the telling."

He watched his mother gather the dolls together and motion to Tom to put them in the pasteboard box Simpson provided. "And now the *Admirable* is in dry dock and I find myself in a strange position for a seafaring man."

"On land and hating it?" Sally asked, her voice soft. She hadn't stirred far from his side, but had continued to work on the doll in her lap.

Twenty-four hours ago, he would have agreed with her, but now he could not say. "Let us say, on land and not certain where to go from here," he told her, "or even what to do." He was deeply conscious of the fact that he was aware of every breath she took, so close there to him.

"Then that makes two of us," Sally murmured. She put down the doll. "Captain Lynch, do you ever wish, just once, that you could be sure of things?"

He shrugged. "Life's uncertain," he told her. "I suppose that is what I have learned."

"Not that it is good?" she asked. "Or at least satisfactory on occasion?"

"That has not been my experience, Miss Partlow," he said, his voice sharp. "If it has been yours—and I cannot see how, considering your own less-than-sanguine circumstances—then rejoice in it."

To his shame, Sally leaped up from the table as though seeking to put real distance between them as fast as she could. If he could have snatched his spiteful words from the air, crammed them back in his mouth again, and swallowed them, he would have, but as it was, Sally only stood by the window, her head down, as far away as the moon.

"That was poorly done, son," his mother murmured.

"I *told* you I had changed, Mother." Where were these words coming from? he asked himself in anguish.

"Not for the better, apparently."

The room was so hot, he wondered if he had been wise to order more coal. "Excuse me, please," he said as he left the table.

He kicked himself mentally until he passed through the copse and could no longer see the dower house. In his mind he could still see the calm on Sally's face, and the trouble in her eyes. It takes a thoroughly unpleasant customer to tread on a woman's dignity, Lynch, he told himself, and you've just trampled Sally's into the dust. Too bad the *Celerity*'s carronade didn't belch all over you, instead of her uncle. She'd certainly have had a better Christmas.

He wanted to cry, but he wasn't sure that he could ever stop if he started, so he swallowed the lump in his throat and walked until he looked around in surprise, the hair rising on his neck.

He stood in the orchard, barren now of leaves, and any promise of fruit, the branches just twisted sticks. How does it turn so beautiful with pink blossoms in the spring? he wondered. I have been so long away from land and the passage of seasons. He closed his eyes, thinking of summer in the orchard and then fall, especially the fall twenty-two years ago when two brothers had squared off and shot at each other.

Why did I let him goad me like that? he thought. Why did I ever think that his fiancée preferred me, a second son, greener than grass, unstable as water in that way of fourteen-year-olds?

He stood a moment more in thought, and then was aware that he was not the orchard's only visitor. He knew it would be Oliver, and turned around only to confirm his suspicion. "Does it seem a long time ago, brother?" he asked, hoping that his voice was neutral.

Oliver shook his head. "Like yesterday." He came closer. "Did you mean to kill me?"

I was cruel only minutes ago, so what's the harm in honesty, Lynch wondered. "Yes. I'm a better aim now, though."

Oliver smiled. "My pistol didn't fire."

"I thought as much. And then you shot yourself later, didn't you?"

His brother nodded. "I wanted to make sure you never returned."

"It worked."

They both smiled this time. Lynch noticed that Oliver was shivering. "Your cloak's too thin for this weather," he said, fingering the heavy wool of his own uniform cloak. "Oliver, why in God's name do you live so cheap? Is the estate to let?"

He didn't think Oliver would answer. "No! It pleases me to keep a tight rein on things," he said finally. "The way Father did."

"Well, yes, but Father lit the house at night and even heated it," Lynch reminded him.

"I control this estate."

To Lynch, it seemed an odd statement. He waited for his brother to say more, but the man was silent.

They walked together out of the orchard and Lynch wondered what he was feeling, strolling beside the person he had hated the most in the world for twenty-two years. "You ruined my life, Oliver," he said as a preamble to the woes he intended to pour out on the skinny, shabby man who walked beside him.

Oliver startled him by stopping to stare. "Michael, you're worth more than I am! Don't deny it. I've checked the Funds. You've done prodigious well at sea. You aren't ruined."

"Yes, but—"

"And you don't have a wife who is so boring that you must take deep breaths before you walk into any room she is inhabiting. And someone damned unfeeling enough to . . . to drop her whelps before they're big enough to fend for themselves!"

"I doubt that Amelia ever intended to miscarry," Lynch said, startled, and wondering if now he had finally heard everything.

"And the deuce of it is, brother, I cannot unburden myself of her and take another wife who might get me an heir!"

Dumbfounded, Lynch could think of no response to such a harsh declaration, beyond the thought that if Amelia Lynch had been a horse with a broken leg and not a wife with an uncooperative womb, Oliver could have shot her. He had the good sense not to mention it. "No heir," was all he could say, and it sounded stupid.

Oliver turned on him. "Oh, I have an heir," he declared, "a by-blow got from the ostler's daughter at the public house, for all the good that does anyone. Naturally he cannot inherit. There you are, damn you, free to roam the world, tied to nothing and no one. As things stand now, you will inherit this estate."

As they walked on, Lynch felt a great realization dawning on him. It was so huge that he couldn't put it into words at first. He glanced at his brother, feeling no anger at him now, but only the most enormous pity and then the deepest regret at his own wasted time.

"Brother, can it be that we have been envying each other all these years?"

"I doubt it," Oliver snapped, but his face became more thoughtful.

"You were the oldest son and successor to the title, and you won Amelia's affection—my God, but I wanted her then—and Father's love," Lynch said. "Didn't you get what you wanted?"

Oliver sighed. "I discovered after six months that Amelia only loves lap dogs. Father never loved anyone. And Mama, who used to be such a scatterbrain, has turned into the most . . . the most . . ."

". . . respected and wise woman in the district," Lynch concluded, smiling at the irony of it all. "You and Father broke her of bad habits out of your own meanness, didn't you? And she became someone worth more than all of us. That must've been a low blow."

"It was," Oliver said with some feeling. "And look at you! Damned if you aren't a handsome big fellow. I've been ill used."

The whole conversation was so unbelievable that Lynch could only walk in silence for some minutes. "So for all these years, you've either been wishing me dead, or wishing to change places. And I've been doing the same thing," Lynch said, not even attempting to keep the astonishment from his voice. "What a pair we are."

If it weren't so sad, he would have laughed. Father sentenced me to the sea, and I was the lucky one, Lynch thought. I've not been tied to a silly, barren woman, forced to endure years with that martinet who fathered us, or tethered to an estate when just maybe

I might have wished to do something else. And Oliver thinks I am handsome. I wonder if Sally does?

He took his brother by the arm, which startled the man into raising both his hands, as though in self-defense. "Settle down, Oliver. I have an idea. Tell me how you like it." He hesitated only a moment before throwing his arm around the smaller man, enveloping him in the warmth of his cloak. "I've given some serious thought to emigrating to the United States. I mean, since I refuse to die and oblige you that much, at least if I became a citizen of that nation, I certainly couldn't inherit a title, could I? Who would the estate devolve upon?"

"Our cousin Edward Hoople."

"Hoople." Lynch thought a moment, then remembered a man somewhat near his own age.

"Yes! He has fifteen or twenty children at least—or it seems that way when he troubles us with a visit—and as many dogs," Oliver grumbled. "But I'd much rather he had this estate than you."

"Done then, brother. I'll emigrate," Lynch said. "At least, I'll do it if I survive another year on the blockade, which probably isn't too likely. My luck has long run out there. That satisfy you?"

"I suppose it must," Oliver said. He looked toward Lynch Hall. "Do you want to put it in writing?"

Lynch shook his head. "Trust me, Oliver. I'll either die or emigrate. I promise."

His brother hesitated, then nodded, and hesitated again. "I suppose you can come to luncheon," he said, his reluctance almost palpable. "I usually only have a little bread and milk."

"I'll pass, Oliver. I think I've promised to take some dolls to the vicarage for Mama."

Oliver sighed. "That woman still manages to waste money!"

Lynch surprised himself by kissing Oliver on the forehead. "Yes, indeed. She must have spent upwards of twenty shillings on all those dolls for orphans. What can she have been thinking? Tell you what I will put in writing. I'll take care of Mother from now on, and relieve you of that onerous burden and expense." He looked at Oliver closely, trying to interpret his expression. "Unless you think you'll miss all that umbrage."

"No, no," Oliver said hastily, then paused. "Well, let me think about it."

They had circled back to the orchard again. Lynch released his brother, and put out his hand. "What a pair we are, Oliver."

Oliver shook his hand. "You promise to die or emigrate."

"I promise. Happy Christmas."

Oliver turned to walk away, then looked back. "You're not going to marry that chit with the red hair, are you? It would serve you right to marry an object of charity."

The only objects of charity are you and I, brother, Lynch thought. "That would please you if I married her, wouldn't it?" he asked. "You'd really think I got what I deserved."

Oliver laughed. "It would serve you right."

"I'll see what I can do," he offered, "but my credit with Sally is on the ground right now. I think she wants me dead, too."

Oliver was still laughing when Lynch turned away. He didn't hurry back to the dower house, because he knew they would have gone on without him. He sat at the table in the breakfast room for a long moment, wondering if it would be better if he just left now. He could make arrangements with his solicitor in Portsmouth for his mother, and add a rider to it for Sally and Tom, even though he knew that scrupulous young woman would never touch it. In only a day or two he could be back on the blockade conning another ship.

The thought of the blockade turned him cold, and then nauseous. He rested his forehead against the

table until the moment passed. He knew that he
needed Sally Partlow far more than she would ever
need him.

The vicarage was much as he remembered it, but
this new man—vicar since his old confidant had died
five years ago—had taken it upon himself to organize
a foundling home in a small house just down the road.
"My good wife and I have no children of our own,
Captain," the man explained, after Lynch arrived and
introduced himself. "This gives us ample time to
help others."

Lynch nodded, thinking of his own childless brother,
who spent his time pinching pennies, denying his
mother, and squeezing his tenants. "It seems so . . .
charitable of you," he said, realizing how lame that
sounded.

"Who among us is not a beggar, sir?" the man
asked.

Who, indeed? Lynch thought, turning to watch Sally
Partlow bend over a crib and appropriate its inmate,
a child scarcely past birth. He watched as the baby
melted into her, the dark head blending into her own
beautiful auburn hair. He thought of years of war and
children without food and beds, left to shiver in odd
corners on wharves and warehouses, and die. "I am
tired of war," he said, his voice quiet. I need that
woman.

"How good that you can leave war behind now,"
the vicar said.

"Perhaps," he told the man as he watched Sally.
She has an instinct for the right thing. I wish I did.
He sighed. If she turns me down flat, then my sentence
is the blockade and I will die.

He shuddered at the thought; he couldn't help himself. The vicar looked at him in surprise, then touched
his sleeve. "*Can* you leave it behind?" he asked.

That, apparently, is the question, he asked himself
as he went to Sally. "Please forgive me," he mur-

mured and without another word took the sleeping
child from her. To his deep need and intense gratification, the baby made those small sounds of the very
young, but did not even open her eyes as she folded
into his chest, too. He felt himself relax all over. Her
warmth was so small, but as he held her close, he felt
the heat of her body against his hand and then his
chest, as it penetrated even the heavy wool of his uniform. He paced up and down slowly, glad of the motion because it reminded him of his quarterdeck. The
baby sighed, and he could have wept when her little
puff of breath warmed his neck.

He wasn't aware of the passage of time as he
walked up and down, thinking of nothing beyond the
pleasure of what he was doing, the softness of small
things, the impermanence of life, its little span. What
would it have cost me to forgive my brother years
ago? Nothing.

Stung by his own hypocrisy, he walked on, remembering the Gospel of Matthew, which he read from
the quarterdeck to his assembled crew on many a Sun-
day, after the required reading of the Articles of War.
With painful clarity, he recalled the parable of the
unmerciful servant, who was forgiven of a great debt,
then inflicted his own wrath on another who owed
him a tiny portion of that which had been forgiven.
" 'Shouldest not thou also have had compassion on
thy fellowservant, even as I had pity on thee?' " he
whispered to the baby.

He never prayed, but he prayed now, walking up
and down in the peaceful room with a baby hugged
to his chest. Forgive us our debts, he thought, as we
forgive our debtors. How many times as captain have
I led my crew in the Our Father and never *listened*?
Forgive me now, Father, he thought. Forgive me,
Sally. Forgive me, and please don't make me go back
on the blockade. For too many years I have nourished
my animosities like some people take food. Let us

now marry and breed little ones like this sweet child,
and walk the floor of our own home, and lie down at
night with each other. Please, not the blockade again.

He stood still finally. The baby stirred and stretched
in his embrace, arching her back and then shooting
out her arms like a flower sprouting. He smiled, thinking that in a moment she would probably work up to
an enormous wail. It must be dinnertime, he thought.
She yawned so hugely that she startled herself, and
retreated into a ball again. He kissed her hair and
walked on until she was crying in earnest and feeling
soggy against his arm. In another moment, the vicar's
wife came to him, crooning to the baby in that wonderful way with children that women possessed: old
women, young women, barren, fertile, of high station,
and lower than the drabs on the docks. "The wet
nurse is waiting for you, little one," she whispered.
"And did you soak Captain Lynch's uniform?"

"It's nothing," he said, almost unwilling to turn
loose of the baby.

She took the baby and smiled at him, raising her
voice so he could hear over the crying, "You're a man
who likes children."

I know nothing of children, he thought, except those
powder monkeys and middies who bleed and die on
my deck. "I think I do," he replied. "Yes, I do."

He stood another moment watching the woman
with the baby, then took his cloak from the servant,
put it on, replaced his hat, and soon stood on the steps
of the vicarage. Sally Partlow waited by the bottom
step, and he felt a wave of relief wash over him that
he would not have to walk back to the dower house
alone, he who went everywhere alone.

"I sincerely hope you have not been waiting out
here for me all this time," he said.

She smiled that sunny smile of hers that had passed
beyond merely pleasing to absolutely indispensable to
him. "Don't flatter yourself! I walked home with your

mama and Thomas, and then she told me to return and fetch you." She tugged the shawl tighter around her glorious hair. "I told her that you had navigated the world, and didn't need my feeble directions. Besides, this is your home ground."

"But you came anyway."

"Of course," she said promptly, holding out her arm for him. "You're not the only biped who likes to walk. The path is icy, so I shall hang on to you."

He tucked her arm in his gladly, in no hurry to be anyplace else than with Sally Partlow. "I am thirty-six years old," he said, and thought to himself, That ought to scare you away. Why am I even mentioning my years to this woman? was his next thought, followed by, I have not the slightest idea what to say beyond this point.

"Only thirty-six?" Sally said, and gathered herself closer. "I'd have thought you were older." She smiled at him.

"Wretched chit."

"I am twenty-five." She gripped his arm tighter. "There, that's in case my advanced years make you want to flee."

"They don't." To his gratification, she didn't let loose of him.

They walked on slowly, Lynch gradually shortening his stride to make it easier for the woman beside him to keep up. I'll have to remind myself to do that, he thought, at least until it becomes second nature.

In far too short a time, he could see the dower house at the bottom of the slight hill. Beyond was the copse, and then the manor house, all dark but for a few lights. It was too close, and he hadn't the courage to propose.

He sighed, and Sally took a tighter grip on his arm. "I hoped this would be a happy Christmas for you," she said.

He shook his head. "Perhaps we can remember this

as the necessary Christmas, rather than the happy one," he replied, then wondered at his effrontery in using the word "we."

She seemed not to even heed his use of the word, as though something were already decided between them. "Well, I will have food for thought, at least, when I return to the blockade," he continued, less sure of himself than at any time in the last decade, at least.

"Don't return to the blockade," she pleaded, and stopped.

He had no choice but to stop, too, and then made no objection when she took the fork in the path that led to the village and not the dower house. "You're going the wrong way," he pointed out.

"No, I'm not," she said in that unarguable tone that he had recognized in her uncle. "We're going to walk and walk until you have told me all about the blockade." She released his arm so she could face him. "You have told us stories of the sea, and personally I thank you, for now Tom has no urge to follow his uncle's career! You have said nothing of the blockade, beyond watch and watch about, and you look so tired."

"Say my name," he said suddenly.

"Michael," she replied without hesitation. "Michael. Michael."

"No one says my name."

"I noticed how you started the other day when your mama did." She took his arm again, this time twining her fingers through his. "I can walk you into the ground, Michael. No more excuses."

You probably can, he told himself. He yearned suddenly to tap into her energy. "I'm tired. Watch and watch about is four hours on and four hours off, around the clock, day after week after month after year. We are a wooden English wall against a French battering ram."

She rested her cheek against his arm and he felt her low murmur, rather than heard it. "At first it is possible to sleep in snatches like that, but after a few months, I only lie in my berth waiting for the last man off to summon me for the next watch."

"You *never* sleep?" she asked, and he could have cringed at the horror in her voice.

"I must, I suppose, but I am not aware of it," he said, after a moment of thinking through the matter. "Mostly I stand on my quarterdeck and watch the French coastline, looking for any sign of ship movement." He stopped this time. "We have to anticipate them almost, to sense that moment when the wind is about to shift quarters, and be ready to stop them when they come out to play in our channel."

"How can you do that?" Her voice was small now. "It is not possible."

"Sally, I have stood on the deck of the *Admirable* with my hat off and my cloak open in the worst weather, just so I won't miss the tiniest shift in the wind."

"No wonder you tell us of fevers."

"I suppose." He took her arm again and moved on. "Not only do we watch the coast, but we watch each other, careful not to collide in fog, or swing about with a sudden wind, or relax our vigilance against those over our shoulders who would sneak in under cover of dark and make for shore."

"One man cannot do all that," she whispered, and she sounded fierce.

"We of the blockade do it." He patted her hand and they walked on into the village, strolling through empty streets with shops boarded for the long winter night. Through all the exhaustion and terror he felt a surge of pride and a quiet wonder at his own abilities, despite his many weaknesses. "We do it, my dear."

He knew she was in tears, but he had no handkerchief for her. I don't even know the right words to court this beautiful woman, and flatter her, and tell her that she is essential to my next breath, he told himself. I've never learned the niceties because they're not taught on a ship of the line. In the middle of all my hurt and revenge, I hadn't planned on falling in love. He knew he had to say something. They were coming to the end of the village. Surely Sally did not intend just to keep walking.

To his amazement, she did, not even pausing as they left the last house behind. She kept walking on the high road, as though it were summer. She walked, eyes ahead, and he talked at last, pouring out his stories of ship fevers, and death, and cannonading until his ears bled from the concussion, and splinters from masts sailing like javelins through the air, and the peculiar odor of sawdust mingled with blood on the deck, and the odd patter of the powder monkeys in their felt slippers, bringing canister up from the magazine to the men serving the guns, and the crunch of weevils in ship's biscuit, and the way water six months in a keg goes down the throat in a lump.

She shuddered at that one, and he laughed and took both her hands in his. "Sally Partlow, you amaze me!" He looked at the sky, and thought he saw the pink of dawn. "I have told you horrible stories all night, and you gag when I mention the water! If there is a man alive who does not understand women, I am he."

Holding her hands like that, he allowed himself to pull her close to him. If she had offered any objection, he would have released her, but she seemed to like what he was doing, and clasped her hands across his back with a certain proprietary air.

"I'm keeping England safe so my brother can squeeze another shilling until it yelps, and . . ." He took a deep breath and his heart turned over. ". . . and you can lie safe at night, and mothers can walk with babies, and Thomas can go to school. Marry me, Sally."

She continued to hold him close. When she said nothing, he wondered if she had heard him. He knew he didn't have the courage to ask again. The words had popped out of his mouth even before he had told her he loved her. "Did you hear me?" he asked at last, feeling as stupid as a schoolboy.

She nodded, her head against his chest, and he kissed her hair. "I love you," he said.

She was silent a long moment. "Enough to leave the blockade?"

His heart turned over again and he looked up to see dawn. He had told her all night of the horrors of the blockade, and in the telling had come to understand his own love of the sea, and ships, and war, and the brave men he commanded. It terrified him to return, but he knew that he could now. With an even greater power than dawn coming, he knew that because he could, he did not need to.

"Yes, enough to leave the blockade," he said into her hair. "I will resign my commission with the new year." He waited for such a pronouncement to rip his heart wide open, but all he felt was the greatest relief he had ever known. This must be what peace feels like, he told himself in wonder. I have never known it until now.

She raised her head to look at him then, and he wanted to drop to his knees in gratitude that for every morning of the rest of his life, hers would be the first face he saw. She put her hands on his face. "You are not doing this because I am an object of charity?" she asked.

"Oh, God, no!" He kissed her until she started to squirm for breath. "My dearest love, *you* are the one marrying the object of charity." He smiled when she did. "Of course, you haven't said yes yet, have you? You're just clarifying things in your Scottish way, aren't you?"

"Of course," she replied calmly. "I want to know

precisely where I stand. Your brother will be horrified, your mother will be ecstatic, and Thomas will follow you about with adoration in his eyes. You've lived solitary for so long. Can you manage all that?"

"Actually, Oliver will be ecstatic. I'll explain later. I wish you would answer my question, Sally, before you start in with yours! My feet are cold, and do you know, I am actually tired right down to my toenails." That was not loverlike, he thought, but it didn't matter, because Sally was pressing against him in a way that sharpened his nerves a little more than he expected there on a cold road somewhere in the middle of Lincolnshire. "Where the deuce are we?" he asked.

"Somewhere in Lincolnshire, and yes, Michael, I will marry you," she said, then took her time kissing him. When they stopped, she looked at him in that intense way that warmed him from within. "I love you. I suppose I have for a long time, ever since Uncle Partlow started writing about you in his letters home."

"Preposterous," he said, even as he kissed her once more.

"I suppose," she agreed, after that long moment. "There's no use accounting for it, because I cannot. I just love you." She held up her hands, exasperated at her inability to explain. "It's like breathing, I think."

"Oh, Sally," he said, and then kissed her again, until even the air around them felt as soft as April.

They learned from a passing carter (who must have been watching them, because he could hardly contain himself), that they were only a mile from Epping. It was an easy matter to speak for breakfast at a public house, admire his blooming Sal over tea and shortbread, then take the mail coach back to Lynch. Pillowed against Sally's soft breast, he fell asleep as soon as the coachman gathered his reins. He probably even snored. Hand in hand they walked back to the dower house. He answered his mother's inquiries with a nod in Sally's direction, then went upstairs to bed, leaving his pretty lady to make things right.

She must have done that to everyone's satisfaction. When he woke hours later, the sun was going down and she was sitting in a chair pulled close to the window in his room, her attention on yet another doll in her lap. He lay there admiring her handsome profile and beautiful hair, and hoped that at least some of their children would inherit that same dark red hue. He chuckled at the thought; she turned in his direction to give him an inquiring look.

"I thought I would prophesy, my dearest," he said, raising up on one elbow.

"I almost shudder to ask."

"I was merely thinking that a year from now it will probably still be watch and watch about."

She put down her needlework and he recognized that Partlow glint in her eyes. "You promised me you were going to give up the blockade."

"I am! Cross my heart! I was thinking that babies tend to require four on and four off, don't they? Especially little ones?"

To his pleasure, she pinked up nicely. She took up her sewing again, and turned back to the window, even as her shoulders started to shake. "I can see that you will be a great deal of trouble on land," she said, when she could speak again.

"I'll do my best."

She finished a seam on the little dress in her lap and turned it right side out. "I think it would be prudent if we don't settle anywhere close to Lynch, my love," she told him. "I'm sure Oliver thinks I am a great mistake."

"I'm open to suggestion," he said agreeably, then shifted slightly and patted the bed. "Let's discuss it."

She shook her head. "Not from there! My uncle Partlow always told me to beware of sailors."

"Excellent advice. See that you remember it."

They were still debating the merits of a return to the Highlands over a bolt across the Atlantic to Charlotte because he liked the Carolinas, when Mama called up the stairs that dinner was ready.

He took Sally by the arm as she tried to brush past the bed. She made not a single objection as he sat her down next to him. Sally leaned closer to kiss him. "I thought your uncle told you to beware of sailors," he reminded her, then pulled her closer when she tried to sit up. "Too late, Sal."

She seemed to feel no melancholy at his admonition, but curled up beside him with a sigh. "I am tired, love! I do not plan to walk all over Lincolnshire tonight."

"Let me make a proposal, dearest Sal."

"You already did, and I accepted," she reminded him, her voice drowsy.

"Another one, then. What do you say if after dinner we hurry to the vicarage, where I can ask about the intricacies of obtaining a special license? We can get married right after Christmas, and I will see that you get to bed early every night."

She blushed, even as she nodded. He folded her in his arms, and to his gratification, she melted into him like the baby he had held yesterday. He thought briefly of the *Admirable* in dry dock, then put it from his mind forever. He smiled to think of the Gospel of Luke, another favorite quarterdeck recitation—"and on earth peace, good will toward men."

"Happy Christmas, Sally," he whispered in her ear, as goodwill settled around him like a benediction, and peace became his second dearest companion.

The Wexford Carol

——◦•◦——

by Emma Jensen

Chapter One

County Wexford, Ireland

The Honorable Elizabeth Fitzhollis had dirt beneath her fingernails. She also had a bruise on her chin and bits of dried plaster in her hair. She didn't think Mr. Dunn, the family's aged solicitor, had noticed. He was glancing nearsightedly at the paper in his hand, beaky nose nearly against it. Lizzie did, however, believe he had noticed the not very pleasant smell emanating from her person. He'd wrinkled his nose upon entering the room, squinted at her, then emptied the contents of his bulging leather satchel onto the already concave desktop.

There hadn't been much Elizabeth could do about the smell. She had been knee-deep in a clogged drainage ditch when Dunn had arrived unexpectedly. She'd only had time to clamber inelegantly from the hole and bolt upstairs to don a worn but appropriate dress before joining him in her father's study. A bath had been out of the question. There hadn't been time. And she was just going back into her discarded clothing and the ditch, shovel in hand, within ten minutes of his departure anyway.

The bruise was from the pantry door. It had been sticking for months, but fixing it hadn't been anywhere near the top of Lizzie's list. Having yanked it open into her own face the day before, she'd moved it up a few notches. The collapsing ceiling in the Lily Room had been much more pressing, hence the plaster in her hair. Had it been the ballroom ceiling, she could simply have closed the door and forgotten about it for the time being. But the Lily Room was where she spent what scant quiet time she had, usually battling with monetary figures that wouldn't budge no matter how many times she rearranged them.

The patch job she'd done on the ceiling was just that. Until the west wing had a new roof, there would be leaks and damp, and sagging plaster . . .

". . . will be arriving in a fortnight."

Lizzie dragged her attention away from the crumbling roof tiles to what Mr. Dunn was saying. He did tend to prattle on about debts—nothing of which Lizzie was not well aware, so she tended to listen with only half an ear. "Who will be arriving, sir?"

The solicitor peered at her over the paper. "Captain Jones."

Lizzie ran through the list of creditors. To be sure, there were quite a few, but that name rang no bells. "And who is Captain Jones?"

"Why, the agent for the new owner, of course."

Oh, no. Please, God, no. Lizzie's stomach did a dizzying flip. She'd been waiting for this day, dreading it, but never quite believing that Cousin Percy would actually sell her home, her beloved Hollymore.

"Captain Lawrence Edward Jones," Mr. Dunn read, squinting at the missive, "representing the Duke of Llans. His Grace plans to set up a hunting estate here, and Captain Jones will be supervising the demolition and subsequent development."

"D-demolition?"

"Mmm. He has no use for the house. Far too large and"—Mr. Dunn cleared his throat apologetically—"er . . . not, shall we say, in the best of repair. He will replace it with a smaller lodge. Now, Captain Jones will expect a room . . ."

Lizzie had stopped listening. Replace Hollymore.

Knock down stones built upon the stones that had sheltered Henry II in 1171, break out the stained-glass windows in the Long Gallery that had been a gift from King Charles mere months before he lost his head. Rip out the wooden paneling in the dining hall that bore the carved names of the twenty-two Fitzhollis men who had died at the Battle of the Boyne.

Yes, the house was tumbling down around her ears. Yes, her father had died without a son to inherit or anything to leave his only daughter. Yes, as the new baron, Percy had every legal right to sell the house. Lizzie simply hadn't expected him to do it. All in all, she thought miserably now, she shouldn't have been surprised.

She loved Hollymore, every damp stone and rotting panel. Percy loved his title, money, and his horse, in that order.

"I am correct in that, am I not, Miss Fitzhollis?"

Lizzie blinked at the solicitor. "I am sorry, sir. I did not hear you."

Dunn clucked his tongue, not unsympathetically. "I was referring to your father's aunt. You will have a home with her, will you not?"

"I will, yes."

Oh, yes. A home in pinch-faced Aunt Gregoria's overwarm little cottage that smelled of cats. A home where each morsel of food was weighed before it went onto a plate and candles were only used for a half hour each evening.

Lizzie practiced economy. Gregoria had turned it into a Holy Crusade.

"Well, then." Dunn began to gather up his belongings. Several papers stuck to the decaying leather blotter, still more had been impaled on the decidedly ugly sculpture of a hedgehog that squatted atop the desk. Lizzie gave the thing a careful pat as she freed the papers. The bronze hedgehog had been part of her great-uncle Clarence's "natural" period. Not one of his more successful sculpting endeavors. But it remained in its place of honor because both Lizzie and her father had been very fond of Uncle Clarence. And because it couldn't be sold as nearly everything else in the house had been. No one in their right mind would buy it.

Lizzie herself retrieved Mr. Dunn's hat and stick from the coatroom. O'Reilly, the ancient butler, was busy replacing the paper stuffing in the first-floor windows, and both maids were doing their best to rescue the parlor furniture. Lizzie peered carefully into the solicitor's hat before handing it over. The coatroom was a bit dark and cobwebby, and the Reverend Mr. Clark had been understandably unhappy on his last visit when he'd donned a very large spider along with his hat. Pity, she'd thought at the time, that it hadn't been her cousin. But Percy kept all of his belongings near to hand when he paid his unwelcome visits.

After a quick check to make certain he wasn't standing on a crumbling bit, Lizzie left Mr. Dunn on the front steps and went off to summon his carriage. Kelly, the groom, was still trying to capture the pair of owls that had flown into the Gallery two nights before. So far, they had been impressively clever at avoiding his net.

Eventually, she got Mr. Dunn into his carriage and waved him down the weedy drive. Only when he was out of sight did she allow her shoulders to slump. It was a brief break, though. She knew the staff would gather at teatime—they always did after his visits—and would want the report. Usually, it was merely the news that their wages would be delayed again. Since none of them had been paid in more than six months, they left those meetings cheerful. This time would be so very different.

And so Lizzie found herself in the warm kitchen two hours later, bathed and better-smelling but exhausted from her moderately successful second round with the ditch, facing her loyal staff over their tea. She studied the beloved faces as they sipped the strong, sweet tea or gnawed on O'Reilly's biscuits. The butler-cook-general factotum was cheerful as ever, eyes bright in his seamed face. But Lizzie knew his rheumatism was acting up again. As hard as he'd tried to hide it, she had seen his grimace as he sat down at the table. Meggie, the ginger-haired maid, had plaster dusting her young face; black-haired, motherly Nuala had a bigger bruise than Lizzie's on her right cheek. And Kelly, who tended the single horse and over-grown gardens as best he could, as well as being resident house wildlife trapper, had a face so red from his exertions with the net that it rivaled the brilliant hair he shared with his sister Meg.

All were regarding her with trust, loyalty, and hope familiar enough to warm Lizzie's heart, and powerful enough to break it.

"It isn't good," she began, and determinedly kept her voice from cracking as she repeated the solicitor's news. That done, she assured them, "I'll find you better posts elsewhere before I leave. I promise you that."

No one spoke for a long moment when she'd finished. Then O'Reilly, undisputed leader of the pack, growled, "Don't you be worrying about us, missy. We'll be just fine." There was a chorus of nods and ayes around the table. "We've all places t'go. 'Tis you who needs the caring for. Stuffed away wi' that bitter old bat. 'Tisn't right, no more than you slaving away at this old pile. Beautiful young girl needs beaux and balls and a house wi'out falling walls."

Lizzie smiled. "You know you love this old pile as much as I do." And they all did. O'Reilly's father and grandfather had been in service to the Fitzhollises before him, as had Nuala's mother and both of Kelly and Meggie's parents. "Besides that, it has been so long since I attended a ball that I wouldn't know where to put my feet, at present all the walls are standing splendidly, and if I wanted a beau, there is always Persistent Percy."

It had its desired effect. There were snorts and smiles all around. Lizzie was grateful for the unbending support. Grateful, too, if amused, by the familiar compliments. She supposed she was young enough; six and twenty was hardly an advanced age. And enough men had called her beautiful. She had inherited her father's rich gold hair and Irish-green, thickly lashed eyes. Along with her mother's heart-shaped, high-boned face, willowy frame—a bit hardened, perhaps, by all the shoring and shoveling and plastering—and quick, wide smile, it was a pleasant enough picture. But her beauty had, for good or ill, not been quite enough to surpass her want of fortune. One after the next, her youthful swains had taken themselves off to wealthier climes. Lizzie suspected that her forthright nature and frank intelligence had something to do with the matter as well, but for whatever reason, no man had come courting in the two years since her father had died. Except Percy, of course, and she would marry his horse before she would have him.

"I will manage perfectly well with Aunt Gregoria," she announced to her staff now. "I will still be close to the good company of the area. And, if I am very well behaved, and manage to remember the names of all eight cats, she will take me to Dublin with her when she performs her good works."

There were more snorts and smiles. Gregoria Fitz-hollis's idea of good works consisted of distributing scratchy woolen gloves and sermons on resisting the drink to Dublin's unsuspecting poor. That she herself was rather partial to sweet sherry was a source of wry amusement to her acquaintances. But a weekly half bottle of genteel after-dinner sherry consumed in the presence of her vicar, Gregoria steadfastly asserted, was as different from whiskey in a tavern as orange and green. She'd never commented on the other five half bottles she consumed during every sennight.

"I still don't like it," Kelly muttered, hunching and bristling in the protective mien he'd always used for Lizzie despite the fact that she was several years older. "Sure, and this captain's a dog for coming to shove you out of your rightful home."

"And just after Christmas, too!" was Meggie's indignant addition. "Couldn't be bothered to wait 'til the holidays had well passed. They're all just the same, they are, the fancy. Sensitive as turf bricks." She gave Lizzie a sweet smile. "We don't count you among them, o' course, Miss Lizzie."

"Thank you." Lizzie took the compliment with a smile of her own. With the exception of her beloved if ineffectual sire and the gentle mother she'd barely known, her opinions of the aristocracy were much the same. Most she'd met were just like Percy. "But I do not suppose we can blame Captain Jones. I imagine he comes and goes at the duke's bidding."

"You're too kind, *cailin*," Nuala scolded. " 'Tisn't this captain having his heart broke during what should be the kindest time o' the year. Bad business for holy days, I say, and may they know it."

Silently Lizzie agreed. It was a sorry thing indeed to conduct such business just after Christmas week. But despite the fact that both Captain Jones's name and the duke's title were Welsh, it was likely that the duke at least was more English than anything and, like members of the English High Society in which he no doubt lived, just didn't care whose holidays were inconvenienced as long as they weren't his own.

As it was, there had been little holiday spirit at Hollymore for a very long time.

"Poor Miss Lizzie," Meggie sighed.

"Poor Miss Lizzie," the others echoed, a mournful toast.

Lizzie shook her head, tried to shake off the weight

of sadness. "Don't be shedding any tears for me." Her brave face lasted only a moment. She whispered, "Save them for Hollymore."

Four heads bobbed dejectedly. "Is there naught we can do?" Kelly demanded.

"Aye, Miss Lizzie." Nuala leaned forward, sweet face furrowed. "Can your cousin be made to change his mind, do you think?"

"Oh, Nuala." Lizzie gripped her chipped earthenware mug tightly and willed her lips not to tremble. "I'm afraid not. Even if he hadn't already sold Hollymore to the duke, it would only be a matter of time before he took the next man's gold."

The older woman harrumphed. "I'd like to see him show a shred o' decency just this once."

"Like to show him the business end of a musket, I would," O'Reilly muttered.

Lizzie fully agreed with both. But any time spent thinking of Percy was wasted time. She had something else in mind. "There's nothing to be done for my future here," she said firmly, "but I've had an idea to save Hollymore."

Her staff all leaned forward eagerly. "Well, go on, miss," O'Reilly prompted. "What would that be?"

"We've at least a sennight before Captain Jones arrives, perhaps more. I know we've had quiet Christmases here since Papa died . . ." The first had been spent in mourning, the next two in the sort of penury that precludes all but the most modest of celebration. ". . . but this year can be different."

"A last hurrah in Hollymore?" Kelly inquired bleakly.

"Well, yes, that. But there's more." Lizzie took a deep breath. She didn't want to sound too hopeful. Didn't want to feel too hopeful. "Perhaps, just perhaps if we can show Hollymore at its best . . . Yes, yes, I know," she murmured when four sets of eyebrows lifted. "The best it can be in its present condition. Perhaps then Captain Jones will see how very wonderful a house it is and will persuade the duke to keep it, to restore it rather than raze it. His Grace could use it as a hunting lodge. At least then . . . well, at least then it will still be here, and there might well be places for all of you in it."

"As if we'd take money from them as put you out," O'Reilly snapped. The others nodded.

"I won't have you even considering making any such foolishly noble stand for me," Lizzie said fiercely. "But you can do this: Help me save my house. Here is how I think we should begin . . ."

Later that afternoon, garbed in an old pair of her father's wool trousers and one of his warm coats, Lizzie stood on the sweep of rear lawn that was more crabgrass than anything, surveying the holly maze below that had been planted in honor of her family name. Dense and glossy green with red berries, the branches growing thickly from ground to top, the holly was a cheery sight. The shrubs had been planted among the maze hedge and, when left untended, made navigating the maze a prickly business. Needless to say, they had been left untended.

Lizzie planned to go at them herself with hedge shears. If she and Kelly put their minds and backs to it, they could make the maze passable—if not perfect—and supply the house with ample decoration all in one day. The problem, of course, was which day. The parlor ceiling wasn't finished, Kelly still hadn't captured the second owl . . .

She jumped as a hand landed heavily on her shoulder. "Bidding it all a fond farewell?"

She shrugged off the hand and turned to face her cousin. It was difficult at times to reconcile the character with the appearance. Short, round-faced, with the blond curls and pink cheeks of a cherub, Percy Fitzhollis—Baron Fitzhollis now—could have modeled for Raphael, and done service to Lucifer.

He was garbed as always in his idea of London fashion. Today it was an azure jacket over an orange-spotted waistcoat and white pantaloons. To Lizzie's eye he looked like a tubby bullfinch. In her mind, she thought of him as more of a reptile.

"Percy, you are a snake," she said wearily. She never bothered mincing her words around him, but neither did she expend more energy than was absolutely necessary.

"No such thing in Ireland," he drawled back as he sidled in to stand much too close. "Can't say the same for temptation, though."

Lizzie crossed her arms over her chest. If he were going to loom and slobber, she wanted at least eight inches between them. "You sold my house."

"My house, actually. Soon to be the Duke of Llans's house."

"Until he knocks it to the ground," Lizzie said bitterly.

Percy grinned, rosebud-mouthed and forked-tongued. "Plans to build a hunting lodge. Invited me for grouse season already. Splendid fellow, the duke."

"And where on earth did you manage to meet a duke?"

"Didn't, actually. Put an advert in the *Journal*. Apparently Clane saw it and passed it on."

Percy had never met the Earl of Clane, either. Lizzie had. They had danced together at several balls, even had a moonlit walk in Phoenix Park once. Lizzie had liked him, even indulged in a few romantic reveries. But she'd been so young, barely seventeen at the time. Then Clane had gone off to serve in the army, and by the time he had returned, Lizzie's father had died and she had been long gone from Dublin Society events. Clane was married now, she'd heard. He'd probably thought the same of her when he'd seen that Hollymore was for sale.

Lizzie had told herself sternly not to cry. She told herself again. It wasn't working. "Oh, Percy," she snapped, cursing the catch in her voice, "how *could* you?"

Her cousin shrugged. "Why wouldn't I?"

"Perhaps because this land has been in the family for eight *hundred* years? Perhaps because you know how much it means to me?"

She knew that was a mistake the minute she'd said it. But emotion had softened her brain and loosened her tongue.

Percy's eyes sparked. "Isn't too late, y'know, Lizzie."

"And what is that supposed to mean?"

"Haven't signed all the papers. Told you before: have me, have your beloved house."

Yes, he'd told her more than once, usually when he was foxed on second-rate Madeira. Even had Percy not been a fool, not been a reptile, and not always spoken in half-formed sentences—only to be expected, Lizzie thought, for someone with half a brain—she wouldn't have had him. Only now, with Hollymore at stake . . . She shuddered at the thought of seeing Percy's face first thing in the morning and last thing at night.

"Makes perfect sense," he was saying now. "Always did . . ."

Had Lizzie seen it coming, she would have been ready with knees, nails, and teeth. But she only had time to gasp in surprise as Percy grabbed her by the upper arms and thumped her into his orange-spotted chest. Her sharp protest was lost to his soft lips and jabbing tongue.

Her first thought was that she was going to be ill. Her second was that if he didn't release her immediately, she was going to box his ears until they rang like Christmas bells.

"Pardon me."

At the sound of the deep voice, Percy released her so abruptly that she nearly went down onto her bottom. She stumbled back, furiously wiping at her mouth with the back of her hand.

"I say," Percy muttered at the man standing not ten feet away, "ain't sporting, that. Interrupting a fellow when he's at play."

A single black brow winged upward, but all the man said was, "I do not mean to intrude, but no one answered the front door. Perhaps you can tell me where I can find Lord Fitzhollis."

No deferential lackey this, Lizzie thought. From the top of his towering dark head to the soles of his booted feet, he exuded arrogance and command. He wasn't a handsome man; the blue eyes were too cold, the jutting nose and jaw too hard, but he was certainly an impressive figure in his naval uniform coat.

At the moment he had his ice-blue gaze fixed on her.

"Captain Jones, I presume," she addressed him. He continued to stare at her. "Captain Lawrence Jones? Oh, dear."

Everyone present jumped as metal clanged loud and hard against the stone terrace. A piece of the gutter had come loose. It wasn't the first. Lizzie gave the two-foot-long section a mournful look. It had shattered the slate tile beneath it.

Captain Jones, when she turned to address him again, was scowling fiercely enough to frighten what stone gargoyles remained on the ramparts. Lizzie sighed. "Forgive me for saying so, sir, but your arrival really is atrociously timed."

Chapter Two

Captain Lord Rhys Edward-Jones studied the almost startlingly beautiful woman who was wearing breeches and had, until a moment earlier, been in the arms of a fussy little cherub, and wondered why the favors he did for his brother never seemed to involve ordinary specimens of humanity. He sighed.

"I am looking for Lord Fitzhollis."

The cherub gave a regal nod that was diminished somewhat by the ridiculous arrangement of his cravat. "I am Fitzhollis."

"I am—"

"Yes, yes," the lady interrupted, briskly brushing the man's lingering pudgy fingers from her waist, "we know. You are Captain Lawrence Jones, representing the Duke of Llans in his purchase of Hollymore. Mr. Dunn told me. He also told me you were scheduled to arrive a fortnight from now."

As Rhys watched, a young man with brilliantly red hair and a bulging sack came trotting into view from the house. The sack seemed to be alternately swelling and deflating in his grasp and, if Rhys wasn't mistaken, was emitting an odd, muffled sort of shriek. Neither Fitzhollis nor his companion seemed to notice. Only when the fellow opened the sack and released a large, screeching owl did the lady turn. She gave a cool, satisfied nod, then swung her emerald gaze back to Rhys.

"I am afraid, Captain," she announced, "that we are not quite ready for you."

Before Rhys could reply, or inquire just who she was to be ready or not, the man on the lawn gave a dismayed yelp. As the party on the terrace watched, the owl did a slightly clumsy turn midair and flew back toward the house, where it abruptly vanished from view. Shoulders slumped, the young man tucked the sack under his arm and shuffled back up the lawn.

"Splendid effort, though, Kelly!" the woman called to him. He gave a dispirited wave and disappeared through a stone doorway.

Rhys waited for an explanation. Instead, the cherub shoved an overlarge pinch of snuff up his button nose, sneezed, and demanded, "Do tell me, Captain, how the duke is faring. Well, I trust, marvelous fellow. Anticipating a smashing grouse season."

Rhys was not aware of his brother Timothy ever anticipating anything about grouse. He was, however, well aware of the fact that Fitzhollis's sole dealings with the marvelous Duke of Llans had been through Timothy's able man-of-affairs. Fitzhollis wouldn't have known the duke if the duke had walked over him. Rhys was spared the necessity of reply, however, by a crash that resounded through the open door behind him. It was followed by several smaller crunches and one pained squawk. Human, he thought.

The lady promptly stepped forward. "I daresay you would like a tour of the grounds, Captain Jones."

What he would like was for her to get his name right and offer her own, along with an explanation of sorts. He had no idea who she was; she clearly had some bungled idea of who *he* was. After that, he wanted a bath and meal. The journey from Wales across the Irish Sea had been uneventful but long. The experience of trying to hire a coach and get to County Wexford had been long and extremely trying. In the end, it had involved a crowded public conveyance containing a ripe and motley collection of travelers, an equally uncomfortable ride from Wexford town in a farmer's wagon, and a long walk up Hollymore's sweeping drive. His valise was still at the bottom, by the listing stone gateposts.

Nor had the sight at the end of the long and bumpy drive improved Rhys's mood. Hollymore was, to put it mildly, a crumbling monstrosity of countless different architectural styles and tastes, a squat, sprawling beast of a house. If his brother were wise, he would raze the thing before setting foot on Irish soil and build himself a nice, solid hunting lodge without a headless medieval gargoyle or frill-less Elizabethan frill to be found on it.

"What I would like, madam," he began, and was interrupted by a discreet cough from behind him. "Ah, yes, of course," he muttered. "We mustn't be unmannerly. Allow me to introduce my nephew, Vi—"

"Andrew Jones, at your service." Seventeen-year-old Andrew, otherwise known as Viscount Tallasey, gave him a small jab in the ribs as he pushed past.

The cherub sneezed again and huffed into action. "Ah, yes. Of course. M'cousin and fiancée, Miss Fitzhollis."

"Oh, Percy," she snapped, "I am not—"

"Of course." A light had gone off in Rhys's head. "The late Lord Fitzhollis's daughter."

"Well, yes," she said with an exasperated sigh, "I am that. Elizabeth. This is my house. But I am not—"

"*My* house," her cousin corrected, winking at the other two gentlemen as he spoke. "Ladies and their notions, you know."

From the mutinous set of Elizabeth's jaw, Rhys decided that statement from her fiancé had not gone over well. He also decided that Timothy's efficient man-of-affairs was not quite as efficient as he seemed. *Aging spinster,* the man's report had read. *Merits little or no attention in the matter.*

If this was anyone's idea of an aging spinster, Rhys was the King of Connaught. He also had a strong suspicion that Elizabeth Fitzhollis would merit at least a little attention. She could not possibly be ignored.

"An honor and a pleasure, Miss Fitzhollis." Andrew, flashing the Edward-Jones smile that made him look exactly like his father and sent most ladies and scullery maids alike into moon-eyed sighing, bent over Elizabeth's hand. She went neither moon-eyed nor breathy. She didn't even smile. Then Andrew announced, "Allow me to say how extraordinary your home is," and suddenly Rhys found his own eyes going a bit crossed.

An irritable-looking Elizabeth Fitzhollis was beautiful. A smiling one was absolutely dazzling. Her cousin, Rhys noted, was nearly slobbering at her side and even his own, ever-poised nephew was goggling slightly.

"Isn't it wonderful?" she breathed, turning that astonishing smile onto the crumbling pile behind them. "There is not a house standing in all the isles to equal it."

There might not be, Rhys agreed silently, making a determined effort to drag his eyes from the lady to the pile of stones behind him. But he'd seen any number of abandoned ruins that were quite on a par with Hollymore.

"So, Miss Fitzhollis," Andrew was asking now, "may I take you up on your offer of a tour?"

"Pushing young pup, ain't he?" the increasingly less cherubic baron demanded.

Andrew's brows went up, but he continued to smile pleasantly at Elizabeth. She, for her part, rolled her eyes. "Oh, Percy. Really. I would be delighted to show you Hollymore, Mr. Jones. And Captain Jones, of course," she added eventually, almost as an afterthought.

This time, the shriek from the house was definitely human, certainly female, and it was followed by a new series of crashes and thumps.

Elizabeth sighed. "Perhaps we ought to start with the grounds."

"Perhaps we ought to set a matter or two straight," Rhys muttered.

He was drowned out by Andrew's, "Splendid!"

And Fitzhollis's dismayed, "But my boots, Lizzie!"

Elizabeth ignored Rhys entirely, but smiled at Andrew as she stalked across the terrace on—Rhys couldn't help but notice, considering her garb—very long, very nicely shaped legs. She stepped over the fallen gutter and pulled the French door closed with a rattling thump. There was paper jammed into several cracked panes.

"Yes, the mud would most certainly ruin the gloss on your boots, Percy," she said matter-of-factly. "I suggest you go home."

"But, I could—"

"You've done more than enough already, thank you. Go home. Come for dinner if you must."

Fitzhollis's mouth pursed in a defiant pout. "Won't have you ordering me about, Lizzie."

"No, of course you won't." She smiled, but it was not even close to the blazing smile that had lit the very air. "I wonder, do you think Aunt Gregoria would care to discuss the state of her sherry reserve?"

Whatever that meant, it had a quick and notable effect on the man. Fitzhollis flushed a bright pink and took himself off so quickly that he nearly left his highly polished, high-heeled boots behind. His fragmented farewells trailed in his wake.

Rhys, watching this display with some amazement, felt a distinct if fleeting surge of pity for Fitzhollis. By all appearances, the pair were a match made somewhat south of heaven. Despite the fact that Elizabeth Fitzhollis was easily the loveliest sight he'd seen in aeons, she seemed a bit scatty. And officious. There was little question of who would be running the household. And judging from what Rhys had seen so far of this household, the lady was not much of a manager.

He ignored the following thought: that there was something under Elizabeth Fitzhollis's surface, something deeper than beauty, that should have been well above the touch of anyone like her cousin.

Rhys thrust away that foolish sentiment and turned his attention back to the matter at hand. "Miss Fitzhollis, I really must inform you—"

"Come along, *Uncle Lawrence*," Andrew interrupted. The little sod was grinning like a fox. "I am all eagerness to see what the duke has done this time. One can always be certain of a surprise or two when he decides to toss his money about."

It was on the tip of Rhys's tongue to reply that it was ultimately part of Andrew's inheritance that Timothy was tossing into this ramshackle heap of stone. Tim had always enjoyed a good jest, and he had passed that unfortunate quirk on to his son. For the first time, Rhys wished this was one of those jests. Pity he knew better. His brother had taken it into his head that he needed an Irish hunting box. Apparently it would be here.

Rhys had willingly enough undertaken the task of overseeing the preparations. Timothy and his wife were visiting friends on some godforsaken little Hebridean island, and Rhys had little to do now that he was in the process of selling out of the navy. His years on the seas had left him wealthy, a bit weary, and heartily sick of salt water. So when his brother had declared the need to visit the Wexford property, Rhys had offered to make the journey. He had sailed from Cork countless times, and had developed an appreciation for Ireland. The landscape, once one got away from the coast, was refreshingly green, the people were pleasant, and the whiskey was exceptional.

He could use a stiff shot now.

What he had on hand was a disapprovingly stiff golden goddess in attire that, against all his good sense and inclination, was making parts of his own anatomy go taut. He tugged his greatcoat closed.

It seemed Andrew's glib comment about tossing

money had struck an unpleasant chord. "I hadn't meant to say this quite so soon," Elizabeth was saying crisply, "but since you've caught us unaware, I don't suppose I have a choice." She turned to face Rhys fully, hands on nicely rounded hips. "I don't mean to speak ill of the duke, especially since I do not know him and he *is* your employer, but he is making a terrible mistake with Hollymore."

"Is he?" Rhys replied. Judging from what he'd seen so far, he was inclined to agree. He suspected, however, that he and the lady of the house would have very different opinions as to why.

"I do not blame His Grace. Or I am trying not to. Men of his ilk are seldom bothered to attend the smaller details of business transactions. I suppose it simply did not occur to him to come see Hollymore himself. He really ought to have done so. Seeing the estate would almost certainly have changed his plans."

So far, they were still in agreement.

"Had he seen the house," she went on, "he would not possibly have considered tearing it down."

And there was the divergence. Had Timothy seen the house, he would most certainly have insisted it be razed before allowing his son anywhere near the place.

"A moot point, I am afraid, Miss Fitzhollis," Rhys said blandly.

She gave a vague hum, then asked, "How long do you plan to stay?"

"A fortnight at most." In fact, he thought it would be somewhat less than that. He'd seen just about all he needed to see.

Elizabeth tilted her glossy head. "Forgive my impertinence, sir, but your idea of a fortnight and mine seem to be different."

Rhys bit back his own sarcastic retort. "I assure you, Miss Fitzhollis, that your Mr. Dunn was informed of my anticipated arrival date in the letter that was posted nearly a month ago."

"A month ago?" She sighed. "Ah, well, that would explain that. Mr. Dunn is not as sharp of mind or eye as he once was. Still, Captain, I confess I find it odd that you would arrange to be here over Christmas."

Andrew, who had expressed much the same sentiment more than once, gave a not particularly discreet snort. Rhys shrugged. "It is just a day, Miss Fitzhollis. I assume we will find a Church of Ireland Christmas service just as long and hymn-filled as one at home. Perhaps you will be so kind as to allow us to accompany you."

"You are assuming I am not Catholic, Captain."

"Are you?"

"No, as it happens, I am not. But most of the nearby residents are. And they take the holidays quite seriously. There is a great deal more to the next fortnight than one long and hymn-filled church service."

Andrew snorted again. "Don't expect him to understand, Miss Fitzhollis. My uncle was off practicing military drills when they handed out holiday spirit."

"Watch your tongue, puppy," Rhys muttered resignedly. In a family that possessed an overabundance of every sort of spirit, he stood alone in his preference for contained emotions. And said family delighted in reminding him of that fact at every opportunity.

"No one is immune to an Irish Christmas," Elizabeth announced. Then, with a decisive nod, she gestured toward the muddy expanse before them, broken only by an oddly shaped copse of spiny holly bushes. "Shall we walk?"

She strode off down the rocky slope on her long legs, Andrew grinning at her side. Rhys followed with less cheer than his nephew, but with a far better view of Elizabeth's pert bottom as it flashed in and out of view. The man's wool coat she was wearing looked to have been mended one too many times. The split above the tails appeared destined to stay split.

Cursing under his breath, he dragged his gaze away.

Of all the views he should be studying, Elizabeth Fitz-hollis's posterior was not among them. With luck, she would complete her tour and take herself off to wherever she was residing and out of his sight. Rhys recalled something about a maiden auntie. He pictured a tidy, rose-covered cottage with a profusion of lace doilies and china shepherdesses. God only knew what sort of havoc Elizabeth would wreak on bric-a-brac with her brisk, arm-swinging movement.

"There," she announced, pointing to a listing stone bench, "is where Jonathan Swift is reputed to have first conceived of *Gulliver's Travels*."

"Attacked by resident leprechauns?" Rhys muttered under his breath.

She heard him. "So he said, apparently," she shot back smartly, "but I expect it was my great-grandfather's whiskey."

Here was the remnant of the moat into which King Henry II had taken an unexpected tumble. "He made a great joke of it," Elizabeth informed them, as if the event had taken place last month, rather than seven centuries earlier, "demanding that a stone tablet be placed to mark the spot of Henry's downfall." She'd then glanced around bemusedly. "I have no idea where that went. The largest piece used to be around here somewhere."

Andrew earned another brilliant smile when he promised to have a look around for it in the coming days. Rhys silently wished him the best of luck. There were enough treacherous looking stones lying about to make one seven-hundred-year-old fragment feel right at home.

Here came the brackish fountain where the pirate Grace O'Malley had sailed a model of her ship and *there* the oak tree under which Wolfe Tone had planned his rebellion. Elizabeth's father, as she explained it, had been instrumental in the strategy, but prevented from participating by her mother, who would not countenance the shedding of any blood, no matter how noble the cause.

A fortunate decision, Rhys thought, as the blood would no doubt have been the baron's.

As they passed Wolfe Tone's oak, Rhys shoved a moss-laden branch from in front of his face, and was promptly forced to scuttle forward in a hurry as the whole thing detached itself from the tree and crashed to the ground. Elizabeth gave him a brief backward glance. "Mind yourself," she murmured, leaving him with the impression that she was scolding him for having attacked the precious tree.

By the time they had done a circuit of the impenetrable maze—Elizabeth had insisted they just have a peek inside the entrance, and Rhys's coat had suffered greatly from the brief experience—and rocky flower gardens and spectacularly muddy ha-ha, the winter light was all but gone and they had met the figurative ghosts of just about every late, illustrious Irish personage.

"The outer grounds will have to wait until tomorrow," Elizabeth announced as she guided them back up the hill, her stride as brisk as when they'd begun. "I shall see to readying a set of rooms for you."

Rhys hoped she would then take herself off and leave them to whatever peace the house offered. "Are you in residence near here, Miss Fitzhollis?"

She stopped and regarded him with obvious surprise. "Not near," she said. "Here."

"You *live* at Hollymore?"

"Of course I do," she said, starting off again. "Where else would I live?"

Where else indeed? Rhys wondered wearily as he pulled a holly spine from his lapel. And vowed to give Timothy's incompetent man-of-affairs a good dressing-down when they got back to Wales.

He had expected a skeleton staff. He most certainly had not expected a lady of the manor, especially not one with an angel face, racehorse legs, and rapier tongue. As far as he was concerned, matters could not get much worse.

Of course he was wrong.

"I think it marvelous," Andrew announced two hours later when they had been settled into their respective moth-eaten chambers and completed their respective lukewarm baths. "Rather like having a holiday in a moldy old Highland castle."

Rhys, eyeing the sagging tester bed on which he was supposed to sleep later, thought of the ancient Highland castle in which his brother and sister-in-law were having their holiday. He doubted it was half as moldy as this place. Nor could he find anything marvelous about the idea.

Other than the faded bed drapes, which he could only hope did not house any owls or other unwelcome creatures, the room had little decoration. It didn't have much in the way of furniture, either. But there were telltale marks on the floor and walls where various objects had once been. Sold off, he decided, like the contents of so many other estates. All that remained was the bed, a wardrobe that probably would have been sold—or fallen—had it not been firmly attached to the wall, a rickety washstand, and a single painting above the mantel. It depicted the front of the house itself, and was every bit as ugly as the subject.

"God help us," Rhys muttered as he wandered over to study the scraggy white dogs painted into the foreground. It took him a minute to realize they were meant to be sheep.

"Are you still determined to correct them as to our identities?" Andrew asked from across the room. He was testing the back of the behemoth wardrobe for a secret door. He enjoyed such pursuits.

"Why are you so determined that I not?"

Andrew tapped away. "Oh, I don't know. I suppose there's something very pleasant about being plain Andrew Jones for a change. Being Lord Tallasey, heir to the Duke of Llans, does get so heavy sometimes. Don't you ever tire of being the ever-formal, ever-proper Captain Lord Rhys Edward-Jones?"

Rhys grunted. As a matter of fact, he was quite happy being the ever-formal, ever-proper Captain Lord Rhys Edward-Jones.

He leaned in to have a closer look at the painting. Yes, definitely sheep.

"A beloved family heirloom, no doubt," his nephew suggested, joining him in front of the painting. "Stop scowling. It is merely old and lacking in taste."

A bell rang faintly from the depths of the house.

"For our sakes," Rhys growled as he and Andrew headed from the room, "let us hope the same cannot be said of our dinner."

Chapter Three

Dinner was awful. The leek soup was cold, the roasted chicken singed to crispy. O'Reilly had done his best, Lizzie knew, but the fates had been working against him. The Joneses had not been expected, his rheumatism was giving him the devil of a time, and his help had been slightly incapacitated.

In the absence of holly boughs to decorate the mantels, Meggie and Nuala had rushed out in search of an alternative. The pine and yew they'd gathered were certainly attractive, bringing a lovely green scent into the rooms. But they'd inadvertently brought home an army of tiny spiders as well. Both women had been bitten from wrist to neck, necessitating salves and compresses and, in Meggie's case, a large glass of restorative wine. The poor girl had still looked a fright as she moved wide-eyed and ointment-spotted around the table to remove the plates.

Beyond all that, Percy had returned, and he had brought Aunt Gregoria with him. The two had not even taken their seats in the drawing room before they proceeded to do untold damage to Lizzie's plan.

"We nearly had our necks broken as we were coming up the drive," Gregoria had snapped as she'd stalked into the drawing room, trailing yards of graying crocheted shawl and pinched disapproval. "Disgraceful, the state of it, all hillocks and holes!"

Scarcely had all the introductions been made when the lady continued sourly, "Honestly, Lizzie, your staff is robbing you blind and doing not a jot of the work for which you pay them their exorbitant wages!"

Nuala, to her vast credit, did not pour the lady's sherry over her tight gray topknot. Nor did she so much as blink when Gregoria snapped, "You have barely covered the bottom of the glass, stupid creature! Lizzie might not be aware of her portion going down your throat, but I am on to you!"

Upon arrival, Percy had promptly settled his rotund bottom onto the settee beside Lizzie. "What are we doing in here?" he asked, gesturing around the drawing room with his own glass, and slopping a generous amount of his own sherry onto one of Lizzie's two semifashionable white dresses. "Thought you'd closed it up."

She had, the winter before. There was no use, after all, in maintaining rooms that were never used. But shabby state aside, the Grand Drawing Room, with its Chinese silk walls and painted ceiling, was one of Hollymore's gems. In honor of the Joneses, Meggie and Nuala had swept, scrubbed, and dusted, and laid a fire in the pine-festooned hearth. Lizzie tried to be optimistic. No spiders and no chimney fires. She couldn't recall when last there had been a fire in that grate. Certainly not since last autumn when Kelly had opened the flue and nearly been brained by a pair of falling bricks.

"This is a lovely room," young Andrew announced sincerely.

"What is that noise?" his uncle demanded.

Lizzie listened. All she could hear was Kelly whistling outside the window. "That," she replied tightly, "is the 'Wexford Carol.' It is one of Ireland's most famous Christmas tunes."

Captain Jones looked down his long nose. His nephew chuckled. "Christmas, Uncle Lawrence. You know, the season to be jolly. A very pretty tune indeed," he said to Lizzie.

What would have been her warm reply was forestalled by Gregoria, demanding, "What wine are we to have with dinner, girl?"

"A nice Burgundy from Lambe's," Lizzie answered. She'd sent Kelly quietly haring into town with a few precious shillings they could scarce afford to spend on something so frivolous as wine. But the Joneses needed to be impressed.

Gregoria snorted. "Washed up on the beach, no doubt, and sold at a tidy price by that reprobate of a wine merchant. Nasty, watery stuff, Burgundy," she remarked to Captain Jones. "Never take it myself, if I can possibly help it." Before the Captain could respond, Gregoria turned on Lizzie again. "Your father had some very nice claret put by. I cannot imagine why you would not be serving that to your guests. Burgundy," she huffed. "An insult, I say."

The truth of the matter was that the very last of the late baron's reserve—which really had been no more than several dozen bottles rendered unsalable by the loss of all means of identifying their type or vintage— had been lost three weeks earlier when the ceiling of the wine cellar had collapsed. Lizzie had no intention of revealing that in front of the Joneses.

Percy did it for her. "Gone under a pile of rubble," he sighed. "Whole bloody ceiling came tumbling down on m'head. Could've done me serious ill."

Unlikely, Lizzie thought. Her cousin's head was hard as marble and just as dense.

And so it had gone on, Gregoria and Percy doing their best, intentional or not, to reveal the state of all but Lizzie's undergarments. Captain and young Mr. Jones had sat politely through it all. Even had he been able to get a word in, Captain Jones seemed disinclined to chat. His nephew had made a few charming efforts to engage Lizzie in stories of Hollymore's lessdamaged days. Percy or Gregoria had been there each time to spoil the moment. So the story of the Charles I windows, the mahogany paneling, the Parma marble had gone untold. Instead, the Joneses heard about Percy's unfortunate encounter with a falling window-sill and the time a trio of mice had scuttled from behind the dining room wall and across Gregoria's feet.

Lizzie had resorted to a second sherry. And she loathed sherry. She might have had a third had Gregoria not effectively drained the bottle.

The meal itself had been worse.

The picture of the polite gentleman, Captain Jones had waited, stiff and expressionless while the ladies had taken their seats around the table. Lizzie felt a surge of pride at the sight: several chairs had been scavenged from around the house to make five, the remnants of her mother's china and Kerry lace tablecloth had been laid—with various candlesticks and dishes covering the holes. There were tapers in all the remaining wall sconces and among the pine and yew boughs.

It was a lovely, cheery scene. Until Captain Jones sat down.

His chair collapsed under him with the speed of a blink. There was a crack, a thump, and there he was, seated perfectly upright against the intact chair back, his own legs straight out in front of him and the four chair legs sticking out from beneath him like the limbs of one of Meggie's spiders.

He didn't say a word, merely sat for a long moment, staring stonily in front of him. Then, slowly, he gathered in his long legs and started to lever himself off the floor. At the sound of the crash, Kelly had rushed into the room. He hurried forward to help, and there was a tense minute as he appeared to wrestle with the captain. Then the wooden splat broke away with a crunch, and Captain Jones was flat on his back.

"Thank you," he muttered upward to the hovering Kelly, sharply waving away the younger man's extended hand, "but I believe it will be best if I manage this myself."

He rose as elegantly as the situation allowed. Kelly, red-faced and wild-haired, rushed off to find another chair. When it arrived, Captain Jones lowered himself rather gingerly. Everyone present held their breath while this chair creaked, shifted, but remained intact. Everyone, that is, except Andrew, who was making faint gasping noises. A quick glimpse in his direction told Lizzie he was making a valiant effort not to laugh. For her own part, she was ready to cry.

"Captain," she managed, voice tight, "I am so very—"

"Miss Fitzhollis." He met her gaze with hard eyes. "Do not mention it."

Just then, Meggie and Nuala bustled in with the cold soup. Percy and Gregoria started flapping their tongues again. Lizzie felt her heart sinking inch by desolate inch.

It didn't take long for both Joneses to give up on their meal, the captain with a deepening scowl and his nephew with an apologetic smile in Lizzie's direction. Then, charming creature that he was, he tried again to engage her in conversation.

"I have been admiring the artwork, Miss Fitzhollis." Lizzie didn't need to look at the pair of hunting scenes on the wall. Both were atrocious. She didn't need to answer, either.

"My brother's work," Gregoria announced. "It's all over the house."

"Ah," Mr. Jones said. "A family tribute."

Percy let out a braying laugh. "Not half. Stuff ain't good for anything but covering the holes in the walls. Good stuff's all been sold."

Lizzie's heart took another sad little dip.

"I . . . er . . . I see." Poor Andrew really was doing his best, she knew. What could he possibly say? He cleared his throat and turned to Gregoria, who was tapping an irritable finger against her empty glass. "I understand Miss Fitzhollis will soon be residing under your roof, madam. That must be a comfort to you."

Gregoria snorted. "As if she'll be with me for any length of time. No, no, off she'll go to take her place in Percy's home, leaving me all alone."

Lizzie closed her eyes for a weary moment. Gregoria didn't want her, never had. Nor was she at all in favor of Percy throwing himself away on his cousin. The splendid boy, she'd declared more than once, could do far better. Meaning, of course, that he ought to be wedding a quiet, malleable heiress. But then, his choosing Lizzie would save him having to make any settlements of his own, so Gregoria had grumblingly resigned herself to the match. Which, of course, was not likely to happen if Lizzie had anything to say about it. If he set his feeble mind to it and was very, very fortunate, Percy might be able to find a woman willing to trade her money for his title. Heaven help her.

"When is the happy event to take place?" Andrew inquired politely.

"Next spring," Percy replied, puffing out his new waistcoat, this one a striped yellow and turquoise.

When swine fly, Lizzie thought. "I do not—"

"*Boy!*" Gregoria bellowed. She'd never bothered to learn Kelly's name.

He had been standing at rigid attention near the door, no doubt waiting to catch the captain should the second chair go the way of the first. He stepped forward. "Yes, ma'am?"

"My glass is empty."

"Yes, ma'am."

Gregoria's ever-pinched face grew more so. "Well, bring me more wine!"

Kelly drew himself up regally. "There isn't more, ma'am."

Gregoria stared him down fishily, but Kelly stood firm. "Hmph." She slapped her napkin onto the table. "Thieves *and* liars, Lizzie. You are a stupid, stupid girl."

And with that, the meal was over.

Now, with her relatives long gone and her guests abed, Lizzie quietly let herself out the back of the house and onto the terrace. She donned yet another of her father's worn coats over her dress and pulled it closely around her as she stepped into the cold Wexford night. In the dark, the maze didn't look quite as overgrown, and it was almost possible to believe that the fountain statue still possessed its head. Almost.

Lizzie crossed the terrace to sit on a cracked step. "Oh, Papa," she whispered, rubbing her cheek against the soft wool of the coat's collar. "I am afraid this is all going very, very badly." Then, unable to stave off the tears any longer, she rested her head on her arms and wept.

She did not see the male figure looking down from the empty window frame above.

Chapter Four

Rhys rose from his slanting and lumpy bed the following morning to find first a cold hearth and thin film of ice on the wash water and later, evidence that some rodent had temporarily nested in one of his stockings. There, too, was a vivid and itchy path of red bumps across his torso where he'd been bitten by some small insect. He added several more red marks to his own face shaving with the icy water.

By the time he descended the creaking staircase, he was in a grim mood, and it was not yet eight o'clock. He assumed his nephew and hostess would still be abed. With any luck, he would be able to order something palatable to eat. After that, he intended to do a quick tour of the house on his own. If Elizabeth insisted on accompanying him around the grounds, so be it. But he didn't need her pointing out each notable nook and cranny inside this decaying monstrosity. Hollymore's days were numbered. Rhys was not going to let Elizabeth make him feel guilty for that. He made a point of never doing anything for which he might later feel guilty. And as he'd had nothing whatsoever to do with either the house's decline or sale, he could do without its mistress's sad little recriminations, silent though they might be.

He would find the entire task considerably more comfortable if he didn't have to look into that lovely, heartbreaking Madonna's face at every turn. Damned if he knew where his well-honed detachment had gone. Elizabeth Fitzhollis was hardly the first beautiful woman he had disappointed in one way or another. And this was just a house. It wasn't as if he had engaged her heart. He didn't owe her anything save some courtesy. There wasn't a reason on earth for the strange, restive feeling in his gut.

He made his grim way to the dining room to find it empty. All the pieces of the broken chair had been cleared away, but Rhys could still hear the crunch and crack echoing around the gloomy space. His jaw tightened. No doubt Andrew would gleefully report the event to the family, who would get endless joy from making Rhys relive it. He would have to remember to sit down carefully for a while. He wouldn't be surprised if his brother had a few chairs altered to collapse.

After an irritable glance at the empty sideboard, he decided he would have to go in search of one of the house's bumbling servants if he wanted to eat. Recalling the meal of the previous evening, he decided he didn't especially *want* to eat, but probably needed to. Hoping the cook couldn't do anything too terrible to several eggs and some toasted bread, he returned to the hall.

The squat little butler with a face like a walnut and an impressive scowl was standing just outside the door. "Can I be of help to you, sir?" he fairly grunted.

"I would like some breakfast, as a matter of fact."

The fellow darted a quick glance at a nearby standing clock. It read, Rhys noted, ten past eleven. Judging from the still pendulum and cracked case, it might well have ticked its last on the night of seventeen December, 1750. The message, however was clear. He was being chastised for rising so early.

"This way." Without waiting to see if Rhys followed, the man stomped off.

Rhys followed. After several halls and turns, the butler tugged several times at a small paneled door.

It creaked outward. Rhys gave a sardonic glance at the little sprig of mistletoe suspended from the lintel. He ducked under it—and felt his jaw going slack in surprise.

The little room was a solarium of sorts. The entire rear wall and part of the ceiling were glass. Cracked glass, certainly, and a few panes seemed to be covered with oilskin, but everything was sparklingly clean and bright. There were vases of winter foliage dotted about, the walls were a sunny yellow with a pattern of plaster lilies, and the graceful marble fireplace was festooned with red ribbon and ivy. The sideboard was loaded with shiny silver serving dishes that were dented and mismatched. And in the midst of it all sat Elizabeth.

She was dressed in a forest-green wool dress, some years out of fashion and visibly mended in spots, but striking nonetheless. The light coming through the windows brought a glow to her fair skin, and picked out fiery lights in her neatly coiled golden hair through which she had whimsically threaded a red ribbon. Titania, Rhys thought, momentarily sorry that he knew the names of no winter holiday faeries, and something warm and wholly unfamiliar wreathed through his chest.

Dear God, she was lovely.

Her glorious smile dimmed somewhat at the sight of him, going cool and polite. "Good morning, Captain."

"Uncle Lawrence!"

Rhys glanced in disbelief at Andrew, very awake, fully dressed, and lounging in his seat across the table. Remnants of breakfast littered his plate.

"Andrew," Rhys said dryly. "You're up a bit early." A good three hours early, as a matter of fact.

"What, sleep through a morning such as this?" His nephew quirked one brow until it nearly met his shock of earth-brown hair. "Perish the thought. Miss Fitz-hollis and I were just about to go out for a stroll. Now you can join us."

"Perhaps the captain would like to eat," Elizabeth suggested. "Help yourself, sir. You will find what you need on the sideboard."

Minutes later, he was settled at the table with a surprisingly appetizing breakfast in front of him, and a cup of marvelously strong coffee in hand. "It appears I am the late riser."

Elizabeth shrugged. "I expect you are accustomed to Town hours."

He wasn't, actually, not of late, but neither was he accustomed to farm hours. "You are not, I see."

"I prefer the morning light," she replied, then blinked as Andrew pushed himself away from the table.

"Back in a tick," the young man said cheerfully. "Then we will go at your convenience, Miss Fitzhollis. Do try the black pudding, Uncle."

He strode from the room, closing the door with a solid thunk behind him. Rhys suddenly found himself alone with Elizabeth in a room that, surprisingly charming as it was, suddenly seemed far too small.

She broke the long silence. "Do you care for black pudding, Captain?"

He did not, but debated fetching some to be polite. He quickly decided against it. There were limits to courtesy. "Perhaps later," he demurred.

Elizabeth delicately wiped her mouth, then set her napkin aside. She propped her elbow on the table and rested her chin in her palm. Her eyes, Rhys noticed, were holly green this morning, and fixed intently on his slightly achy, certainly itchy person. He shifted in his seat.

"Are you married, Captain Jones?"

He blinked at the unexpected question. It was one he loathed as it was usually asked by mothers with marriageable daughters lurking nearby. But as far as he knew, no one lurked, and the question was being asked by a woman with her own nuptials looming.

"No. I am not."

"Why?"

This startled him even more. Women never asked that bit. It just wasn't . . . proper? It was certainly personal. He gave the terse, stock answer. "I have been at sea for the better part of ten years."

"Mmm." She hummed thoughtfully. "That sounds rather lonely."

"Hardly" was his dry retort. "It tended to be among several hundred other men in very cramped quarters."

"Yes, I know that. I meant that being away from home, away from the people who care for you would be lonely."

It had been expected. Rhys shrugged. "Home was always where I left it. Whenever I was on land, it was waiting for me, the same brick and stone, filled with the same faces."

"That," Elizabeth murmured, "is what matters." She shook her head with a small sigh, pulled a holly sprig from a small vase, and played with it absently. "I suppose I ought to apologize, Captain. You certainly did not see the best of Hollymore, or of me yesterday."

"You were not expecting me," he said graciously.

"I was wishing you to Hades, actually."

So very blunt. And so very, very pretty. For some odd reason, Rhys smiled. "You would be far from the first."

"Be that as it may, I was discourteous. You see, Captain Jones, this is my home—"

"Miss Fitzhollis, I . . ."

She waved her free hand. "Yes, yes, Hollymore is Percy's to sell. An unfortunate quirk in the entail. The property could only go to the male heir, but there was nothing to make him keep it."

"Most inconvenient." He hadn't meant to sound glib.

"Indeed." Elizabeth lifted a bronze brow. "Most inconvenient. My father tried to have the matter altered to no avail." She shrugged. "The first Baron Fitzhollis had eight sons, so he saw no need to make any provisions for female inheritance of property. But that is neither here nor there now. Percy had a right to sell Hollymore, and he exercised that right. What I need to say is that it broke my heart."

Curious behavior for a besotted fiancé. But then, Rhys mused, the man would not want to be second in his wife's affections to a pile of stone. There was also the strong possibility that the new Baron Fitzhollis simply did not have the funds for the upkeep.

"I am sorry for that, Miss Fitzhollis." He hadn't meant that to sound glib, either. Especially not when he had seen her crying on the terrace the night before. He hadn't been able to hear, but he hadn't needed to hear to know the sobs were wrenching ones. Heartbroken ones. "I am sorry."

"You don't need to be." Elizabeth removed her face from her hand and sat up very straight. "But there is something I would like from you."

"And that would be?"

"Give Hollymore a chance."

"How?"

"Get to know it. Allow me to show you its great value. Then tell the duke that he mustn't tear it down."

Rhys paused with his coffee cup halfway to his mouth. "Miss Fitzhollis. I simply cannot—"

"Try." Elizabeth faced him squarely, chin up. "The first stone was laid at Hollymore seven hundred and eighty-six years ago. That is a tremendous amount of history to eradicate for little more than sport."

They sat in silence for a long minute. Then Rhys set his cup down. "I don't think I can help you, Miss Fitzhollis. But"—he raised a hand when she started to speak—"I will keep what you've said in mind."

She nodded. "I know that is all I can ask, Captain."

Then, rising to her feet, she announced, "I'll see if Kelly can prepare the cart. We'll be able to cover more ground that way."

Rhys hastily set his cup down and rose. There was no servant to open the door for her, so he reached smoothly around her to do so. As his hand closed around the doorknob, his arm brushed warmly against hers. He could feel the soft friction of wool against wool, could smell the clean, honey scent of her hair. "Elizabeth."

"Yes?"

He hadn't realized he'd spoken aloud. And to be so forward as to speak her name . . . She didn't seem to mind, didn't even appear to have noticed. Rhys shook his head and tried to think of something more appropriate to say. She waited, a slender golden beam in the sunny room.

"For what it's worth," he said gruffly, "this is a lovely room."

"Yes" was her simple reply. "It is."

Rhys turned the knob to open the door. It didn't budge. He pushed. The door still remained resolutely closed.

"It sticks." Elizabeth sighed. "Some of the doors have a tendency to stick . . . every once in a while."

Rhys raised a brow and tried again. When nothing happened, he stepped back and, putting his weight behind it, thumped his shoulder firmly against the paneling. The door groaned, but opened.

"Thank you." Elizabeth stepped past him into the hall. "I—"

The plaster bouquet that decorated the space above the door frame missed Rhys's head by an inch. It fell heavily past his nose and shattered against the floor. He lifted his eyes from his plaster-dusted ankles to Elizabeth. She was staring at him wide-eyed. For a long moment, neither said anything.

Then she sighed, a small, desolate sound. "Oh, dear."

"Yes," Rhys said tersely, pulling the sprig of mistletoe from where it had landed on his shoulder. Mistletoe. *Ridiculous,* but . . . He jerked his gaze away from Elizabeth's soft, mobile mouth, and tossed the sprig away. Then he stepped back into the room.

As he walked stiffly back to the table, he heard her footsteps receding down the hall. "Good God," he muttered, and poured himself more coffee.

Andrew bounded back into the room several minutes later. "Well?" he demanded, dropping solidly into a chair. It, of course, stood firm.

"Well, what?"

"Well, did you kiss her?"

Rhys frowned and shifted in his seat. "That is a ridiculous question."

Andrew looked at the doorway, took in the sight of the fallen plaster ornament and discarded mistletoe. "*Christmas,* Uncle," he sighed. "*Carpe diem* and all that. Oh, well. Did you and Elizabeth at least have a nice chat?"

"*Miss Fitzhollis,*" Rhys said pointedly, "and I . . ." He paused. "What *is* that noise?"

Andrew listened. "Kelly," he said, "singing outside the window. I believe Elizabeth called it the 'Wexford Carol.' Pretty. I'm certain Kelly would gladly teach it to us."

"God forbid."

Andrew shrugged. "*Christmas,* Uncle. So, what did you and Elizabeth discuss?"

"Nosy brat," Rhys muttered with more affection than rancor. "As it happens, our lovely hostess and I don't have a great deal to say to each other."

"Mmm. She wants to save her house and you want to reduce it to rubble."

Rhys glanced at the shattered flowers near the door.

"I don't *want* . . . Oh, for pity's sake. It hardly needs any help in that quarter. And lest you forget, puppy, it is your dear father who wants to raze this behemoth. Even if I cared, it is not my decision."

Andrew appeared to ponder this for a moment. When he opened his mouth, Rhys expected an argument. Instead, his nephew demanded, "Do you know what time Elizabeth gets up in the morning?"

"That is hardly my concern."

"Five o'clock. Do you know what she does at five o'clock in the morning?"

"Of course I don't. Andrew—"

"She does a candlelight tour of the house to see what has broken, disintegrated, or fallen during the night. After that, she fixes what she can. It rained last night."

"And?"

"And this morning when it was barely light she was on the *roof*, Uncle Rhys, trying to nail down loose shingles. After that, she cleaned out the gutters. And yesterday morning, before her solicitor arrived to tell her that her house had been sold, she was trying to dig out a blocked drainage ditch."

Rhys slowly digested this information and found himself growing angry. The image of Elizabeth shoveling out a drainage ditch sent his hackles up. He couldn't even begin to contemplate her clambering around three stories above the hard earth. "What are they thinking," he growled, "to let her do such things?"

"Not *let* her!" Andrew gave a short laugh. "From what I understand, she threatens to sack the lot of her staff—all four persons who are left, that is—every time one of them tries to stop her. And that is nearly every day."

"I suppose you're going to tell me that she doesn't pay them quite enough to climb the roof themselves."

Andrew snorted. "She can't pay them at all, hasn't been able to in more than half a year. They love her," he added quietly. "She loves them. And she loves this place. Desperately."

"How did you learn all this?" Rhys demanded. "Did she pour it out along with the coffee this morning?"

Andrew's handsome face hardened uncustomarily. "You know, Uncle Rhys, sometimes you are hard as nails in a frozen pail."

"I refuse to take that as an insult. And a bit of respect wouldn't be amiss, puppy."

"I respect you, Uncle. I simply do not always understand you."

"You are your father's son," Rhys muttered.

"So I am." Andrew tapped long fingers against the tablecloth. "As it happens, Elizabeth talked about the building of Hollymore. She didn't say a word about how she spends nearly twenty hours of every day trying to keep it from tumbling down. No, I heard the story from O'Reilly."

"Who?"

"The butler—and cook and window fixer. Joseph O'Reilly. I've just cornered him in the hallway. Surly fellow until you get to know him; he's really quite charming. Poor man suffers terribly from rheumatism. Ghastly this time of year. And Kelly says—"

"Who?"

"Kelly. Corcoran. The footman, groom, and gardener. And owl trapper this week, as it happens. Elizabeth would never have told me any of this. So they did."

Rhys closed his eyes wearily and leaned back in his chair. A creak made him think better of it, and he lowered the chair legs carefully to the floor. His nephew always got to know people—the names of spouses and children and family dogs. Rhys barely knew the Christian name of his butler. He had no idea if the man had children or a dog.

"What is it you want me to do, Andrew?"

Andrew opened his mouth, then closed it again. After a moment he announced, "Christmas is next week. Bad enough that we're here at all, but far worse the reasons. Can we simply not spoil the holidays for Elizabeth and her household?"

Rhys knew he'd done that already, just by arriving. And he could hardly be expected to traipse around decking the halls and wassailing, or whatever it was these people did at Christmas.

Mistletoe. *Ridiculous.*

"Andrew . . ."

"Please, Uncle Rhys."

Rhys reached for his now-cold coffee. "I will not sing," he muttered.

"Fair enough," his nephew shot back, and began whistling as he checked the sideboard for hidden drawers.

Chapter Five

Lizzie cleared the top of the desk with a dejected sweep of her arm. The sheaf of bills thudded heavily into the waiting drawer, which she shoved closed. It hardly mattered anymore. In the six days Captain Jones had been in residence, he had not shown so much as a smidgen of interest in saving Hollymore. He had strode about the house and grounds on his long legs, militarily stiff and forceful, taking notes and occasionally muttering to himself or his nephew.

He had been polite. Too polite, really. Lizzie had found conversing with him rather like talking to a very well-trained parrot. He fixed her with his cool blue gaze, tilted his head as she spoke, and repeated back the occasional phrase. He had not appeared in the least impressed by the Charles windows or the Boyne paneling. Lizzie's spirits had lifted somewhat when he'd stood thoughtfully in front of the green marble fireplace in the Great Hall. Massive and ancient, it had the family symbol: the holly bough, carved into its surface. Now, in honor of Christmas, the top was festooned with entwined holly and ivy. It was a beautiful piece, saved from sale by the simple fact that removing it would have been impossible without destroying the entire hearth and chimney.

Captain Jones had soon dashed Lizzie's hopes by announcing, "Perhaps my brother will want this salvaged for the new lodge."

Small blessings, she tried to convince herself. At

least the marble wouldn't be reduced to rubble with the stone surrounding it.

She'd caught the captain watching her often, sometimes with surprisingly—and, she had to admit, appealingly—softer eyes. Each time, he had glanced quickly away, and for that Lizzie was grateful. She couldn't have borne seeing the pity she knew was there. Captain Jones was a hard man, but not, she'd come to believe, a wholly unfeeling one. There was certainly an abundance of affection for his nephew in those ice-blue eyes. He might try to cloak it, just as Lizzie did her anguish over her home, but as she saw the flashes of emotion in him, she expected she wasn't any better at hiding hers.

She didn't want his pitying glances. She didn't really want him looking at her at all. It made her feel skittish and slightly warm and came with the inexplicable and absurd urge to check her reflection in the nearest tarnished mirror.

Lizzie glanced up now as the bells from the local church sounded faintly in the distance. It was noon on Christmas Eve. No more work would be done outside today in the county. Inside, even here at Hollymore, kitchens would be filled with the smells of the holiday, and the last of the decorations would be laid.

Her hopes for her house were all but dashed. It had been the hardest admission she'd ever had to make, but she had been forced to silently acknowledge that beneath the greenery and candles, behind the red of holly berries and scent of cloves, Hollymore was still a slowly crumbling pile of stone, beloved as each stone might be.

She had one last hope. It wasn't a great one, but it was all she had.

After that . . . The day after Christmas was St. Stephen's Day. She would hand over the house to Captain Jones and, while the festivities of the day went on through Wexford County, she would slip quietly into her place in Gregoria's house. No fuss, no dramatic farewells. She would just as quietly start perusing the Dublin newspapers she would borrow from the Reverend Mr. Clark—Gregoria refused to pay so much as a penny for something so frivolous as the printed word—and if she were very lucky, would find a post as a companion or governess by the new year.

"Well," she said aloud, standing and patting Uncle Clarence's bronze hedgehog on its misshapen head, "enough of that."

Her staff would see to most of the traditional Christmas Eve activities, but there was one she insisted on doing herself. Propped just outside the French doors was a stack of small holly and yew wreaths, twenty-six of them to be exact, strung together with twine. She gathered them up, ignoring the prick of holly spines through her worn wool coat, and set off through the gardens. The little family chapel hadn't been used in decades, since its roof had collapsed, but the ground was still consecrated, still the resting place of departed Fitzhollises.

Lizzie placed the first wreath on the grave of the first Baron Fitzhollis. The marker had long since been lost to the earth, but each generation had taught the next where the right spot was. Lizzie's father had brought her, year after year on Christmas Eve, to lay the wreath. Now she wondered who would take on the hallowed task. She couldn't bear to think that the precious Christmas tradition would be lost. Perhaps she could tell Andrew. Or Captain Jones. Strange as it was, she had a feeling that he would understand.

No, she thought. He might understand, but there was no more reason for him to care about her long-gone Fitzhollis ancestors than for their house.

"I'm sorry, my lord," she whispered to the first Baron's headstone. "I . . . I tried."

The next twenty-two wreaths went carefully, reverently one by one onto the graves of the Fitzhollis men who had died at the Battle of the Boyne. "I'm sorry," she offered to each. And, as she went, found a precious and growing comfort in the task and in the quiet around her.

Of the last three wreaths, the first went to her great-uncle Clarence. She didn't apologize to him. He'd been a jolly little man who'd lived for his art, and for the next day of eating, drinking, and being merry. "Happy Christmas, Uncle," Lizzie offered to the stone marker he had carved himself. It depicted him as a sort of cheery Irish Bacchus, wearing a holly laurel and holding a chisel, a paintbrush, and a bottle of wine. *"Sláinte."* She had surreptitiously saved a little vial of claret from the previous night's dinner, and tipped its contents now onto the earth at the base of the stone.

The second wreath was for her mother. And the last, the fourth she had placed on its spot, was for her father. She sank down beside it, not caring about the cold or damp and pulled her legs up to her chest, wrapping her arms tightly around them.

"I've done nearly all I can, Papa," she told him. "I wish I could have done more or better—but that's neither here nor there now. I love Hollymore with all my heart, but then, I loved you, too, and I've managed to carry on without you, hard as it has been at times."

She rested her chin on her knees. "I'm thinking I'll go to Dublin, if I can find a post. Or England, perhaps. Yes, yes, I know what you think of England, but I've never been out of Ireland and I should like to see London. And you never know. Perhaps I will find a family with a well-stocked library and constant fires in the hearths." She smiled as a brisk breeze lifted the curls around her face. "Fair enough. I don't mind a bit of cold. But I cannot stay with Gregoria. You wouldn't want me to."

She fell silent for a long moment, listened to the wind rattling in the trees and whispering through the cracks and crevices of the fallen chapel. "It isn't much, Papa," she continued softly, "but I will say a prayer, make a wish tonight. I've never wished for something so big as a house before. It was always for candy on Christmas, or new puppies in the stable. I suppose I was afraid of being disappointed if I asked for something larger." She recalled the mountains of sweets she and her father had shared every Christmas, gorging themselves until they were both ill. "Oh, Papa. Well, they say no wish made on Christmas Eve in Ireland goes unanswered."

She patted the hard earth. "There's never any harm in trying. You taught me that."

A crunch from behind her made her start. She turned to find Captain Jones not twenty feet away and wondered if he'd heard her conversing with her father. Not that it would matter if he had, she supposed. He was the one who was intruding.

He seemed to realize that. He cleared his throat. "I am sorry. I am interrupting a private moment."

Elizabeth shrugged. "I was nearly done." She patted the earth again, and made sure the wreath was centered. "Happy Christmas, Papa," she murmured. "I love you."

Then she rose to her feet and brushed some lingering dirt from her heavy skirts. "Can I help you, Captain?"

He was looking, she noted, rather less starched than he had during his first several days at Hollymore. Living without a valet, she assumed. Much to his credit and amid much grumbling, O'Reilly had surpassed himself in the kitchen, but had adamantly drawn the line at acting as manservant to the guests. "I'll feed him," he'd muttered of the captain, "but damned if I'll put my hands on his things. Let him wear dirty drawers. It'll serve him right enough."

Lizzie had no idea about the state of Captain Jones's drawers, but the rest of him had become appealingly rumpled of late. His cravats had wilted, softening the line of that formidable jaw, and his buttons and boots had lost their sharp, almost painful gleam.

It was clear he'd been out walking in the cold. His midnight hair was wind-tousled, his skin given a virile glow. He might not be a handsome man, but Lizzie, try as she might, couldn't help appreciating the sight of him. She busied herself rewinding her father's fraying old muffler about her neck.

"I have been having a last stroll around the grounds," Captain Jones remarked. "Andrew and I will be leaving on Monday."

The faint flare of disappointment startled her. She decided she would miss young Mr. Jones's genial presence. It had been so long since there had been infectious cheer in the house. She certainly would not miss his uncle's stern, stolid presence. Of course she wouldn't.

"You'll be leaving on St. Stephen's Day," she said. "Is that significant?"

"The day," she replied. "Not your leaving. It commemorates the day that a wren betrayed St. Stephen to his enemies by singing loudly in the bush behind which he was hiding."

Rhys raised a brow. "Interesting event to celebrate."

Elizabeth tucked the last errant strand of wool into her collar. It should be ermine, he found himself thinking, or the finest, softest kasimir. Not that the dun-colored wool detracted in the least from her beauty. She was glorious, shining gilt and ivory in the cold winter air.

"It is a day for song and mummery," she replied. "Boys dress up in costume and traipse through the villages, collecting money and gaming. I thought Andrew might enjoy it."

"Yes," Rhys said automatically, "he probably would. But we'll be on our way back to Wales."

"Mmm. Pity." She glanced around. "Where is Andrew?"

Rhys knew she wouldn't ask the same question should Andrew be present and he himself nowhere to be seen. He promptly quashed the twinge of regret. "He is in the house somewhere, tapping and prying at the paneling, looking for hidden passages. Foolish boy."

"Oh, not at all."

"Ah. Should I take it you have been encouraging him in this endeavor?"

Elizabeth smiled. "I haven't actually, but only because I wasn't aware he was searching. I hope he finds something."

"Do you expect him to?"

"Well, I have been searching all my life and have found nothing more exciting than a secret drawer in my father's desk." She smiled again. "It was full of spare quills, or rather, the remains of them. Papa and I decided the drawer had last been used by Great-Grandfather Seymour. He hoarded everything except gold, more's the pity. When he died, my grandfather found three hundred forks stashed away in various parts of the house. Heaven only knew what sort of entertaining my great-grandfather was planning on doing . . . Anyway, Andrew ought to find what he's searching for if he tries hard enough. Hollymore is like that."

Apparently it occurred to her that she'd belatedly hit upon one more of Hollymore's charms: its mysteries. She launched into, "There are priest holes from the fifteenth century. And certainly some passageways used by various Fitzhollises in smuggling activities. I'm certain if Andrew explored that part of the old dungeon that hasn't caved in, he might find an oubliette or two . . ." She broke off at the sight of Rhys's scowl. "Oh. Oh, dear. I do not mean to say he is likely to fall *into* an oubliette . . ." She gave up. "I believe I will return to the house. O'Reilly will be needing help in the kitchen."

"Allow me to escort you."

He offered his arm. She took it—with some reluctance, he thought, but she took it. He could see a hole in the thumb of one woolen glove, and he found the sight oddly charming, even as he found himself cursing the wastrel men of her family for allowing such a prize to be reduced to wearing much-mended clothes and holey gloves.

As they started back to the house, he pondered the scene upon which he had clumsily intruded. The sight had first stopped him in his brisk tracks, then had had him literally creeping closer. He didn't think he had ever actually crept before. But she had been so beautiful, heartbreakingly so, first settling the wreaths carefully on the graves with a quiet word or two, then, seated like a child on the cold earth, legs tucked up, conversing with a headstone and little green twist of holly and yew. He hadn't meant to eavesdrop. He wished he hadn't.

It isn't much, Papa, but I will say a prayer, make a wish tonight. I've never wished for something so big as a house before. It was always for candy on Christmas, or new puppies in the stable. I suppose I was afraid of being disappointed . . .

"What are you going to wish for?" he asked, and was startled by his own question. Embarrassed, too, that he had given himself away.

Elizabeth, however, glanced up and gave him one of her stunning if fleeting smiles. "You overheard me talking to my father," she remarked, seemingly not angry in the least.

"I didn't mean to eavesdrop, Miss Fitzhollis. I certainly—"

"Elizabeth."

"I beg your pardon?"

She stopped beside a particularly ugly little statue

of a cherub, pulled her hand from his arm, and turned to face him fully. "It is Christmas Eve. I think such formality seems wrong somehow, when we should be thinking of peace and goodwill, and can be suspended for two days. Don't you?"

She rubbed a bit of grime from the cherub's head with her sleeve. Then she removed a cluster of holly berries from her pocket and deftly arranged them on the stone curls. That done, she looked expectantly back to Rhys. He fought the urge to rub a faint muddy smudge from her cheek.

"Well?" she demanded pleasantly.

He'd never spent much time contemplating peace on earth and goodwill to men. After all, he'd been a naval officer at war for so many years. "That is an appalling cherub."

"Isn't he?" she answered, fondly patting the thing's fat cheek. "My uncle Clarence's work."

"Ah. I should have known." Then, without thinking, he said, "Rhys."

Her smooth brow furrowed. "I beg your pardon?"

He was not going to have *Lawrence* falling from those inviting lips, not if Andrew and St. Stephen and all the heavenly hosts demanded it. Not when he could hear her saying his proper name. "If I am to call you Elizabeth, you will call me Rhys."

"Rhys." She pondered that quite seriously for a moment, then laughed briefly, a wonderful, silvery sound. "It suits you. Far better than Lawrence, if I may say so without giving offense to your parents."

His late father hadn't given a damn what his second son was called as long as he responded and the first son stayed healthy. His mother, Rhys decided, would find the entire story vastly entertaining. He might even tell it to her when he got back to Wales, although he wasn't much of a bard. That was yet one more of Tim's talents.

"No offense at all. Elizabeth." He felt his hand lifting of its own accord toward a loose gold curl. He clenched his fingers into a fist and shoved it into his greatcoat pocket. "What are you going to—" He broke off and shook his head, wondering where his impeccable sense of propriety had gone. "No. I should not even think of asking."

She laughed again. "I rather like that you did. And I am glad that you overheard that particular tradition. Everyone should know to make a wish on an Irish Christmas Eve. You included, Captain. It might very well come true."

"Ah, the simplicity of superstition."

She gave him an exasperated glance, but didn't take umbrage. "They could be far worse," she chided mildly. "Another says that if you die on Christmas Eve, you go straight to Heaven."

"Is that what you will wish for, then? My speedy demise?"

"Goodness. A jest. Very good, Captain." As he watched, surprised, charmed, and increasingly warm, she removed another sprig of holly from her pocket, tucked it into a buttonhole on his coat, and briskly patted his chest. "As you could easily guess, I will make a wish for Hollymore."

With that, she stepped back, draped an arm around the cherub, and surveyed her handiwork on Rhys's coat. She gave a satisfied nod.

In that brief moment, Rhys was enchanted to his toes.

And suddenly angry. "Did you inherit nothing at all?" he heard himself demanding harshly. "I cannot believe your father left you with nothing . . ."

This time her smile was slow and sad before it turned blithe. "Of course I did." She patted the stone shoulder. "I inherited all the remaining artwork at Hollymore. And that is something worth more than all the gold in the world to me. Now, I really must see how O'Reilly is getting on with our dinner."

She hurried off. Rhys followed. As he went, he noticed something he had not before: There was mistletoe hanging from a good many of the scrubby trees that lined the scrubbier lawn. Sighing, he continued on his way. He caught up with Elizabeth in the Great Hall where she appeared to be supervising the maneuvering of a better part of the local woods. Andrew, the young footman, and the elderly butler were wrestling with a massive, slightly feral-looking log. They were trying to cram it into the fireplace, which, despite its own mammoth proportions, seemed to be resisting the intrusion.

Rhys studied an arm-sized twig that jutted from the log and was sticking out from under his nephew's elbow. "What," he demanded, "is that?"

"It's the blockna . . . blockna . . ." Andrew replied, panting somewhat as he hefted his end in a different direction, trying to make it fit. "One more time, if you please, Kelly."

"Bloc na Nollag," the footman grunted from his side.

"The Yule log," Elizabeth explained as she, too, joined in the fray. "Now, Andrew, if you lift there, and Kelly, you turn it there . . . O'Reilly, at the risk of having you snarl and snort at me, might I suggest that this is not the best activity for your rheumatism. Perhaps you ought to relinquish . . ." The butler did, just as Rhys stepped forward to help. The behemoth of a log landed squarely on his booted toes.

Andrew would later report that the responding long, lurid, and decidedly inventive curse had been heard all the way to Wexford town. By the time he had hobbled up the stairs to see how many of his ten toes were intact, the unfortunate *bloc na Nollag* had been relegated to the woodshed. When Rhys hobbled back down several hours later on ten unbroken but complaining toes, it had been replaced by a much smaller, much less interesting specimen. From the po-faced looks the staff gave him as they served the meal, he surmised that it all had been a sad disappointment, the responsibility for which landed squarely on his uniformed shoulders. Elizabeth, at least, inquired after his feet. She then cast a mournful look at the Hall hearth as they passed on the way to the drawing room. It was almost a relief to retire.

Once settled in bed, Rhys stared grimly into his own fire. Thirty-six hours. In thirty-six hours, he and Andrew would be safely on their way back to Wales. By the time Rhys returned, demolition should have begun. He wouldn't have to set foot in Hollymore again. He wouldn't have to suffer the recriminating glares of the scowling O'Reilly, or endure Andrew's silent but potent opinions on the matter of his empty rib cage. He had a heart, damn it. It simply refused to bleed on demand. Not even for someone like Elizabeth.

Thirty-six hours, and he would never have to face Elizabeth again. Only, he found himself thinking as his eyes drifted shut, a man could do far worse than face Elizabeth closely and often. For a fleeting second, Rhys wished that once, just once, she would look at him with the same dreamy eyes she had for her sad if splendid ruin of a house . . .

His own eyes sprang wide as the door to his bedchamber creaked open. Andrew stood in the doorway, candle in hand, eyes wide. "I think," the young man announced without preamble, "that you'd better come with me now."

"Andrew—"

"Please, Uncle Rhys. It's important."

Rhys couldn't have refused the plea if he'd tried. Sighing, wincing, he climbed from the bed and donned his dressing gown. He followed Andrew into the hall. There were candles lit everywhere in the house, and they were being allowed to burn all night. Another Irish tradition, Elizabeth had explained. A fire hazard,

Rhys thought, but certainly an attractive one. With their light, Andrew didn't need the single taper he carried. Not, Rhys realized, until he entered an empty bedchamber down the hall.

It was one they'd seen briefly during their early tour of the floor. Apparently Andrew had been back. The wardrobe door stood wide, and Rhys watched as his nephew disappeared through it. "Well, come along!" came impatiently from the depths. Rhys poked his head in. Where Andrew should have been was another door—or rather several panels standing open. A scuffling echoed from the space behind it.

"Andrew," Rhys growled, "come out of there now. You cannot know if it is safe—" He then grunted as a heavy, sheet-shrouded object came sliding out to thud into his shin.

"Take that into the room," Andrew commanded, "and come back. There are three more."

Several minutes later, uncle and nephew stood staring at the four paintings they had uncovered and propped against the bed. Rhys had collected more candles from the hallway. He leaned in close to the first painting and couldn't stop himself from letting out a low whistle.

"Is it . . . ?" Andrew whispered.

The face of a not especially pretty young girl looked back at them sourly. Yes, Rhys thought, an ugly child, but a very distinctive style. "Gainsborough," he announced.

"I thought so. And that one."

There was little question that the long-faced Madonna was El Greco. The dark supper scene could only be Rembrandt. But it was the final piece, the delicate lady in silk and ermine with the unmistakable emblems of English royalty surrounding her, that had Rhys's jaw going slack. It could have been Elizabeth, but he suspected that he was looking at the ill-fated Catherine Howard, fifth wife of Henry VIII.

"Holbein," he murmured.

"Valuable?" Andrew whispered.

"Extremely."

It appeared Christmas had arrived early at Hollymore. *Allelujah,* Rhys heard in his head. In chorus. Elizabeth Fitzhollis was about to become a very wealthy young woman. She would be able to give Timothy every penny he'd paid for her home—and more. *Allelujah.*

Then it occurred to him that perhaps this gift of some quirky magi was not something to celebrate.

Chapter Six

On Christmas morning, Elizabeth gave herself the ultimate luxury and stayed in bed past seven. Then, after a quick and chilly wash, she donned the one wool dress, the soft green, she possessed that had neither stains nor mended spots, and headed downstairs.

"Happy Christmas, Miss Lizzie!" Meggie chirped as she hurried by with an armful of holly.

"Happy Christmas." Lizzie lifted a brow at the maid's departing back. Such a hurry.

The Lily Room was empty, but breakfast was laid out on the sideboard. There was chocolate this morning, a rare treat, and Lizzie stood for a moment, steaming cup held to her face so she could breathe in the rich aroma. She noted with a smile that someone had replaced the mistletoe. It might have been a silly gesture, but it was a charming one.

Now, if only a knight would come along, tall and strong, armor shining, for one sweet kiss . . .

"Happy Christmas, miss." Kelly poked his face into the room. "Is there anything I can fetch for you?"

"No, Kelly. Thank you. Happy . . ." But he had already gone. "Well," Lizzie said to the empty doorway. There would be no knight, shining or otherwise, on this day, she thought, and resolutely pushed the image of aquamarine eyes and a poet's mouth in a warrior's face from her mind. She would settle for old friends.

She took her time with breakfast, doing her best to

savor what would be her last Christmas in her beloved home. Somehow, though, it didn't seem to be working. It was, she decided, being alone that was dampening her festive mood.

She nearly sighed with relief when Andrew bounded in a half hour later. Seeing the mistletoe, he grinned and blew her a saucy kiss from the doorway. He had a sprig of holly tucked into his lapel and a winning smile on his handsome face. He stopped at her side and bowed with a charming flourish. "Good morning, Elizabeth, and a very happy Christmas to you!"

Feeling much better, Lizzie returned the greeting. Then, "Will your uncle be joining us soon?"

Andrew rolled his eyes. "Oh, Uncle Lawrence. I doubt we'll see him for some hours yet."

"But it's Christmas morning."

"So it is. And a glorious one at that. There is frost on the ground and a glimmer in the air."

Yes, Lizzie had stood at the window, drinking in the sight. But the glimmer had dimmed. "Captain Jones will not be joining us for church, then?"

"Unlikely." Andrew tucked cheerfully into his sliced ham. "I, however, am very much looking forward to it. When do we leave? And can we walk?"

She always had, but had assumed they would take the dog cart. "If you don't mind a mile in the cold."

"Mind? On the contrary." Both glanced up as O'Reilly stomped into view. "Ah. Good morning, O'Reilly, and a happy Christmas."

"Happy Christmas, Miss Lizzie. And to you, young sir." The butler appeared to wink. But no, Lizzie thought. He never winked. She worried that the poor man might be developing a palsy. No one knew precisely how old O'Reilly was, but he certainly would not see sixty again. "We'll be off to Mass, miss. Is there anything you'll be needing afore we go?"

"No, thank you, O'Reilly. Happy . . ." And he was gone, too. "Hmm. Curious."

Andrew shoved a last forkful of eggs into his mouth, then jumped to his feet. "Shall we be off, then?"

Bemused, Lizzie rose. "Certainly. But—"

"Splendid. Now you go fetch yourself something warm to wear. It's frightfully chilly out there. I felt it right to my toes."

Lizzie couldn't imagine what he had been doing outside, but didn't have the chance to ask. Andrew was hustling her out of the room and into the hall. A few minutes later, booted and cloaked, Lizzie joined him on the front steps. A distinct crunching sound caught her attention. Andrew didn't seem to notice.

"What is that noise?" she asked. It seemed to be coming from behind the house. But when she started toward it, Andrew grasped her hand and tucked her arm through his. "Oh, Kelly puttering about before they go," he commented cheerily. "Come along now, before I freeze on the spot."

He whistled a tune as they headed down the drive. Lizzie recognized it. "That is the 'Wexford Carol.' "

"Indeed. Lovely piece. Now, do tell me, will I be allowed to sing very loudly in church this morning . . . ?"

He did, much to the disapproval of Aunt Gregoria and to the vast delight of most of the congregation. Lizzie was grateful for his genial presence by her side as she said her fervent prayers. And when she, along with the rest, chose a wisp of straw from the manger— a symbol of blessing and luck that she so needed— Andrew tucked one of his own into his pocket.

When the service was over, he did a charming social circuit, pumping the hand of a bemused but delighted Reverend Clark, chatting with Josiah Lambe, tickling the Kinahans' baby under the chin, and sending pretty young Ann Dermott into a blush with his cheeky grin.

He even offered his hand and merry greetings to Percy, who was sporting a truly ridiculous combination of purple-striped waistcoat and green coat. "And may I say that is a very fetching hat, ma'am," he complimented Gregoria on her storm-gray bonnet. Whether because the milliner had sewn it on too tightly to remove or in honor of the day, the thing sported a rather prickly looking collection of black feathers.

To Lizzie's astonishment, Gregoria actually grunted a thank-you. Followed, not surprisingly by, "I trust you have managed to obtain something potable to serve with dinner, girl."

It was only more Burgundy, actually, but Lizzie smiled and replied, "Of course, Aunt." In truth, she hadn't been expecting her relatives for dinner, but she probably should have. They always came when they were least wanted. O'Reilly could be counted upon to prepare more food than was necessary on Christmas. With luck, Percy would leave some for the rest of the party. "We shall see you this afternoon, then?"

"Not a bit of it." Percy thrust his familiar snuff up his nose and sneezed onto Andrew's coat. "Coming now, of course."

"Of course." Lizzie swallowed her sigh. "Well, shall we go?"

Gregoria's beady eyes slewed around. "Where is the carriage?"

"We walked, Aunt."

"Walked?" was the disbelieving response. "Good heavens, why? Has that good-for-nothing groom of yours driven the cart into the ground?"

"We walked," Andrew cut in with his winning smile, "for the sheer pleasure of it. I would be honored if you would take my arm, madam, or I will certainly run and have your carriage readied."

Lizzie could almost see the wheels turning behind her aunt's eyes. To subject her ancient carriage to the winter roads . . . "Give me your arm, young man," the lady said imperiously. "We shall walk."

It was not a particularly merry group who arrived at Hollymore an hour later. Gregoria had carped about the state of the roads, the wear on her shoes, and the paucity of the fires at Hollymore. Percy, for his part, had snorted and sneezed, and spent the entire walk trying to slip an arm around Lizzie and suggesting various dates for a spring wedding. Through it all, Andrew maintained his goodwill and charm. Lizzie wanted to cry.

Nuala greeted them just inside the door. She cheerfully accepted coats and cloaks, not so much as batting an eyelash when Gregoria snapped, "And don't you be going through my pockets! I know precisely what is there."

"Has Captain Jones come down?" Lizzie asked quietly.

Nuala nodded. "And up again. Now, Kelly's got a fire going in the blue parlor, and there's cider and eggnog ready. You just go have a nice sit, miss, 'til he's ready."

"He . . . Kelly?" Lizzie began, but Nuala was bustling off. "Well."

"Marvelous. Eggnog!" Andrew was all but pushing Gregoria across the floor.

"Yes. Eggnog," Lizzie murmured. "Very nice. But we haven't any brandy . . ."

Percy got a grip on her arm just as Kelly appeared briefly in the facing hall door. Elizabeth knew she was mistaken, but the objects in his arms looked just like champagne bottles. That was quickly forgotten when Meggie scuttled through a far archway, a steaming basin in her hands and what appeared to be the medicine basket tucked precariously under her arm. She disappeared through the door leading to the back stairs.

"Really must insist on speaking with you, Lizzie," Percy insisted, casting a nervous glance toward the grand stairway. "Matters to be settled, y'know."

"Oh, Percy!" Lizzie blew out an exasperated breath. "There is nothing to be settled. Now, if you would let go of me . . ."

He didn't, and tried to pull her right past the parlor door. Sighing, she tugged her arm free of his grasp and followed Andrew and Gregoria into the room. The holly decorations seemed to have multiplied overnight. There were bunches and garlands and little wreaths with bright candles in them on every surface. There was a large fire burning merrily in the grate and, as promised, mulled cider and eggnog on the side table.

"Mistletoe!" Percy cried. Lizzie elbowed him smartly in his well-padded ribs.

"Eggnog." Gregoria plunked herself down in the seat closest to the fire. "And don't be stingy, young man!" she commanded as Andrew hurried to fill a cup for her.

"No later than April, Lizzie." Percy rubbed his rib cage as he made his own quick way to the refreshments. Lizzie closed her eyes for a weary moment, then smiled as Andrew pressed a warm cup into her hands.

"Have a little faith in this blessed day," he murmured, then was off again to refill Gregoria's waving cup.

A long quarter hour later, footsteps sounded outside the door. Kelly opened it with a flourish and stepped aside to admit Captain Jones. Lizzie's heart, heeding no message her brain was sending, gave a cheery little thump at the sight of him. His coat shone richly in the light, his boots gleamed with new polish, and he'd combed his hair back so it gleamed like ebony above his brow. Where, Lizzie noticed, he had several angry-looking scratches.

His eyes met hers, warm blue, and he smiled. It was a smile like his nephew's: swift and startling in its power. This time, Lizzie's heart did a dizzying flip.

"Happy Christmas," he announced huskily. "I think, Elizabeth, that you should come with me. You need to hear the decisions I have come to regarding Hollymore."

He held out an arm, over which was draped her cloak. His hand, she noticed as she rose a bit shakily to her feet, bore more scratches. Confused, pulse skittering, Lizzie met him halfway and allowed him to help her into her cloak. "Where are we going?"

"Outside," he replied. "This needs to be done outside."

"Now, see here"—Percy hauled himself to his feet—"Can't just be taking m'fiancée off like th—"

"I can and I will. Elizabeth?"

She did not protest as he guided her out the door. In fact, she didn't say anything at all as they left the house. Rhys kept his eyes on her as they reached the terrace steps. He wanted to see her expression every step of the way. His determination almost had him going tip over tail when he stepped on a loose slate. But it was worth it, worth the stumble and every painful scratch on his body, when she saw the maze.

"What . . . ? Who . . . ?" Her eyes were wide, brilliant as she surveyed the dramatically if not particularly neatly trimmed hedge. "Did you do this?"

"I had help." And he had. Every member of the staff had pitched in, working by his side. "When were you last inside?"

She shook her glossy head. "I don't quite recall. Years."

"Do you remember the way?" He guided her through the entrance.

"I . . . I'm not certain."

"Trust me." Tucking her arm firmly through his, not feeling a single one of the deep holly scratches that the little maid had carefully bandaged, he walked until they met the first turn. "Now, first, you must allow me to introduce myself before we go any farther."

She stared at him, brow furrowed. Damn, but she was beautiful. It was all Rhys could do to keep from hauling her into his arms there and then. "But I know who you are," she insisted.

He smiled and stepped away. Bowing low before her, he said, "Captain Lord Rhys Edward-Jones at your service, Miss Fitzhollis."

"Lord . . ." She blinked. "Oh, dear. Truly?"

"Truly. Your solicitor's eyesight is apparently rather poor."

"Oh, dear. Yes, it is. But why did you—"

"Never mind that." Rhys took her arm again and

guided her to the next turn. "My brother is the Duke of Llans."

She pondered this for a moment. Rhys half expected her to rail at him. Instead, she sighed. "So Andrew . . ."

"Andrew is Viscount Tallasey. He will someday be the Duke of Llans." Before she could speak again, he changed the subject and demanded, "Why on earth would you even think of marrying Percy Fitzhollis?"

This earned him a small, heartbreaking smile. "Have him, have my house," she answered quietly.

Rhys muttered something rude. Elizabeth shrugged. "If I said yes, he would not sign the final papers selling Hollymore to your brother."

"He lied. All the papers were signed, sealed, and delivered."

Once more, to his surprise, Elizabeth did not rail. Instead, she sighed again. "Yes, I rather thought so."

"So?"

"So, I was *never* going to marry Percy. Not even for Hollymore. I am selfish, perhaps, Captain . . . er, I beg your pardon. Lord Rhys."

"Rhys," he said gruffly. "And you are not selfish. You are a splendid, brave, clever woman." They walked to the next turn.

"Now what?"

"Now this." He reached into his pocket and withdrew the sprig of mistletoe that Andrew had pushed into his hand early that morning. All four members of Elizabeth's staff had had spares on hand in the last hour.

He gently tucked the mistletoe into Elizabeth's braided coronet. And finally, at last, not a moment too soon for his liking, he hauled her into his arms, up onto her toes, and kissed her. She gave a small, surprised squeak. Then she was kissing him back, sweetly, sensually, and every inch of his taut body went to flame. "God," he murmured against her lips. "Dear God, Elizabeth."

It seemed an aeon later, yet far too soon, when he

gently held her away from his chest—where, he noted, his heart was pounding strongly enough to burst free. "I have a gift for you."

Her eyes were slightly unfocused as she replied, "That wasn't it?"

He gave a pained chuckle. "No. No, this is something far better."

"I don't think it could be," she said hazily, and Rhys almost grabbed her again.

"Trust me." He satisfied himself by holding her hand this time. "Now, this isn't really from me. I would say it is a gift from Hollymore. I am hoping, of course, that you'll allow me to take care of the matter of the house, but if you'd rather, this ought to more than pay for all you wish."

"What *are* you talking about?"

"Wait," he commanded, and used his free hand to cover her eyes as they approached the final turn.

He'd had Kelly build makeshift easels for the paintings. It had occurred to him that a half hour in the winter air wouldn't precisely be good for a Rembrandt, but he'd needed to have things just this way. There were blankets to cover the paintings as soon as Elizabeth had seen them, and no doubt all of her staff was lurking nearby. They could haul off the art. He intended to have his hands full of Elizabeth.

"My lord . . . Rhys," she protested as he kept his hand over her eyes.

"Hush." He guided her into the center of the maze and directly in front of the paintings. "Miss Fitzhollis, allow me to present Hollymore's salvation: Misters Gainsborough, El Greco, Rembrandt, and Holbein. Happy, happy Christmas, Elizabeth."

He removed his hand.

Elizabeth stared. "Oh. Oh, my." He heard her breath catch. "Where on earth did you find these?"

"Andrew discovered them, actually, behind a secret panel in one of the bedchambers. I assume one of your ancestors tucked them away for some reason, and they've been waiting for you to find them."

He stood back, heart swelling for her.

She glanced up. "You're whistling."

She was right. "So I am."

" 'The Wexford Carol.' " Elizabeth reached up and stroked her hand quickly down his cheek. Then she stepped forward to the Holbein queen and gently touched a fingertip to the face that was so much like hers. "Oh. Oh, Rhys."

He thought she was crying. He was wrong.

To his utter amazement, she began to laugh. It started as the light, lovely, silvery sound he knew. A minute later she was gasping and holding her sides. In the end, as he watched slack-jawed, she was forced to grope for the broken stone bench in the center and perch precariously on the edge.

"Oh, Rhys," she gasped. "I love you!"

"I am very glad to hear that," he muttered, "as I am rather alarmingly in love with you, too. But perhaps you will tell me just what is so funny."

She drew an audible breath and wiped at her eyes with the hem of her cloak. "Those." She pointed to the paintings.

"I fail to see the amusement in four masterworks of art."

"No. No, I don't suppose you would. They're very good, aren't they?"

"Very."

"And not worth a penny." Elizabeth rose and waved at the Gainsborough. "Don't you recognize her?"

Rhys scowled at the unattractive young lady. "Should I?"

"The pinched lips? The little eyes?"

Now that she mentioned it, there *was* something familiar in the face. "It is . . ."

"Aunt Gregoria! Of course, I didn't know her then, but I daresay it's a spitting image."

Rhys made the calculations in his head. He supposed a young Gregoria could have sat for the famous painter. He didn't know precisely when the family's fortunes had turned.

"And this one." Again, Elizabeth gently touched the lovely blonde.

"An ancestress?"

"My mother." Her eyes were soft when they met his. "My great-uncle Clarence painted these. All of them."

Rhys felt his jaw dropping. "Uncle Clarence of the cupid and the god-awful hunt scenes?"

"The very same. He was a very skilled copyist, you see, but it never gave him half the satisfaction of letting his creative impulses run wild. And you thought . . . Oh, dear." Shoulders shaking again, she returned to the bench. Rhys lowered himself to sit beside her. "Are you very angry?"

"To be honest . . ." He lifted her chin and stared sternly down into her heartbreakingly beautiful face. "I am bloody delighted."

"Good heavens, why?"

"Because," he replied, "this means you are still poor as a church mouse."

"And that makes you happy?"

"Deliriously so." He kissed her again, a quick, light touch, and grinned when she hummed with pleasure. "You see, I cannot imagine you having me otherwise. Now I can offer my fortune along with my humble person."

"Oh, Rhys."

"You will have me, won't you, Elizabeth? I am rather disgustingly rich."

"I would have you," she said softly against his lips, "if you hadn't a shilling to your altogether too-grand name."

This time, it was she who pulled his face to hers.

"What did she say?" came sharply from the hedge behind them. Kelly.

There was a rustling and shushing. "Get yourself off my shoulder, you daft eejit," O'Reilly muttered. "Are you after flattening me?"

"Hush!" Nuala hissed. "I want to hear how she answered."

"Sure and she answered yes!" came Meggie's pronouncement.

There was a loud scuffling and a yelp from the other side. "Ouch. Can't go this way." Percy. "Lizzie? Won't wait forever for your answer, y'know."

"Oh, shut up, boy!" Gregoria snapped. "Just push through. And stop whining. It's only a little scratch. *Lizzie*? You come out right now! Do you hear me? Oh, give me your flask, Percy. I feel faint . . ."

Just then, Andrew's grinning face appeared around the corner. "Well?" he demanded. "Did you kiss her?"

"Go away, puppy," Rhys muttered.

His nephew didn't budge. "*Christmas*, Uncle. So, what did she say?"

The rustling grew louder on all sides. Rhys sighed. Then grinned. "She said yes," he shouted.

"That's the spirit!" Andrew crowed, coming to give Elizabeth a resounding kiss on her cheek. Then he poked Rhys solidly in the chest. "*There's* the spirit. And merry well about time, too. Now come and have some champagne. Mr. Lambe's finest."

"Champagne?" Gregoria's voice carried stridently through the hedge. "Washed up on the beach, no doubt. For God's sake, Lizzie, when *are* you going to have some decent spirits in this hovel? Oh, do stop sniveling, Percy. It is merely a scratch . . ."

Epilogue

Letter from the Earl of Clane to the Duke of Llans, 4 November 1813:

My Dear Llans,

Call me the worst of meddlers, but I have a scheme brewing in my head and, as it will not go away and I cannot figure how to manage it myself, I am appealing to your sense of friendship and your brotherly devotion.

The enclosed is an advert from yesterday's paper. As you will see, it is for a Wexford estate. It belongs to a family I knew in my youth. The daughter, Elizabeth Fitzhollis, lives there now. She is a lovely girl; I fancied her madly for a bit in my much younger days. I have only recently learned that her father died several years ago and, due to the typical nasty legalities, left her virtually nothing at all. Everything—lock, stock, and her beloved, crumbling pile of a house—went to a perfectly awful cousin who is advertising it for sale.

I would offer my assistance in a heartbeat, but it would look rather dodgy and Elizabeth wouldn't accept it anyway. She is proud and lionhearted and, I have learned, so determined to keep her moldering Hollymore standing that she shores and mends and digs herself. A mule shouldn't have to work so hard.

Now, generous a soul as I know you are, still let

me assure you that there is something for your family in this as well. I know how fond you are of your brother, as are we all of Rhys, despite his damnable starchy deportment. I also know that you, Susan, and the rest of the realm have despaired of his ever finding a woman to suit him. I think Elizabeth Fitzhollis just might be that woman.

Buy the pile; send Rhys to look at it. If all goes as I expect it will, not only will you have a lovely sister-in-law and a happy brother, but he'll insist on taking said pile off your hands quicker than you can say "felicitations."

If all does not go as I expect, and that is a very rare occurrence indeed—oh, cease with the guffaws, sir—I will buy Hollymore from you at a profit. If Rhys does not come back with Elizabeth, perhaps he will come back with some Christmas spirit. Heaven knows he could do with a bit.

Ailis sends her love to you and Susan, and thanks you again for the marvelous Welsh hospitality during our honeymoon. She cannot abide England and is vastly relieved whenever I reveal a close acquaintance in a Celtic clime. She also bids me inform you that if you do not bring your sorry selves to Dublin in the new year, she will feature you prominently in her next set of caricatures. Trust me, my friend, you do not want that.

A Happy Christmas to all.

Clane

The Wexford Carol

Good people all, this Christmastime, consider well and
 bear in mind
What our good God for us has done, in sending his
 beloved Son.
With Mary holy we should pray to God with love this
 Christmas day;
In Bethlehem upon that morn, there was a blessed
 Messiah born.

The night before that happy tide, the noble Virgin and
 her guide
Were long time seeking up and down, to find a lodging
 in the town.
But mark how all things came to pass; from every
 door repelled, alas!
As long foretold, their refuge all was but a humble
 ox's stall.

There were three wise men from afar, directed by a
 glorious star,
And on they wandered night and day until they came
 where Jesus lay,
And when they came unto that place where our beloved Messiah was,
They humbly cast them at his feet, with gifts of gold
 and incense sweet.

Near Bethlehem did shepherds keep their flocks of
lambs and feeding sheep;
To whom God's angels did appear, which put the
shepherds in great fear.
Prepare and go, the angels said. *To Bethlehem, be
not afraid,*
*For there you'll find, this happy morn, a princely babe,
sweet Jesus born.*

With thankful heart and joyful mind, the shepherds
went the babe to find,
And as God's angel had foretold, they did our savior
Christ behold.
Within a manger he was laid, and by his side the vir-
gin maid,
Attending on the Lord of Life, who came on earth to
end all strife.

Mistletoe and Folly

Sandra Heath

Sir Richard Curzon left Lady Finch's Christmas ball unexpectedly early. The diamond pin in his starched muslin neckcloth flashed in the light of a street lamp as he strolled slowly along the snowy Mayfair pavement of Pargeter Street. His fashionable Polish greatcoat was unbuttoned as he walked through the starry December night toward nearby Park Lane, and his town residence overlooking Hyde Park.

It had been Christmas Eve since the stroke of midnight, and the sounds of revelry followed him as London's *haut ton* danced the night away. They'd do the same the next night at the lavish masquerade to be held at Holland House, and Richard's name figured prominently on that guest list as well, but given the mood he was in at present he didn't know if it would be advisable to attend.

He breathed deeply of the keen winter air. The December of 1819 had been bitterly cold so far, almost as cold as the winter of 1814 when the Thames had frozen over, and somehow he didn't think it would improve before the new year. Lifting his cane he dashed some snow from an overhanging branch. Pargeter Street was a place of elegant mansions and high-walled gardens, and tonight it was filled with that air of excitement that always accompanied Christmas. A line of fine carriages was drawn up near Finch House, red-ribboned wreaths adorned all doorways, and more greenery could be seen through brightly lit windows, for it was as traditional to decorate one's house in Mayfair as it was any country cottage. Richard strolled on, feeling no excitement at all, just an unsettling restlessness, as if something of tremendous importance was about to happen to him.

His tall-crowned hat was tipped back on his blonde hair, and the astrakhan collar of his greatcoat was turned up. Beneath the coat he wore the tight-fitting black velvet evening coat and white silk pantaloons that were *de rigueur* for a man of fashion, and altogether he presented the perfect picture of Bond Street elegance. He was handsome, charming, and much sought after in society, but tonight there was a pensive look in his blue eyes, and an unsmiling set to his fine lips.

The ball would continue until daylight, but he hadn't been enjoying the diversion, not even when he'd held Isabel in his arms for the waltz. Miss Isabel Hamilton was the woman he was to marry, and he loved her very much, but that hadn't prevented him from behaving aloofly all evening, so much so that in the end he'd felt obliged to remove himself. Isabel hadn't understood, indeed she'd been so displeased that she'd tossed her head in that willful but fascinating way of hers, and, much to the annoyance of that lord's shrew of a duchess, had promptly requested the good-looking young Duke of Laroche to partner her in a cotillion. She'd given Laroche her full and flattering attention, and hadn't glanced again at the fiancé who'd displeased her so.

With a sigh Richard jabbed his silver-tipped cane into the deep snow at the side of the pavement. Things weren't going well in his private life, for of late there'd been far too much friction and misunderstanding. Isabel was the belle of London, having taken society by storm when she'd arrived from her home in Scotland the year before. She had no title or fortune, but was very beautiful and from a good family, and she'd been besieged by admirers from the moment she arrived. With her shining short dark curls and melting brown eyes she was quite the most heart-stoppingly lovely creature in the realm, and he was the envy of his many rivals for having won her hand. But as the months of the betrothal had passed he'd begun to see a side of her of which his rivals knew nothing. She could be flirtatious, capricious, selfish and untruthful, and these traits had rubbed a little of his happiness away. He still loved her, but deep in his heart he was beginning to have grave doubts about the wisdom of making her his wife.

But tonight he'd behaved boorishly, and she'd been perfectly justified in showing her displeasure. They were due to take a ride in Hyde Park in the morning, and he'd do his best to smooth her ruffled feathers. He'd do the same at the Holland House masquerade, which he reluctantly accepted he'd have to attend if he was to put matters entirely right with Isabel. But it all depended on his being able to shrug off this damned restlessness.

Something made him pause suddenly and whirl about to look swiftly back along the pavement. He had the strong feeling that he was being followed, but all he could see was the line of elegant carriages drawn up at the curbside outside Finch House, and the small groups of coachmen laughing and talking together as they whiled away the long hours of the ball. He continued to look back, for the feeling was so strong that every instinct told him someone was there, but there was nothing, just the empty pavement and the entrances to the mansions he'd passed. Someone could be hiding in one of those entrances. . . . For a moment he considered going back to look, but then decided against it. He had his cane and was well able to take care of himself against any footpad.

The sounds of the ball began to dwindle away behind him as he walked on again, but as the night became more quiet, there was a new sound as a travel-stained post-chaise turned the corner from Park Lane, driving toward him at the sort of weary trot that told of a long and arduous journey. The yellow-jacketed postboy scanned the houses on either side of the street until at last he saw the address he sought, and with relief maneuvered his tired horses to a standstill outside number forty-four, a few yards in front of Richard.

The owners of the house, Mr. and Mrs. Josiah Fitz-haven, were acquaintances of his, and he half-expected to see them in the chaise as he glanced toward it, but instead he saw two women, a rather elderly maid in a poke bonnet and prim brown mantle, and a young woman in a hooded crimson velvet cloak. He caught a glimpse of the latter's sweet profile by the light of a streep lamp opposite as she prepared to open the chaise door.

Instinctively Richard hastened forward to open it for her, extending his white-gloved hand to help her out. She slipped her fingers from the warm depths of her white swansdown muff, and as she accepted his hand he was conscious of the hardness of her wedding ring. The fragrance of lily-of-the-valley drifted over him as she stepped down to the snowy pavement; it was a perfume that evoked the past with a poignancy that was almost as tangible as her ring. Memories of a lost love were all around as she turned to thank him, and her hood fell back to reveal a face he'd never expected to see again.

His heart almost missed a beat. "Diana?" he whispered. "Diana, is it really you?"

With a gasp she stared at him, her magnificent green eyes wide with shock. "Richard?" she breathed, withdrawing her hand as if burned by his touch.

He gazed into the face he'd once adored to distraction. Her eyes were of a fathomless emerald, and she had a cascade of rich burnished chestnut curls which had always defied the efforts of pins to restrain them. She was that rarest of creatures, a flame-haired beauty with a flawless creamy-white complexion, and as he looked at her again, he knew there wasn't a woman on earth to compare with Miss Diana Laverick.

For the space of another heartbeat he was under her spell again, captivated by emotions he'd striven so desperately to deny since the last bitterly cold winter in 1814. But as he drank in the sweetly remembered face, the spell snapped suddenly, and reality rushed over him. She wasn't Miss Diana Laverick anymore; she was Mrs. Robert Beaumont, and she didn't deserve his love. She deserved his loathing.

All these years before in his home county of Cheshire, when he'd been a second son without hope of inheriting his father's wealth or title, he'd been unbelievably happy when he'd fallen in love with her. He'd been foolish enough to think she returned his love, but she was too ambitious and grasping to regard him as more than an idle fancy, and on Christmas Eve 1814 he'd learned of her sudden marriage to Robert Beaumont, a fabulously wealthy plantation owner who'd immediately swept her away to a life of luxury in Jamaica. She'd remained out of England ever since, and her heartbroken lover had at last managed to put his life in some sort of order again, but here she was on another Christmas Eve, stepping down to bring back all the torment he'd suffered at her hands. Perfidious, cold, calculating Diana, the bane of his life.

Bitter resentment gripped him anew, and his blue eyes were suddenly ice-cold. "So, London is to be honored with your presence, is it? May I enquire if Mr. Beaumont is with you?"

She glanced back at the chaise, from which the elderly maid was alighting. "As you can see, Richard, Mr. Beaumont is not with me."

"Will he be joining you?"

"No." She gave the maid a warning look, as if to

prevent her from saying something which might be out of turn.

The maid met her mistress's gaze, and remained silent, but she looked at Richard in an unsmiling way that conveyed her disapproval of him. He knew her. Her name was Mary Keating, and she'd been in Diana's service for many years. She was a small, slight person with sharp gray eyes and a questing nose, and she always guarded her mistress as fiercely as any mother cat defending her kitten. In the past she hadn't disapproved of him, but she obviously did now.

Diana nodded at her. "See that Mr. and Mrs. Fitzhaven are informed of our arrival, and have their butler instruct some men to assist with the luggage."

"Yes, Miss Diana." Mary went to the door of the mansion, reaching up past the wreath of holly and mistletoe to rap the lion's head knocker.

Richard glanced at the house. "You're staying with the Fitzhavens?" he asked Diana.

"Very fleetingly."

"I had no idea you knew them."

"Mrs. Fitzhaven is my mother's second cousin, and she very kindly invited me to stay with them during my . . . She invited me to stay with them," she finished, as if deciding against a further explanation of her presence in London. She looked at him again. "I understand that you are now Sir Richard?"

"Yes."

"I was very sorry to learn that both your father and brother were lost on board the *Wanderer*."

He didn't reply.

"Are you married?" she asked.

"I'm betrothed to Miss Isabel Hamilton."

"The name means nothing to me." She gave the faintest of smiles. "As you may remember, I never left Cheshire before my marriage, and this is the first time I've been to London."

"I'm afraid I don't recall the details of your life,

Mrs. Beaumont," he answered coolly. Anger bubbled beneath the surface of his calm. It was preposterous to be standing here exchanging pleasantries when he really wished to shake her and make her say she was sorry for all the hurt and anguish she'd caused him.

She couldn't ignore the chill in his voice, or the resentment in his eyes. "Richard, I'll only be here for a day or so, and I don't anticipate that you and I will meet again . . ."

"I sincerely trust not," he replied cuttingly.

The door of the house had been opened now, and light flooded out as footmen hastened to attend to the luggage at the rear of the chaise. Mary stood at the top of the steps, watching Richard and her mistress.

Diana gave him a ghost of a smile. "Given what you've just said, it would obviously be inappropriate to say that I'm glad we encountered each other like this."

"Very inappropriate indeed, madam." The rancor he felt was suddenly so great that he couldn't trust himself to prolong the meeting a moment more. "Goodbye, Mrs. Beaumont," he said tersely, "I trust this Christmas brings you everything you so richly deserve." Inclining his head in a gesture calculated to be insulting, he strolled on, his cane swinging as if nothing of any consequence had occurred.

Diana watched him until he turned the corner into Park Lane, where she remembered his town house was to be found. How full of resentment he still was, and how little he understood, even after all this time. Tears stung her eyes, and she blinked them back. He'd never forgive her—he'd made that plain enough when he'd ignored the letter she'd sent explaining her swift marriage to Robert. Oh, how sad Christmas always made her feel now. It was the time of year she dreaded most of all. She took a deep breath. The sooner all this was over and done with, the better for all concerned.

Mary came down the steps toward her. "Come inside out of the cold, Miss Diana."

"I'm coming, Mary."

"Mr. and Mrs. Fitzhaven have been called away unexpectedly because Mr. Fitzhaven's father is unwell, but they've left word that the house is entirely at your disposal."

Diana was about to reply when something made her look back along the pavement toward the crush of carriages outside Finch House. She'd heard a soft sound, a small scuffling noise as if someone was hiding in the shadows nearby.

"What is it, Miss Diana?" asked Mary, looking anxiously at her.

"I thought I heard something. Mary, I think there's someone watching us."

Mary shivered. "Then come inside straightaway, Miss Diana," she said firmly, ushering her mistress toward the steps.

Diana allowed herself to be drawn into the brightly lit entrance hall, where a kissing bunch of mistletoe, holly, red apples, and lighted candles was suspended low beneath two glittering chandeliers. The walls were a cool classical blue-and-white, and the floor patterned with black-and-white tiles. Two sapphire-blue brocade sofas were placed on either side of a white marble fireplace, where a huge yule log burned slowly in the hearth. Elegant console tables stood against the walls, each one presided over by a tall gilt-framed mirror adorned with girandoles, and at the far end a grand staircase led up to the floor above, vanishing between tall Corinthian columns that emphasized the spaciousness and grandeur of the house.

Mary led her across to some handsome white-and-gold double doors, opening them to show her into the sumptuous drawing room beyond. There was rose-pink silk on the walls, and gilded French furniture, and more chandeliers that cast a rich, warm glow over everything.

Mary relieved Diana of the crimson velvet cloak

and the swansdown muff, and watched as she went to
hold her hands out to the fire burning so brightly in
the magnificent black marble fireplace. The maid's
eyes were sad. "It will be over soon, Miss Diana, and
then we can go home again."

"Home?" Diana turned to give her a rather wry
smile.

"Well, it is, isn't it?"

"I suppose so."

Mary was worried about her, for she'd been through
so much recently. The long journey hadn't helped, for
although she, Mary, had been able to sleep when the
chance arose, she knew that her mistress had had very
little rest. "Miss Diana, I've asked the cook to prepare
you a warm drink and a light supper, and there's a
maid attending to your bedroom right now, so that
when you've had some refreshment, you can get some
sleep at last. I'm sure you'll feel a great deal better in
the morning."

"In readiness for my fateful meeting with the lawyer
in the afternoon," murmured Diana, thinking of how
they'd traveled at breakneck speed from Falmouth in
order to be in London in time.

"It may not be all bad news, Miss Diana," said
Mary as reassuringly as she could.

"I wish I could feel that optimistic," replied Diana,
turning to hold her cold hands out to the fire again.

Mary went sadly out, closing the doors softly behind her.

Diana gazed down into the hearth, but it wasn't the
glow of flames that she saw, it was the ice in Sir Richard Curzon's blue eyes.

As the hired chaise at last pulled away from the
curb outside, a secretive figure emerged stealthily from
the shelter of some snowy laurels in front of a nearby
house. The Honorable Geoffrey Hawksworth, son and
heir of Viscount Hawksworth, cursed beneath his

breath as snow slithered down the back of his neck and over his fashionable clothes. Standing on the pavement, he carefully brushed the black fur trimming on his elegant ankle-length redingote.

He was a tall young man, thin-faced and pale, with long-lashed hazel eyes and full lips. His curly brown hair was abundant, and cut in an extravagantly modish style. Beneath his redingote he too wore evening clothes, for he'd been following his adversary, Richard, from the ball when the intriguing encounter with the enigmatic Mrs. Beaumont had taken place.

As he looked up at the bright windows of number forty-four, there was a slyly thoughtful expression on his face. Pure chance had caused him to follow Richard, whose puzzling conduct tonight and sudden departure had aroused his curiosity; pure chance had also caused Mrs. Beaumont to step down from the chaise right in front of her old love. Geoffrey was one of the few people in London who knew about Diana, for he'd once been Richard's close friend, and Richard had told hardly a soul about his heartbreaking affair in Cheshire in the frozen winter of 1814, and he certainly hadn't told Isabel. He'd told his good friend Geoffrey, however, because Isabel hadn't entered their lives then, but when she'd arrived in London, and both men had fallen in love with her, they'd fallen out beyond all redemption. In the end she'd given her favor to Richard, but Geoffrey had never given up. Until she became Lady Curzon, the battle was far from over.

Geoffrey's hazel eyes glittered in the light from a street lamp as he pondered the engrossing encounter he'd just eavesdropped upon. The past had suddenly invaded Richard Curzon's present, and it was a past that still had the power to destroy that gentleman's equilibrium. Geoffrey had often wondered what his former friend's false-hearted Diana had looked like, and now he knew. She was bewitchingly beautiful, and if Richard's stung reaction had been any gauge, he was far from over her.

Turning, Geoffrey began to stroll back toward the ball, congratulating himself upon so fortuitously choosing to follow Richard. Diana Beaumont's arrival in town presented the perfect opportunity for driving a wedge between Richard and Isabel, whose dealings with each other hadn't been going sweetly of late. A plan was already forming in his scheming mind, a plan so simple that it could not possibly fail. He began to hum to himself, and his cane twirled as he walked. He gave no thought to Diana, whose marriage might be put in jeopardy by his machinations. He was only concerned with wresting Isabel from Richard.

Reaching Finch House, he left his top hat, gloves, cane, and redingote in the room provided, and then reentered the dazzling ballroom, where a sea of elegant, bejeweled guests danced beneath a canopy of chandeliers and Christmas garlands. No expense had been spared in the extravagant decorations; there were even German fir trees, their branches laden with tiers of colored wax candles, a continental fashion brought over by Lady Finch from her native Hanover.

Another waltz was playing, and Isabel was again dancing with Henry Daventry, Duke of Laroche. She wore a low-cut cerise silk gown, its hem modishly stiffened with rouleaux and bows, and there was a white feather boa trailing on the sand-strewn floor as she moved. Diamonds sparkled at her throat and trembled from her ears, and flouncy white ostrich plumes, her favorites, sprang from the circlet around her short dark hair. She was laughing at something Laroche had said, and her brown eyes were soft and teasing as she looked up into his good-looking face.

Geoffrey paused at the foot of the ballroom steps, toying with the lace spilling from his black velvet cuff. His adoring, intense gaze followed her every step, lingering on her exquisite face. Soon she would be his, he didn't doubt it for a moment now that he possessed such invaluable information about her loathed fiancé.

Stepping on to the crowded floor, he pushed his way toward her, tapping the duke on the shoulder. Laroche was an old acquaintance from school days, and no one ever called him by his first name; he was always simply Laroche. "Come now, Laroche, you're being greedy," said Geoffrey. "You mustn't hog the loveliest lady in the room, it's my turn now, besides, I've just seen your wife, she's looking for you. I suggest you adjourn to the card room, she's already searched there." It was a deliberate lie, for Geoffrey hadn't seen the duchess at all, but he knew the thought of his wife's approach would be sufficient to get rid of Laroche, whose dalliances outside the marriage bed had made the duchess an extremely jealous and suspicious woman.

Laroche swiftly relinquished Isabel to Geoffrey, and melted away into the press of guests. Isabel pouted after him, and then gave Geoffrey a reproachful look.

"You haven't seen the duchess at all, have you?" she said in her soft Scottish voice.

"Would I tell fibs at Christmas?" he replied, whirling her away into the waltz.

"Yes, Geoffrey, you would, just as you'd tell fibs on any other time of the year if it suited you," she answered, smiling coquettishly.

"You look breathtakingly lovely tonight, Isabel," he whispered.

"Why, thank you, sir," she said in that teasingly flirtatious way that always played havoc with him. "It's so very agreeable to be paid compliments by an admirer, instead of having to endure one's fiancé's contrariness."

"Have you and Curzon quarreled again?"

"Not exactly, he's just seen fit to take himself home. He was in a most beastly mood, quite the surly bear, and I wish now that I'd told him not to call on me again until he's improved his manners. However, I didn't say any such thing, so he'll be taking me riding in Hyde Park tomorrow morning, and to the masquerade tomorrow night. Or should I say tonight? It's Christmas Eve now, isn't it?"

"It is indeed," he replied, exulting not only in the pleasure of holding her, but in the fact that she was quite obviously very disenchanted indeed with the man she was to marry. "Isabel, if you were mine I'd never be a surly bear, and I'd certainly never leave early."

"I know you wouldn't, Geoffrey, for you're the most of an angel I ever knew."

"You should have chosen me."

"I know." She sighed, her lips pouting a little again. "Richard's been so very hurtful of late, he's even declined to buy me the little Christmas gift I crave more than anything else in the world."

"Little Christmas gift?"

"It's only a little brooch, a golden sunburst that would look the very thing on the tartan sash I intend to wear with my new white silk gown, and he knows how much I want it, but this morning it was still in Cranford's window."

"Oh, my poor darling," murmured Geoffrey, drawing her just a little closer. His mind was racing, for he'd just thought of a way of adding to his plan in order to make it even more assured of success.

As dawn began to lighten the eastern sky, and Lady Finch's guests departed, Geoffrey's carriage drove slowly down Bond Street, drawing up outside the premises of Messrs Cranford, the fashionable jewelers. Stepping down, he looked in at the exquisite items shining in the light of a street lamp. The sunburst brooch reposed in a little red leather box, and, as Isabel had said, it would indeed look perfect with her tartan sash. Tartan accessories were all the rage now because of Sir Walter Scott's popular novels, and no one wore them to better advantage than Isabel.

Returning to the carriage, he instructed the coachman to drive to Piccadilly, and the premises of Messrs Duvall & Carrier, fanmakers and glovers to royalty. A few minutes later he alighted again, this time to study a window display of dainty gloves and fans of every description.

It wasn't long before his glance fell upon a fan that fitted his requirements in every way, for not only was it made of Isabel's adored white plumes, but it was also trimmed with little tartan bows. Next to it there was a small folding fan with gold-embroidered gray satin fixed upon sticks of gilded, carved ivory. He didn't know Mrs. Diana Beaumont, but intuition told him that she'd find such a fan very much to her liking.

He returned to the carriage again, and it drove away along the virtually deserted street toward his Mayfair residence in North Street. It would be several hours yet before the shops opened for the hectic business of Christmas Eve, and in the meantime he had much to do. It would be a long time before he could get some sleep, but somehow he didn't feel even remotely tired. He had far too much on his mind for that.

As his carriage drove slowly along Park Lane, past Richard's imposing town house, the church bells of London began to strike seven.

The sound of the bells died away, but everything was quiet in the sumptuous green-and-gold drawing room where Richard had fallen asleep in a fireside chair, an almost empty cognac glass resting precariously in his hand.

The only light came from the fire, and shadows moved softly over the hand-painted Chinese silk on the walls, and over the rich green velvet curtains drawn across the tall windows overlooking Park Lane and Hyde Park. The whole room was in the Chinese style, with life-size porcelain figures, pieces of jade, dragon- and chrysanthemum-embroidered chairs and sofas, and lotus-blossom carved on every wooden surface.

Richard didn't hear the church bells, for the windows were shuttered. His evening coat had been idly discarded on a nearby sofa, and his lace-edged shirt and white satin waistcoat had been partially unbuttoned. His crumpled neckcloth hung loose, and the diamond pin had been left on the marble mantelpiece amid the sprays of seasonal holly, mistletoe, ivy, and myrtle arranged with such care by the maids.

He was dreaming about Diana, and the Christmas five years before when he'd last held her in his arms. She'd been wearing a lilac gown, with a low neckline and long diaphanous sleeves gathered in rich frills at her slender wrists. Her cloud of chestnut hair had been brushed loose, tumbling down about her shoulders in that wanton way he loved so much. They'd slipped away from her family to the seclusion of the minstrels' gallery above the great hall of her parents' Cheshire manor house, and masked mummers from the nearby village had been playing in the hall below. He and Diana had been engrossed only in themselves as they stood in each other's arms in the holly-garlanded shadows. Her lips had tasted so sweet as her supple body yielded against his, and she'd felt so warm and alive through the soft stuff of her gown. His love had never been stronger or more sure than it had been in those magical minutes, and yet within a day or so he was to learn of her marriage to Robert Beaumont, a man of whose existence he knew nothing.

The fire shifted in the hearth, and the flames began to crackle loudly around a half-burned log. Richard awoke with a start, and the glass fell from his fingers, shattering on the polished fender. For a moment he was confused, the tentacles of the dream still coiling around him, but then it faded away, and he remembered.

He leaned his head back wearily. Why had Diana come back to torment him again? Why couldn't she have stayed in Jamaica? He wished he'd been able to put her firmly in the past, but now that he'd seen her again, he knew that he'd never be able to turn his back finally upon his first great love.

Getting up, he crossed to one of the windows, drawing the curtains back and then folding the shutters aside to look out at snowy Park Lane and Hyde Park. A few tradesmen's carts were making their way along the street toward the fashionable shops of Oxford Street and Piccadilly, where soon the most profitable day of the year would be in full swing.

His gaze moved across to the park with its ghostly white trees. Would Isabel still be prepared to ride with him later on, or had he offended her too much? He wished now that he hadn't given in to his strange mood, but had remained at the ball, for then he'd have been spared the encounter with Diana. Damn her for coming back, and damn her even more for still being able to stop his heart with a glance.

In Pargeter Street, Diana was sleeping the sleep of the exhausted. Her flame-colored hair spilled over her pillow like molten copper, and there were no dreams to disturb her slumber. She had no idea of the stir her return was about to cause due to the underhanded intentions of one Geoffrey Hawksworth, who, the moment he'd entered his residence in North Street, had sat down at the great writing desk in his library with pen, ink, and many sheets of quality vellum upon which to perfect a more than passing resemblance to Sir Richard Curzon's rather distinctive writing. Letters had been exchanged during the days of the two men's friendship, and so Geoffrey did not lack examples from which to copy. It was painstaking work, but in the end he was satisfied that the only person who would be able to tell his work from the real thing would be Richard himself.

While this clandestine activity was taking place, Diana slept on, not waking until the ormulu clock on the mantelpiece struck nine, and Mary came in with a dish of morning tea, which she placed on the elegant marquetry table beside the four poster bed before going to draw back the curtains and fold the shutters aside.

It was a sunny morning, made brighter by all the snow, and the fresh light flooded into the bedroom, lying in sunbeamed shafts across the aquamarine-canopied bed, the brocade curtains of which were tied back with golden ropes. There was gray-and-white-striped silk on the walls, and a dressing table that was lavishly draped with frilled white muslin. A dressing room lined with wardrobes led off to one side, and a lacquered Chinese screen shielded the alcove where the washstand stood. There were two comfortable chairs by the fireplace, and above the mantelpiece was a mirror so large that Diana could see herself in the bed as she sat up.

Mary came to the foot of the bed. "Good morning, Miss Diana."

"Good morning, Mary," replied Diana, picking up the dish of tea and sipping it.

Mary went through into the dressing room, and emerged in a moment with a very odd assortment of clothes, an apricot velvet spencer, and a lightweight cherry wool riding habit.

Diana stared at the garments. "Mary, what are you thinking of . . . ?"

"It's not as foolish a choice as you may think, Miss Diana, for I've learned that there is an excellent riding school in the mews behind here, where fine horses can be hired for riding in Hyde Park. I know how much you like riding, and I also know that such exercise would do you good, so I've taken the liberty of ordering a saddle horse for you."

Diana stared at her in dismay. "Oh, Mary, the last thing I want to do is be seen somewhere as public and undoubtedly crowded as Rotten Row!"

"No one here knows you, except for Sir Richard Curzon, and it's doubtful if he would acknowledge you anyway." Mary draped the clothes over the back of one of the fireside chairs. "It's much colder here than in Jamaica, which is why I thought this spencer would go neatly under the coat of your riding habit. No one will know it's there, but it will keep you warm while you're out."

"Mary . . ." began Diana again, but the maid fixed her with a stern look.

"A ride will do you good, Miss Diana, you need a little diversion to take your mind off the appointment with the lawyer this afternoon."

For a moment Diana considered arguing, but she recognized that look, and knew it signified that Mary Keating would keep on until she gave in. "Oh, very well," she said with a sigh, "I'll go riding if you insist."

It was a decision that was to play right into Geoffrey Hawksworth's hands.

As Diana dressed for riding after breakfast, Geoffrey set off in his carriage, first of all for Messrs Duvall & Carrier in Piccadilly, and after that for Cranford's in Bond Street. The carriage blinds were lowered, for he didn't wish to be seen, and he wasn't alone in the vehicle, his reluctant valet was with him.

The carriage drew up at the curb in Piccadilly on the first part of the stratagem, and Geoffrey took a letter of authority, two sealed notes, and a fat purse from his pocket. He pushed them all into the valet's hands.

"I trust that by now you know exactly what you are to do. You are to tell the assistant that you are Sir Richard Curzon's man, and you are to hand over the letter of authority. It describes exactly the two fans in question, and it gives clear instructions as to the names and addresses of the two ladies to which they are to be sent. It also says that the fans are to be despatched without delay. You must be sure to give them the purse and see that they put the correct sealed note with the correct fan."

"Yes, sir."

The man's response was half-hearted, and Geoffrey gave him a testy look. "Is there something wrong?"

The valet swallowed, taking his courage in both hands in order to stand up to his master just a little. "Is it not just a little dishonest for me to pretend to be Sir Richard's man?"

Geoffrey's gaze was frozen. "If you wish to remain in my employ, I suggest you forget your conscience and just do as you're told."

"Yes, sir."

"Then get on with it!" snapped Geoffrey, leaning across to fling open the carriage door.

The noise of the busy street leapt in at them, a mixture of voices, footsteps, hooves, and wheels. A fiddler and a blind penny-whistler were playing *Good King Wenceslas,* a pieman was ringing his handbell and shouting the virtues of his hot pies, and a stage-coach was just leaving the nearby Gloucester Coffee House, its horn ringing out sharply. The valet climbed out, pausing on the pavement for a moment before turning to carefully close the carriage door again and then go into the shop.

Geoffrey held the blind slightly aside so that he could see what was happening. He could just make out the silhouette of the valet, and that of the young man behind the counter. The assistant was nodding, and then came to the window, opening the glass case and removing the two fans Geoffrey had selected at dawn.

A satisfied smile played on Geoffrey's full lips. It was going without a hitch. But then the smile was abruptly cancelled, for a formidable female face looked in through the carriage window barely inches away from him. He gave a start, drawing back and releasing the blind so that it fell back in place, but almost immediately the carriage door was opened, and the same fearsome face appeared again. It belonged to his great-aunt, his father's aunt, and a personage who was undoubtedly the scourge of the Hawksworth family, for she always demanded, and got, her own way. Small, rosy-faced and possessed of a curiously sweet smile, she was nevertheless a harpy of the highest order, and she seemed to take particular delight in imposing upon him whenever the mood took her. The mood had evidently taken her now.

"Ah, so it *is* you skulking in here like a felon, Geoffrey! What on earth are you up to?"

"Er, nothing in particular, Great-Aunt."

"No? Excellent, for that means that you can be of singular assistance to me."

"It does?" His heart sank. What did the old harridan want him to do? Whatever it was, he'd have to bow to her wishes, for she had considerable influence with his father, and therefore with the family purse strings. Geoffrey had no intention of risking a reduction in his allowance simply because this medusa had been mildly offended.

"Yes," she said, opening the door fully and holding out her hand to him for assistance. "Well, help me in, sir, or would you see me struggle?"

Reluctantly he took the hand, and in a rustle of piped damson silk, she climbed in and took the seat opposite him. Her pelisse and matching gown were tightly fitted at the throat and cuffs, and her hands were plunged into a fur-lined muff of the same piped damson silk. She wore a plain black hat with a small black net veil through which her button-bright eyes were clearly seen. Her hair was tugged back in a knot at the back of her head, and she wore no jewelry at all.

As she made herself comfortable, Geoffrey was dismayed still further to see that she wasn't alone, but was accompanied by two maids carrying bundles of Christmas purchases. They proceeded to enter the carriage as well, taking up the two remaining seats. Now there wasn't any room left for his valet.

Geoffrey began to protest. "I say, Great-Aunt . . ."

"You said you weren't doing anything in particular, Geoffrey, and so I expect you to convey me home to Hampstead. My fool of a coachman has managed to break the wheel of my barouche on a corner curbstone, and I require transport. I saw your carriage waiting here, and knew that you'd been heaven sent to assist me in my predicament."

Geoffrey stared at her, too appalled to speak. Hampstead was over four miles away, and uphill through snow all the way! He still had Cranford's to visit, but could hardly do that with the old biddy watching his every move. Plague take her, for she was interfering with his plans! For a moment he considered getting out and leaving her the use of his carriage, but almost immediately he discounted such a course of action, for she'd regard it as a slight, and his father would be regaled with the tale of his son's disappointing manners.

The old lady's eyes were upon him. "Well, Geoffrey? Are we to remain here all day? Instruct the coachman to take us to Hampstead."

There was nothing for it but to do as she ordered. With ill grace, Geoffrey leaned out of the door to tell the coachman what he was to do, and the carriage pulled away just as the valet emerged from the shop, his errand completed. He stood on the curb, staring

after the carriage as it vanished amid the crush of
Piccadilly.

With a sigh, the valet turned to make his way back
to his master's residence in North Street. He'd done
all he'd been instructed to do, and soon the two fans
would be on their way. He didn't know what his master was up to, but he did know that it wasn't to any
good.

While Geoffrey unwillingly commenced the short
but arduous journey to the heights of Hampstead,
Diana had set out on her ride in Hyde Park.

In spite of the snow, Rotten Row was a throng of
fashionable riders, both ladies and gentlemen. Gleaming horses were handled with excellence, and there
was a display of high fashion that was second to none
as the *beau monde* rode to and fro along the famous
way where it was only the reigning monarch's preroga-
tive to drive in a carriage.

There was skating on the frozen Serpentine, and
nearby there was a great deal of interest in an American horsedrawn sleigh driven with consummate skill
by a gentleman from Washington. A party of mounted
Bow Street Runners was making its way west toward
Kensington Palace, and numerous people were simply
taking in the air as they strolled in the snow. Diana
had at last gained the measure of the bright chestnut
horse provided by the riding school. It had proved a
surprisingly mettlesome mount, tossing its head and
capering as if it would seize the very first opportunity
to get the better of her, but as she rode into Rotten
Row, she had it firmly under control.

She attracted many admiring glances from the gentlemen, for she was very eye-catching in her cherry
wool riding habit, her flame-colored hair almost
matching the sheen on her mount's chestnut coat. There
was a jaunty black beaver hat on her head, black
gloves on her hands, and she carried a riding crop that

she had no need to resort to. She appeared to great advantage, and she knew it, and under other circumstances she would have reveled in all the admiration, but today her real wish was to blend into the background, which was something she'd failed abysmally to achieve.

There was a second lady who looked particularly delightful in Rotten Row that morning, for she was beautifully turned out in a ruffed lime-green velvet riding habit trimmed with black military frogging. She rode a pretty strawberry roan mare, and her lovely dark-eyed face was sweetly framed by the lime-green gauze scarf encircling her little wide-brimmed black hat. Miss Isabel Hamilton was used to being the center of attention in the park, and she was vain enough to deliberately incite her easygoing mount to dance around a little, in order to show off her riding skills.

She rode with Richard, with whom she'd at first been sulky and difficult when he'd called upon her at the Hanover Square house of the wealthy relatives with whom she lived, she most definitely being from the poor branch of the family. She'd been offhand and awkward whatever Richard had said, but it was virtually impossible to remain in a sulk with him when he was disposed to exert his immense charm. If he'd been in a strange mood at the ball, he was certainly endeavoring to make up for it now, for no gentleman could have been more gallant and attentive than he. If she hadn't known him better, she'd have concluded rather uncharitably and suspiciously that he had a guilty conscience, and *not* concerning his manners at the ball! But Richard wasn't the sort of man to play her false with another, and so she could only believe that the transformation this morning was due entirely to his acceptance that he'd behaved badly the night before.

At her side, Richard rode a large black Hanoverian that few others would have cared to take on, for it could be a savage beast at times, given to snapping its bared teeth at other nearby mounts. He had it under a tight rein, for he wished to concentrate upon sweetening Isabel, not upon the caprices of a disagreeable horse. He tipped his top hat back on his blonde hair, and took a deep breath of the icy morning air. He wore a pine-green coat and tight pale-gray breeches, and the shine on his top boots bore witness to his valet's devotion to duty. He was beginning to feel he'd smoothed the troubled waters of his dealings with Isabel, and no one could have been further from his thoughts than Diana, who was at that very moment riding through the crowds toward him.

Isabel was talking about the masquerade that night. "What shall you wear, Richard? I think you would make a splendid cavalier."

"I think I'll just content myself with my ordinary evening wear and a mask," he replied, for if there was one thing he loathed it was dressing up. The invitation from Holland House hadn't stipulated fancy dress, and that was sufficient excuse for him. He smiled at her. "What do you intend to wear?"

"Oh, I haven't decided yet," she replied vaguely.

He was more than a little surprised. "You haven't decided? But I thought such matters were considered long before the actual day!"

"Well, I haven't made up my mind, and that's the end of it," she replied rather shortly.

He fell silent. It was strange that someone as particular as Isabel had yet to make up her mind about something she would normally have regarded as vitally important. Matters of clothing usually preoccupied her to the exclusion of all else.

It was Isabel who first became aware of the slight stir among the riders in front of them. The ladies looked far from pleased about something, and the gentlemen were equally far from being displeased. Then she saw the cause of it, a dainty red-haired figure in cherry, mounted on a spirited chestnut. Isabel's lips became set in a sour line, for the last thing she wanted was a rival in the beauty stakes, and this stranger was definitely as head-turning as she.

Diana rode toward them without realizing, but then something made her look directly at Richard, and with a gasp, she reined in. Her face became suddenly pale as she gazed at him. Her gloved hands tightened on the reins, and for a moment it seemed she would speak to him, but then her glance flickered toward Isabel, whose cold gaze was very pronounced. Diana kicked her heel, and urged her mount on past them, swiftly vanishing among the riders behind.

Isabel had reined in as well, and turned in the saddle to gaze after her. Then she looked sharply at Richard, whose discomfort was only too plain. "Who was she?" she demanded.

"Er, I believe her name is Beaumont, Mrs. Beaumont," he said lamely.

"I've never seen her before, and I don't believe I know the name. Do you know her well?"

"Hardly at all."

"Then don't you think her reaction to you was somewhat strange?" Suspicion burgeoned in Isabel's heart, for his responses were hardly reassuring. She wondered again about his remarkable attentiveness this morning. Was there something going on?

"I really have no idea why she behaved as she did," he said, meeting her eyes. "As I said, the woman is hardly known to me."

"I thought her rather vulgar, didn't you? So much red is hardly tasteful."

He didn't reply, for in truth he'd thought Diana looked magnificent, so magnificent that she'd stopped his breath with admiration. Oh, damn Diana, how he wished she'd stayed out of his life!

His silence displeased Isabel still more, and she too fell into a heavy silence as they rode on. A moment

later they were joined by the familiar figure of Laroche, who presented a dashing sight on his highly
bred bay Arabian horse, his greyhounds padding faith-
fully at the horse's heels. He wore a corbeau-colored
riding coat and beige breeches, and he gave them both
a lazily good-natured grin.

"*Eh, bien, mes enfants,* did you see the fair incognita
on the chestnut? I vow several gentlemen turned their
heads so sharply they almost severed them on their
stocks!"

It wasn't a remark calculated to please Isabel, who
gave him a stormy look. "Are you referring to the
loud creature in scarlet? Richard knows her, he says
her name is Mrs. Beaumont. Perhaps he also knows
if she is indeed as brash as she looks. Is she, Richard?"
There was a challenging note in her voice, and her
dark eyes were accusing.

Richard's lips pressed angrily together for a moment.
"Isabel, I told you, I hardly know her. As to her character, I promise you that it is of no interest to me."

Isabel searched his face, and evidently found something there she did not trust. "You're a liar, Richard
Curzon!" she declared suddenly, in a tone loud enough
to carry to several riders nearby. "That odious creature is known to you far more than you're saying!"
Kicking her heels, she urged her startled mount away
from them.

Richard made no move to follow her, and Laroche
looked at him in surprise. "Hadn't you better make
your peace with her, dear boy?"

"I don't think that at this precise moment she's
open to reason, do you?"

Laroche pursed his lips, and then shrugged. "Richard, she's the loveliest woman in London, and you've
snapped her up. You can't afford to rest on your laurels, not when the *monde*'s wolves are always prowl-
ing about."

"Isabel can be very unreasonable."

"But, in this particular instance, I wonder if her suspicions aren't just a little justified?" Laroche gave him a sly look. "How well *do* you know that proud Titania, eh?"

"There's nothing between Mrs. Beaumont and me, Laroche, and I'd thank you not to hint to the contrary!" replied Richard sharply.

"Alright, alright, don't bite my head off, I believe you!" protested Laroche, pretending to put up his hands in self-defense. "But if you love Isabel and wish to keep her, then I suggest you pay more attention to her wishes."

"Her wishes?"

"In matters such as that brooch she covets."

"So she's told you about that, has she?"

"She confides a great deal in me."

"Then let me explain that the brooch in Cranford's doesn't stand up to a close inspection, indeed it is somewhat inferior, which is why it still reposes in their window, and why I've taken the step of ordering an alternative which I intend to take delivery of this afternoon. I'll give it to her at the masquerade tonight, and when she sees it, I rather think she'll forget about the tawdry bauble she's convinced herself is essential to her happiness. I'm not an uncaring monster, Laroche, indeed I'm far from it."

Laroche looked at him for a long moment. "Do you love her, Richard?" he asked quietly.

Richard hesitated, and then lowered his eyes, for when he tried to picture Isabel's face, all he saw was Diana.

The silence was eloquent, and Laroche shifted uncomfortably in his saddle. "I, er, think I'd better be toddling along," he said, gathering his reins.

"No doubt I'll see you tonight at the masquerade."

"Er, no, I fear not. I have other plans."

Richard looked at him in surprise. "But I thought your wife was looking forward to it."

"She is, and as far as I'm concerned she can go, but I have something else to attend to." Laroche touched his top hat, and then urged his Arabian horse away. Followed by his greyhounds, he disappeared in the crush of riders.

Richard remained where he was, the only motionless figure in a moving sea of equestrians. Faced with the direct question about whether or not he loved Isabel, he hadn't been able to answer. This morning he'd striven to placate her, but the moment Diana appeared . . . His thoughts trailed away in confusion. What in God's name *did* he feel?

Isabel rode furiously back to Hanover Square, thrusting the reins of her sweating horse into the hands of the groom who waited in front of the house, and then hurrying into the rather austere white marble entrance hall, where tall Doric columns rose toward a lofty ceiling. Following Lady Finch's lead, Isabel's aunt, Mrs. Graham, had had German fir trees placed on either side of the fireplace, their tiers of colored wax candles shining softly in the gloomy light cast down from the window above the main doorway. The Doric columns were festooned with seasonal branches, and an enormous bunch of mistletoe was suspended low from the ceiling, turning slowly in the draft caused by her entry.

There was a beautiful inlaid table standing in the center of the red-and-cream-tiled floor, and on it there was a large bowl of red-berried holly, and a silver dish for visiting cards. There was also a brown paper package, and Isabel was drawn to it like a pin to a magnet.

Putting her gloves on the table, she picked up the parcel, swiftly opening it as she saw that it was addressed to her. Oh, how she loved opening packages! Her breath caught with delight as she saw the fan inside, and she ran her fingertips over the soft white plumage and dainty tartan bows. It was the most perfect thing imaginable! Her glance fell on the sealed note that had fallen out on to the table, and her eyes softened a little as she recognized Richard's writing. Maybe he had some redeeming qualities after all . . .

Breaking the seal, she began to read the message inside. *My darling Diana, Words cannot say how overjoyed I am that you are part of my life again, nor can they convey the yearning I feel for the moment I've set you up in a house where I may visit you whenever I wish. My marriage will make no difference to my love for you. You are my heart, my mistress, and my life, and if you were free I'd make you mine forever. I adore thee. Richard.*

Thunderstruck, Isabel stared at the note. His darling Diana? A house? His mistress? The note dropped to the table and she clutched the exquisite fan to her breast, trying to gather her scattered composure. So he *was* up to something behind her back! Oh, the monster! He had a mistress and had been found out because he'd made the foolish mistake of sending the wrong note to Hanover Square!

Fury seized her, and she flung the fan across the floor where it came to rest at the foot of one of the German fir trees. Her eyes flashed and her lips were a thin line of rage. How dared he! How *dared* he!

Unbidden, a vision of the creature in the cherry wool riding habit entered her head. Was that brazen Mrs. Beaumont his precious inamorata? If she was it would certainly explain the odd way both she and Richard had reacted on seeing each other. Isabel hurried to retrieve the fan, examining the handle as she searched for the maker's mark. She soon found the name of Messrs Duvall & Carrier. If she guessed correctly, then there had been a second fan, one intended for the unknown Diana, only it contained the message intended for Hanover Square! A visit to Piccadilly was most definitely necessary in order to establish all the

facts, before Sir Richard Curzon could be faced with
his vile infidelity and deceit!

She called for a footman, and one emerged hastily
from the shadows, quailing a little at the blazing fury
in her eyes. "Yes, Miss Hamilton?"

"Have another horse saddled for me without
delay!"

"Yes, Miss Hamilton." Turning, he almost ran from
her presence.

She pulled on her gloves, flexing her fingers like the
claws of a cat. So, Richard was making a fool of her,
was he? He was keeping a mistress *and* paying court
to the belle of London society! Well, he was about to
find out that Miss Isabel Hamilton couldn't be treated
like that. If anyone was going to be made a fool of,
it was Richard himself!

With sudden decision she hurried through into the
library, where she sat at the writing desk and dipped
a quill in the ink. She wrote a very hasty note, and
immediately sanded and sealed it, then she wrote a
gentleman's name on it. She'd been hesitating about
taking such a shocking course as the one she now
intended, but Richard's duplicity had made her mind
up for her. London was about to be scandalized, and
Sir Richard Curzon would be left looking very foolish.

Reentering the hall, she found the footman waiting.
"Have this delivered immediately," she said, giving
him the note.

"Very well, Miss Hamilton. Your horse has been
brought around to the front."

She nodded, but hesitated before going out. "See
that the note is given to the gentleman himself, for it's
important that it doesn't fall into the wrong hands."

"Very well, Miss Hamilton." The footman was the
soul of discretion, giving no hint at all of his intense
curiosity as to why she should be sending messages to
such a gentleman.

A moment later she left the house again to ride to

Piccadilly, and the premises of Messrs Duvall & Carrier.

No sooner had the sound of Isabel's horse died away in Hanover Square, than Diana returned to the riding stables in the mews behind Pargeter Street. She walked back to the house through the garden at the rear, where a stone nymph stood in frozen nakedness in the center of an ice-covered pool. The trees were heavily laden with snow, and a robin redbreast sang his heart out from the wall, his bright eyes watching her as she made her way toward the house.

She was still thinking about the encounter in the park. The lady in lime-green must be the Miss Hamilton Richard was to marry. She was very beautiful indeed, and unnecessarily jealous and suspicious, for Richard hadn't been even remotely warm toward his former love, in fact he'd looked right through her. Diana sighed, recalling the chill in his gaze. If it hadn't been for that invisible barrier he'd placed so firmly between them, she'd have spoken to him, for what point was there in prolonging the bitterness of the past? But he'd given her no encouragement at all, and so she'd ridden on. But, oh, how she wished it could be different.

Entering the house, she found Mary waiting for her in the drawing room. "What is it, Mary?" she asked quickly, sensing that something had happened.

Mary went to a table and picked up a small brown paper package. "This was delivered a short while ago. It's addressed to you."

"To me?" Diana put her riding crop down, and began to tease off her gloves. "But who would send anything to me?"

"I don't know, Miss Diana," replied Mary unhappily, for every instinct told her that the package meant trouble.

Diana took the package and opened it, pausing in

astonishment as she saw the exquisite gray silk fan inside. "Why, it's beautiful," she breathed, then she glanced down to the floor as the sealed note fell. Her face became still as she recognized Richard's writing.

Mary recognized the writing as well, for in the past she'd seen many letters written to her mistress by Sir Richard Curzon. Bending, she retrieved it. "It's from . . ."

"I know who it's from, Mary," replied Diana quietly, putting the fan and the brown paper wrapping on the table.

"But . . ."

"Mary, I've just encountered him in the park, and he looked through me so coldly that I could have turned to ice. Whatever this fan is, it isn't sent kindly, of that I can be sure."

"Perhaps you're wrong. Shouldn't you at least read the note?"

"I'm not wrong, but I'll read it," replied Diana, taking the note and breaking the seal. She read it aloud.

> *My beloved,*
> *Let this Christmas be the signal for a new future together. Let us forget the misunderstandings of the past and accept our undying love for each other. I will adore you throughout eternity.*
> *Richard.*

She dropped the note on to the fan, and began to wrap the package up again. "That Richard Curzon was resentful I've always known, but I didn't think he was also unspeakably petty and spiteful."

"Oh, Miss Diana . . ."

"I want this sent back to him at his Park Lane residence, with the message that I wish him to refrain from communicating with me again."

"Yes, Miss Diana."

Turning, Diana left the room, but as she hurried up the grand staircase there were tears in her eyes.

The church bells were sounding midday as Isabel reined her horse in by the doors of Messrs Duvall & Carrier. Giving the reins and a coin to a man selling mistletoe, she entered the dark confines of the exclusive establishment, and a superior young man came to assist her. He was dressed in a charcoal coat and starched blue-and-white-spotted silk neckcloth, and he placed his fingertips very precisely on the dark oak counter. He stood directly beneath a very pretty Christmas kissing bunch, and was so filled with a sense of his own importance that he made Isabel more furious than ever.

"May I be of assistance, madam?" he inquired.

"Possibly," she replied icily. "I have been sent a fan that was purchased at this establishment, but I believe there must have been a mistake made with the order, and that I've been sent the wrong fan."

"Mistake, madam?" He evinced amazement that anyone could believe such hallowed premises capable of perpetrating an error of any kind.

"Yes, sir, a mistake, sir," she said coldly. "The fan was purchased by Sir Richard Curzon."

"Ah, yes, I recall the order, indeed I handled it myself. Sir Richard sent his man to act on his behalf."

"And there were two fans concerned in the order?" She asked the question lightly, as if she already knew all about it and was just confirming the facts.

"Yes, madam, there were indeed two fans."

"As I thought, and you, sir, have sent the wrong one to me."

"Oh, that cannot possibly be so," he replied vainly, "for the letter of authority was quite specific."

"May I see it?"

He stared at her. "*See* the letter? Oh, I'm afraid that would be a little irregular."

"Then be irregular, sir, or else I shall make such a noise that you will very swiftly regret your obstinacy!"

He blinked, and then decided that discretion was the better part of valor, for she did indeed look as if she was capable of making a fuss to end all fusses. "Very well, madam, I'll go and get it now."

Turning, he went through a door at the rear of the shop, reemerging a moment later with the letter in his hand. As he held it out to her, she almost snatched it from him. Richard's telltale writing leapt out at her, as did the name of the recipient of the second fan: Mrs. Diana Beaumont. So, the creature in the park and his beloved Diana seemed to be one and the same, indeed the coincidence was too great for it to be otherwise. No wonder Richard had affected such vagueness in Rotten Row when they'd come face to face with his doxy! He must have thought himself undone! Well, he hadn't been undone then, but he most certainly was now!

Thrusting the letter back into the assistant's hand, she turned on her heel and marched out again, slamming the door so fiercely behind her that the little kissing bunch began to revolve on its scarlet ribbons. The mistletoe-seller saw the glint in her eyes and hastily held out the reins of her horse before retreating to what he felt was a safe distance. It was a wise move, for she mounted very swiftly, turning the horse actually on the pavement itself, much to the alarm of the unfortunate pedestrians nearby. Employing her riding crop on the horse's flank, she urged it away toward Park Lane, riding like a demon through the heavy Christmas traffic.

Piccadilly paused in amazement to watch the progress of the fury in the lime green riding habit. She rode without any thought for others, weaving her nervous horse between the crowded vehicles and managing to knock a hamper and a brace of Christmas pheasants from the back of a stagecoach. She stopped some carolsingers in mid-song by cutting the corner into Park Lane and thus riding straight through them, and she was very nearly the cause of a spillage of yule logs all over the London street when she forced a heavily laden cart to swerve in order to get out of her way.

She reined in outside Richard's elegant town house, only just managing to control her lathered horse, which was now thoroughly upset. Dismounting, she dropped the reins and gathered her skirts to advance furiously on the front door.

Her angry knocking brought the butler as quickly as his legs could carry him, and he stood aside in astonishment as she strode in.

"M-Miss Hamilton . . . ?"

"Have someone attend to my horse," she answered shortly, glancing around the entrance hall with its Chinese paintings and lotus blossom chandeliers. "Where is Sir Richard?"

"In the conservatory, madam. Shall I announce . . . ?"

"That won't be necessary," she replied, marching away determinedly toward the rear of the house.

The butler gazed uneasily after her, for her mood didn't bode at all well for his master.

The conservatory was a lofty, spacious place, its many glass panes facing over the snowy gardens. Tropical leaves pressed all around, and the air was warm, fragrant, and damp. Richard was lounging on one of the white-painted wrought iron chairs set by a matching table. A decanter of cognac stood on the table, and he was sipping a glass as he glanced through a newspaper. Hearing her angry steps approaching, he put the glass and the newspaper down quickly, and rose to his feet.

"Isabel?"

"Good afternoon, sir."

A light passed through his eyes at her cold, angry tone. "Is something wrong?" he asked.

"Wrong, sir? Oh, yes, something is indeed wrong. You've been found out!"

"Found out? I don't understand . . ."

"I know all about your *belle de nuit!*"

He looked blankly at her. "I'm afraid I don't understand. What *belle de nuit?*"

"Your precious Mrs. Beaumont!" she snapped.

His eyes cleared. So that was it: somehow she'd found out about Diana's part in his past. "Isabel, I can explain all about Diana . . ."

She flashed him a look so bright and furious that it was as if her eyes were on fire. "So, you admit it! You *admit* she is more to you than a person with whom you are vaguely acquainted."

"Yes, I admit that much, but I assure you she . . ."

"Don't attempt to lie to me, sir, for it won't wash. You've been found out, and you have only yourself to blame. How foolish and careless of you to address the wrong note to me!"

He stared at her. "Isabel, what on earth are you talking about? What note?"

"I'm not a fool, sir, so don't treat me like one! You know perfectly well what note, for it can only be the one you penned to your vulgar little inamorata, but which you managed to send to me instead! How dare you deceive me, how *dare* you keep a mistress!"

His face became very still. "Isabel, I swear to you that I have no idea what you're talking about. I haven't written any notes, not to you or to anyone else!"

"And I suppose you didn't send your man to Duvall & Carrier's to purchase the two fans you'd picked out?" she replied frostily.

"No, damn it, I most certainly did not!" he snapped.

"Then the letter of authority in your handwriting just conjured itself out of nothing? As did the note for your precious Diana? No doubt she is at this very moment gazing upon the *billet doux* meant for me!"

For a long moment he was silent, then he spoke in a quietly incensed voice. "Are you telling me that someone has purchased two fans in my name, and had one sent to you and the other to Diana Beaumont?"

"Does it amuse you to ask something you know only too well, sir? Of *course* that's what I'm telling you! How long did you imagine you'd get away with it? Obviously you meant to continue keeping her after our marriage. . . ."

"Isabel, I am not keeping her, and I never have!"

"Monster! How can you face me and utter such manifest untruths!" she cried. "In the park earlier you said that she was hardly known to you, and yet now it's rather clear that that was a bare-faced lie. How long have you known her?"

"Over five years."

Isabel stared at him. "Are you telling me you've been keeping her all that time?"

"No, I'm just telling you how long I've known her. She was Diana Laverick then, and if I could have married her, I would, but she chose a wealthier husband and went with him to live in Jamaica. She returned to England yesterday, and that is the extent of my recent knowledge of her. She is not my mistress, I'd swear that on the Bible itself! Someone is up to something, Isabel, for I did not write any letter or any notes. I did not order any fans, and I did not send my man to Duvall & Carrier's."

"The note I received and the letter are both in your handwriting, sirrah."

"Then someone has forged my writing!" he replied shortly. "Damn it, Isabel, do you really imagine I'd conduct myself in such a way as to keep a mistress when I am betrothed to you? Do you honestly believe that I'd be so low and deceitful as to see someone else behind your back?"

She lowered her eyes. "Such things have been known, sir," she replied softly.

"You should trust me more, madam."

"Should I? Why, when you've lied already where that brazen doxy is concerned?"

"Isabel, Diana Beaumont is neither brazen nor a doxy. She is a respectably married woman who has done nothing to warrant being involved in this . . . this whatever it is. Someone has seen fit to meddle in our affairs, and I intend to find out who." He held her gaze. "Do you trust me, Isabel?" he asked softly.

She met his eyes, still remembering the encounter in the park. "No," she replied. "No, I don't trust you, sir."

"Then I think our betrothal must be at an end, don't you?" he said coldly.

"As you wish, sirrah," she replied, her chin raised proudly. For a moment she considered making the grand gesture of tossing his ring at him, but then she thought better of it, for the ring was very valuable, and she liked it a great deal. Conflicting emotions crossed her lovely face, but then she turned on her heel and left him. So, he thought to end the betrothal, did he? Well, she didn't intend to tell the world about it; she just intended to teach him the lesson of his life, making him the laughingstock of society in the process! The shoe was about to be on the other foot, oh, *how* it was to be on the other foot!

As she flung from the conservatory, Richard turned to gaze angrily out at the snow-covered gardens. What was going on? Who was scheming against him like this? An obvious name came to mind, Geoffrey Hawksworth, but how would Geoffrey know about Diana? Then he remembered, in the days before Isabel, when he'd been intimate enough with Geoffrey to confide in him. Yes, Geoffrey knew all about Diana, and, coincidentally, Geoffrey also happened to covet Isabel. If that same Geoffrey had somehow learned of Diana's return to England . . . Richard took a long breath. He'd lay odds that Geoffrey Hawksworth was behind all this, and the best way to start making enquiries was to adjourn to Messrs Duvall & Carrier to see what was what.

First things first, however, for there was the matter of setting Diana straight concerning the fan *she* had apparently received in his name. The lord alone knew what message had accompanied it, but . . .

"Sir Richard?"

He turned to see the butler standing there with a crumpled brown paper package in his hand. "Yes? What is it?"

"This has just been delivered from Mrs. Beaumont of Pargeter Street, sir."

Richard lowered his gaze to the package. "Indeed?" he murmured, going to take it. As he opened it, he saw the exquisite gray silk fan inside, and the note that purported to come from him. Oh, it was a clever forgery, that was for sure. No wonder Isabel believed it to have come from him. He read the brief but loving message.

> *My beloved,*
> *Let this Christmas be the signal for a new future together. Let us forget the misunderstandings of the past and accept our undying love for each other. I will adore you throughout eternity.*
> *Richard.*

He closed his eyes for a moment. Diana had received *this?*

The butler cleared his throat. "Sir, I fear there was an, er, communication from the lady."

"Communication?"

"The fellow who brought it said that he was instructed to say that Mrs. Beaumont does not wish to receive any further gifts, and that she wishes to be left alone." The man looked hugely embarrassed at having to repeat such a message.

Richard tossed the package and the note down on the table. "Have my horse saddled."

"Very well, sir."

"I won't be out for long, but if I'm needed urgently you'll find me either at Duvall & Carrier's in Piccadilly, or at 44 Pargeter Street."

"Yes, sir." The butler withdrew.

Richard stood looking down at the package. If Geoffrey Hawksworth was responsible for this, he'd pay dearly for such unwarranted meddling! Picking up his glass, Richard drained it of the cognac he'd been drinking before Isabel's arrival, but as he put it down on the table again, the incredulous realization flooded over him that his betrothal was at an end. He'd severed the engagement to the woman he'd pursued for so long, and he felt nothing, nothing at all.

Diana was at that moment leaving the house in Pargeter Street to enter the hired chaise that was to convey her, with Mary, to the lawyer's chambers in Lincoln's Inn. She wore a peach woolen mantle richly embellished with beaded black embroidery, and a wide-brimmed peach hat adorned with small black plumes. The distress caused by the arrival of the fan and its accompanying note had subsided a little now, and she was quite composed as the chaise drew away to set off east toward the city. Opposite her, Mary sat quietly in her corner seat thinking about Sir Richard Curzon. He'd taken refuge in his hurt pride five years before when he'd ignored Diana's long, tear-stained letter, and now he was exacting spiteful revenge. In the past Mary had believed him to be all that was right for her mistress, but she'd been forced to make a reappraisal of his character. That second opinion of him was now proving to be only too correct, for he was a mean-hearted, shabby toad to do such a monstrous thing to someone as sweet as Miss Diana.

The chaise drove swiftly eastward through the Christmas traffic, through streets that tingled with seasonal excitement and anticipation, but Diana kept her eyes downcast. She knew only too well what the lawyer was going to tell her, but she couldn't help, deep in her heart of hearts, hoping that there would be a little good news as well.

In Piccadilly, which was soon far behind the chaise, Richard reined his horse in outside Duvall & Carrier's, and, as chance would have it, tossed a coin to the same mistletoe-seller to look after the animal while he made enquiries inside. The very same assistant came to wait upon him, and evinced an ill-placed air of bewildered irritability on being asked yet again about the order for the fans.

"Sir, I am not at liberty to . . . !"

His words were choked in mid-sentence as Richard leaned across the counter to seize him by his immaculate blue-and-white-spotted neckcloth. "Now listen to me, my fine fellow," breathed Richard through clenched teeth, "someone has been playing fast and loose with my name, and I intend to get to the bottom of it. Either show me the letter I am supposed to have written, or I will suspend you from the ceiling alongside that damned kissing bunch! Do I make myself crystal clear?"

"Yes, sir!" squeaked the assistant, closing his eyes with relief as Richard relaxed his grip.

A moment later the letter had again been produced, and a nerve flickered angrily at Richard's temple as he read it. Geoffrey Hawksworth's name still came to mind, for somehow it had that sly gentleman's disagreeable mark all over it. He looked at the red-faced assistant, who was rubbing his throat as if he'd been half-strangled. "I understand my man is supposed to have brought this?"

"Yes, Sir Richard."

"Describe him to me."

"Well, sir, he was small and wiry, like a groom or a jockey, and. . . ."

Hawksworth's valet to a tee! Without another word, Richard turned on his heel and strode out again, leaving the assistant to stare thankfully after him. The kissing bunch swayed a little in the draft from the doorway, and the man's eyes moved nervously toward it. There had been something in Sir Richard's tone that had suggested most strongly that the threat hadn't been uttered idly.

Richard rode to Geoffrey's residence in North Street, but was told that he wasn't at home. He was also told that Geoffrey's valet wasn't in the house, although if the truth were known that nervous fellow was at that very moment peeping down through the marble bannisters from the floor above, from whence he'd been about to descend with some of his master's clothes. Hearing Sir Richard Curzon's name announced, and detecting the anger in his voice, the valet had stayed wisely well out of sight. It was obvious that Sir Richard had put two and two together, and had come up with the correct answer, which meant that it had all suddenly become a little hazardous for the likes of the Honorable Geoffrey Hawksworth's unfortunate man.

Thanking his stars that the footman who'd answered the door really did believe him to be out of the house, the valet emerged from hiding as Richard rode away again. A gentleman in such a justifiable fury was to be avoided at all costs, so maybe now was the perfect moment to pay a visit to the family in Newmarket. The valet drew a long breath. Yes, London was a dangerous place now, and Newmarket a haven of peace and tranquility! He'd leave as soon as he possibly could.

At Pargeter Street, Richard's next destination, he was told that Diana was keeping an appointment with her lawyer in Lincoln's Inn and wouldn't be back for at least another hour, so he returned to Park Lane. As he entered his house, Geoffrey Hawksworth's carriage was at that very moment turning from Brook Street into Hanover Square, having at last returned from the lengthy and unwanted visit to Hampstead. His great-aunt hadn't been content with merely insisting upon being driven home, she'd made it plain that she'd be very displeased indeed if he didn't stay for a while. He'd therefore had to kick his heels drinking tea and nibbling wretched wafers until at last she'd relented and allowed him to leave. The Devil take the old tabby, for if ever there'd been a day when he'd wished her on another planet, this was that day!

But at least he'd now managed to complete the preparations for his stratagem, having stopped at Cranford's in Bond Street to attend to the business of the sunburst brooch. There hadn't been time to return to North Street for his valet, so he'd had to do it himself. He'd astonished his coachman by demanding the use of his box coat and wide-brimmed hat, but it was a necessary precaution in a shop where he'd recently made two purchases, and might be recognized. Disguising his voice, he'd pretended to be Richard's man, and had handed over a second letter of authority, together with a purse and another sealed note. The shop had readily agreed to despatch the brooch to the lady concerned, and now he was at liberty to proceed with the rest of his plan.

The afternoon light was just beginning to fade as the carriage turned the corner out of Brook Street. Geoffrey glanced out and was just in time to see a face he knew riding past on a gleaming Arabian horse. Swiftly lowering the glass, he leaned out.

"Laroche! I say, Laroche!"

The carriage halted, and Laroche turned in the saddle, reining in as he recognized Geoffrey. He glanced back across Hanover Square, but then rode toward

the carriage, followed by his greyhounds. "Good afternoon, Geoffrey."

"About last night at the ball . . ."

"Ah, yes, and the fact that you lied to me about
my wife."

Geoffrey gave him an apologetic grin. "It was all I
could think of to get you away from Isabel."

"And it worked handsomely."

"Forgive me. I promise not to resort to such trickery
again tonight."

"Tonight?"

"The Holland House masquerade."

Laroche gave a slight smile. "Resort to whatever
you wish tonight, dear boy, it's immaterial to me."

"Immaterial?"

"Because I will not be there. And now, if you have
nothing further to say, I fear I have to be on my way.
I've got a great deal to do before tonight."

"Oh, very well, if that's the way of it," replied Geoffrey. "Perhaps I'd better take this opportunity to wish
you a very happy Christmas."

Laroche laughed. "My dear Geoffrey, I intend this
to be the happiest Christmas of my life. Goodbye."
Touching his top hat, he rode on into Brook Street,
his greyhounds still padding at his horse's heels.

Shrugging at the fellow's somewhat odd manner,
Geoffrey sat back again, and the carriage drove
around Hanover Square, coming to a halt at the curb
outside the Graham residence.

Geoffrey paused for a moment before alighting. Isabel must by now have received the fan and read the
note, which meant that she'd have leapt to the conclu-
sion that Richard was keeping Diana Beaumont as his
secret mistress. What developments had there been?
If it hadn't been for his old biddy of a great-aunt he'd
have been here much sooner than this, and would
have been able to manipulate things with a few well-

chosen words here and there, but as it was he knew nothing about what may or may not have been going on, and he'd have to play it by ear.

Taking a deep breath, he climbed down from the carriage, looking up at the house. As the shadows lengthened, so the lights were being lit inside, and already the houses in the gracious square were bright for Christmas Eve. A girl was selling little kissing bunches on the pavement nearby, and her sweet, clear voice rang out. *Kissing bunches, kissing bunches for your sweetheart.*

Geoffrey smiled to himself, for if things went as he'd planned, he and Isabel would have no need of a kissing bunch to encourage them this Christmas . . .

He rapped his cane on the gleaming door, and the butler opened it almost immediately. "Ah, your grace, I was about to send your . . ." The man's face changed as he recognized Geoffrey. "Oh, forgive me, sir, I thought you were the Duke of Laroche returned for his riding crop."

Laroche had been here? Geoffrey was about to speak when Isabel herself appeared at the top of the grand staircase, looking delightful in a pink sprigged muslin gown that had a lavishly stiffened hem. A black-and-gold cashmere shawl trailed behind her as she hurried down the staircase, and there was a vivacious smile on her lips. She hesitated then, seeing Geoffrey.

"Oh, it's you," she said, her smile becoming a little fixed.

"Yes, it's me." He hardly noticed her lack of enthusiasm on seeing him, he was too surprised by her manner immediately prior to that. She'd looked positively blooming, and there was certainly no sign of the distress he'd expected. Had Duvall & Carrier failed to deliver the fan? It had to be something like that, for what else would explain her light-hearted manner? If she'd read his carefully worded note, she'd by now believe that Richard was Diana Beaumont's protector, and the last thing she'd be was light-hearted!

Geoffrey's mind raced in those few seconds, and he decided that there was nothing for it but to put the second part of his plan into action. He smiled at her. "I've come to take you to buy your Christmas gift."

"Christmas gift?" She returned the smile. "Why, Geoffrey, how sweet of you. What are you going to buy me?"

"That I will not say, but suffice it that it is something from Cranford's."

She clapped her hands in delight. "Oh, Geoffrey! You absolute darling! Are we going now?"

"I am at your disposal," he replied, sketching her a bow.

"I'll put some outdoor clothes on," she replied, gathering her skirts and hurrying back up the staircase, the shawl still dragging prettily behind her.

She returned a few minutes later wearing a gray three-quarter-length velvet pelisse over the pink muslin gown. A gray jockey bonnet rested on her shining dark curls, with a pink gauze scarf tied around the crown and hanging down to her hem at the back. Linking her little hand lightly through his proferred arm, she allowed him to lead her out into the increasingly dark late afternoon.

The streetseller's sweet cries rang out again. *Kissing bunches, kissing bunches for your sweetheart . . .*

In nearby Pargeter Street, Diana's hired chaise had just returned, and she and Mary had entered the drawing room. Diana teased off her gloves, and faced the maid.

"It was as bad as I always feared. Oh, why was I foolish enough to let myself hope . . . ?"

The butler came to the doors. "Begging your pardon, Mrs. Beaumont, but Sir Richard Curzon has called."

Without ceremony, Richard strode past him into the drawing room. "I wish to speak to you, madam," he said, tossing his hat, gloves, and cane on to a table.

Diana nodded at Mary. "That will be all for the moment, Mary."

"But, Miss Diana . . ."

"Please leave us."

Mary looked at her, and then gave Richard a cold glance, before going out. The butler closed the doors, and Diana was left alone with Richard. She turned away from him, for just being in the same room made her tremble. "We have nothing to say to each other, sir."

"On the contrary, madam, we have much to say, especially apropos the fan you are under the impression I sent to you."

"Under the impression? Sir, you *did* send it!" she cried, whirling to face him.

"No, madam, I did not," he replied shortly, but all the while he couldn't help thinking how exquisitely lovely she was.

"I recognized your writing, sir, and it may surprise you to know that I think you quite capable of malicious and spiteful acts."

"Malicious and spiteful? Is *that* how you see me?"

"How else? I wrote to you five years ago explaining my marriage to Robert, but you declined to acknowledge it in any way. I think you very shabby, sir, especially now that you've stooped to that cruel trick with the fan."

"I didn't receive any letter, madam, because you didn't send one. You tossed me aside because you found a better match, that's the beginning and end of the story." Bitterness rang in his voice, and shone in his clear blue eyes as he looked reproachfully at her.

Her green eyes were large and hurt. "You wrong me, sir," she whispered, taking off her hat and placing it gently on the table. Her hair, too heavy for its pins, fell loose, tumbling down in a flame-colored cascade. The fragrance of lily-of-the-valley drifted sweetly over him, stirring the desire he'd struggled so long to subdue. He still wanted her. He still wanted her as much as ever . . .

She looked at him. "Please leave, Richard, for we only hurt each other more all the time."

He turned to go, but before he knew it he'd reached out to seize her, dragging her roughly into his arms and kissing her on the lips. His fingers curled in her hair, and he crushed her slender body against his. Her perfume was all around him, alluring, beguiling, heart-breakingly poignant . . . He bruised her lips with the force of his passion, but nothing mattered except the sheer ecstasy of holding her again. She was the only woman he'd ever wanted like this, the only woman who'd ever pierced his heart and made him vulnerable. His feelings for Isabel were as nothing compared to the towering emotion Diana Beaumont could arouse in him with just a glance.

She was struggling to escape, trying to beat her fists against him, but he was too strong. Then sanity began to return. He was wrong to do this, wrong to compel her by force . . . Abruptly he released her, and she dealt him a stinging blow, leaving red marks on his cheek. Her eyes were bright and full of unspoken emotions. She didn't say anything, but shook visibly as she again turned away from him.

For a moment he could only stare at her, drinking in the way her hair fell in such heavy, curling tresses, and the way her figure was outlined by the cut of her clothes. But he didn't say anything either. Instead he snatched up his hat, gloves, and cane, and left the house.

In the drawing room, Diana hid her face in her

hands, her lips still tingling from his kiss. Tears stung her eyes. "Oh, Richard," she whispered, "Richard, I still love you so very much . . . ."

Mary came in and found her. "Oh, Miss Diana . . . ."

"I want to leave London as quickly as possible, Mary. Have the butler send out to see if a chaise can be hired."

"But it's Christmas Eve, Miss Diana, there won't be a chaise to be had anywhere. And with tomorrow being Christmas Day . . . ."

"Just do it, Mary."

"Very well, Miss Diana." As Mary left the drawing room again, her thoughts of Sir Richard Curzon were very dark indeed. He had a great deal to answer for, a great deal.

The bell at Cranford's rang out prettily as Geoffrey ushered Isabel inside, and the proprietor himself came to assist them.

"May I be of service, sir, madam?" he inquired. He was a plump man with a balding head, and was much given to wearing bright blue clothes. Today he had on a sky-blue coat and matching cravat, with a frilled white shirt and indigo brocade waistcoat. He thought himself very much the thing, which indeed he was, being Mayfair's most exclusive and sought after jeweler.

Geoffrey leaned an elbow on the shining counter. "You have a brooch in the window, a sunburst made entirely of gold."

"Ah, you mean the one in the red leather box, sir?"

"Yes, that's the one."

"I fear it's already sold, sir. Sir Richard Curzon purchased it a short while ago, and it is just about to be delivered."

"Who to?" asked Isabel suddenly.

"Madam, I hardly think that that is information I am at liberty to divulge."

She glanced around, and her glance fell upon a

silver-gilt bowl containing a bouquet of Christmas greenery, holly, mistletoe, ivy, and Christmas roses. Picking it up, she held it aloft, as if about to dash it to the stone-tiled floor. "Tell me, Mr. Cranford, or it will be the worst for your lovely bowl, which I'm sure will be greatly damaged if it accidentally falls."

The jeweler gaped at her, and then nodded quickly. "Very well, madam, I'll tell you. The brooch is to be delivered to Mrs. Beaumont at 44 Pargeter Street."

"Thank you," she replied, putting the bowl carefully back on the counter.

Geoffrey waited for the outburst of speechless fury, but it didn't come. Instead Isabel was smiling at him. "What a shame about the brooch, Geoffrey, but I'm sure Mr. Cranford has more from which I can choose. Don't you, Mr. Cranford?"

"Oh, indeed so, madam," that gentleman replied with alacrity, producing a selection which he displayed swiftly before her.

Now it was Geoffrey who was speechless. She'd just learned that Richard had purchased for another woman the brooch *she* wanted, and yet she was dismissing it as being of no consequence! What was going on? It was inconceivable that Isabel should respond in such a fashion, and yet that was precisely what had happened.

A few minutes later they emerged from the shop, and Geoffrey's purse was measurably lighter as a consequence of purchasing a delightful little trinket studded with rubies. Isabel hadn't mentioned Richard again, indeed it was as if he'd ceased to matter in any way. This impression was made more noticeable than ever when she smiled again on settling back in the carriage.

"Oh, Geoffrey, you're such a *darling* for giving me this little present. I must think of some way of rewarding you. I know, you shall escort me to the masquerade tonight!"

"Escort you to the masquerade? But what of Curzon?" He was utterly bewildered.

"Richard? Oh, I really have no idea." She pouted. "Don't you want to take me to Holland House tonight?"

"Yes, of course, it's just that . . ."

"Then it's settled, you will take me there. Come to the house at eight, yes, eight should about do it." She smiled again, fixing the brooch on to her pelisse.

Still utterly bewildered, Geoffrey said nothing more. He was completely at a loss to understand her, and totally at a loss for words.

Darkness had fallen, and the *beau monde* was preparing for the masquerade at Holland House. Fancy dress purchased specially for the Christmas Eve occasion was put out in readiness, and at Holland House itself Gunter's were attending to last minute details of the veritable banquet that was to be served to the hundreds of guests. The orchestra was tuning up, and the house was brilliantly illuminated, every single window boasting festive candles and festoons of yuletide leaves.

At 44 Pargeter Street, everything was quiet. Diana was in the drawing room endeavoring to read one of Sir Walter Scott's popular novels, and the only sound was the gentle fluttering of the fire in the hearth. She wore a dark green velvet gown, and gazed at the page without really seeing it, for all she could think about was Richard.

She heard someone knock at the front door, and then voices in the entrance hall. A moment later the butler brought her a small packet.

"This has just been delivered, madam," he said, giving it to her.

Her heart sank as she closed the book, for the arrival of this packet bore a marked similarity to the

arrival of the fan a little earlier in the day. Reluctantly
she opened the packet, and found the little red leather
box inside. As she opened the box, she found herself
gazing at a pretty sunburst brooch. There was, as she
fully expected, another note in Richard's handwriting.

> *You're mine, my darling Diana, just as you al-*
> *ways were and always will be. The future could*
> *be ours.*
> *Richard.*

Fresh tears stung her eyes, but she willed them
back. She nodded at the butler. "Thank you, that will
be all."

"Madam." He bowed and withdrew.

Diana put the brooch and its packing on the table
next to her chair, and reopened the book. She
wouldn't succumb to her tears again, she *wouldn't!*
But the tears were stronger than she, welling hotly
from her eyes and down her cheeks. She felt so unut-
terably wretched that she wished she were dead. She
curled up in the chair, burying her face in the rich
upholstery.

Mary came in shortly afterward, having learned of
the brooch's delivery from the butler. Uneasy on her
mistress's account, she'd hastened immediately to the
drawing room, where her worst fears were realized as
she found Diana weeping so heart-brokenly in the
chair.

Diana was too distressed to even know the maid
was there, and she knew nothing as Mary picked up
the note that had come with the brooch, read it, and
then replaced it. The maid's eyes were stormy as she
withdrew from the room again. It was time that Sir
Richard Curzon was set right on certain important
points, and she, Mary Keating, was just the one to
do it!

Five minutes later, clad in her plain but serviceable

cloak, Mary left the house, stepping out into snowy darkness and making for Park Lane.

As Mary's angry, determined steps took her toward Richard's residence, Isabel was fully occupied in her apartment at the house in Hanover Square. The line of wardrobes in her dressing room were all open, and, together with her long-suffering maid, Isabel was surveying the array of garments inside.

"I'll take the salmon brocade, the white satin, and the plowman's gauze. No, not the plowman's gauze, I'm a little tired of it. I'll take the green organdy muslin instead."

"But, madam . . ."

"That takes care of the gowns," interrupted Isabel, not listening. "Now we come to the outer garments. I shall wear the black fur-lined cloak over my vermilion wool, but I shall also need the mantle, the pelisse, and probably the buttercup dimity paletot as well."

The maid was appalled. "But, madam, it's only a very small valise!"

"Not that small. Is it?" Isabel looked sharply at her. "Well? *Is* it that small?"

"Yes, madam, it is."

"Then we'll take a larger one."

The maid sighed inwardly. "Yes, madam."

"And of one thing we must be absolutely certain: we must not forget a single item of my jewelry."

"No, madam."

Isabel went through into her bedroom, and flung herself on her white silk bed, gazing up at the exquisitely draped canopy. Oh, what a cat was about to be set among the pigeons of Mayfair! And how very foolish Richard was going to look. It served him right, for having the audacity to keep that Beaumont demirep!

Mary was conducted to the conservatory, where Richard received her. He was standing by the white wrought iron table, and had been about to pour himself another glass of cognac when his butler had informed him that Mrs. Beaumont's maid was insisting upon seeing him. One of the last people on earth he wished to see was Mary Keating, who'd have nothing pleasant to say to him, but he knew he behaved more than badly when he'd called at Pargeter Street earlier, and if Mary had come to berate him, then it was no more than he warranted.

He faced her, his blonde hair very golden in the light from the solitary candelabrum standing on the table. Leafy shadows pressed all around, and outside the snowy garden looked almost gray-blue in the night.

"You wished to speak to me, Mary?" he said.

Maid or not, in that moment she stood up to him as his equal. "Yes, Sir Richard, I wish to speak to you, and I trust you will hear me out to the end, for it's important that you know the truth. You told my mistress that you didn't receive her letter five years ago . . ."

"I didn't."

"Then, since she will not tell you about it herself, it falls to me to do it for her. You didn't know it, sir, but five years ago Miss Diana's father, Mr. Laverick, was in very severe financial difficulties, indeed he was an inch away from debtor's jail. His debts had to be settled without delay, and they were such that Miss Diana could not have turned to you for help, for you were at that time your father's second son. Mr. Beaumont had been making his interest known, and he somehow found out about Mr. Laverick's debts. He offered to settle them without delay, provided Miss Diana agreed to be his wife, and returned with him to his plantation in Jamaica. It broke her heart to agree to such a contract, Sir Richard, but she had to save her father. She wrote to you, because you'd come back here to London for a day or so, and it was a long, tear-stained letter that took a great deal of courage to send. She loved you with all her heart, she felt nothing for Mr. Beaumont, and yet she was prepared to spend the rest of her life as his wife." Mary held his gaze. "She wrote that letter, sir, and when she'd sealed it I took it to the letter carrier myself. I *know* it was sent."

"It didn't arrive."

"So you say, sir."

Anger stirred through him. "If I say it didn't arrive, then it didn't arrive!"

"You show wrath that someone should dare to cast doubt on your word, sir, and yet you think nothing of casting doubt on my mistress's word about that same letter."

He met her eyes, and then nodded. "The point is taken, Mary. Please proceed."

"You may think that Miss Diana has been enjoying a life of happiness and plenty since her marriage, Sir Richard, but that is not the case. Mr. Beaumont was a monster, he gambled heavily and drank still more heavily, and when he'd lost at the first and overindulged at the second, he was a very violent man. She endured it as best she could, for she'd meant her wedding vows, but he made it impossible. He was frittering away his fortune, and the plantation was in increasing difficulty. She had no one to turn to, no one to help her, and after one terrible night, when he'd drunk even more than usual, she knew that she couldn't go on anymore. She told him that she was leaving and coming home to England. In his fury he attacked her and tried to throw her down the stairs, but instead he lost his balance and fell down himself and was killed in an instant."

Richard stared at her. "Is all this true?" he breathed.

"Would I lie about such things, sir?"

"Tell me the rest."

"Well, as I said, on the night he died he'd been drinking far more than usual, and it turned out after-

ward that it was because he'd just gambled away his
entire estate. Miss Diana was left with nothing at all,
save her clothes, she had to sell what jewelry she had
to settle bills he'd left outstanding. As soon as she
could, she left Jamaica to come back here. She's going
home to her parents in Cheshire, but first she had to
come to London to see Mr. Beaumont's lawyer and
finalize the remainder of his estate. She hoped there
might be a small amount left at the end of it all, but
there isn't. She's absolutely penniless, Sir Richard, but
at least she's free of the man who made her so
wretched for five long years. She vowed she wouldn't
wear black for him, not even at his funeral, for he
hadn't earned that tribute from one he'd used so
shamelessly during their time together. Now she just
wants to live her own life, Sir Richard, and she doesn't
deserve to suffer all over again now, this time at your
hands. You shouldn't keep sending her those gifts, sir,
for such spite ill becomes you."

"Gifts? I only know of the fan I'm supposed to
have sent."

"And the brooch, sir. It came tonight, and it upset
her so much that that was when I decided to come
to you."

"I didn't send the fan, and I didn't send the brooch,
I swear that I didn't."

Mary searched his face, beginning to wonder if he
was telling the truth after all.

"Mary, I'm innocent of all this, but I think I know
who is behind it. There is someone who would move
heaven and earth to win Miss Isabel Hamilton from
me. He is also someone who happens to know of Diana's part in my past."

"Well, maybe this man is the guilty one, Sir Richard, I wouldn't know about that, but I do know that
Miss Diana is already desperately unhappy, and is
being made more unhappy."

He leaned his hands on the wrought iron table, his head bowed. "If only I'd known all this before, if only that damned letter hadn't gone astray . . ."

"Then you concede that there was a letter?"

He nodded. "I have no choice."

"Well, it's over and done with now, and you are about to marry Miss Hamilton . . ."

"No, Mary, I'm not marrying her. The betrothal was ended earlier today." He straightened, and looked at her. "There is one woman who will ever really mean everything to me, and I looked into her eyes last night when I assisted her down from her chaise. I still love her, and I think I always will."

Mary stared at him. "Do you really mean that, sir?"

"With all my heart."

"Then tell her so yourself, I beg of you."

"Do you think she'll wish to hear?"

"I know she will." Mary smiled. "Come back with me now."

An unlit carriage waited in the mews lane behind Hanover Square. It was drawn up by the rear entrance of the Graham residence, and its blinds were lowered. The Christmas Eve night was bitterly cold, and there were clouds covering the stars. A few stray snowflakes fluttered silently down.

Suddenly the rear gate of the Graham house was quietly opened, and two women, a lady and her maid, emerged, the latter struggling with a heavy valise. The coachman clambered down to assist the maid, and the lady hastened to the carriage door. She wore a black fur-lined cloak over a vermilion wool gown and matching pelisse, and there was a stylish beaver hat on her short dark hair.

The carriage door opened, and the gentleman inside leaned out. "Isabel, my darling . . ." He reached out to take her outstretched hand.

"Laroche," she whispered, allowing him to draw her up into the vehicle, where she was soon enclosed in his loving embrace.

"Oh, my darling," he breathed, his voice husky with desire. "I thought you'd change your mind. I thought Richard would win after all."

"Never, for my heart has always been yours," she murmured softly, her eyes dark.

"When I received your note today, I couldn't believe you'd decided to come away with me after all."

"I'm not just another diversion, am I? Please tell me that you love me."

"I love you," he replied immediately, just as he had to other sweethearts since his marriage.

A moment later the carriage was driving away, the maid seated up beside the coachman. Inside, Isabel and Laroche were wrapped in each other's arms, whispering sweet words. Isabel smiled to herself in the darkness. Before the night was out the whole of London would be talking about the astonishing flight of Miss Isabel Hamilton with the married Duke of Laroche. She'd be notorious for a while, but in the end she'd triumph, for Laroche had promised to divorce his wife and make her his duchess. How important, wealthy and fine a lady she'd be then, far more important and wealthy than she'd have been as mere Lady Curzon. Her smile became sleek as she pondered Richard's reaction to the scandal. She'd turned the tables on him, instead of he making a fool of her, she'd made one of him! Oh, what a wonderful Christmas this was!

Diana was still curled up in the chair in the drawing room. Her tears had dried now, but her heart felt as if it had been shattered into a thousand unhappy fragments. She didn't hear the front door being opened, nor did she hear footsteps approaching the drawing room, she knew nothing until Mary spoke.

"Miss Diana?"

She looked up, her glance going immediately past the maid to where Richard stood. Slowly Diana rose to her feet. "Sir, I think we've said all there is to say."

Mary stood aside for him to enter, and then closed the doors upon them.

Richard halted a few feet away from Diana. "Mary has told me everything," he said quietly.

"She had no right." Diana turned away as hot color rushed into her cheeks.

"I wish you'd told me earlier, instead of letting me . . ."

"Would you have believed me? I think not, for you'd have preferred to continue thinking ill of me."

"Forgive me," he said softly, coming a little closer.

"Please go, sir, for I'm sure Miss Hamilton would not understand if she knew you were here."

"I'm no longer betrothed to her, Diana."

She turned. "Why?"

"We were ill-suited, and besides . . ."

"Yes?"

"Besides, I still love you."

She stared at him, her emerald eyes large and uncertain.

His heart tightened with love for her. "Diana, I love you so much that I can't bear to think how you've suffered."

"Please don't toy with me, Richard, for I couldn't bear it."

"I'm not toying with you, I'm telling you the absolute truth. I love you, and I want you to be mine. I want the last five years to be wiped away, and for us to begin again."

Fresh tears shone in her eyes, and she took a hesitant step toward him. He needed no second bidding, but swept her into his arms, his lips seeking hers in a kiss so passionate and consuming that it was like a flame flaring through them both. Her perfume was all around, lily-of-the-valley, so delicate and exquisite that it seemed as if there was magic in the air. She was his again at last, returning his love just as he'd always dreamed.

Geoffrey's carriage drew up at the curb outside the Graham house in Hanover Square. He sat inside for a moment, adjusting his costume. He was dressed as Harlequin, and would have felt quite the thing had it not been for the unease caused by the discovery of Richard's angry visit to his residence. The fact that Richard had asked specifically if his valet was available was all the proof Geoffrey needed that Richard had discovered the truth, and as a consequence Geoffrey was very much in two minds about attending the Holland House masquerade. The thought of being confronted by a furious Richard was almost too alarming to contemplate, but now that Isabel was so nearly his, Geoffrey was very loath to forfeit the chance of escorting her. He was in a quandary, and so hesitated before alighting.

His glance fell on the wrist favor he'd purchased for her. It lay on the seat opposite, and was a delightful concoction of velvet mistletoe and holly, to be tied on with a dainty scarlet ribbon. It was such a pretty thing, and he'd been charmed with it the moment he saw it. He must take his courage in both hands, and risk the possibility of Richard's fury. Isabel was worth it all and more.

Taking a deep breath, he alighted, presenting a strangely lithe figure as he hurried up to the door of the house. Some carolsingers were on the corner, their lusty voices echoing around the elegant lamplit square, where a number of carriages were setting off for the masquerade. The singing was so very redolent of Christmas that Geoffrey turned for a moment to listen. *God rest ye merry, gentlemen, Let nothing you dismay . . .*

He rapped on the door, which in a moment was opened by a footman, but as Geoffrey made to step inside, the man shook his head. "I fear Miss Hamilton is no longer here, sir."

"Eh? What's that?" Geoffrey stared at him, for it was such an odd choice of words. No longer here? What was the fellow saying?

"She asked me to give you this note, sir," said the footman, holding out a sealed letter.

Puzzled, Geoffrey opened it and read. *Mr. Hawksworth. By the time you read this, I shall be long gone from London with the Duke of Laroche, whom I love with all my heart. He is to make me his duchess. Goodbye. Isabel Hamilton.*

Geoffrey stared at the letter, a thousand conflicting emotions tumbling through him. Isabel and *Laroche?* Numb, he looked at the footman, who was all civility.

"Will there be anything else, sir?"

"Er, no."

"Good night, sir, and the compliments of the season to you."

"Thank you. And to you." In a daze, Geoffrey turned away from the door. Isabel and *Laroche?* Oh, what a fool she'd made of him, and of Richard!

Richard. Suddenly Geoffrey thought again of the awfulness of a confrontation with that gentleman. Perhaps now was the time to show discretion, rather than the proverbial valor. Yes, indeed, a Christmas visit to his family in Great Yarmouth would seem to be the wisest move under the circumstances.

Suddenly Geoffrey wished he hadn't been moved to meddle so. The old adage simply wasn't true, it *wasn't* all fair in love and war; it certainly wasn't fair to Geoffrey Hawksworth, that was for sure! With Isabel as his prize at the end of it, maybe it was worth the hazard, but now that she'd flitted off with that philanderer Laroche, it had all come to nothing!

The carolsingers were still in full voice on the corner

as Geoffrey resumed his place in his carriage. As the vehicle drew away, his glance fell again on the pretty wrist favor. Mistletoe and holly? Mistletoe and *folly,* more like! He gave it a savage scowl, and then leaned his head back against the upholstery. Suddenly he wasn't enjoying Christmas at all, in fact it was the most disagreeable season of the entire year!

As the church bells struck midnight, and then began to peal out joyfully across London, Richard and Diana were locked in each other's arms in the house in Pargeter Street.

He drew back, putting his hand tenderly to her cheek. "It's Christmas Day," he whispered, "so will you make me the happiest man on earth by agreeing to be my wife?"

"Oh, Richard." Her eyes shone with joy.

"Will you?" he pressed.

"Yes, oh, yes."

"My darling . . ." He kissed her again, loving her so much that he felt weak. She was his forever now, and suddenly Christmas was a time of unbelievable happiness.

Upon a Midnight Clear

Amanda McCabe

Chapter One

"Oh, Aunt Antoinette, *please* won't you come to Bath with us? Christmas won't be *Christmas* without you!"

Lady Penelope Leighton's childish voice piped into the fire-warmed air of the sitting room. Her large, green eyes were wide and beseeching as she leaned against Antoinette's knees.

"Grandmama's house in Bath is always jolly, but it won't be if you're not there," added Penelope's brother, Edward, hanging off the back of Antoinette's chair with his sturdy, chubby little hands. "We're going to see a pantomime."

"*And* a lecture on Greek theater," said Penelope, her eyes growing even larger, if that was at all possible. She reached out to clasp a handful of Antoinette's red silk robe. "Or, if you don't care for Greek theater, there is sure to be something on philosophy or theology at Aunt Chat's Philosophical Society."

"Or herbs!" cried Edward. "You always like to hear about herbs."

Baby Louisa, still scarcely able to toddle, glanced up from her building blocks and gurgled an agreement.

"Oh, *mes petites*," Antoinette said softly, putting an arm about Penelope and Edward and drawing them close to her. "You know I would love nothing better than to spend Christmas with my favorite children in all the world. But, as I have said, I must finish this new book on winter herbs very soon, or my publisher will be most unhappy with me. And in Bath there would be far too many 'jolly' things to distract me."

"We would not distract you, Aunt Antoinette!" Penelope declared, going up on tiptoe to loop her small, slender arms about Antoinette's neck. "We would be so good and so quiet when you were working."

Antoinette laughed, for she knew all too well that the Leighton children's idea of "quiet" consisted of tiptoeing while they shouted out about their newest discovery in Greek history (Penelope), horses (Edward), and solid food (Louisa). She pressed a quick kiss to Penelope's tousled dark curls. "I know you would, dearest, but the lectures and dances would not be resisted. We will have a grand party when you return home next month."

As Antoinette hugged them close, she caught a glimpse of their little group reflected in the gilt-framed mirror hung above the fireplace. Anyone looking at them would realize immediately that she was not the children's *true* aunt. Not their blood aunt. Their milky-white complexions, Edward's silvery blond cap of hair, were in sharp contrast to Antoinette's own coffee-colored duskiness, her midnight eyes, and the thick, wavy fall of her matte-black hair. They were as far opposite as people could possibly be.

Except in their hearts. In Antoinette's deepest soul, they *were* her nieces and nephew, and she loved them beyond all else. They never watched her with doubt or curiosity or hostility, as so many others did. In their clear eyes there was only love and respect.

Or beggary—as there was now. It hurt her heart to see them, to know that they would go away in only a very few moments and leave her alone at the one time of year when *all* families should be together. She almost jumped up, grabbed a valise, and shouted, "Of course I will go to Bath with you!"

But she could not. Some urges were too strong, some hurts too deep for even Christmas to heal.

"We will find you the most wondrous Christmas present, Aunt Antoinette," Penelope said. "I promise. And I will write you every day."

"So will I!" Edward said stoutly.

"You do not know your letters yet," Penelope said, disdain heavy in her young voice. "And that is because you don't apply yourself to your lessons. You only think about horses."

"I do not!" Edward shouted, and the two siblings were off on their oft-repeated quarrels.

Little Louisa used her tiny sticky hands to pull herself up by Antoinette's skirt, adding her babble to the fray.

Thus was the room full of chaos when the cottage door was pushed open and Cassandra Leighton, Countess of Royce, the children's mother and Antoinette's best friend, appeared. A heavy, fur-lined white wool cloak swathed about her so that she appeared a ghostly apparition. Everyone at Royce Castle knew a great deal about ghosts. One could not avoid them in one of the most haunted houses in Cornwall.

The illusion faded, though, when Cassie pushed back her hood and stomped dew from her stout half boots. She took in the fray with one sweeping glance, and laughed. "Ah! I see I have come just in time. My children are obviously being carried away by naughtiness."

"Mama!" Penelope cried imperiously, propping her tiny fists on her hips. "We were not doing anything *naughty*. We simply asked Antoinette to come to Bath with us for Christmas."

"Did I not tell you, before I let you come here, that you were not to bother your auntie?" Cassie scooped up Louisa into her arms, and leveled her steady, motherly gaze on her eldest daughter.

Penelope's pugnacious stare faltered. "Yes, Mama. But . . ."

"No buts. You were quite clearly disturbing her. There is no time to discuss it now, though. The carriage is waiting, and if we do not hurry your papa will vanish back into his library for another hour. So, kiss your auntie, and be on your way. Papa will settle you in the carriage with warm bricks and blankets."

Penelope turned back to Antoinette and dropped her a perfect little curtsy. "Good-bye, Aunt Antoinette. I will write to you every day and tell you what we are doing." The image of impeccable young ladyhood was ruined, though, when Penelope threw her arms around Antoinette's neck and kissed her once, twice, three times. "We'll miss you! But we *will* have a party when we return home, right?"

Antoinette kissed her back. "Of course, my dear. Be a good girl for your grandmama, and enjoy yourself."

"I love you, Aunt Antoinette."

"And so do I!" Edward piped up, kissing Antoinette's other cheek.

Louisa just gurgled, and thrust a silk tassel from her mother's cloak into her little mouth.

Antoinette's throat tightened, and she blinked hard against the sudden rush of hot tears behind her eyes. "I love you too, *mes petites*."

With one last kiss, the children dashed past their mother and out the cottage door. Their shouts and laughter could be heard clearly on the crisp, cold air until they turned the corner on the pathway to the castle and were gone.

Cassie leaned against the doorway, Louisa still propped on her hip. Her dark eyes were shrewd and all-seeing as she watched Antoinette. They had known each other for far too long for Antoinette to hide much from Cassie, or Cassie from her. It had been ever thus, since they were little girls running on the beach in Jamaica, neither caring that one was the daughter of an English landowner and one the child of a freed slave.

Antoinette tried to give her friend a light smile. She pulled her Kashmir shawl closely about her shoulders, yet could not entirely rid herself of her chill.

The chill that was always with her. It could not be banished by the crackling fire, and did not melt with the English snows in the spring. It was a chill in her very soul.

"The children are not the only ones who would beseech you to come to Bath with us," Cassie said. "There is still time, you know. Phillip would not mind waiting one jot while you packed a trunk. Christmas in Bath is so jolly!"

"I know. Edward told me." Antoinette stood from her chair, and took up the cast-iron poker to stir at the fire. Tiny orange-red embers crackled and fell out onto her stone hearth, almost catching the hem of her robe. "And I have been there with you every Christmas for the last five years."

"But not this year?"

Antoinette smiled back over her shoulder at Cassie. "Not this year."

"Because you must work."

"Indeed. Because I must work. My last book on herbal soaps and lotions did so very well that my publisher is eager for a volume on growing herbs in winter. He is willing to pay me twice as much if I can send it to him next month. I would be too distracted to write in Bath."

Cassie shifted Louisa to her other hip, still frowning. "If it is a question of money . . ."

"It is not!" Antoinette cried, a sharp pain pricking behind her eyes. She whirled back to face the fire, pressing her fingers to her temples. She loved Cassie as her own sister, she truly did. But she was seized with such a need to be alone, a desperation for silence. She could not bear to talk about money, or Christmas, any longer, to try to explain yet again.

And, really, how could she explain something to her friend that she did not understand herself? If she tried to voice these strange, unvoiceable feelings she had been having of late, it would only worry Cassie, and to no good end. Her friend could not help Antoinette; no one really could. And Cassie deserved a joyous holiday with her husband and children, enjoying all the delights Bath could offer.

And Antoinette needed this time alone.

She felt a soft touch on her sleeve, and turned to see that Cassie had drawn nearer, reaching out to Antoinette with her gloved hand. Her pale, heart-shaped face was creased in worry—which was the last thing Antoinette wanted to cause.

She forced herself to give another merry smile and a light laugh, and reached up to press Cassie's hand with her own. "Don't look so melancholy, my friend. I will be fine here, truly. I will work, and rest, and finish a new batch of lotions for Mrs. Greeley's store in the village."

Cassie still did not appear happy, but something shifted behind her eyes. Some sort of surrender, some giving-in, which was quite amazing. Though Cassie was a full foot shorter than Antoinette's own towering six feet—and a full year younger, to boot—she still tried to be the arranger, the overseer.

"If you are certain this is what you want . . ."

"It *is*," Antoinette answered firmly.

"Then we will honor your wishes." As if she had any choice.

"Thank you, Cassie. I will write to you often and assure you that all is well here."

"If you get too lonely, at least go up to the castle.

Cook will be delighted to ply you with her cinnamon cakes, and your guest suite is always prepared."

"I shall probably avail myself of the cakes, but I cannot stay there. The eternal quarrels of Lady Lettice and Jean-Pierre would be too great a distraction."

Cassie had to laugh at the reminder of the noisy antics of Royce Castle's resident ghosts—an Elizabethan lady and her faithless French swain. "Indeed they *are* a distraction. I sometimes wonder when they will move on, but Lady Lettice is so good with the children."

"Yes. And I know someone else who must 'move on' now," Antoinette said. "Your journey is a long one, and if you do not leave soon you will never make it to your first stop by nightfall."

Antoinette reached for one of the small willow baskets arrayed on her sitting room shelves, and took out a little black muslin bag stuffed with fragrant herbs and tied with a pink ribbon.

She pressed it into Cassie's hand. "Take this. The black is for protection, and it is filled with rose for friendship, lavender for even more protection, and marjoram for happiness. I know this will be the happiest of holidays for you."

Cassie stood on tiptoe, much as her daughter had, and kissed Antoinette's cheek, holding the precious bag out of Louisa's grasping reach. "I will keep it close by me. Happy Christmas, Antoinette."

"Happy Christmas, Cassie." Antoinette kissed Cassie's cheek in return, and urged her out the door and back into the wet morning.

She leaned against the wooden frame, tucking her hands into the sleeves of her silk robe for warmth as she watched her friend hurry along the narrow path leading from Antoinette's cottage to the castle. Cassie turned just before disappearing at the bend and waved, along with little Louisa. For just an instant, the baby's chortles could be heard. Then they turned away and were gone.

The only sound was the wind in the bare trees around the cottage, the winter's whispers on the faintly salty Cornwall air.

Antoinette was alone.

She hugged her arms closer about her waist and moved to the edge of her small front garden. The herbs and flowers were mostly sleeping for the winter, but a few things flourished still, including a tough clump of rosemary beside the low stone wall. Antoinette picked a stem, toying with it between her fingers as she leaned against the cold wall. The wind caught at her loosely tied-back hair, tossing the dark, coarse strands about.

Antoinette pushed them back impatiently and studied the scene spread out before her. She could not see the cliffs or the sea from her cottage; they were hidden by thick stands of trees, precious trees that gave her solitude and camouflage. But she could hear the song of the waves, chill gray and pale blue water crashing against the rocky shore.

A shore so very different from that of her birthplace, Jamaica. As different as if they were on another planet. The sea in Jamaica was turquoise and emerald green, always shifting, sparkling under a warm golden sun. She and Cassie had often run across the sand, white sand as soft as a baby's breath under their feet. The thick breezes had borne the scents of jasmine and plumeria to them, as well as the rich spices from the kitchens. From the open doors there, they could hear the cook and her assistants singing the old Trinidadian song "The Virgin Mary Had a Baby Boy."

Antoinette thought she heard an echo of their song on the cold breeze now. It was a song her mother used to sing at this time of year, as her nimble needle created her exquisite gowns and shawls. "Ah, Antoinette, *ma belle*, one day you will find your own destiny," she would say, when Antoinette expressed a desire to sew like her. "Greater things await you than stitchery. One day, you will see. One day they will find you. . . ."

Well, it had not found her yet. Nothing she would call *destiny*, anyway. Yet a part of her mother's prophecy had come true. She did not make her way by the needle. She made it by her pen, by the herbs she grew in this garden and in the small conservatory behind her cottage. Her books about the uses of herbs sold well in London bookshops. Many women swore by her lotions and tinctures, vowed they made their skins younger and softer. She was glad of that—glad that her knowledge made her the money to buy this cottage, to be independent.

She did not share *all* of her knowledge of herbs, of course. That would be foolish in a place where her acceptance was so very precarious anyway. She could not share it with the white English who, in their ignorance, would call her a witch. Only Cassie and her family knew the true power to be found in an ancient, secret book hidden beneath Antoinette's bed.

It was the greatest gift of Marie-Claire Duvall to her daughter. The secrets of the Yaumumi priestesses were safe in Antoinette's hands. And they had served her well in many ways.

Antoinette tipped her head back to stare into the empty, slate-gray sky.

"Oh, Maman," she whispered. "Why could you not have taught me to cure an unsure heart, as well? How to fill an emptiness, when I do not even know where the wound lies?"

There was no answer, of course. Antoinette had not expected any, yet there was always a half-hidden hope. A hope for a reply, a *sign* that she was doing the right thing in her life.

She did not regret leaving Jamaica to accompany Cassie to England when Cassie's father died and his plantation was sold. Antoinette's mother had died many years ago, and she had no other family. Only Cassie, who was like her sister. And Cassie's family was likely the only one Antoinette would ever know— there were not very many suitors in southern England for women such as her!

Antoinette could have stayed in Jamaica, of course, could have purveyed her herbs and spells to people of her own sort. But she knew she would have been just as alone there, in a hut on the beautiful beach, as she was here. Just less cold.

Antoinette shook her head hard and laughed, trying to push away her sudden rush of self-pity. She was usually far too busy to wallow in maudlin thoughts. Indeed, she ought to be busy now, tending her conservatory, writing, brewing a new batch of lavender-rose lotion. She had no time to loll about, moaning like some hapless heroine in one of the horrid novels Cassie loved so much.

She pushed back from the wall and strode back down the pathway to her cottage door, brushing off her dew-dusted sleeves. It was only Christmas making her feel so sad, she thought. Christmas was a time for families, for children, for evergreen boughs and holly wreaths and red-ribbon bows. Not for strangers in strange lands.

It was chilly in the sitting room again, the fire died down to mere embers in the grate. Antoinette grabbed the poker and stirred them back to life, while she shivered under her robe.

Why was this blasted country always so *cold*?

Chapter Two

Cold. Freezing cold, like ice or snow. Or death.

The nightmare was the same as it always was, the full horror of those moments rushing back onto him as if eleven years had not passed. As if it were happening again—and again. He always knew it was a nightmare, yet he could never pull himself out of it, pull himself back into the reality of his life now. He just had to watch it once more, until the bitter ending.

The explosion that tore half his ship away hurled him into the churning waves. At first, he welcomed the chill of the water, the freezing bite of its depths. The entire left side of his body burned with a frigid, heavy flame, his uniform torn away, the gold braid cutting into his raw flesh. But then the full force of the cold salt water slapped against him, bringing new agony.

He began to sink, dragged to Davy Jones' locker by an inexorable force. He welcomed it, welcomed the dark, sweet oblivion that he knew waited for him there, promising to soothe away the unbearable pain. He was a sailor; had been since he was a boy of fifteen. It was a fate he was familiar with and had always half-expected.

Then, as the waves closed over his head and he shut his eyes against the waning of the light, he saw her face. *Elizabeth*. His fiancée, his love. Her golden curls glowed with all the brilliance of the sun. Her violet-blue eyes beckoned to him, begging him to stay with

her, to not leave her, not lose their love. She reached
out to him, as if to pull him back to the land of the
living.

Her eyes were stronger than the force of the sea.
He reached out for her beckoning fingers—and his
hand brushed the hard, splintering wood of a piece of
flotsam. A plank from his ship. He grasped it and,
with every bit of strength left in him, every ounce of
willpower, pulled himself up into the air.

Into a new hell.

His ship was dying, sinking fast, but all around him
the battle still raged. Cannon fire turned the air thick
and rancid, the black clouds mingling with flames and
blood. Shouts and cries swirled above him, while all
about him was the detritus of the ship he had been
entrusted with. Burning wood, guns, bits of steel—the
bodies of his men.

He recognized Lieutenant Bridgers, as the young
man's body floated past him, eyes wide open yet un-
seeing. He stared down at his own arm that wouldn't
seem to move, and blinked in disbelief at the sight of
raw, red flesh where his blue wool sleeve was torn
away.

Bits of burning sail landed on that arm even as he
watched, bringing fresh waves of agony. He gasped,
and fell back onto his lifesaving plank. The battle
around him, the cacophonous noise, the light fading
left him with only one thought.

Elizabeth.

Mark Payne sat straight up in his bed, a shout strangled in his throat. *Of course.* A nightmare. That was
all it was, all it ever was. It was not real.

But once it had been. It had been a real hell, fresh
and hot around him, burning his nose with its stink.
Eleven years. Eleven years he had been haunted by
that day. Would the memory of it, of his failing, never
leave him?

Mark longed for it to be gone, yet he knew it never would be. Not until he could lose the ache of guilt that gnawed at his belly.

At least here, in his isolated little house in Cornwall, there was no one to be disturbed by his nighttime shouts. Or the endless pacing on the nights when he could not sleep at all. Here, he could hurt no one.

He knew that the villagers speculated about him, made up tales, as they had ever since he came here seven years ago. He knew they asked endless questions of the old woman who came in to cook and clean for him, questions she could not answer, though she certainly tried to with fantastical speculation. Perhaps he was a werewolf? A devil, cursed and cast out of hell? An exiled prince from a faraway land?

Mark laughed now to think of those stories—and they were only the ones that had come to his own ears. He could not even begin to imagine the ones he had not heard. The Cornish were ever fond of wild tales. Perhaps that was why he had come here, and not to one of his family's estates in Kent or Devon. Here, he was only one more haunt among many.

Even his nearest neighbor, the grand and ancient Royce Castle, was said to be haunted. Full of ghosts and spirits and devils of all sorts—even an island witch. Though Royce Castle was above two miles away from Mark's small abode, on clear days he could glimpse the turrets and speculate about those creatures, speculate about what an island witch could possibly want with such a cold and desolate land.

Such speculations were one of his life's few amusements.

Mark threw back the heavy bedclothes. He knew he would find no more sleep this night. The fire in the grate had died away, leaving the small bedchamber chill and dark. He lit the candle on the bedside table, casting a small circle of light in the gloom, and reached for his dressing gown. The fur-lined velvet slid over his nakedness, caressing his damaged flesh with its softness. As he tied the corded sash, he turned to the window, pushing back the draperies to let the night in.

And such a night it was, as different from the landscape in his nightmare as it could possibly be. He might have suddenly landed on the moon. The same moon that peeked from behind thick clouds to cast a brief, silvery glow over the night.

Rare snow from early in the evening lay in a thin white layer, light as an eiderdown, over the ground, shimmering in the new light. Frost hung from the bare branches of the trees in his sadly overgrown and tangled garden, and a new snowfall drifted like magic from the skies. It was not yet thick; every flake could be seen in its own individual perfection.

It was a breathlessly beautiful scene. Mark was reminded of a story his mother used to tell him and his brother and sister when they were small children. A tale of an ice princess, who was incredibly lovely but very, very lonely. She lived all alone in her palace made of winter, because no one understood her or her magic. They all shunned her. So she spent all her time creating snowflakes, no two alike, each a picture of cold perfection.

Thoughts of his family—his mother, and Charles and Edwina—far away in London, reminded him that it was very nearly Christmas.

Christmas. The holiday the ice princess and her snow minions—and his own mother—loved above all others. When had he last thought of it? Not for a very, very long time.

His mother always wrote to him at this time of year, of course, urging him to come home, to share the holiday with them. Yet how could he? How could he ruin this time of year for his family, the people he loved the most, by showing his face in their elegant drawing room? He did not belong around their pianoforte, singing Christmas ditties, or around their table with roasted goose and berry tarts.

Every time he was tempted to go back, he remembered the revulsion that swept over Elizabeth's beautiful face when she first beheld him after the battle. He heard again her scream of despair, remembered how she had turned away.

No. He would not put his family through that. They deserved the perfect Christmas.

Mark pushed back his brocade sleeve and stared down at his left arm. By some miracle, it had been saved from the surgeons' knives, but the skin was puckered, criss-crossed with scars and welts. In the sunlight, it was a strange, shell-pink color; in the moonlight, it was pale, disguised. The left side of his face was the same, scarred, marked forever by what had happened that day. He could usually hide from it, by being alone, by having no mirrors in his house except the tiny one above his shaving stool.

At night he was exposed for what he was: A living haunt.

Mark laughed roughly at the fanciful thought. He was so very rarely *fanciful*. "You are moon-mad, Captain Payne," he muttered to himself. "Or perhaps bewitched? There are many curses floating about in Cornwall. One must have landed on you."

He started to turn away, to reach for the bottle of brandy sitting on the bedside table, when some noise startled him. He swung back toward the window.

"What the devil was that?" he said out loud, peering into the night. It had sounded like some low cry or moan. Not a scream or shout; something beckoning, enticing. Like the ice princess's lonely song.

There was nothing else. Only the silence of the snow-blanketed night. But Mark's nerves still rang. Something was out there. He could sense it, just as he had once sensed enemy ships lurking in the sea fogs.

He suddenly felt alert, alive, as he had not in months and months. He had to find whatever was in the night.

He shrugged off his dressing gown and reached for the clothes he had carelessly piled on the chair before retiring. As he tied back his overlong dark hair and searched for his greatcoat, one thought reverberated in his mind.

He was moon-mad, indeed.

Chapter Three

Antoinette sat straight up in bed, gasping for air. She felt the edges of some tantalizing dream floating away from her, snatched away before she could grab onto it. What *had* she been dreaming? It dissipated like so much smoke, leaving her with only the remnant impressions of something unbearably sweet.

The blankets fell away from her shoulders, and she shivered despite her long-sleeved muslin night rail. The cottage was chilly and dark, the scents of her dried herbs and flowered soaps heavy in the crisp air. Antoinette shrugged her thick braid back over her shoulder and collapsed against the piles of feather pillows. She closed her eyes and breathed in slowly until she felt her fevered blood slow in her veins.

The dream was completely gone, and she was all alone in her familiar cottage. The moonlight spilling from the mullioned windows cast a glow over her brightly colored silk quilts, the bottles and pots on her dressing table, the bundles of dried herbs suspended from the ceiling beams. She could see the snow falling out there—the first snow she had seen in a very long time.

Antoinette had always felt safe in the cottage. The whitewashed walls seemed to embrace her from the first day she saw them. But right now, in this quiet midnight, it seemed as if those very walls were closing about her. She needed air. She needed to talk to someone. She needed . . .

She needed her mother. Her mother would be able to help her decipher all the strange feelings that were swirling inside her of late. Antoinette had tried before to contact her mother, but it had always been in vain. Maybe now, on this strange night, the winter solstice, it would work. Antoinette felt the magic in the snow-dusted moonlight on her very fingertips.

She climbed down from the high bed, and without even lighting the lamp, pulled open the doors of the carved wardrobe. The moonlight fell on the array of gowns, cloaks, and robes hanging there, the bonnets and slippers and shawls arranged on the shelf. One silvery beam glistened on the sleeve of one of her robes.

Green. Emotional healing and growth, the Great Mother in her nurturing form. *Perfect.*

Antoinette drew the soft silk of the robe over her night rail and fastened the gold frogs up the front. As she slipped on her sturdiest half boots, she reached into a small box under the bed and pulled out her most cherished possession. The red leather binding of the book was worn to a satin smoothness by all the women's hands that had touched it over the years. Her mother. Her grandmother. Her great-grandmother, who had inscribed much of the ancient knowledge on its parchment pages.

Antoinette smoothed her palm over the book's precious cover before placing it carefully in an oilskin pouch. She added candles, a flint, an array of herbs.

She was ready.

The night was colder than Antoinette expected. Cornwall was usually quite mild, at least compared to the rest of the freezing island of England, but not this night of rare snow. Her breath escaped into the air in tiny smokelike puffs, and her boots crunched on the thin layer of moisture underfoot. New flakes, delicate as the lace many of the local villagers made, landed on the hood of her cloak and caught in her eyelashes and the braid of her hair. The sky had become strangely clear, though, stars blinking down at her like diamonds from between a wide break in the clouds.

She had no idea where she was going. She simply turned out of her garden gate and walked, letting her feet lead her where they would. She would not be surprised to discover she was still in her bed, dreaming. It was not like her to leave the safety of her house to go wandering alone in the night, especially since some villager on his way home might see her and carry the tale of her midnight ramblings back to his neighbors. People there were suspicious enough of her, despite the friendship of Cassie and her family, and of the vicar and his wife.

"Do not be silly, Antoinette," she told herself, turning down a different pathway. "No one is fool enough to be out on such a night. No one but you."

Indeed, it *was* silent. So silent she could almost hear the new snow falling on the ground. She heard no supernatural whispers, no one calling to her. Even the ghosts of Royce Castle were asleep, as all sensible people—human or spirit—should be.

Antoinette laughed softly. It felt a bit like when she was a child, and she and Cassie would slip out to go swimming in the ocean at night—exciting, a strange fluttering deep in her stomach. Only back then their environs had been considerably warmer.

Her laughter faded when she saw where her steps had led her. She was atop one of the steep, rocky cliffs that fell straight down into the roiling winter sea. She stared out over the water, mesmerized for an instant by the waves and the sky.

She came to the shore often, of course. The rocky sand was a favorite picnic spot of the Leighton children, and the old smugglers' caves there contained very strong ghostly vibrations. But she seldom came here at night, and never like this—all alone, in the snow and cold, atop the sharp cliffs.

She shivered, yet somehow this felt *right*. This was where she was meant to be, for this moment.

Tucking her woolen cloak beneath her knees, she knelt down on the ground and took her treasures out of the pouch. Candles—white, silver, purple, blue, gold—were neatly arrayed, protected by their glass globes. Antoinette lit them, and sprinkled thyme, lavender, meadowsweet, and dried rose petals in the snow around them. As she did this, she closed her eyes and focused all her thoughts toward the love of her mother, toward all her mother's teachings. She rose and, at her feet, the ancient book fluttered open, the pages shuffling in the cold breeze.

"Mother of all days," Antoinette called, "come to us this night, touch us with your presence. Bring me your wisdom, your peace, your power. Help me to find the right path."

Help me to find my way out of this loneliness, she added silently, with every ounce of her being.

She held out her arms, and the hood of her cloak fell back. A new wind arose around her, sweeping at her skirts, skittering the candles' flames, though they did not go out. Indeed, they seemed to glow even brighter.

The cord binding her braid fell and her hair blew free, the waist-length strands whipping across her face and throat. A warmth kindled deep inside her, growing hot and brighter.

Antoinette raised her arms higher, palms up to catch the moonlight. "Come to me," she chanted. "*Help* me!"

She lurched a step forward, and another. She felt light, so very light, as if she could fly free of all her confusion . . .

"*No!*" she heard a man shout. At first disoriented,

she thought it was part of the spell. A strange part, one she had not conjured herself, but many times things happened she had not counted on when she was in a meditative state. She did not have the powers of her mother. She closed her eyes tighter, trying to will the strange voice away.

Yet it came again, closer this time, more insistent. "No, miss! Please!"

Antoinette opened her eyes and spun around, seeking the source of that shout. The magic of the night dissipated, the wind faded to a mere cold embrace.

She turned too quickly, though. The soles of her boots slid on the coating of snow, and she felt them slipping beneath her. Almost as if time had slowed down, allowing her to see herself falling, she coasted backward. Her arms flailed, trying to grasp onto something, *anything*.

There was nothing behind her but empty air.

She fell toward the earth. The sky arched overhead, black and cold and void. Something hard struck at the back of her head—and then she saw nothing at all.

Oh, *blast*! He had killed her!

Mark ran from the ring of trees toward the edge of the sea cliff, his boots slipping on the new layer of snowfall. The woman lay there, so very still, a crumpled heap of silk and wool.

He dropped to his knees beside her just as the moon disappeared behind a veil of clouds, leaving them in deepest midnight shadows. The only light was from the flickering ring of candles, sheltered from the cold by glass globes. The scent of lavender and dried rose was sweet and rich—and strange, in the middle of winter.

Mark had no time to ponder such oddities as candles and flowers, though. His only thought, his entire being, was concentrated on the woman lying still on the ground.

"I'm sorry I startled you," he muttered. "Please don't be dead."

Very carefully, he bent down toward her, watching her for any sign of breath and life. He took her hand in his, and pressed his fingertips to her slender wrist. "Thank you," he whispered, when he detected the thready hum of her pulse. Her chest rose in a steady, though shallow, rhythm.

So she was not dead, but not yet out of danger. Mark recalled how, on the second ship he sailed on, a cabin boy had been struck on the head by a falling bucket. The lad had remained unconscious for many days before dying, never once awakening. Head injuries were quite perilous and unpredictable.

He quickly stripped off his greatcoat and made a cushion of it on the ground. Slowly, gingerly, he moved her head onto its softness, probing gently for an injury. There was a small knot near the base of her neck, but none of the stickiness of blood.

He had been quite right all these years to resist his mother's letters urging him to come home. Look what happened when he ventured outside his door! He was a menace to other people. A curse. Here he had merely meant to prevent the girl from throwing herself over the cliff, and instead he had nearly killed her.

He should go for help, he thought, as he reached for one of the woman's candles and brought it closer. But where could he go? The nearest house after his own cottage was Royce Castle, and the woman who came in to keep house for him had said that the Leighton family had gone to Bath until after the New Year, and most of the servants were home in the village with their families. The physician was in the village, too, more than thirty minutes' ride from here. Mark would just have to take care of her himself.

He lifted up the candle so he could see her better— and gave a strangled gasp. It wasn't merely that she was beautiful, though she certainly was, extremely so.

It was that she was so completely unlike anyone he had ever seen before, and not at all what he would expect to find here in this remote corner of England.

She was more like something he would find in a dream, a fantasy of warm seas, waterfalls, and jasmine flowers. Maybe she *was* a dream, truly. This whole bizarre night was a dream.

His fingers tightened on her wrist. No, she was too warm, too solid to be a dream. Or a ghost.

The woman's skin, though ashen at the moment, was a dark, burnished color, like cream in coffee, undulating like smooth silk over high cheekbones and an aquiline nose. Her hair, spread around her on the snow, was a wild riot of thick, black waves. She was dressed unlike anyone else, too. Her dark cloak had fallen back to reveal a strange robe of green silk, embroidered in gold with exotic flowers and symbols, fastened up the front with gold braid frogs. She was very tall. If she was standing, she would probably be about as tall as Mark's own six foot three, yet she was slender as a reed.

"You must be an illusion," he whispered to her. "What else would you be doing on this godforsaken shore?"

Then he remembered—the island witch. Of course. This must be she.

When Mark first joined the Navy at age fifteen, he was sent to the West Indies station, where he stayed for over five years. Jamaica, Barbados, Bermuda. There he had seen many women like this one, dusky, willowy, impossibly exotic. He had never seen one to approach her aura of elegance, though. Even unconscious, she exuded a certain power surely unknown to any English lady.

"Who are you?" he asked her. "How did you come to be here?"

And *was* she a witch? Mark was certainly not a man to put stock in village gossip. He had been the subject of it far too often himself. But something odd had been happening here this night. Look at her robe, the candles.

The necklace she wore. It was a heavy silver pendant, suspended on a long chain, etched in its center with a crescent moon image, surrounded by a circle of rough-cut gemstones. They glowed in the candlelight, seeming to entice him, to beckon him. . . .

The tips of his fingers were grazing the cold silver, when she let out a soft moan. Her long fingers stirred and reached up toward her temple.

"You're awake!" Mark shouted in jubilation, a relief unlike any he had ever known rising up in his heart. She was *not* dead, nor in an endless stupor. He had not killed her.

"Am I?" she whispered roughly. Her eyes opened, focusing up on him. They were wide, as black as the night around them, and as clear as if she was simply waking from the most refreshing of slumbers.

Her brows, as silken and arched as a raven's wings, drew down slightly when she saw him, as if puzzled. Too late, Mark realized he held the candle near to his face—his ruined face. It was sure to send this goddess back into her unreachable sleep to see *that*! And he had not put his gloves on, either. He hastily blew out the candle and cast it away into the snow.

She did not scream or gasp or turn away, as other ladies often did. Nor did her expression dissolve into pity. She simply watched him, that tiny puzzled frown on her brow.

Perhaps her wits were still addled from the fall.

"Who are you?" she asked, her voice low and soft, touched with a French island lilt. She stared up at him warily, her slender body stiffening. "What happened to me? Are you a ghost?"

He swallowed hard past the sudden dryness in his throat. "No, I am not a ghost. Not yet. My name is Captain Mark Payne, madam," he answered her, the words escaping before he could even catch them. Captain? He had not called himself by that title in many years. But there it was, the sound of it hanging in the air between them. "I fear you took a fall and hit your head. I thought you were about to jump off the cliff, and I called out to you. I fear I startled you—I'm sorry."

"A fall?" Carefully, wincing a bit, she turned her head to see the sputtering candles, the scattering of herbs now being covered by the new snowfall. "I remember coming here now. Do you live nearby?"

"Yes. In Thornbush Cottage. I could not sleep, so I came out for a walk. I thought no one would be about."

She studied him very carefully, her dark eyes narrowed. He did not know what she saw there, but whatever it was obviously somewhat reassured her. She finally nodded, and said, "You saved me? Thank you very much."

Mark could only nod brusquely, unable to take his gaze from her. She appeared to be waiting for him to say something. Her perfect stillness, her very aura of some unfathomable serenity, seemed to invite confidences of all sorts. Even from a man who had confided in no one, relied on no one, for seven long years.

But she was far too fragile to listen to any of his nonsense, and he would be even more of a boor than he already was to burden her with his apologies. *She* was the one he must take care of.

"You're welcome," he said simply.

"Well, Captain Mark Payne," she said, her voice a bit stronger though still shaky. "I am Miss Antoinette Duvall, and pleased to meet you, despite the less than auspicious circumstances. Do you always walk in the snow in your shirtsleeves?"

Mark gave a bark of laughter, suddenly realizing that he was indeed in his shirtsleeves, and it was demmed cold. "No, madam. I am not quite as foolish as all that. My coat at present resides beneath your head."

"Oh!" Her trembling hand darted up to feel the soft, crumpled wool of his greatcoat. "Here, sir, you must take it back. I would not have you catch a chill for your good deed. You must be freezing. Unless you really *are* a ghost? Then you would not be cold at all."

He *was* cold, but she was probably much more so, lying on the ground. The snow was drifting thicker and faster around them. And he worried about her rambling talk of ghosts. "Do you feel well enough to rise, Miss Duvall?"

"I feel as if my bones have turned to jelly."

"Put your arms around my neck," he told her. As she wound her silk-clad arms weakly about him, he slid his own beneath her legs and lifted her carefully as he rose to his feet. He was glad to find all of that wood-chopping he had done, all the new thatching on his roof, the evening rides along the cliffs, had not been for naught. Antoinette Duvall was not a small woman, but she fit easily into his arms.

With a low, pained sigh, she rested her head on his shoulder. Her hair smelled of jasmine and candle smoke. "Thank you, Captain Payne," she whispered. "You are truly a knight in shining armor."

"Rather tarnished armor, I fear."

"Not at all." She still clutched his coat in her shaking hand, and awkwardly shook it out to spread it over one of his shoulders.

He carried her away from the cliff, toward the meager shelter of the trees. Once on the pathway, though, he was struck by a sudden doubt—where to take her, where she would be safe and cared for? The Leightons at the castle were gone; he had no idea where Miss Duvall lived. The closest residence was his own cottage.

His thoughts were interrupted by her sudden panicked cry. "My book!"

"Your what?"

"My book. I left it back in the snow. Oh, it cannot be ruined! It's all I have."

Mark glanced around them, and saw a fallen log that was as yet only lightly dusted with snow. "If I put you down here, can you sit for a moment while I go to fetch it?"

"Yes, of course."

He was not sure he completely believed her; her head bobbed against him weakly. But he could not argue against the urgency in her voice. She obviously *needed* that book, whatever it was, and she would not be easy until she had it. He placed her carefully on the log, making certain she would stay upright and that her cloak was tucked warmly beneath her.

Mark turned and ran back toward the cliff, thrusting his arms into the sleeves of his greatcoat. The book was indeed there, beside the dying candles. A few flakes melted on the antique parchment pages, but it appeared to be undamaged. As he brushed off the moisture, he saw printed there words in some strange language, the dark brown ink faded with age.

He had no time to ponder the volume's mysteries, though. He closed it with a snap and pushed it inside his coat. There was Miss Duvall he had to return to with all haste, or she would surely faint away again.

Indeed, she was listing quite alarmingly when he returned to the fallen tree; her head wobbled on her slim neck. She smiled radiantly, though, when he handed her the book. She cradled it against her as if it was made of the rarest rubies.

"Thank you," she said. "That is twice you have saved me this night, Captain Payne."

"Ah, but my rescue will have been in vain if we do not get you home this minute. You will surely catch a chill," Mark said, scooping her up into his arms again. "Do you have a maid or companion waiting at your house? You should not be alone with a head injury. You need someone to keep you awake until a physician can be summoned."

"No, I live alone," she answered, her voice soft, almost drowsy. Her head drooped back against his shoulder. "There is a girl who comes to clean for me, but only in the afternoons."

Mark cursed beneath his breath. That was what he was afraid of, that she was as solitary as he.

"What is it?" Antoinette asked complacently, not at all fazed by any use of impolite language. He wondered nonsensically if she had perhaps grown up around sailors and become used to their ways. "Is something amiss? Beyond the obvious, of course."

"If there is no one where you live, then there is only one place for you to go, Miss Duvall. At least for this night."

"Oh? And where is that?" Her tone held only casual curiosity, as if her immediate future held only marginal interest for her. He sensed her deep weariness.

"My house. Thornbush Cottage, it's called. Someone must look after you for the next few hours. They are the most vital after someone sustains a head injury."

If he had expected missish protests, cries, or tears, he was to be pleasantly disappointed. She merely gave a quiet laugh, and said, "That is *three* times now you have rescued me, Captain Payne. I am so very sorry to inconvenience you, but I fear you are correct. I have some knowledge of healing myself, as you obviously do, and I know I should *not* be alone right now. I feel so very—odd."

Her arm tightened about his neck, and she cuddled closer with a gentle sigh. Her breath was cool against his bare throat.

He had indeed been correct, Mark thought, as he turned down the hidden lane toward his cottage. Miss Antoinette Duvall was unlike any other woman he had ever met.

Chapter Four

Antoinette's head throbbed with a low, dull ache, giving a fresh twinge every time her rescuer took a step. The cold wind blew her cloak and robe about her, and her senses hummed with the force of her interrupted spell. Yet none of those discomforts were stronger than the one thought reverberating in her mind . . .

How very intriguing her rescuer was.

She rested her head against his hard shoulder and studied him carefully in the moonlight. She was certain she had never seen him before, or she certainly would have remembered him. He was quite unforgettable, and not only because of the scars tracing a delicate white pattern over the left side of his sun-bronzed face. Her heart ached at the knowledge of the pain he must have suffered, the agony that etched those marks on his flesh.

Even with those scars, he was a handsome man, with a strong jaw shadowed by a day's growth of beard, a slightly crooked nose, and eyes that glowed a strange pale silver even in the night. His hair was dark and overlong, falling over his collar in rich waves that escaped from their loose tie and tickled softly at Antoinette's fingers. He was very tall, and strongly built—strong enough to carry her over the uneven ground, and she knew she was no featherlight female. The muscles that moved and bunched across his shoulders and arms were as powerful as those of any farm laborer.

He was no laborer, though; she knew that for certain. She had never met a farmer with such an air of command, of aristocratic self-possession.

It was not just his good looks, but his innate strength that drew her to him, that made her quite unable to look away from him. It was the deep, cutting sadness she saw hidden deep in his eyes, a despair deeper than any she had seen before.

Antoinette longed to know who he was, where he came from. What sorrows he carried in his heart. Whatever they were, she would vow they made her own loneliness, her own sense of displacement, seem insignificant indeed.

But her powers of discernment were muted by the pain in her head, and by a sweeping wave of exhaustion threatening to drown her beneath it. She closed her eyes, and felt the heavy weight of her limbs.

She must have sighed out loud, for she sensed his gaze upon her. "We are very nearly there," he said gently. "I'm sorry for jostling you."

"I am fine," Antoinette assured him. "Just very, very tired."

He lifted her higher in his arms, and beneath her skirts she felt him reach out and push open a squeaking gate. "You must be exhausted after everything you have been through this night, Miss Duvall, but you must not go to sleep yet. Not until we can ascertain the true extent of your injuries."

"I know," she answered, her words breaking off on a wide yawn. She grimaced when she realized she had not even covered her mouth. "Forgive me. You must think I was raised in a barn somewhere."

Captain Payne gave a low chuckle, which vibrated warmly through her body. "I will confess to a curiosity about where you were raised, Miss Duvall, but I think you are in no condition to answer at the moment. You should be quiet, and rest as well as you can."

Antoinette opened her eyes at the sound of a soft

click and a thud. He had opened the door of what appeared to be a cottage. It was smaller than her own abode, and darker, covered with a thick climbing ivy that concealed even the windows. The captain ducked his head down as he took them through the narrow doorway into a room even darker than the night they left behind.

Antoinette could see nothing in the gloom, but it was obvious that he knew his way easily. With a gracefully balanced movement, he bent down and gently deposited her on a soft settee.

"Wait here, Miss Duvall, and I will light a fire. We'll have you warm in no time," he said.

"I'm warmer already," she answered. The room still held the memory of an earlier fire, and already the chill was receding from her fingertips and earlobes. The pain in her head was also muted, yet the fatigue only grew greater now that she was warm and still. Antoinette untied the ribbons of her cloak and pushed it back from her shoulders, settling against the cushions of her new seat.

She listened to the sounds of the captain's movements, her senses heightened by the rich darkness. He was near, she could feel that. She heard the hollow thunk of wood being piled in the grate, the rustle of paper, and the click of a flint—once, twice. A flare of light broke the gloom, and soon a merry blaze glowed in the fireplace.

Still kneeling before the grate, he turned to look at her, his expression solemn. In the orange firelight, his scars were more pronounced, a puckered pale pink, and she saw that his left hand and wrist were also damaged. They were injuries that were healed, though, and nothing at all to some of the wounds she saw in Jamaica.

And they could not compare to the glory of his hair, autumn-brown, waving to his shoulders, or to the wary intelligence shining from his eyes.

"So this is your home?" she asked, slowly shifting her gaze from his to examine the room around her. The whitewashed walls and gray stone hearth were the same as those in her own home, but there the comparison ended. Where hers was full of pictures, books, and the scent of herbs, his was just—bare. The few pieces of furniture were old and shabby; there were no rugs, no draperies at the windows. The only painting was a print of a frigate cutting through the churning gray waters.

It gave her no clues whatsoever as to the personality of her rescuer, yet its clean starkness did confirm one thing she had suspected, even before he gave her his rank—he was a military man. Judging from the print, a navy man.

"It is very cozy," she added, when he was silent.

He gave her a half smile, sitting back on his heels to watch the flames he had kindled grow brighter. "Tiny, you mean."

"Hm, yes, that is one way to put it. But, as I reside in a rather small cottage myself, I am keenly aware of the advantages of a less than grand space. Not so much dusting, for one. And, even better, it is easier to keep the dreadful English chill away."

His smile widened just a fraction, slowly, as if his mouth had grown rusty from a long lack of mirth. He seemed to fear his face might crack if he dared smile further, or, God forbid, laugh aloud. Antoinette decided that when she was not so tired, she would wrack her brain for the most ridiculous jests she knew, just to see if he could indeed laugh.

"Compared to the cramped conditions aboard a ship, Miss Duvall, this cottage is a veritable palace," he said. "And everything stays where you put it, with no pitching or rolling about."

"Ah, so you *are* a navy man. I suspected as much."

His faint smile faded away altogether, and he glanced away from her into the fire. "*Was* a navy man.

A very long time ago." He pushed himself to his feet and sat down in the only other chair in the room, a twig rocker by the side of the mantel. He closed his hands on the chair's wooden arms, curling his long fingers tightly. The only sound in the room was the crackling of the flames, the rasp of their breathing, and the rhythmic ticking of a strange, oval-shaped gold-and-ivory clock on the mantel.

Antoinette gazed up at its pale face. It was after one o'clock, still hours until the dawn. It was obvious that Captain Payne was not a man for light chatter, but Antoinette was itching to talk, to make *some* sort of noise. Otherwise, the warmth and the ticktocking of the clock would send her straight to sleep.

"Have you lived very long in the neighborhood, Captain Payne?" she asked him, rubbing at her temples. The pain was already muted, receding away. "I myself have been here for five years, yet I am sure we have never met."

He turned to her, very careful, Antoinette noticed, to keep the left side of his face in shadow. "I have lived here for seven years now, but I do not mix very much in society."

"Nor do I. Not that there is very much of what most people would call 'society' hereabouts. Not very many balls or routs. Though there are some agreeable people."

The corners of his mouth turned down a bit in obvious doubt. "Indeed, Miss Duvall? You do not find them to be a rather—gossiping lot?"

Antoinette thought of the individuals who had tried so very hard to make her feel at home here, such as the vicar and his wife, Lady Paige, Mrs. Greeley. Then she thought of the others, too many to count, who stared at her wide-eyed as she walked through the village, whispered behind her back as she passed.

She hated that so much, hated always having to hold her head high and pretend she did not hear them.

Were they really so very different, though, from the people in Jamaica, people of her own sort, who whispered and speculated about her friendship with the white Richards family?

"They are no more gossiping than any other set of people, I suspect," she said.

"That is too true. London, a ship, Cornwall—there is truly no escaping the curiosity of others. Not even, I imagine, in an Indian jungle. At least I have found what I was looking for in Cornwall."

"What were you looking for, Captain Payne?"

"As you say, Miss Duvall, a lack of society."

"And where did you come from before?" Antoinette suddenly noticed how very uncomfortable her damp boots had become. She bent to unhook them—and winced at the fresh wave of pain in her head.

"Here, let me do that. You should remain still." He left his chair and knelt down at her feet, his elegant fingers deftly unhooking the pearl buttons from the stiffening leather. "I fear I am out of practice at playing host. You ought to have something warm to drink. I think there may be some tea about."

"Tea would be most welcome, Captain Payne. Yet I fear you are evading my question."

He looked up at her, that tiny, rusty half smile on his lips again. In the firelight, his hair glowed with the burnish of October leaves, waving damp and silky to his shoulders. Antoinette longed with a sudden, tingling passion to touch that hair, to sink her fingers through its softness and trail them down his damaged cheek to his jaw, his lips. . . .

She tightened her hands into fists before they could go wandering of their own accord, and sat back in her chair.

"If you are so perceptive with a head injury, Miss Duvall, I should hate to see you with all your wits about you," he said. "You must be formidable indeed."

Antoinette's throat was suddenly so dry, she wasn't

sure if she could speak clearly. Sitting here, with this strange, glorious man at her feet, the night and the fire wrapped around them, she did not feel like her usual sensible self at all. "I am not sure about formidable," she managed to say hoarsely. "But I am incurably curious. Some might even say a busybody."

Captain Payne gave a low chuckle that was really no more than a rumbling deep inside his chest. He slid her boots from her feet and lined them up neatly next to the fire, then stood up to stroll away through a narrow, half-hidden doorway. Antoinette surmised, from the rattling of china and metal, that that must be the kitchen.

"You cannot possibly be half the busybody my housekeeper is, Miss Duvall," he called back to her. "But in answer to your question, my family lives mostly in London. They have country estates, also, which I am sure they still travel to now and then."

"You do have family, then?" Antoinette asked, her breath held with the apprehension that she had gone too far, asked too much. His silence stretched on too long.

Distance, though, seemed to lessen Captain Payne's obvious reticence. Perhaps it was the fact that he could not see her face while he spoke from the kitchen. Or perhaps he sensed, as she did, the odd intimacy of this midnight, this feeling that they were the only two people in the whole world.

Probably not, though. That was surely all a product of her head injury, her disordered brain.

"I do have family," he said finally. "I am the younger son of the Earl of Havelock. My brother, Charles, is the earl now, and my mother and sister live with him at Havelock House in Portman Square. Edwina, my sister, is much younger than Charles and myself—she is to make her bow in the spring. I am sure she will be quite the toast of the Season if she is as beautiful as I remember."

There was obvious affection in his tone as he spoke of this family, yet Antoinette saw nothing of them in his house. No portraits, no mementos. Nothing arranged on the mantel except the clock. "They do not care to visit you here?"

"No. They do not." There was cold finality in the words, his previous, ever so brief words gone like so much candle smoke.

Captain Payne came back into the sitting room with a tray arrayed with mismatched china cups and saucers and a plate of biscuits, as well as a kettle which he placed on the hob to warm.

"There is no sugar or milk," he said, with that stiff formality he had only barely begun to throw off.

"That is quite all right," Antoinette answered, not sure what else she could say to continue to draw the captain out.

Much to her surprise, *he* was the one who continued the conversation. "And where is your family, Miss Duvall? You are obviously not a native of Cornwall."

Antoinette gave a little laugh. "Ah, so you noticed that, did you? No, I am not English. I was born in Jamaica. My mother was a freed slave from Saint-Domingue. She and my father came to Kingston before I was born, and he died shortly thereafter. He was a blacksmith, I believe, the son of a French merchant and his placée, though I have no memory of him at all. My mother was a seamstress, a very fine one."

Antoinette had *never* told anyone of her family. Not even Cassie knew the truth about Antoinette's father. Most English people would be shocked to their core by this litany of slavery and illegitimacy. Captain Payne, though, was not like other Englishmen; she had sensed that the moment she first saw him. He merely nodded at her words, and reached for the kettle to pour hot water into their cups.

"Your mother, too, is deceased?" he asked, carefully steeping the tea.

"Yes."

"And how ever did you come to find yourself here?"

"That is a long story, Captain Payne."

"We have all night, Miss Duvall." He passed her the cup, and gave her a wry grin. It seemed less stiff now, as if he was remembering at last how a smile went.

"It is a dull story, as well."

"Ah, but I am seldom bored."

"Very well, then." Antoinette stretched her stockinged feet out toward the fire, and sipped at the strong, bracing tea. She told him of how her mother was employed as seamstress to Cassie's mother, of how their families became close and Cassie became like her sister.

"So, when her father died and she came here to live with her aunt, she asked me to come with her," Antoinette finished. "I could not say no."

He nodded thoughtfully. "You were very brave to come to a new land."

Antoinette gave a disbelieving snort. "Brave? Nay, Captain, I was a coward, unable to make my own way in life without my friend to cling to."

Captain Payne shook his head. "I lived in the West Indies for five years, Miss Duvall. I know what you left behind; I know how very different it is from this place. It is warm, full of flowers and sun and strange, compelling music. To have that, and come to this cold, narrow-minded, inhospitable place—that is courage indeed."

There was a sudden passion in his voice, a pain, a longing, that seemed to echo that in her own heart. "I have not always found England to be so terrible."

His head swung toward her, his gaze, like quicksilver, piercing her to her very core. "Do you not?"

"I—no. It is not all one could wish for, of course, but what is? I often miss the sun, and the way the sea looks there, so very different from the cold waves here. But there are compensations. Such as tonight."

His dark brows drew down. "Tonight? You enjoy being knocked unconscious and falling in the snow, then? You *are* a strange female."

Antoinette laughed, feeling an odd rush of sudden lightness. "Of course not! Snow is *horrible*. So cold. But if all that had not happened, I would not have met a new friend."

Those brows arched up in surprise, as if the word "friend" was one he had not heard in a very long time. Then he chuckled, a sound more warming than the fire and the tea. "Indeed, Miss Duvall. I would have been most unhappy to be deprived of making your acquaintance."

"And, considering everything we have been through this evening, could you perhaps call me Antoinette? Just for tonight?"

"If you will call me Mark."

"It is a bargain—Mark." Antoinette took a biscuit from the plate and settled back happily in her chair. Despite everything—her injuries, the cold, her spell gone awry—she felt more content here in this tiny, bare cottage than she had in a very long time.

"I think that captaining a navy vessel is far braver than anything *I* could have ever done," she said. "And far more exciting besides."

"It was mostly deadly dull," he answered.

"I do not believe that. You must have a great many tales to tell."

Mark shrugged, and reached for a biscuit of his own. "A few. But they are hardly suitable for a lady's ears."

"Ah, yet as we have established, I am not your typical English lady. Come now, Mark. We have many hours until dawn. Tell me some of your sea tales."

He gazed into the fire, perhaps trying to recall a story that was not too gruesome, or too personal. Antoinette doubted he would tell her how he came to get his scars—not yet, anyway. Their friendship was too new, too delicate.

Antoinette was a patient woman, though. One day, he would tell her. And it was the Christmas season, after all—a season when anything was possible. She had not believed that before, but now she was beginning to.

"When I was a mere ensign," he began, "I was sent to the West Indies, to Jamaica in fact, and there an old sea captain told me a most fanciful story indeed. . . ."

Chapter Five

Dawn was just beginning to break over the landscape with the palest pinks, lavenders, and or-
anges when Antoinette made her slow, careful way
out of Mark's cottage door. She leaned on his arm,
steadying herself against residual waves of dizziness.
Mark had wanted to carry her out, tried to scoop her
up out of her chair into his arms. She laughingly resisted, insisting that she was not an invalid. She *had*
been sorely tempted to give in, though. To feel his
arms about her one more time, holding her safe above
the earth and all its mundane cares.

It was a most extraordinary night that had just
passed, she thought, as she moved slowly down the
uneven stone walkway to where Mark's saddled horse
waited. They had talked for hours, of nothing in particular. She told him stories of the Leighton children's
antics, the beauties of her island home, the books on
herbals she wrote, and the lotions and soaps she made
for stores in the village and in London. He related
tales of his years at sea and all of the exotic lands he
had seen. But only light tales he thought might amuse
her, make her laugh; nothing of what had caused his
scars, what had driven him from a life of seafaring
adventure he obviously loved to one of isolation in
Cornwall. Nothing more about his family.

She wanted so much to know all those things, to
know *everything* about this intriguing man. But she
did not want to press, and ruin this lovely night they

shared. For it had been a lovely night indeed, filled
with talk and tea and firelight. She had not felt so—
so *light* in a very long time.

Strange, considering that it was all thanks to a man
whose heart was the heaviest she had ever sensed.

Antoinette paused to lean against Mark's rusting
garden gate, watching as he untethered the horse.
"The snow has ceased," she said.

He gave her a small smile. "So it has. Judging by
that sunrise, we should have a clear day. Warmer."

"I thought the saying was 'red sky at morning, sailors take warning,' " she answered, remembering a little rhyme her mother had sometimes recited. "Can we
look for new storms?"

"Ah, but that is not quite red, is it? More like—
pinkish." His strong hands came around her waist, lifting her carefully and easily into the saddle. All too
briefly, his warm touch, soothing and incredibly exciting at the same moment, landed on her leg, smoothing
the silk of her robe. "If it is clear tonight, will you go
back out to the cliffs to finish what you began last
night, Miss Duvall?"

Antoinette turned her face up to the glories of the
sunrise. Last night, when she ran out to the cliffs in a
dark fit of loneliness, seemed so very far away now in
this new dawn. She went there wanting to find
something—what, she knew not. She relied on her
book and her herbs to send her an answer.

She began to think now that they had done just
that, though in a manner she could not have predicted.
She felt so strange, so uncertain—so tired.

"I thought I asked you to call me Antoinette. And I
do not know," she answered him. "I rarely go walking
along those cliffs at midnight, though I often do so in
the early evenings. There is no one about then, and the
sounds of the sea and the birds are very peaceful."

He smiled up at her. "I am quite fond of a good
evening walk, myself."

"Are you indeed, Captain? Well. Perhaps one evening we shall meet there."

"Perhaps we shall." Mark swung himself up into the saddle behind Antoinette, his arms coming around her to take the reins. She leaned back against him, savoring that sensation of warm safety. His breath was cool, scented of the spice from their tea, as it brushed against her temple and stirred her hair. "Now, Miss Duvall—Antoinette. Would you be so kind as to give me the direction to your home?"

Mark stood outside the garden gate of Antoinette Duvall's cottage long after she disappeared through the door, turning to give him a wave and a smile before the red painted wood closed behind her. The draperies at the old-fashioned mullioned windows never opened, but in good time a plume of silver-gray smoke rose up from the chimney.

He knew he should rush back to his hideaway before the countryside stirred to life and someone saw him lurking there. Her maid would be coming in soon, or a woodsman might pass by on the way to his morning's task. Even worse, Antoinette herself might glance out of the window and see him still there, and wonder with growing horror just what sort of shambling beast she had let into her life.

But he found he could not leave. Not yet. He felt like a beggar child, gazing longingly into the window of a warm bakery. There were delights of all sorts there—comfort, beauty, good humor, intrigue. But not for the likes of him.

Antoinette's cottage looked much like his own—small, square, built of rough gray stone. There the resemblance ended. Where his garden was wild and overgrown, hers was trim and perfectly ordered, with beds outlined in red brick. It was cut back for the winter, but in the summer it would be a riotous glory of color and scent. Her walls were free of choking ivy, her gate neatly painted and oiled.

He wondered what she would do if he walked up to her door, knocked on it, and begged admittance as he longed to do. He even took one step forward, his hand reaching for the latch on her gate, before he remembered himself and fell back. She was exhausted. She needed to sleep and recover from her fall—a fall *he* had caused—not to be pestered by a retired sailor begging for just another moment in her company.

In the firelight he could pretend she could not see him clearly, that he was as he had been eleven years ago. In the daylight, his flaws were all too obvious.

Mark swung back up into the saddle and turned the horse toward home. Yes, indeed—firelight and shadows could conceal much, could even allow a foolish man to pretend he was not as he was. Those long hours of night had been a precious time out of time, where he could enjoy the company and the laughter of a beautiful woman. He told her half-forgotten tales of the sea and basked in the musical cadence of her voice as she told him stories of her own.

Stories that were funny, and interesting, and even a bit eerie, as when she related ghost stories from her homeland. But nothing that told him what she had been doing on the cliffs last night, what she thought of her life in England. It could not be easy for her. Her skin marked her as an outsider, just as his scars marked him. There was only the merest trace of that in her wide smile, in the dark pools of her eyes.

He had the sense, though, that she would understand about his own life, his own pain. She would listen, and *know*. If he could just tell her, which of course he could not. He didn't even have the words to explain it to himself. Long years in the navy had frozen off that part of himself, and not even Antoinette Duvall's Jamaican sun could thaw it.

He liked conversing with her, though. He liked looking at her, at her exotic beauty and the elegance of her long hands. She never glanced away from him uneasily, as everyone else did, as Elizabeth did. Antoinette watched his face as they conversed, touched his damaged left hand as he lifted her from the horse. It was as if she noticed not a thing amiss. They were merely two neighbors, sharing an amiable chat and a pot of tea by the fire.

Perhaps he *would* go strolling along the cliffs one evening soon, where they could meet and talk and walk together in the fading daylight.

And perhaps he would not. For Mark Payne, who had faced the French navy and fierce squalls at sea without flinching, found he was an abject coward before a beautiful woman.

Chapter Six

"Oh, Miss Duvall, I vow your lotions smell more luscious every time!" Mrs. Greeley gazed down at the array of bottles and pots on her store counter, and inhaled deeply of a dab of chamomile cream. "I cannot tell you how happy I am for a new batch. These fly off the shelves as quickly as I can put them there."

Antoinette smiled, deeply gratified by the compliment. She had worked long and hard over these preparations, concocting exactly the right recipes and mix of herbs. "There are soaps too, Mrs. Greeley," she said, reaching into the large hamper and bringing out small, muslin-wrapped squares. "Rose, lavender, sandalwood. I am working on some toilette water; it should be ready to bottle after the New Year."

"Lovely, Miss Duvall! These soaps will be just the thing for customers looking for Christmas gifts."

Antoinette thought of the little fragrant bars she had carefully wrapped up at home, waiting for Cassie and Penelope. "Indeed you are right, Mrs. Greeley. The sachet bags would be very nice too. Perhaps you could make a pretty display of them here on the counter? Then people coming up to pay for their purchases would see them, and you could persuade them that their mother or daughter needs just one more sweet little gift."

Mrs. Greeley laughed. "How clever of you, Miss Duvall! I shall do just that." She turned the small, colored glass bottles so that their facets caught the sunlight from the windows. Her store was quiet at this time of day, and she was obviously primed for a bit of chatter. "Now, Miss Duvall, speaking of the festive season, I hope you are not working so very hard that you cannot enjoy it. It *is* Christmas, after all, and it only comes about once a year."

Christmas. Of course. How could Antoinette forget it, when every shop in the village was bedecked with greenery over the doors, every window festooned with ribbons, every horse's bridle merry with bells? She had even given into it herself, bringing holly and evergreen in to decorate her fireplace mantel and staircase balustrade.

Much to her blushing shame, she went so far as to make a kissing bough to hang in her sitting room, just on the slight chance that Captain Mark Payne might come calling. She thought better of it as soon as it was made, though, and tossed it in the fire.

A very good thing too, for Captain Payne had *not* called. She had not seen even a glimpse of him in the past two days, not since he left her at her garden gate. She went walking in the evenings along the cliff, just as they had talked of, and he was not there either. Now tomorrow was Christmas Eve, and it seemed the holiday would pass without another meeting with the intriguing captain.

Not that she cared, of course, for she did not. Not one jot. Truly.

"Of course I am enjoying the season, Mrs. Greeley," she said, with a smile that even she could sense seemed overly bright and false. "Who could not?"

The shopkeeper gave her a shrewd glance. "We heard that the family up at the castle has gone to Bath to visit the dowager countess."

"Yes, that is true. They go every Christmas."

"Since they are your nearest neighbors, and your

cottage lies such a distance from the village, it must get very quiet there. Very lonesome."

Antoinette peered closely at Mrs. Greeley, wondering what the lady was insinuating. Had she seen Mark leaving Antoinette's cottage at daybreak? Was there gossip?

That would be the very last thing Antoinette needed. It was difficult enough to overcome the villagers' suspicions as it was. But Mrs. Greeley merely looked complacent and innocent, her faded blue eyes wide as she peered up at Antoinette.

"I do well enough in my home, Mrs. Greeley," Antoinette said cautiously. "I am very cozy."

"Yes, but one shouldn't be alone at Christmas, Miss Duvall. You should come to the assembly tomorrow evening at the Hare and Hound. Mr. Greeley and I would so enjoy it if you came with us."

"An assembly?"

"Yes, for Christmas Eve. Lady Paige is sponsoring, and the whole village is ever so excited—the assembly rooms haven't been used in an age, and they are so much more spacious than the old rooms we used for the Christmas Eve assembly last year! There will be supper and dancing and cards."

Quite against her will, Antoinette was tempted. She generally disliked social events, where everyone watched her and whispered, and only a few people actually conversed with her. She usually only attended parties at Royce Castle or supper at the vicarage. She never went anywhere without the Leightons.

But she did love to dance, and was not averse to cards either. And she had not really been looking forward to a solitary holiday. She had hoped, oh so briefly, that perhaps she could invite Mark for a Christmas supper and a hand of piquet. Since that appeared to be a distant possibility, she should go to the assembly with the Greeleys and try to enjoy herself.

Be brave for once, Antoinette, she told herself.

"Thank you, Mrs. Greeley," she said. "I happily accept your kind invitation."

Mrs. Greeley's smile lit up her round, lined face. "Excellent, Miss Duvall! We will see you tomorrow evening, then."

Antoinette tucked the payment for the soaps and lotions into her reticule, and stepped out onto the walkway, the bells on the Greeleys' door jingling merrily behind her. It was a quiet time of day for the village, and not very many people were out and about on the street, going in and out of the half-timbered shops. Only the vicar drove by in his gig, raising his hat in greeting to Antoinette, and Mrs. Brown, the dressmaker, was arranging a new display of fabrics and ribbons in her bow window.

Antoinette turned her steps toward home, but then paused, considered, and glanced back at Mrs. Brown's window. The mantua-maker sometimes had gowns ready to purchase, or at least some shawls and dancing slippers or headdresses. Something new, and dashingly attractive, might be in order for the assembly. After all, Mark Payne might, just *might*, attend.

Antoinette laughed at herself, and forced her feet to turn once more toward the outskirts of the village without going back to the shop. She was acting like a silly schoolgirl, mooning about for a man who cared nothing for her. She had thought, after their evening together, that they were forming a new friendship. But his silence these past two days gave the lie to that.

Ah, well, she thought, as she walked briskly along the clifftop pathway. So she had been wrong about the captain. She was certainly no worse off than she had been before.

And, with the winter wind whipping at her hems, the cold, pale sun shining down on her, she could almost believe that. She hummed a bright tune under her breath, a Christmas carol in honor of the season.

"It came upon a midnight clear, that glorious song of old, from angels bending near the earth to touch their harps of gold. Peace on the earth, goodwill to men . . ."

The tune quite died away in her throat as she turned the corner that led to her cottage and she saw the tall figure waiting by her garden gate.

Captain Payne. *Mark.* He had come after all. Her heart gave a flutter in her breast, and she felt a very foolish grin catch at the corner of her lips. For an instant, she feared he might be an illusion, a phantom with his back toward her, tall and broad in a dark blue greatcoat.

Then he turned, and she could clearly see his strong, scarred face, half-shadowed by his hat brim. He gave her a slow, tentative smile.

"Miss Duvall—Antoinette," he said, his rich, rough voice carried to her on the wind. "I have called to see how you fare."

"Mark," she answered, through her own silly smile. "I fare very well indeed."

He should not be here. Mark knew that very well. Antoinette Duvall had enough to contend with in her life without him adding to her troubles by tagging along at her skirt hems. She was far from home, making her life among strangers who whispered of "island witches."

He had resolved to leave her alone. She was a beautiful lady, obviously busy with her work, and this would be for the best.

That lasted only two days. Two days of chopping firewood and shoveling snow, of scything back the undergrowth from his garden. He worked himself hard during the day, worked until his muscles burned and the sweat trickled in itchy rivulets down his back and shoulders.

But at night—at night there was nothing to occupy

his mind. He tried to read, yet he just ended up staring
into the fireplace, remembering the dark mystery of
Antoinette's eyes, the way her face lit with a smile as
she recounted some antic of the wild Leighton children. He wanted to know more about her, more of
what lay beneath her smiles and her amusing stories.

Sometimes, when she thought he was not looking,
her smiles faded a bit and some shadow of loneliness
lowered over her fine eyes. A loneliness he knew all
too well, and one he would banish from her eyes for
all time if he only could.

He had not thought so much about a woman since
the heady early days of his courtship of Elizabeth.
Elizabeth. He grimaced now to think of her, to remember how he had been foolish enough to fall for
her golden loveliness, her air of light charm. How he
had never seen the shallowness behind her pretty, flirtatious manners.

Antoinette was nothing like Elizabeth. Mark would
stake his ship—if he still had one—on that. She had
charm, but there was no heartlessness in it. She was
marked by life, as he was, and that left no room for
a shallow heart. Her dark eyes spoke of miseries and
joys that a girl like Elizabeth, now safe in London as
Lady Penworthy, could know nothing of.

It was that gleam in Antoinette's gaze that drew
him here today, when he could stay away no longer.
It was why he found himself standing outside her garden gate, wearing his best coat, a dark blue superfine
the height of fashion twelve years ago, his boots
shined and his hair neatly tied back.

Yes, he had done his best to make himself appear
presentable (a hopeless endeavor on the best days).
But now it appeared his efforts were in vain, as Antoinette was not at home. There was no smoke from her
chimney, no stirring at the window draperies.

"Well, now," he said to his waiting horse. "It appears I *am* a foolish old sailor after all."

He gathered the reins up, and turned to mount the horse when he heard a lightly lilting voice call, "Good afternoon, Captain Payne—Mark! I trust you have not been waiting too long?"

His heart gave a jolt to hear that voice, crisp and sweet in the cold air. Grinning like an idiot, he stepped back to see Antoinette hurrying down the pathway toward him. She was not dressed in her green silk robe today, but instead wore an ordinary walking gown and pelisse of burgundy-and-cream-striped wool. Her glorious hair was tucked beneath a burgundy turban, and the dark fur collar of her pelisse lay sleekly against her throat.

In the pale winter sunlight, dressed as a respectable English lady, she did not have the wild, untamed beauty of her midnight self. Yet her eyes still glowed, her tall figure radiated energy and vibrant good health. He felt his own spirits rise just watching her, and his reticence of the past two days seemed foolish indeed.

His life held little enough cheer. Why should he not enjoy the company of a lovely lady, if she was willing to bestow it?

He resolutely pushed back the niggling doubts, the revulsion of Elizabeth and her ilk, and returned Antoinette's smile with one of his own.

"I have only just arrived," he answered her. "But I saw you were not at home, so I was about to take my leave."

"I am glad I returned in time, then," she said. As she reached his side, she held her hand out to him, and he bowed over it. She smelled of jasmine and the fine kid of her glove, and he wanted so much to hold onto her hand, to absorb her warmth into his own flesh.

She withdrew it even before his clasp could tighten, though, still smiling, her cheeks painted with a pink flush over the coffee and cream.

"Won't you come inside, Mark?" she said, pushing

open the garden gate and leading the way to her door. "I gave Sally the afternoon off, but I'm sure I can find some tea to offer you."

"Thank you, Antoinette," he answered, following in her jasmine-scented wake. He was afraid his tone and demeanor were ridiculously stiff, but he was not accustomed to paying polite calls. Even before his injuries, he had been poorly equipped to perform social niceties. Life aboard a ship held little in common with a drawing room.

Antoinette did not appear to notice, though, and he relaxed as soon as he stepped through her door. Her home was not grand, as his mother's was; there was no delicate gilt furniture for him to worry about smashing, no porcelain gewgaws. Antoinette's abode was filled with fine Jacobean antiques and glowing garnet and blue rugs, fine paintings of seascapes and portraits of small children, and rich draperies at the windows. But it was all very welcoming and cozy. The air was scented with the bundles of herbs hanging from the ceiling rafters and the leather bindings of books.

Not the book she had with her on the cliff, though. That volume was nowhere to be seen.

Antoinette took his coat and hung it on a peg beside her pelisse. "Please, sit down, Mark," she said, gesturing toward the chairs drawn up by the banked fire. She went to open up the draperies, letting light spill into the sitting room, before joining him there.

Mark instinctively drew back away from the light, into the shadows where she could not see his face so clearly.

"I wanted to see how you were faring after your— adventure," he said.

Antoinette laughed. "Oh, I am quite well! I had a terrible headache the day before yesterday, but it is gone now. I walked into the village, to deliver some of my special lotions to Mrs. Greeley's store. She wanted them before Christmas in case any of her customers needed last-minute gifts." She reached for the fireplace poker and stirred the embers, coaxing them to flame anew.

Mark leaned back against the velvet cushions of his chair. He felt his qualms of the past two days fading away at the sense of *rightness* in this moment. It felt so pleasurable and strangely comfortable to sit here with her, feeling the soft magic of her presence around him. Her ease in his presence, her informality, gave him a sense of comfort he had not known in a long while.

"Actually, Mark," she said, "I am very glad you came to call. I was going to send a note around to you this afternoon."

He smiled at her, ridiculously pleased that she thought to write to him. "Were you?"

"Indeed. You see, Mrs. Greeley invited me to an assembly at the Hare and Hound Inn tomorrow evening. It is in honor of Christmas Eve. I believe they have it every year in different locations, yet I have always spent the holiday in Bath until now. I would like to attend, and I need an escort. Would you care to come? I know it is not at all the thing for a lady to invite a gentleman, but perhaps I could be excused by my island upbringing."

Mark stared at her, aghast. An *assembly*? At the village inn, where there would be dozens of people in attendance? People who would stare and whisper.

He liked *this*, just sitting with her by a quiet fire, listening to her speak, enjoying her smiles. It was comfortable. It was—safe. He could not imagine walking into a dance, where everyone would wonder how such a damaged cripple had found such a rare and exotic beauty.

Besides, his dancing skills were beyond rusty.

"An assembly, Antoinette?" he asked her, still wondering if perhaps he had misheard her. "Where there will be—dancing and such?"

She just nodded serenely. "Of course. And cards too, for those who do not care for dancing. I confess I myself quite enjoy a lively country dance."

"I thought you did not care much for mixing in society."

"Generally, I do not. In such a small place, someone as—different as I can have a difficult time finding a niche. I am sure you have found the same. But Mrs. Greeley said, and I concur, that it *is* Christmas. A time for new beginnings, new friends. It would be too sad to spend it all alone when one could spend it with music and dancing."

Mark felt himself being swayed, even against his very instincts. The thought of dancing with Antoinette was too much for a red-blooded male to resist.

She gave him a cajoling smile. "Come, Mark, for me? I have a ballgown I am aching to show off, and if you are not there I shall sorely lack for partners."

Mark was sure *that* was not true. Yet he found he was nodding, and saying, "Of course, Antoinette. I would be honored to escort you to the assembly."

Chapter Seven

In the daylight, the Hare and Hound was a perfectly ordinary village inn. Cleaner than most, perhaps, with a fine ale and a friendly landlord, but still like dozens of other half-timbered, stone-chimneyed relics of the Tudor era.

On this Christmas Eve evening, though, it was quite transformed. Golden light spilled from every window and doorway onto the innyard, covering everything with a fairy-tale sparkle. Laughter and chatter rose and fell like music from the revelers making their way up to the third-floor assembly rooms. Strains of actual music also floated down from a village orchestra demonstrating little finesse but a rich abundance of enthusiasm. The entire tableau was one of great frivolity and holiday good cheer.

Antoinette began to think that this had not been such a good idea after all. The crowd was large, loud with merriment. What would happen when they saw *her* here?

She stood on the front steps of the inn behind the Greeleys, who had paused to greet some acquaintances of theirs, staying back in the night shadows for as long as she could. Her hand, encased in her most elegant silk evening glove, was tucked into Mark's elbow, and, much to her embarrassment, she felt that hand tremble.

He peered down at her, his lips tilted down in a slight frown. He looked very distinguished and quite elegant in his black-and-white evening clothes, a fur-lined cloak tossed back from his shoulders, and a bi-corne hat tucked beneath his arm. His hair was brushed back and tied with a black velvet ribbon, shin-ing chestnut-brown in the candlelight. Yet, despite all his handsome looks, he, too, seemed distinctly ill at ease. His face was taut, expressionless as a stone statue.

As her own was, she was sure. Her skin felt like it would crack if she stretched it even further.

She saw his free hand reach yet again toward his scarred cheek, and she pulled at his elbow.

He gave her a startled glance, as if he had quite forgotten she was watching him. Then he smiled at her ruefully.

"Are you certain you want to attend this assem-bly?" he whispered. "We could go back to my cottage and share some brandy. You could tell me more tales of Jamaica."

Of course she didn't want to attend this assembly! How could she have once thought she did? A nice fire, a snifter of brandy, and some convivial conversation seemed far preferable to staring crowds. Especially now that she was actually faced with that crowd—the farmers and shopkeepers and local gentry who whis-pered about her. Why had she thought this was a fine idea in the first place? She must have been addled by her head injury.

Antoinette glanced back over her shoulder. They were apparently the last to arrive, for no one waited behind them in the innyard. It would be easy to make their excuses to the Greeleys and depart. . . .

Except that Antoinette's mother had not raised her to be a coward. She would not become one now. She had wanted a Christmas party, and here it was. She would hold her head up, and laugh and dance and chat. And she would make Mark Payne do it with her.

She gave him a mischievous smile, and tugged again

at his arm. "Certainly not, Captain. You promised me a dance, and I intend to hold you to it. Besides, I have not yet had a chance to show off my ballgown."

He laughed, and laid his free hand over hers, briefly squeezing her fingers. "Quite right, Miss Duvall. I will happily dance with you, if you do not mind ruined slippers. I am not as light on my feet as I used to be."

The Greeleys moved forward then, and Antoinette and Mark followed them into the inn's common room. After surrendering their cloaks to a waiting attendant, they made their way up the stairs to the assembly rooms.

Antoinette paused just outside the door to glance into a mirror. She had only this one ballgown, but she loved it, loved the inky-blue color of the silk, the shimmering gold embroidery on the low-cut bodice, the Elizabethan slashing of the tiny puffed sleeves. Now she only wondered—what did *Mark* think of the way she looked in it?

Her gaze met his in the glass, and she had her answer. His quicksilver eyes warmed like a summer sky, and his polite smile turned slow, sensual.

"You look most elegant tonight, Miss Duvall," he said deeply.

Antoinette gave him an answering smile. "As do you, Captain Payne." She reached up to untangle her long earring from her blue silk turban, and then turned back to clasp his arm again.

Somehow, with his warm, muscled strength beneath her hand, she no longer feared the crowd. She no longer feared *anything*.

"I believe I hear a Scottish reel starting," she said.

The long, wide assembly room was filled with gaily dressed revelers; young couples joining the dance, matrons watching them, chattering together; old men speculating on sport and the weather. On a table along one wall was arrayed a variety of delicacies, salmon patties, roast goose, mushroom tarts, a large plum pudding, and three punch bowls.

Yet the room did not feel crowded or overly warm. It sent out an atmosphere of holiday cheer and welcome. Even Antoinette felt it, deep inside of herself, and for the first time since their arrival at the Hare and Hound she felt some small flame of—was it *excitement*?

She gazed around, and noticed that while some people did give Mark and her startled glances, most did not even notice them.

Yet.

"Miss Duvall!" she heard someone call out, and she turned to see Mr. Lewisham, the vicar, hurrying toward them. His plump, cheerful wife followed, artificial holly woven into her pale blond hair in honor of the holiday. "Miss Duvall, how very charming to see you here. We thought perhaps you had gone off to Bath with the Leightons, until I saw you in the village this morning."

"It is good to see you as well, Mr. Lewisham, Mrs. Lewisham," Antoinette answered. "I stayed behind this year to finish some writing."

"Work? At Christmas? I thought only the vicar had to do *that*!" declared Mrs. Lewisham. "We are glad you had time to join this evening's revels."

"As am I," Antoinette said, and found, rather to her surprise, that it was true. The music, the holly, Mark's arm beneath her touch, all conspired to give her a rather breathless Christmas warmth she had not felt since childhood. "I do not believe you have met Captain Payne. Mr. and Mrs. Lewisham, this is a neighbor of mine, Captain Mark Payne, late of His Majesty's Navy. He came here with the Greeleys and myself this evening. Mr. Lewisham is incumbent of St. Anne's." She pulled Mark from the shadows into the flickering candlelight, fully to her side.

Mr. Lewisham only gave a welcoming smile, and

reached out to shake Mark's hand, but Mrs. Lewisham's eyes grew wide at the sight of his face. Her
glance darted from Mark to Antoinette and back
again.

"It is always a pleasure to meet a newcomer to the
neighborhood, Captain Payne," said Mr. Lewisham.

"Thank you, Mr. Lewisham," Mark answered, not
bothering to correct the vicar and say he had actually
been in the neighborhood for seven years.

"And, of course, any friend of Miss Duvall's . . ."
added Mrs. Lewisham, a sly undercurrent of speculation in her voice. The vicar's wife fancied herself the
village matchmaker, and she had not had a "victim"
in quite a long while.

"Perhaps we will have the honor of seeing you at
St. Anne's tomorrow, for Christmas services," said
the vicar.

"Thank you," Mark answered slowly. The music
changed from a reel to a schottische. "Ah—a dance I
believe I can manage. Miss Duvall, may I have the
honor?"

"Of course, Captain Payne. Please do excuse us, Mr.
Lewisham, Mrs. Lewisham." Antoinette gave them a
smile, and followed Mark to take their places in the
set. She could feel the interested gaze of the vicar and
his good wife all the way across the room. As she
and Mark took their places in the dance, conversation
hushed around them. Ladies whispered behind their
fans.

She ignored them as she smiled across at Mark. No
gossip could bother her at all this evening—not with
the lively tune making her toes tap and Mark's silver-
blue gaze on hers.

"The Lewishams seem quite—congenial," he said,
as their hands met and they made a turn and a leap.

"Indeed they are. They have been quite kind to me
ever since my arrival in Cornwall."

"Unlike certain others?"

"Perhaps."

They were separated by the patterns of the dance. When they came back together, to promenade the length of the set, Mark leaned closer to her and whispered, "They were surely only jealous."

Startled, Antoinette stared up at him, almost missing the step. "Jealous? Of *what*?"

"Of your beauty, of course. Of how very—special you are." His voice was deep, touched with a sweetly surprised ardor.

Antoinette wanted to kiss him more than she had ever wanted anything in her life. She wanted to lean over and place her lips on his, to hold on to him and never, ever let him go.

If he meant what he said—what could it mean for her? For them?

She felt the very foundations of her life shift and re-form beneath her feet.

Mark did not know where his words came from. He meant them. By Jove, but he *did* mean them! She was beautiful, beyond beautiful, and so special. He had realized that the moment he saw her on the cliff. And now, seeing how radiant and glorious she was, laughing in the dance, her deep blue gown flowing around her like the night, he knew she was a veritable goddess. A goddess of the sea and the wind. She made him see the beauty of life again.

No other woman could help but be jealous of her. She was more magnificent than any mortal woman could hope to be. But he hated it—hated it with a rage—that she had been hurt by any ignorance or lack of understanding. And she *had* been hurt; he could see it in the hidden depths of her eyes.

He wanted her only to have joy in her life from now on. Yet he was the last man to bring joy to any lady.

He did not regret his words, though, even as he was

not a man given to poetic sentiment. He meant them—and more. So much more.

The dance ended, and Mark led Antoinette to the edge of the room, his arms already aching to hold her again. "Would you care for another dance, Miss Duvall?"

"Later, perhaps," she answered, with a gentle smile. "Right now, I'm in need of some refreshment. The claret cup looks inviting."

"Of course. Allow me to fetch you a glass."

They found two chairs in a quiet corner where they sipped in silence at the watery punch. Mark listened to the laughter, the movement around them, and urged himself to speak to her. Speak *now*.

"Miss Duvall—Antoinette," he began. "There are things I must tell you . . ."

She turned to him, her eyes wide with expectation, her body leaning slightly toward him. But anything he might have said was drowned out by a burst of music, a rush of voices raised in familiar song.

"*The holly and the ivy, when they are both full grown, of all the trees that are in the wood, the holly bears the crown.*"

Several of the villagers had joined the musicians on their dais, and sang out the old carol with great enthusiasm and holiday cheer. Antoinette looked to them, her eyes shining with enjoyment of the song.

And Mark knew that whatever he wanted to say could wait, *should* wait until a quiet moment. A moment when he could clearly decipher his own emotions toward this most unique lady. He sat back in his chair, carefully situated in the shadows, to watch her as she listened. Just—watch. And greedily drink in her beauty.

More voices joined in as the song came to its close. "*The rising of the sun, and the running of the deer, the playing of the merry organ, sweet singing in the choir.*"

A half smile touched Antoinette's rose-pink lips, and she swayed slightly in her chair, whispering the lyrics. She obviously loved music; it seemed to infuse her entire body, lifting her from the dim surroundings into a realm no one else could invade.

As the carol ended, Mrs. Greeley leaned toward Antoinette and said, "Miss Duvall, why do you not favor us with a song? Lady Royce has told us you have a beautiful voice indeed."

The smile faded from Antoinette's lips, and her shoulders stiffened. "Oh, no, Mrs. Greeley," she protested. "I have a mediocre talent at best. And I am sure no one would be interested . . ."

"Nonsense!" Mrs. Greeley interrupted. "Mr. Greeley and I would so enjoy hearing you, as, I am sure, would Captain Payne. Is that not so, Captain?"

Mark would more than "enjoy" hearing Antoinette sing—he would pay his last farthing to do so. To hear her voice moving around him, showing him what music, what *Christmas*, could truly mean. He was only just becoming aware of the truth of so many things.

"Yes, please, Miss Duvall," he said. "Do favor us with a song. Something from your homeland, perhaps?"

She stared into his eyes long and hard, her own dark pools unreadable. Finally, she nodded. "Very well, Captain Payne. To please you. But please do not ask me to go up on the dais!"

"You may sing right here, Miss Duvall," Mrs. Greeley answered her. "We will be near."

Antoinette slowly rose from her chair, her head held high, hands folded at her waist. The candlelight glittered on the gold embroidery of her gown, and her gaze swept over the swiftly quieting crowd. She looked like a princess, Mark thought. No—a queen. A grand, magnificent queen. Only the slight trembling of her gloved fingers betrayed any nervousness.

She closed her eyes and parted her lips, and the most astonishing sounds, lively and bright, emerged.

"*The Virgin Mary had a baby boy . . . and they say that his name was Jesus. He come from the glory, He come from the glorious kingdom, oh, yes, believer! The angels sang when the baby born . . . and proclaim him the Savior Jesus.*"

As she sang words and melodies that were strange, exotic, yet achingly familiar, Mark could not turn his stare away from her face. She sang of love, redemption, transcendence, her eyes closed, a rosy glow on her cheeks. Her hands fluttered, raised in the joy of the song, the season. Her body swayed. She did not look at him, yet the words seemed only for him. They called to him—they told him that he was not alone, that someone else understood the agony of having one's world torn to bits with nothing to replace it, nothing beautiful to cling to.

Before him stood something beautiful beyond anything he could have imagined.

And he knew then, without a shadow of a doubt, that he was falling in love with Antoinette Duvall. She was an angel, a goddess, a woman of infinite understanding. She was beyond him—perfection did not mate with a monster, he knew that. But he also knew that he was compelled to tell her what she had brought him. What she meant. He had to try to bring her some surcease from her own loneliness, no matter how meager.

"*He come from the glory, He come from the glorious kingdom!*"

The last jubilant notes died away, echoing into the profound silence of the room. The revelers stared at Antoinette, dumbstruck. Many jaws gaped most inelegantly, and more than a few ladies wiped at damp cheeks. Something had shifted in the crowd, just as something had shifted in Mark's own soul.

Yet Antoinette clearly did not see that. Her shoulders were stiff, and slowly, painfully, her eyes fluttered open. Her hands twisted together. She appeared ready to flee, like a wounded gazelle.

Then a clapping began, slow at first, growing as it swept across the room, a tidal wave of emotional sound. A tentative smile again touched her lips, and she made a small, elegant curtsy.

Mark stepped up to her and took her gloved hand in his, bowing over it. "Miss Duvall—Antoinette," he murmured, so no one else could hear. "I must talk to you—I must tell you something. May I come to your cottage tomorrow? To speak to you privately?"

She stared at him for a moment, silent. Then something shifted behind her eyes, something that told him she understood his sudden desperation. She nodded, and her fingers tightened on his for a fleeting instant. "Come to my cottage later tonight," she answered. The last word barely escaped before she was swept away by people demanding another song.

Yes. Later tonight.

Chapter Eight

Antoinette moved one porcelain ornament from the left side of one of her pier tables to the right then back again. It was the fourth time she had done so since she returned to her cottage from the assembly more than an hour ago. Mark had left before she departed with the Greeleys, saying he preferred to walk home, and she began to think she imagined his words to her.

Imagined the entire strange evening. The dancing, the music—the tentative conversation of people she always imagined disliked and suspected her. Above all, she must have imagined the way Mark looked at her as he bowed over her hand.

He looked as if he—admired her. Yet how could that be? He was the son of an earl, a naval captain who had bravely served his king and country, even though he seemed determined to forget all that, to bury himself forever here in Cornwall. She was a nobody. Less than a nobody.

Yet that could not erase the indisputable fact that she also—admired him. *Admire* was an inadequate word for what she felt. There could be no words. She felt she knew him in a way she could never have imagined. The lonely ache of her soul filled up when she met him, and every encounter added to that warmth.

For the first time, she felt at home in England, felt there could be no place else for her.

Soon, Mark would surely go back to his family, his

true place, and she would stay here with her work and her friends. But it would not be the same as before. Her memories of this brief time with this very special man would sustain her, and she intended to seize every moment she could with him.

If he would just appear, as he had promised he would!

Even as she thought this, a low knock sounded at the door. She spun away from the table and dashed to open it, her heart rising in a wild flutter of giddiness.

Mark stood on her doorstep, wrapped in his greatcoat, hat in hand. He smiled at her, yet he seemed rather unsure, as if now that he was here he was not certain what to say to her. Antoinette would have none of that. If their time was to be short, she would, by heaven, make the most of it!

She reached out, took his hand, and pulled him into her sitting room. As the door clicked shut behind him, he took her into his arms and held her close, so close they could not possibly be parted. Not yet. Antoinette looped her arms about his neck and closed her eyes, inhaling his scent of sandalwood soap, leather, and night air. They were much of a height, and she could turn her head to kiss his rough, scarred cheek, his strong jaw. Her lips trailed over the faded burns, healing them with all the love she had in her heart.

"I missed you," she whispered.

Mark gave a hoarse moan, and his lips claimed hers. Their kiss was not gentle—it was full of desperation, of passion, of all the love and need they possessed.

"Antoinette," Mark muttered, his kisses trailing along her throat. "Antoinette, I must . . ."

"Shh," she whispered. "You do not need to talk. I know."

"I *do* need to talk," he protested. He stepped back from her a fraction, his strong hands sliding up to hold her face between them. "I have been a coward for far too long, but you—you extraordinary, perfect woman—make me brave again."

"You? A coward? No!" Antoinette protested. She grabbed at his hands, holding them tightly in hers. "Never, Mark. You fought in battle, you were horribly injured!"

"I did fight, for many years, and I thought nothing of it. But I vow to you I *am* a coward. I have hidden from life—from myself—for all these years because I could not face myself, could not face that my life had changed so irrevocably."

"Yes," she answered quietly. "Yes, I know how that feels."

"I know you do. And that is why I feel I can tell you about what happened to me. About how I came to be—as I am."

Mark took her arm and led her to the settee. She went without a protest, though she was not certain she truly wanted to hear what he would say. She could not bear to think of the terrible pain he must have endured, both of the body and the heart, the soul. But she sensed his need to tell her this, and she would listen.

They sat at opposite ends of the settee, only their hands touching in the middle. "I was the captain of the *Royal Augusta* at Trafalgar, a forty-four-gun frigate with almost three hundred crewmen. Things were going well, or well enough for the heat of battle, anyway. We had lost very few men, and we had already destroyed two French ships. Victory was in our grasp, and then . . ." His voice faded.

Antoinette folded her hand about his. His clasp tightened, but he did not look at her.

"One of our guns exploded, and I don't know how it could have happened. But there was a fire, an explosion, and many—most of my men were killed."

"It was not your fault," Antoinette said softly, hearing the bitter tone in his voice, the self-recrimination he carried after all these years. "Terrible things happen in war, but you are a good man. I know you were a good officer."

"I did my best," he answered. "And that day—it was simply not enough. I know I did not cause that explosion. But I will carry the knowledge of that failure with me always. As well as the knowledge that I am not fit for proper society."

"What happened when you returned home? Was your family not—welcoming?" Antoinette could not imagine how a family could not welcome back such a son. Yet she knew—knew all too well—the immense capacity for cruelty some human beings could possess.

"Oh, no. They were quite welcoming, quite solicitous. Quite—pitying." He gave a wry little smile. "It was my fiancée, Lady Elizabeth Morton-Haddon, who found that her feelings for me had changed quite utterly. She took one glance at my new face and cried off. One could hardly blame her."

Hardly blame her? Antoinette jolly well could. A fire of anger at the unknown Lady Elizabeth burned in her throat. "She was a fool." Antoinette leaned forward to kiss Mark, the softest, gentlest touch of her lips on his. "A great fool to lose a wonderful man such as you."

His arms came about her waist, holding her close. "Most would have called her a fool if she stayed."

"Not I."

"No. Not you, Antoinette. You are quite unlike anyone I have ever met. But I have not told you this story to gain your pity, or even to get another kiss from you."

Antoinette grinned up at him, twining a long strand of his hair about her finger. "Oh, no?"

He laughed, his head thrown back against cushions of the settee. "Well, perhaps just a bit. I do enjoy your kisses. But I told this to you because I wanted you to know I understand what it is like to be lonely. I saw how people treated you when we first arrived at the assembly, whispering behind their fans and staring. Did their parents never teach them proper manners?"

Her grin faded. She did not want to be reminded of the cold winter world outside her door. She only wanted this moment, this perfect time. "It is of no matter," she said, striving for a light, careless tone. "I have my own friends, my own life. The gossip of people so wholly unconnected to me means little."

His arms tightened. "Your life here cannot have been an easy one."

"Who does truly have an *easy* life? Everyone has trials and tribulations, and mine have not been so great." She cuddled closer to him, resting her cheek on his strong shoulder. "No one has thrown rotten vegetables at me as I walk along the street or anything of the sort. They respect the family at the castle far too much. But most of them do keep their distance, I admit. They do not understand me—they don't know where I came from, my customs. I cannot blame them. I do not understand myself most of the time."

"What do you mean?"

Rather than answering, she disentangled herself from his arms and stood up from the settee. She went to the small, locked cabinet in the corner and carefully withdrew her precious book, clutching the silk-wrapped bundle protectively in her arms. Slowly, she turned back to face him.

"I have told you about my family," she said. "Yet there is one thing about my mother I never speak about, something very precious and secret."

He slid to the edge of the settee, his folded hands clasped before him and dangling between his knees. His expression was still and solemn, as if he sensed the true seriousness of her words. "Of course, Antoinette. You may tell me anything you wish. All your secrets are safe with me."

"You'll remember this book, I think," she said, "since I sent you back to rescue it from the snow on the night we met." She placed the bundle carefully on a low table and folded back the silk.

He watched her closely, his expression unreadable in the firelight. "Yes. I remember it."

"This book belonged to my mother, and to my grandmother before her. I do not know where it came from originally. Africa, my mother said, but I don't know if that is true." She opened the book to the pages in the middle, and caressed her hand over the soft, smooth vellum. She could feel the slight indentations of the ancient words written there, the stiffness of the painted images. The pages seemed to warm under her touch, leaping to life.

"What is this volume about, Antoinette?" Mark asked quietly.

Antoinette lifted her gaze from the pages and met his across the table. He looked serious, but not alarmed, merely curious. But she had never shared the book with anyone before, had only ever shown it to Cassie, and her stomach lurched with anxiety.

"It is about many things," she answered. "My mother was a great woman, a powerful woman. She knew many things, things ordinary people cannot conceive of, and she learned them from this book. She could heal people, could see beyond this world to others we know nothing of."

"Witchcraft?" he whispered.

"No!" Antoinette cried, recoiling from the word. "My mother was not a *witch*. She was a devout Christian; she brought me up in the church to be one as well. These were just—gifts she had, abilities that not every person possesses. She said they were gifts from God, given to her so she might help His people on earth. And that is what she did. She healed people; she never harmed anyone!"

Antoinette could feel a frenzy rising up in her as she defended her mother, tried to explain her powers. It was always thus when she spoke of or remembered Marie-Claire Duvall. But now it was more vital than ever that she should make Mark understand. It was the only way she could help him. Help *them*.

He reached over and caught her hand in both of his, cradling it against the warmth of his skin. She calmed at his touch, and felt her breath slow in her lungs.

"I see," he said. "Your mother was a—a priestess of sorts."

"A Yaumumi priestess," Antoinette explained. "It is an ancient tradition, from Africa."

"And she cured people of their illnesses?"

"Yes. Of both the body and the heart, the spirit."

Mark nodded slowly. "I met women of that sort when I was in the West Indies. What they could achieve was remarkable."

Perhaps he *did* understand, then, at least a little. And soon he would see more. Antoinette stepped around the table to stand before him, framing his face in her long fingers. She traced the pattern of his scars gently with her thumb, feeling the silky tightness of the damaged skin. He flinched, but did not pull away.

Antoinette caught and held his stare with her own, not letting him go. She felt a strength, a power growing in the center of her being. She could do this. She *must* do this. The future of the man she loved depended on it.

It would be a future away from her, back with his family, his old world. But she had to do this. She had to try to set him free.

"I do not have the powers of my mother," she said. "I am weak compared to her. But she can help us now, if you will let her."

Mark stared up at her, and covered her hands with his, clutching at her tightly. "What do you mean?"

"Do you trust me, Mark?" she whispered.

"Yes," he answered, not even hesitating for a heartbeat.

"Then all will be well." Antoinette was far from believing that herself. For, truly, how could all be well if she had found true love only to cast it from her? But she *did* love Mark—she saw that so clearly now, as she looked down upon him in the firelight. He was brave and caring. He deserved better than this solitary life he had been living, a life whose pain and loneliness Antoinette understood all too well.

She had to try to set him free.

She stepped back away from him. He reached out for her, trying to catch her back. "Antoinette . . ."

"No," she said. "Trust me. It is Christmas. The most magical time of year."

She quickly gathered candles from the cupboard, red, pink, white. She arrayed them about the book and lit them. Then she gathered herbs—cinnamon, clove, lilac—and sprinkled them along with salt between the candles, whispering all the while, calling on her mother for help. Mark watched her, a small frown tight on his brow, but he said nothing and never moved.

Finally, all was in readiness. Antoinette released her hair from its pins, letting the thick mass float about her shoulders. She lifted her hands above the book and closed her eyes, keeping the image of Mark in her mind. The familiar tingling sensation grew, spreading from her toes to her fingertips. Her thoughts turned misty, and she turned her hands toward Mark, palms upward.

"Be renewed from this day," she chanted. "All pain, all fear, all loneliness washed away. Carry my love to where he'll be best, let his heart be open and free.

Cleanse and consecrate our hearts, and lead us forward from the pain into the light."

A brilliant warmth such as Antoinette had never known suffused her, shooting energy and joy and even pain from her heart until she cried out with the force of it. A bright golden light flooded her mind—and then it was gone. The burst of magic ebbed away from her, and her legs were as weak as a new kitten's. She felt herself falling, yet before she could collapse to the floor, she felt powerful arms catch her, lifting her and holding her close, safe.

Mark had rescued her, just as he had on the night they met. He held her safe in his warm strength.

Antoinette's head sank against his chest. She was so very weak she could not even hold it up. She felt his lips press to her temple, her cheek, her mouth. And there, as his kiss met hers, she tasted the salty wetness of tears.

She opened her eyes to see that he was indeed crying, silent, crystal tears that fell onto her own cheeks in a sort of baptism of released pain and new freedom.

"No, no," she murmured. Her own voice seemed to echo from a very long way away. Exhaustion flowed through her veins like a heavy syrup, and she gave in to it, allowing the darkness of healing sleep to overcome her, right there in Mark's arms.

Chapter Nine

Mark sat by the window in Antoinette's cottage, watching the sun come up on a new day—Christmas Day. He had seen many a dawn, over the waves of the sea, over rooftops of London and cliffs of Cornwall. Yet never had he seen a dawn so exquisitely lovely. Pink and orange and soft lavender swirled in the morning sky, pierced by arrow-pricks of purest gold light, like a halo crowning the heavens.

As exquisite as the sunrise was, though, it could in no way compare to the lady he held cradled in his arms.

Antoinette slept, her head resting on his shoulder, her breath soft against his throat where he had loosened his neckcloth. Her beautiful silk gown was rumpled now, covered by the paisley shawl Mark had drawn warmly around her. Her hair fell in a loose, wild cascade over his arm. Earlier, at the assembly, she was the perfect lady, fashionable, poised, elegant; now she seemed the wild island girl she was born.

And Mark loved both aspects of her. He loved *her*, Antoinette, in a way he had long surrendered hope for. As he sat there in her house, the scent of her jasmine perfume all around him, he felt more at peace than he ever had. Even before the fateful battle that ended his life as he knew it, he had always been seeking, striving, moving. Never still, not even for an instant. His heart could never be serene, never trust that things were right just as they were.

Now he knew that all was right. A quiet contentment settled over his mind, his very soul. The pain of the past was gone. It was behind him, and there was only the future to be faced, full of—of whatever he wanted it to be! And what he wanted, now and always, was Antoinette. By his side, for the rest of his days.

He did not know if this new peace was due to the spell she performed. But he *did* know that when he saw her face as she chanted those words, so intent, so focused, he realized he loved her truly. And she had feelings for him too. Feelings of love? He was not certain. It had been many years since he had even thought about romance; his facilities in that direction were rather rusty.

He had to sharpen them now, though. He had to persuade Antoinette to marry him and go with him to face his family again. It would not be easy. She was as settled in her solitary ways as he had been for so many years. It would be frightening for her to go to London with him and meet his grand family, though they would surely accept her as his wife. But she *had* to do it. She must!

For he could never do it without her.

Antoinette stirred in his arms, her eyes blinking open as the morning sun washed over her. Her hands drew the shawl closer about her shoulders, and she gave him a small smile. "Good morning," she murmured.

"Merry Christmas," he answered. "My love."

His love? Had Antoinette heard aright, or was she still dreaming?

She sat up straight, pushing slightly away from his warmth so she could study him closer. He seemed—different this morning. Younger, somehow. More open. His silvery eyes were clear as he looked back at her, his smile wide and brighter than the morning sunshine.

Had her spell worked, then? Was he free? Were they *both* free?

It was what she had wanted, more than anything. But now that he was free of the past, would he fly away from her?

She reached out to touch his face, her fingers light against his scars. He did not flinch or draw away, ducking into the shadows as she had often seen him do. He turned his head to kiss her fingertips, raising his own hand to hold her there.

"Merry Christmas," she whispered, echoing his own words. *My love.*

"I vow it must be the finest Christmas ever," he answered. "With sunlight, and the sea, and the most beautiful lady by my side."

Antoinette's head spun, making her giddy. This change, this new brightness, was all too much for so very early in the morning. "I fear I have no roast goose, no plum pudding, and no gifts. It is a very shabby Christmas indeed."

"You have the most valuable gift of all, right here." He cradled her hand in his, her palm up.

"What do you mean?"

He bent his head to plant a kiss right there, in the center of her palm. It lingered, warm in the cool morning air. "Antoinette Duvall, will you do me the great honor of giving me your hand in marriage?"

Marriage! Antoinette pulled away from him, startled—no, *shocked*. She jumped to her feet, holding the shawl protectively around herself.

She was not sure what she had been expecting or hoping for. But this was beyond anything she might have dreamed! To be Mark's *wife* . . .

For one moment, she let herself believe that it could be, that they could love each other, make a home together, a *family*, just as she had dreamed.

But then reality came in, like the cold waves of the English sea. He might be a recluse like her, but he came from a titled family, a family who would welcome him back into their fold. She was a nobody, an "island witch." It would be selfish of her to grab at her own happiness at the expense of his.

"Mark, I . . ." she began.

But he sensed her wavering, and jumped up to catch her in his arms before she could go on. "No! No, Antoinette, I won't let you do this. I won't let you refuse me."

"I can do nothing else," she said, feeling her own heart wavering. It felt so good to be in his arms, so safe. So *right*. "Your brother is an earl. Your family would never want to see you wed someone like me."

"My family would want to see me wed any woman who makes me whole again—as you do." He drew her even closer, his hands buried in the mass of her hair, cradling her against him. "Even if they do not, I am my own man; I have been making my own way in the world since I was fifteen. My choice of wife is my own. Please, Antoinette. I was in darkness before you—you are my light. Do not take that away from me. Say you will be my wife, that you will never leave me."

Antoinette shook her head, confused. How could she ever think straight, with his arms around her and his words pouring over her like gold from heaven? She felt tears spilling down her cheeks onto the loosened folds of his neckcloth, and she could not stop them. "I only want your happiness," she choked out.

"*You* are my happiness!" He framed her face in his hands, forcing her to look up at him. "And if you marry me, I will spend the rest of my days making you happy too. We do not have to stay here in Cornwall, or even in London. We can go back to Jamaica together, anything you want."

Antoinette's heart surrendered then, completely. Yes, there *would* be hardships in their future, obstacles aplenty. But she knew now that she—*they*—could face anything at each other's side. They would not be alone anymore, not ever again. Whether here, or on a beach in Jamaica or a town house in London, it did not matter. Only their love mattered. Now and forever after.

The magic had worked. She felt its sparkle in her own heart, and she knew it would never fade away.

"I do not care where we make our home," she told him, "as long as we are together. Yes, I will marry you, Mark. I love you, with all my heart."

Mark gave a loud, whooping laugh of joy, and swept her up into his arms, swinging her about. "As I love you! I told you this was the finest Christmas ever, Antoinette."

Antoinette laughed too, her soul overflowing with exultation. "And so it is! The finest, most *magical* Christmas ever."

And, as they kissed beneath the swags of holly and red ribbon, the pages of her mother's book flickered gently and closed with a soft, satisfied sigh.

Read on for excerpts from some other delightful Christmas Regency romances from Signet.

Available at www.penguin.com or wherever books are sold.

FATHER CHRISTMAS

Barbara Metzger

The Duke of Ware needed an heir. Like a school-yard taunt, the gruesome refrain floated in his mind, bobbing to the surface on a current of brandy. Usually a temperate man, His Grace was just a shade on the go. It was going to take more than a shade to get him to go to Almack's.

"Hell and blast!" Leland Warrington, fifth and at this point possibly last Duke of Ware, consulted his watch again. Ten o'clock, and everyone knew Almack's patronesses barred its doors at eleven. Not even London's premiere *parti*, wealth, title, and looks notwithstanding, could gain admittance after the witching hour. "Blasted witches," Ware cursed once more, slamming his glass down on the table that stood so conveniently near his so-comfortable leather armchair at White's. "Damnation."

His companion snapped up straighter in his facing seat. "What's that? The wine gone off?" The Honorable Crosby Fanshaw sipped cautiously at his own drink. "Seems fine to me." He called for another bottle.

Fondly known as Crow for his anything-but-somber style of dress, the baronet was a studied contrast to his longtime friend. The duke was the one wearing the stark black and white of Weston's finest evening wear, spread over broad shoulders and well-muscled thighs, while Crow Fanshaw's spindly frame was draped in magenta pantaloons, saffron waistcoat, lime green wasp-waisted coat. The duke looked away. Fanshaw would never get into Almack's in that outfit. Then again, Fanshaw didn't need to get into Almack's.

"No, it's not the wine, Crow. It's a wife. I need one."

The baronet slipped one manicured finger under his elaborate neckcloth to loosen the noose conjured up by the very thought of matrimony. He shuddered. "Devilish things, wives."

"I'll drink to that," Ware said, and did. "But I need one nevertheless if I'm to beget the next duke."

"Ah." Crow nodded sagely, careful not to disturb his pomaded curls. "Noblesse oblige and all that. The sacred duty of the peerage: to beget more little aristocratic blue bloods to carry on the name. I thank heaven m'brother holds the title. Let Virgil worry about the succession and estates."

"With you as heir, he'd need to." Crow Fanshaw wouldn't know a mangel-wurzel from manure, and they both knew it.

The baronet didn't take offense. "What, ruin m'boots in dirt? M'valet would give notice, then where would I be? 'Sides, Virgil's managing to fill his nursery nicely, two boys and a girl. Then there are m'cousin's parcel of brats if he needs extras. I'm safe." He raised his glass in a toast. "Condolences, old friend."

Ware frowned, lowering thick dark brows over his hazel eyes. Easy for Crow to laugh, his very soul wasn't engraved with the Ware family motto: *Semper servimus.* We serve forever. Forever, dash it, the duke unnecessarily reminded himself. His heritage, everything he was born and bred to be and to believe, demanded an heir. Posterity demanded it, all those acres and people dependent upon him demanded it, Aunt Eudora demanded it! God, King, and Country, that's what the Wares served, she insisted. Well, Leland made his donations to the church, he took his tedious seat in Parliament, and he served as a diplomat when the Foreign Office needed him. That was not enough. The Bible said be fruitful and multiply, quoted his childless aunt. The King, bless his mad soul, needed more loyal peers to advise and direct his outrageous progeny. And the entire country, according to Eudora Warrington, would go to rack and ruin without a bunch of little Warringtons trained to manage Ware's vast estates and investments. At the very least, her annuity might be in danger.

Leland checked his watch again. Ten-ten. He felt as if he were going to the tooth-drawer, dreading the moment yet wishing it were over. "What time do you have, Crow?"

Crosby fumbled at the various chains crisscrossing his narrow chest. "I say, you must have an important appointment, the way you keep eyeing your timepiece. Which is it, that new red-haired dancer at the opera or the dashing widow you had up in your phaeton yesterday?" While the duke sat glaring, Fanshaw pulled out his quizzing glass, then a seal with his family crest before finally retrieving his watch fob. "Fifteen minutes past the hour."

Ware groaned. "Almack's" was all he could manage to say. It was enough.

Fanshaw dropped his watch and grabbed up the looking glass by its gem-studded handle, tangling ribbons and chains as he surveyed his friend for signs of dementia. "I thought you said Almack's."

"I did. I told you, I need an heir."

"But Almack's, Lee? Gads, you must be dicked in the nob. Castaway, that's it." He pushed the bottle out of the duke's reach.

"Not nearly enough," His Grace replied, pulling the decanter back and refilling his glass. "I promised Aunt Eudora I'd look over the latest crop of dewy-eyed debs."

Crosby downed a glass in commiseration. "I understand about the heir and all, but there must be an easier way, by Jupiter. I mean, m'brother's girl is making her come-out this year. She's got spots. And her friends giggle. Think on it, man, they are, what? Seventeen? Eighteen? And you're thirty-one!"

"Thirty-two," His Grace growled, "as my aunt keeps reminding me."

"Even worse. What in the world do you have in common with one of those empty-headed infants?"

"What do I have in common with that redhead from the opera? She's only eighteen, and the only problem you have with that is she's in my bed, not yours."

"But she's a ladybird! You don't have to talk to them, not like a wife!"

The duke stood as if to go. "Trust me, I don't intend to have anything more to do with this female I'll marry than it takes to get me a son."

"If a son is all you want, why don't you just adopt one? Be easier in the long run, more comfortable, too. M'sister's got a surplus. I'm sure she'd be glad to get rid of one or two, the way she's always trying to pawn them off on m'mother so she can go to some house party or other."

The duke ignored his friend's suggestion that the next Duke of Ware be anything less than a Warrington, but he did sit down. "That's another thing: No son of mine is going to be raised up by nannies and tutors and underpaid schoolmasters."

"Why not? That's the way we were brought up, and we didn't turn out half bad, did we?"

Leland picked a bit of imaginary fluff off his superfine sleeve. Not half bad? Not half good, either, he reflected. Crow was an amiable fribble, while he himself was a libertine, a pleasure-seeker, an ornament of society. Oh, he was a conscientious landowner, for a mostly absentee landlord, and he did manage to appear at the House for important votes. Otherwise his own entertainment—women, gaming, sporting—was his primary goal. There was nothing of value in his life. He intended to do better by his son. "I mean to be a good father to the boy, a guide, a teacher, a friend."

"A Bedlamite, that's what. Try being a friend to some runny-nosed brat with scraped knees and a pocketful of worms." Crosby shivered. "I know just the ticket to cure you of such bubble-brained notions: Why don't you come down to Fanshaw Hall with me for the holidays? Virgil'd be happy to have you for the cards and hunting, and m'sister-in-law would be in alt to have such a nonpareil as houseguest. That niece who's being fired off this season will be there, so you can see how hopeless young chits are, all airs and affectations one minute, tears and tantrums the next. Why, if you can get Rosalie to talk of anything but gewgaws and gossip, I'll eat my hat. Best of all, m'sister will be at the Hall with her nursery brood. No, best of all is if the entire horde gets the mumps and stays home. But, 'struth, you'd change your tune about this fatherhood gammon if you just spent a day with the little savages."

Ware smiled. "I don't mean to insult your family, but your sister's ill-behaved brats only prove my point that this whole child-rearing thing could be improved upon with a little careful study."

"Trust me, Lee, infants ain't like those new farming machines you can read up on. Come down and see. At least I can promise you a good wine cellar at the Hall."

The duke shook his head. "Thank you, Crow, but I have to refuse. You see, I really am tired of spending the holidays with other people's families."

"What I see is you've been bitten bad by this new bug of yours. Carrying on the line. Littering the countryside with butterstamps. Next thing you know, you'll be pushing a pram instead of racing a phaeton. I'll miss you, Lee." He flicked a lacy handkerchief from his sleeve and dabbed at his eyes while the duke grinned at the performance. Fanshaw's next words changed that grin into so fierce a scowl that a lesser man, or a less loyal friend, would have been tempted to bolt: "Don't mean to be indelicate, but you know getting leg-shackled isn't any guarantee of getting heirs."

"Of course I know that, blast it! I ought to, I've already been married." The duke finished his drink. "Twice." He tossed back another glassful to emphasize the point. "And all for nothing."

Fanshaw wasn't one to let a friend drink alone, even if his words were getting slurred and his thoughts muddled. He refilled his own glass. Twice. "Not for nothing. Got a handsome dowry both times."

"Which I didn't need," His Grace muttered into his drink.

"And got the matchmaking mamas off your back until you learned to depress their ambitions with one of your famous setdowns."

"Which if I'd learned earlier, I wouldn't be in this hobble today."

The duke's first marriage had been a love match: He was in love with the season's reigning Toast, Carissa was in love with his wealth and title. Her mother made sure he never saw past the Diamond's beauty to the cold, rock-hard shrew beneath who didn't want to be his wife, she wanted to be a duchess. There wasn't one extravagance she didn't indulge, not one risqué pleasure she didn't gratify, not one mad romp she didn't join. Until she broke her beautiful neck in a curricle race.

Ware's second marriage was one of convenience, except that it wasn't. He carefully selected a quiet, retiring sort of girl whose pale loveliness was as different from Carissa's flamboyance as night from day. *Her* noble parents had managed to conceal, while they were dickering over the settlements, that Lady Floris was a sickly child, that her waiflike appeal had more to do with a weak constitution than any gentle beauty. Floris was content to stay in the shadows after their wedding, until she became a shadow. Then she faded away altogether. Ware was twice a widower, never a father. To his knowledge, he'd never even sired a bastard on one of his mistresses, but he didn't want to think about the implications of that.

"What time do you have?"

Crosby peered owl-eyed at his watch, blinked, then turned it right side up. "Ten-thirty. Time for another drink." He raised his glass, spilling only a drop on the froth of lace at his shirt-sleeve. "To your bride."

Leland couldn't do it. The wine would turn to vinegar on his tongue. Instead, he proposed a toast of his own. "To my cousin Tony, the bastard to blame for this whole deuced coil."

Crosby drank, but reflected, "If he was a bastard, then it wouldn't have mattered if the nodcock went and got himself killed. He couldn't have been your heir anyway."

His Grace waved that aside with one elegant if unsteady hand. "Tony was a true Warrington all right, my father's only brother's only son. My heir. So *he* got to go fight against Boney when the War Office turned me down."

"Protective of their dukes, those chaps."

"And *he* got to be a hero, the lucky clunch."

"Uh, not to be overparticular, but live heroes are lucky, dead ones ain't."

Leland went on as though his friend hadn't spoken: "And he was a fertile hero to boot. Old Tony didn't have to worry about shuffling off this mortal coil without a trace. He left twins, twin boys, no less, the bounder, and he didn't even have a title to bequeath them or an acre of land!"

"Twin boys, you say? Tony's get? There's your answer, Lee, not some flibbertigibbet young miss. Go gather the sprigs and have the raising of 'em your way if that's what you want to do. With any luck they'll be out of nappies and you can send 'em off to school as soon as you get tired of 'em. Should take about a month, I'd guess."

Ware frowned. "I can't go snabble my cousin's sons, Crow. Tony's widow just brought them back to her parents' house from the Peninsula."

Fanshaw thought on it a minute, chewing his lower lip. "Then marry that chit, I say. You get your heirs with Warrington blood, your brats to try to make into proper English gentlemen, and a proven breeder into the bargain. 'Sides, she can't be an antidote; Tony Warrington had taste."

The duke merely looked down his slightly aquiline nose and stood up to leave. "She's a local vicar's daughter."

"Good enough to be Mrs. Major Warrington, eh, but not the Duchess of Ware?" The baronet nodded, not noticing that his starched shirtpoints disarranged his artful curls. "Then you'd best toddle off to King Street, where the *ton* displays its merchandise. Unless . . ."

Ware turned back like a drowning man hearing the splash of a tossed rope. "Unless . . . ?"

"Unless you ask the widow for just one of the bantlings. She might just go for it. I mean, how many men are going to take on a wife with *two* tokens of her dead husband's devotion to support? There's not much space in any vicarage I know of, and you said yourself Tony didn't leave much behind for them to live on. 'Sides, you can appeal to her sense of fairness. She has two sons and you have none."

Leland removed the bottle and glass from his friend's vicinity on his way out of the room. "You have definitely had too much to drink, my tulip. Your wits have gone begging for dry land."

And the Duke of Ware still needed an heir.

Heaving breasts, fluttering eyelashes, gushing sim-
pers, blushing whimpers—and those were the hopeful
mamas. The daughters were worse. Aunt Eudora
could ice-skate in Hades before her nephew returned
to Almack's.

Ware had thought he'd observe the crop of debu-
tantes from a discreet, unobtrusive distance. Sally Jersey thought differently. With pointed fingernails
fastened to his wrist like the talons of a raptor, she
dragged her quarry from brazen belle to arrogant heiress to wilting wallflower. At the end of each painful,
endless dance, when he had, perforce, to return his
partner to her chaperone, there was *la* Jersey waiting
in prey with the next willing sacrificial virgin.

The Duke of Ware needed some air.

He told the porter at the door he was going to blow
a cloud, but he didn't care if the fellow let him back
in or not. Leland didn't smoke. He never had, but he
thought he might take it up now. Perhaps the foul
odor, yellowed fingers, and stained teeth could dis-
courage some of these harpies, but he doubted it.

Despite the damp chill in the air, the duke was not
alone on the outer steps of the marriage mart. At first
all he could see in the gloomy night was the glow from
a sulphurous cigar. Then another, younger gentleman
stepped out of the fog.

"Is that you, Ware? Here at Almack's? I cannot
believe it," exclaimed Nigel, the scion of the House
of Ellerby which, according to rumors, was more than
a tad dilapidated. Hence the young baron's appearance at Almack's, Leland concluded. "Dash it, I wish
I'd been in on the bet." Which propensity to gamble
likely accounted for the Ellerbys' crumbling coffers.

"Bet? What bet?"

"The one that got you to Almack's, Duke. By Zeus,

it must have been a famous wager! Who challenged you? How long must you stay before you can collect? How much—"

"There was no wager," Ware quietly inserted into the youth's enthusiastic litany.

The cigar dropped from Ellerby's fingers. His mouth fell open. "No wager? You mean . . . ?"

"I came on my own. As a favor to my aunt, if you must know."

Ellerby added two plus two and, to the duke's surprise, came up with the correct, dismaying answer. "B'gad, wait till the sharks smell fresh blood in the water." He jerked his head, weak chin and all, toward the stately portals behind them.

Leland grimaced. "Too late, they've already got the scent."

"Lud, there will be females swooning in your arms and chits falling off horses on your doorstep. I'd get out of town if I were you. Then again, word gets out you're in the market for a new bride, you won't be safe anywhere. With all those holiday house parties coming up, you'll be showered with invitations."

The duke could only agree. That was the way of the world.

"Please, Your Grace," Ellerby whined, "don't accept Lady Carstaire's invite. I'll be seated below the salt if you accept."

No slowtop either, Leland nodded toward the closed doors. "Tell me which one is Miss Carstaire, so I can sidestep the introduction."

"She's the one in puce tulle with mouse brown sausage curls and a squint." At Ware's look of disbelief, the lordling added, "And ten thousand pounds a year."

"I think I can manage not to succumb to the lady's charms," Ware commented dryly, then had to listen to the coxcomb's gratitude.

"And I'll give you fair warning, Duke. If you do

accept for any of those house parties, lock your door and never go anywhere alone. The misses and their mamas will be quicker to yell 'compromise' than you can say 'Jack Rabbit.' "

Leland gravely thanked Lord Ellerby for the advice, hoping the baron wasn't such an expert on compromising situations from trying to nab a rich wife the cad's way. Fortune-hunting was bad enough. He wished him good luck with Miss Carstaire, but declined Ellerby's suggestion that they return inside together. His Grace had had enough. And no, he assured the baron, he was not going to accept any of the holiday invitations. The Duke of Ware was going to spend Christmas right where he belonged, at Ware Hold in Warefield, Warwickshire, with his own family: one elderly aunt, two infant cousins.

Before going to bed that night, Leland had another brandy to ease the headache he already had. He sat down to write his agent in Warefield to notify the household of his plans, then he started to write to Tony's widow, inviting her to the castle. Before he got too far past the salutation, however, Crow Fanshaw's final, foxed suggestion kept echoing in his mind: The Duke of Ware should get a fair share.

ONCE UPON A CHRISTMAS

Diane Farr

The vicarage was small and shabby, and so was the girl. But when Her Grace placed an imperious finger beneath the girl's chin and tilted her face toward the light, the better to see her features, a certain something flashed in the child's expression—a look of astonished reproach—that slightly altered Her Grace's opinion. The girl met the duchess's eyes fearlessly, almost haughtily. *Just so,* thought the duchess, a faint, grim smile briefly disrupting the impassivity of her countenance. *This milk-and-water miss may be a true Delacourt after all.*

The duchess dropped her hand then, remarking idly, "You are offended by my examination. Do not be. A woman in my position must be careful. I am forever at risk of being imposed upon."

Ah, there it was again. The flash of swiftly suppressed anger, the unconscious stiffening of the spine. She had spirit, this unknown grandchild of the duke's Uncle Richard.

She spoke then. Her voice was sweet and musical. At the moment, however, it was also crisp with annoyance.

"I am sorry, Your Grace, that I must contradict you, but there is little risk of your being imposed upon by me. I have not sought you out in any way. You have come to my home, ostensibly on a visit of condolence, and asked me the most extraordinary questions—

scrutinized me as if I were some sort of insect—all but placed me under a microscope—"

Her Grace's brows lifted. "*Not* sought me out? What can you mean?"

Miss Delacourt's brows also lifted. "I mean what I say. I have not pursued your acquaintance. You came to me. How, then, can you suspect I wish to impose upon you? Forgive me, but the notion is absurd!"

The duchess gazed thoughtfully at the girl. Her confusion seemed sincere. An interesting development.

Her Grace sank, with rustling skirts, onto a nearby chair. "We have evidently been speaking at cross-purposes," she said calmly. "I received a letter, begging me to interest myself in your fate. Were you not its author?"

Miss Delacourt appeared amazed. "A letter! No. No, Your Grace, I have never written to you. I would never presume to— Good Heavens! A letter! And it begged you to—what was it? *Interest* yourself in—in—" She seemed wholly overcome; her voice faltered to a halt as she struggled to suppress her agitation.

The duchess lifted her hand, knowing that Hubbard would be anticipating her need. Sure enough, Hubbard immediately glided forward to place the letter in her mistress's palm, then noiselessly returned to her place near the door. "This is the letter I received," said Her Grace. "Someone has been busy on your behalf, it seems."

She handed the folded sheet to Miss Delacourt and observed the girl closely as she sat and spread the paper open with trembling fingers. Miss Delacourt then bent over the letter, cheating the duchess of a view of her face. Only the top of her head, crowned with a mass of dark brown curls, remained visible.

The duchess took the opportunity to look more closely at the girl's person. Although she lacked height, her figure was pleasing. Her fingers were smooth and finely tapered, the hands of a lady of quality. She kept her back straight and her ankles neatly crossed, even in an extremity of emotion. Despite the ill-fitting black dress, the cheap shawl, and the frayed ribbons on her slippers, there were marks of breeding in the girl. Given enough time, the right surroundings, the right company—and, naturally, the right wardrobe— she might yet prove adequate.

Given enough time. But how much time would be given? These days, the duchess tried not to think about time in general, and the future in particular. *Would there be enough time?* The thought was disquieting, but Her Grace had a lifelong habit of steely self-control. This rigidity of mind enabled her to banish unpleasant thoughts—a skill that was proving useful of late.

She turned her thoughts away from the fearsome future, therefore, and studied the room about her. She required information about Miss Delacourt. Obtaining it firsthand was the whole purpose of her visit. What might the vicarage tell her about its occupant?

One assumed that a person of rank would be entertained in the best room in the house. If this was the best room in the house, it spoke volumes for what the other rooms must be like. The parlor, or whatever this was, was spotless, but oppressively small and low-ceilinged. Blackened plaster over the fireplace gave mute testimony that the chimney smoked. Those old-fashioned casement windows were completely inadequate; it was growing quite dark in here as the afternoon closed in. The single candle that was burning was tallow, not wax. And the furniture! Someone had polished all the wood until it gleamed, but the duchess's sharp eyes were not deceived. All of it was old, most of it fairly worn, and several pieces were visibly scarred.

Quite a comedown for a branch of the illustrious Delacourt family! Her Grace wished for a moment that her sole surviving son could see it. It might give him pause. This, *this* is what lies in store for those who defy the head of the house and indulge themselves in foolish rebellion! Poverty and ostracism, banishment from all the elegancies of life—not only for oneself but for one's descendants. It was a lesson in filial obedience just to see the place.

But the girl's face was lifting from her perusal of the letter. It seemed to the duchess that she had turned quite pale. "Do I understand you correctly, Your Grace? You have come here in answer to this?"

"Certainly I have. Quite an affecting letter, I thought. Do not be offended by my arrival so many weeks after its date. I am sure you will understand that the assertions it contained required investigation before I permitted myself to reply in any way. In my position, I receive appeals of this nature on a regular basis. One grows quite tired of them. But this one contained the ring of truth. I thought it my duty, as a Christian and a Delacourt, to investigate—and eventually, as you see, to respond. Our connection may be distant, but it is not so distant that I could, in good conscience, ignore it. The tale related in that missive is factual, is it not?"

Miss Delacourt pressed her fingertips against her forehead, as if trying to make sense of all this by main force. "Yes. But—why did you think I sent this letter? It is written entirely in the third person."

"I assumed, naturally, that that was merely a convention on your part."

Miss Delacourt gave a shaky laugh. "Oh! Naturally. As if I had my secretary write it! You will be astonished to learn, ma'am, that I have no secretary in my employ. I suppose that must seem strange to you."

"On the contrary, I did not expect that a girl enduring the circumstances described in that letter would keep a staff of any kind." The duchess glanced fleetingly at the nondescript female who was trying to make herself invisible in the darkest corner of the room. "It is not unheard of, however, for the author of such a letter—which is, if you will pardon my frankness, nothing more than a bald appeal for charity—to phrase the message in such a way that it gives the impression it has come from a third party when it has not. The signature is quite illegible."

The girl glanced briefly back at the letter in her hand. "Yes, I suppose it is. I recognize it, however. It is Mr. Hobbi's signature." She sighed, rubbing her forehead again. "I am sure he meant well. His conscience must have pricked him when he engaged the new vicar. I don't know why it should. What else could he do? He had a duty to the parish. It was kind of him to allow me to stay so long in a house that does not belong to me."

The girl's eyes traveled around the ugly room, her expression one of naked sorrow. She even seemed to be fighting back tears. Was it possible she was mourning the loss of this insignificant little house? Her Grace devoutly hoped that Miss Delacourt did not suffer from an excess of sensibility. There were few things more tiresome than to be subjected to continual displays of sentiment, particularly the sentiments of one's inferiors. True, the child had just suffered a series of tragic misfortunes, but it was high time she recovered the tone of her mind. Her Grace did not approve of persons who unduly indulged their emotions.

The duchess was not, by nature, playful, but in an attempt to lighten Miss Delacourt's mood she offered her a thin smile. "I am glad to hear that you are accustomed to dwelling in a house that is not your own. You will not find it objectionable, I trust, to remove to another house that is not your own."

The girl did not laugh, but Her Grace did not resent Miss Delacourt's lack of comprehension. She, herself, frequently misunderstood when those around her were joking. Miss Delacourt would understand the duchess's modest jest when she saw her new home. The absurdity lay in speaking of such a drastic change for the better as *objectionable*.

The duchess rose, shaking out her cloak. "I shall send members of my personal staff to assist you in packing. You will find them most efficient. I expect, therefore, to receive you at Delacourt this Thursday week. Henceforward, you may address me as Aunt Gladys, and I shall address you as Celia. I am neither your aunt nor your great-aunt, of course; I am the wife of your father's cousin, but that is neither here nor there. The disparity in our rank renders it disrespectful for you to address me as cousin."

Silence greeted this pronouncement. The duchess glanced at Celia, her brows lifting in frosty disapproval. "Well? Have you some objection?"

Celia had automatically risen when the duchess did, but she appeared to have lost the power of speech. Her mouth worked soundlessly for a moment before she managed to say, "I'm afraid I do not understand you, Your Grace. Are you really inviting me to Delacourt? What of the bad blood that existed between— between my grandfather and his family?"

The duchess waved a hand in languid dismissal. "You need not consider that. We shall be pleased to let bygones be bygones. The present duke has no interest in prolonging the estrangement. In fact, I am told that your grandfather was quite my husband's favorite uncle before the . . . unpleasantness. Do not fear that he will object to your presence. I can promise you that he will not."

Celia flushed prettily. "Why, then, I suppose I—I have to thank you. Pray do not think me ungrateful, ma'am! I am just so surprised that I—I suppose I was taken aback for a moment. My grandfather always spoke of Delacourt with great affection, but I never thought to see it with my own eyes. Thank you! I shall look forward to my visit with pleasure."

The duchess eyed Celia for a moment, considering

whether she ought to correct the child. She decided against it. Let the girl think she was coming for a visit. Once she saw Delacourt, she would naturally be loath to leave. It would be an easy matter, once she was actually on the premises, to extend Celia an invitation to make her home there—and once she had seen Delacourt, Celia would understand the enormity of the gesture and be properly grateful.

It was extremely important that Celia be properly grateful. Nothing could be accomplished unless Celia was properly grateful. She seemed to have little understanding, at the moment, of the generosity being extended to her, nor any appreciation of Her Grace's condescension. Her Grace found this vaguely irritating, and had to remind herself that Celia's ingratitude arose from ignorance. That was easily mended. All in good time, she promised herself.

Time. There was that word again. The ghastly specter she must face, and face soon, immediately clamored for her attention. It was, again, swiftly banished. Pish-tosh! She would cross the bridge when she came to it, and not an instant before.

She bade Celia Delacourt a gracious farewell and was pleased to see the degree of deference in the girl's curtsey. She may have sprung from the black sheep of the family, and she might be ignorant of the glories in store for her, but at least she was not one of those brass-faced young women one encountered so lamentably often these days.

The nondescript female who had admitted them emerged from the shadows, showed Hubbard and the duchess to the door, and quickly effaced herself. Hubbard adjusted Her Grace's cloak and tightened the wrap round her throat. The duchess avoided Hubbard's sharp, worried eyes and placidly smoothed the creases on her gloves.

But the more devoted one's servants were, the more impossible it was to hide anything from them. As usual, Hubbard read her thoughts. "Will she do, Your Grace?" she asked gruffly.

It was a fortunate circumstance that Hubbard was so completely loyal. Her uncanny percipience would be embarrassing otherwise. The duchess smiled serenely. "Oh, I think so. She seems a trifle strong-minded, of course, but I daresay that's the Delacourt in her." Her smile faded as she voiced the unpleasant fact possessing both their minds. "She'll have to do. There's no time to find another."

When Celia heard the door closing behind her visitors, she let her breath go in a whooshing sigh of relief and collapsed nervelessly onto the settee. "What a terrifying woman!" she exclaimed. "Why do you suppose she asked me all those impertinent questions? My heart is hammering as if I have just run a race."

Elizabeth Floyd emerged from the shadows to flick the curtain aside. "Be careful, my dear!" she urged in an agitated whisper. "They have not yet gone."

Celia rolled her eyes. "Well, what of that? Even if she could hear me, which I sincerely doubt, I cannot picture the duchess unbending far enough to come back and ring a peal over me."

"I can," asserted Mrs. Floyd nervously. "There! The coach is moving off, and we may be easy. Well! I don't know what she meant by putting you through such a catechism, but it seems you passed the test. Oh, my dear little Celia! What an astonishing stroke of good fortune for you! At last!"

Celia did not move from her collapsed position on the settee, but turned her head far enough to peer at her former governess with a skeptical eye. "Are you serious, Liz?"

Mrs. Floyd's round eyes grew rounder. "Quite, quite serious! Why, how could I not be? I think it amazing, and really quite affecting, that you should come to such a delightful end after all your travails."

"I am not sure this is any sort of end, let alone a delightful one," Celia pointed out. "I own, it will be interesting to visit Delacourt—which I never expected to see—but do not forget that the duchess is in residence there! How am I to face her on a daily basis? I hope she does not mean to pepper me with personal questions every time we meet, for I am likely to say something rude to her if she does." Indignation kindled in Celia's brown eyes and she suddenly sat upright again. "How dared she question me on my religious beliefs? As if Papa might have neglected his duties! And why do you suppose she wanted to know my medical history? I almost offered to let her examine my head for lice. Do you think that would have satisfied her?"

"Oh, dear. Oh, dearie dear. I am so glad you did not. Think how affronted she would have been!"

"Yes, but what was her *purpose*? I don't believe she was worried about . . . what happened to my family. Nothing contagious was responsible for—"

Mrs. Floyd interrupted quickly when she heard the catch in Celia's voice. "No, certainly not. Not a contagion at all. No question of that. Very odd of her, very odd, indeed! But many people are nervous about illness, you know. I daresay she wished to feel quite, quite sure that you would not communicate some dread disease to her household. Smallpox, or typhus, or something of that nature."

"Well, I like that! Of all the—"

"Now, Celia, *pray*! You should be blessing your good fortune, and instead you are looking a gift horse in the mouth! She has invited you to Delacourt—*Delacourt*, my dear! Nothing could be more exciting. I declare, I am in transports! You shall have a family again, for they *are* your very own relatives, however grand and strange they may be. And you shall be surrounded by luxury—which I'm sure is no more than you deserve—and *I* shall be able to go home for

Christmas, something I had not thought possible a quarter of an hour ago. Oh, I am so happy!" She whipped a handkerchief from her sleeve and dabbed briskly at her eyes.

Celia saw that her old friend was really beaming with joy. "Oh, Liz, what a wretched friend I have been to you!" she exclaimed remorsefully. "I have been so taken up with my own troubles, I never gave a thought to yours. Of course you would rather be home for Christmas than cooped up here, bearing me company for propriety's sake."

"For friendship's sake," said Mrs. Floyd firmly, perching her plump form on a nearby chair. "I have not begrudged a single moment of my time here, and well you know it. Why, Celia, you are like a daughter to me! I would no more think of abandoning you than—than anything."

The cap on the little governess's head fairly quivered with indignation. Celia smiled affectionately at her. "Even friendship has its boundaries, however. Am I to keep you from your family forever? You ought to have told me you wanted to go home for Christmas."

"I will be glad to go home, there is no denying it, but my brother's wife takes better care of him than ever I can, and I am only Aunt Liz there. Had you needed me for another month or so, they could easily have spared me. But, my dear, now that the crisis is past, I do not hesitate to tell you how worried I have been—for I was at my wit's end to imagine what would become of you when the new vicar arrives. I could not offer you a place with me, since I do not have a home of my own. There was no possibility of the new vicar being able to spare you a room, with such a large family as he has. And only think how difficult it would be to see another family move into the house where you have lived all your life—the house where you were born! After everything else you have been through, I feared for you, my dear, I really did. How unfortunate, that both your mother and your father had no siblings! With no aunts, no uncles, no cousins—where were you to go?"

Celia tried to smile but failed. "I suppose I would have found myself thrown on the parish. Although I do have four hundred pounds safely invested in the Funds, which will bring me the princely sum of—what is it?—about twelve pounds per annum, I think. And I might double that income if I hire myself out as a scullery maid."

Mrs. Floyd shuddered. "Do not even jest about such a thing. I have been so anxious! And when we received that message from the duchess informing you that she intended to pay you a visit, I was thrown into such a fever of hope it was almost worse than the fear! And then she asked you so many questions, just as if you were being interviewed for a position of some sort, which struck me as so very—but now everything is settled, and quite comfortably. Celia, I congratulate you!"

Celia frowned. "Settled? Surely you do not think that dragon of a female means to offer me permanent residence at Delacourt?"

Mrs. Floyd nodded vigorously. "Oh, yes! Yes, indeed! That is what I understood her to say. Did not you?"

"Certainly not! What an idea! After all—why should she? Her Grace did not strike me as the benevolent sort. In fact, I thought her the coldest fish ever I met."

"Well, she is, perhaps, a little high in the instep—"

"High in the instep! That woman has held her nose in the air for so many years, it's my belief she can no longer bend at the waist."

Mrs. Floyd fluttered agitatedly. "Celia, *really*! You mustn't be disrespectful. After all, she *is* a duchess. It would be wonderful if she did *not* acquire a great opinion of her own importance, the way everyone round her must bow and scrape. Such a handsome woman, too! I daresay she is accustomed to an extraordinary degree of deference."

Celia's eyes sparkled dangerously, and Mrs. Floyd hurried to forestall whatever remark her former charge was about to make. "Do not forget she is your aunt! Or something like it. And she will be showing you a great kindness."

"Aunt." Celia shivered dramatically. "I shall never be able to address her as 'Aunt Gladys,' try as I might."

"Oh, pooh. I daresay she is perfectly amiable when one comes to know her. And they do say blood is thicker than water."

Celia chuckled. "Yes, they do, but she's no more related to me than you are. She simply married my father's cousin—whom he never met, by the by! The old duke booted my grandfather out of the house without a farthing, cut him out of his will, and never spoke to him again after he married my grandmother. We never encountered anyone from that branch of the family, and never cared to. And now I know why! If that stiff-rumped Tartar is the present duke's choice for his life's companion, only think what *he* must be like! After a se'nnight in their house, I daresay it will be a relief to hire myself out as a scullery maid."

"I wish you would not talk in that flippant way, my dear, about matters that are quite, quite serious! And besides, Delacourt is not a house," said Mrs. Floyd severely. "I would own myself astonished if you encountered the duchess above once a month in that great sprawl of a place. Apart from dinner, that is."

"Gracious. Will it be so very splendid, do you think?"

"My dear Celia—! Delacourt is *famous*!"

"I suppose it is." Celia rubbed her cheek tiredly. "In that case, I've nothing suitable to wear. It is a bit much, I think, to have to take something so trivial into consideration just now."

Mrs. Floyd reached out and patted her young friend's knee consolingly. "Depend upon it, my dear, they will understand that you are in mourning."

"They will have to," said Celia defiantly, "for even if I had the inclination to purchase a new wardrobe right now, I haven't the funds." Her eyes widened in alarm as another thought struck. "What about Christmas? I hope I am not expected to arrive bearing gifts for a houseful of persons I have never met. And I cannot afford anything remotely fine enough!"

"Oh, they don't keep Christmas in the great houses the way we humbler folk do. A pity, I always thought— as if Christmas could go out of fashion! But that's what one hears."

"Yes, but we don't *know*. The way my luck has been running, I shall arrive to find every room decked with holly and mistletoe, and discover that I must give expensive presents to all my unknown relatives—and their servants! Well, that's that. The instant I step through the door I shall tell the duchess that I have other plans for the holidays."

Mrs. Floyd looked uneasy. "But you don't, my dear. They will think it odd when Christmas approaches and no one sends a carriage for you."

"Perhaps they will offer me the use of one. They doubtless have a dozen."

"How will that mend matters? You will have to direct the coachman to take you somewhere. Where will you go?"

Celia bit her lip. "I think I feel an attack of influenza coming on," she said mendaciously, pressing a hand to her forehead and falling back on the sofa cushions. "What a pity! I fear I shall not be able to visit Delacourt until the second week of January. At the earliest."

Mrs. Floyd's face fell. "Well, of course, you *could*

plead illness," she admitted. "And Mr. Hobbi has promised us a goose," she added valiantly, "so I'm sure we will have a very merry Christmas here at the vicarage, just the two of us."

Celia's conscience immediately pricked her. She sat up. "No, no, I was only funning," she said hastily, and forced a smile. "The duchess is expecting me next Thursday week, and Thursday week it shall be. I would not dare to gainsay her."

Mrs. Floyd's relief was palpable. She immediately brightened and began chattering of her nieces and nephews, and how pleasant it would be to give them their little gifts in person rather than sending them through the post, and how there had never been a figgy pudding to equal the figgy pudding her sister-in-law made every year.

Listening to her, Celia felt ashamed. Her grief had made her selfish. It hurt to see how much her friend was looking forward to leaving her. But it was only natural, after all. Anyone who had a home would want to be home for Christmas.

Celia had not given Christmas a thought. Now she realized that she simply had not wanted to think about Christmas, any more than she had wanted to think about Mrs. Floyd leaving. Both thoughts gave her a painful, even panicky, sensation. But she would make an effort to hide that. She owed it to her friend, to let her leave for home with a happy heart, untroubled by the notion that Celia still needed her.

But she did. Oh, she did indeed.

Mrs. Floyd was the last person left alive whom Celia loved. The thought of Liz going back to Wiltshire and leaving her alone, completely and utterly alone, filled Celia with a blind and brainless terror.

It was useless to tell herself how silly she was being. She knew there was no logical reason to fear that Liz, too, would die if she let her out of her sight. But logic had no power over the formless dread, monstrous and paralyzing, that seized her every time Mrs. Floyd left the room. Since the first week of September she had been all but glued to Liz's side, following her about like a baby chick. How would she feel when Liz left the county? Could she smile and wave her handkerchief as the coach bore her only friend away? Or would she make a spectacle of herself, weeping and screaming like a child?

This surely was going to be the worst Christmas of her life.

SUGARPLUM SURPRISES

Elisabeth Fairchild

Bath, 1819

Fanny Fowler, an accredited beauty, one of Bath's *bon ton,* slated to be the most feted bride of the Christmas Season, was not in her best looks when she burst through the door of Madame Nicolette's millinery shop, on a very wet December afternoon right before closing. The violent jingle of the bell drew the attention of everyone present. And yet, so red and puffy were Fanny's eyes, so mottled her fair complexion, so rain-soaked her golden tresses, she was almost unrecognizable.

"Madame Nicolette!" she gasped, noble chin wobbling, sylvan voice uneven. Bloodshot blue eyes streamed tears that sparkled upon swollen cheeks almost as much as the raindrops that trickled from her guinea gold hair. "It is all over. Finished."

Madame Nicolette's elaborate lace-edged mobcap tipped at an angle, along with Madame's head. The heavily rouged spots on her heavily powdered cheeks added unusual emphasis to the puzzled purse of her mouth. She spoke in hasty French to her assistant, Marie, shooing her, and the only customer in the shop, into the dressing room.

Then, clasping the trembling hand of this, her best customer, she led her to a quiet corner, near the plate glass window that overlooked the busy, weather-drenched corner of Milsom and Green Streets.

"Fini, cheri?" she asked gently, taking in the looming impression of the Fowler coach waiting without, the horses sleek with rain, their harness decked with jingling bells to celebrate the season. Gay Christmas ribbon tied to the coach lamps danced in the wind.

"The wedding is canceled!" Fanny wailed, no attempt made to lower her voice. "He has jilted me. Says that nothing could induce him to marry me now. Ever."

The distraught young woman fell upon the matronly shoulder, weeping copiously. Madame Nicolette, green eyes widening in alarm, patted the girl's back. *"Vraiment!* The cad. *Abominable* behavior. Why should he do this?"

"Because I told the truth when I could have lied." Fanny gazed past Madame with a sudden look of fury. "I should have lied. Might so easily have lied. Any other female would have lied."

She burst into tears again, and wept without interruption, face buried in the handkerchief in her hands, shoulders heaving.

Madame offered up her own handkerchief, for Fanny's was completely sodden. "What of the *trousseau*?" Madame asked, for of course this was the matter that concerned her most.

Fanny wept the harder, which brought a look of concern to Madame's eyes, far greater than that generated by all previous tears.

"Papa . . ." Fanny choked out. "Papa is in an awful temper. He refuses to p-p-pay." This last bit came out in a most dreadful wail, and while Madame continued to croon comfortingly and pat the young woman's back, her lips thinned, and her brows settled in a grim line.

"And your *fiancé*? Surely he will *defray* expenses."

"Perhaps." Fanny made every effort to collect herself. "I do not know," she said with a sniff. "All I know is that he intends to leave Bath tomorrow morning. Now, I must go. Papa waits."

"Allow me to escort you to the coach." Madame solicitously followed her to the door.

"But it is raining." Fanny wielded both sodden handkerchiefs in limp protest. "And Papa is in such a mood."

Madame insisted, and so the two women ran together to the coach, under cover of Madame's large black umbrella, and Madame greeted Lord Fowler, his wife, and younger daughter standing beneath her dripping shield just outside the fulsome gutter. "An infamous turn of events," she called to them.

"Blasted nuisance," my lord shouted from the coach. "Frippery female has gone and lost herself a duke, do you hear!"

"Fourth Duke of Chandrose, and Fourth Marquess of Carnevon." Lady Fowler's voice could barely be heard above the pelter of the rain that soaked Madame's hem, but as the door was swung wider to allow Fanny entrance, her voice came clearer. "A fortune slips through her fingers."

"Silly chit," her father shouted as Fanny climbed in, cringing. "I credited you with far too much sense."

Fanny's sister kept her head bowed, her eyes darting in a frightened manner from parent to parent.

Fanny resorted to her handkerchief as she plopped down into her seat.

"Do you know what she has done to alienate him?" Lord Fowler demanded of Madame Nicolette as if she should know, as if he were the only one in Bath who was not privy to his daughter's thinking.

Madame shook her head, and gave a very French shrug as she leaned into the doorway of the coach. "My dear *monsieur, madam,* I sympathize most completely in this trying *moment,* and while I understand you have no wish to pay for the *trousseau* that has taken six months' work to assemble, the *trousseau* Miss Fanny will not be wearing, I wonder, will you be so good—"

Lord Fowler sat forward abruptly, chest thrust forth, shaking his walking stick at her with ferocity, the sway of his jowls echoing the movement. "Not a penny will I spend on this stupid girl. Not one penny, do you hear? More than a hundred thousand pounds a year she might have had with His Grace. Not a farthing's worth shall she have now." Like a Christmas turkey he looked, his face gone very red, his eyes bulging, his extra set of chins wobbling.

"I comprehend your ire, my lord," Madame persisted calmly. "But surely you intend to offer some compensation for my efforts, my material?"

His lordship's face took on a plum pudding hue. "Not a single grote. Do you understand? Not one. Make the duke pay." He thumped the silver head of his cane against the ceiling, the whole coach shaking. "Jilting my daughter." Thump. "Disgracing the family name." Thump. "Two weeks before the wedding, mind you." Thump-thump. "Bloody cheek."

With that, he thumped his cane so briskly it broke clean through the leather top so that rain leaked in upon his head, and in a strangled voice, the veins at his temples bulging, he ordered his coachman, "Drive on, damn you. Drive on. Can you not hear me thumping down here?"

The horses leapt into motion with an inappropriately cheerful jingle, and Madame Nicolette Fieullet leapt back from the wheels.

"Fiddlesticks," she muttered in very English annoyance as the coach churned up dirty water from the gutter in a hem-drenching wave. She took shelter in the shop's doorway to shake the rain from her umbrella.

The wreath on the door seemed suddenly too merry, the jingle of the door's bell a mockery. *Christmas.*

Dear Lord. Christmas meant balls and assemblies, and dresses ordered at the last minute, and she must have fabric and lace and trim at the ready. But how was she to pay for Christmas supplies now that so much of her capital was tied up in Fanny's *trousseau*?

"*Madame!* You are soaked," her assistant, Marie, cried out as she entered.

"*Oui. Je suis tout trempe.*" Madame kept her skirt high, that she might not drip, her voice low, that their customer might not hear. "You will give Mrs. Bower my excuses while I change?"

Marie followed her, a worried look in her deep brown eyes. "Is it true, Madame? He refuses to pay?"

"*Oui.*"

"*Mon dieu!* The material arrives tomorrow. However will we pay?"

"I shall think of something. Do not torment yourself." Madame sounded confident. She looked completely self-assured, until she locked herself in the back room, pressed her back to the door, and sinking to the floor, wept piteously at the sight of Fanny's finished dresses.

More than a dozen beautiful garments had been made up to Miss Fowler's specific measurements, in peacock colors to flatter Fanny's sky blue eyes and guinea gold hair. Thousands of careful stitches, hundreds of careful cuts, and darts. How many times had she pricked her fingers in the making of them? How many times had she ripped seams that they might fit Fanny's form more perfectly? It was heartbreaking just to look at them. Tears burned in Madame's eyes. Her breath caught in her throat.

The masterpieces were, of course, the wedding dress, and two ball gowns, one in the colors of Christmas, an evergreen satin bodice, vandyke trimmed in gold satin cord, Spanish slashed sleeves that had taken several days to sew, a deeply gored skirt of deeper green velvet, with a magnificent border of gold quilling, and twisted rolls of satin cord that had taken weeks' worth of stitching.

"Fanny must have something entirely unique," her mother had insisted, "something worthy of a duchess."

The results were exquisite. Madame's best work yet. They were the sort of dresses every young woman dreamed of. Head-turning dresses, and yet in the best of taste, the perfect foil for youth and beauty. They were the sort of dresses she had once worn herself in her younger days. Gowns to catch a man's eye without raising a mother's eyebrows. Gowns to lift a young woman's spirits and self-esteem as she donned them. She had hoped these dresses would be the making of her name, of her reputation.

Now they were worthless, completely worthless. Indeed, a terrible drain upon her purse.

Defeat weighed heavy upon Madame's shoulders. Tears burned in her eyes. Sobs pressed hard against her chest, her gut, the back of her throat. What to do? Panic rose, intensifying her feelings of anger and regret.

She had believed the future secure, the holiday fruitful, her worries behind her at last.

But no! Life surprised her most mean-spiritedly, at Christmastime, always at Christmastime.

The tears would not remain confined to her eyes. It had been long since she had allowed them to fall. They broke forth now in an unstoppable deluge.

She clutched her hand over her mouth, stifling her sobs, choking on them. But they would not be stopped. Disappointment surged from the innermost depths of her in a knee-weakening wave. She was a child again, unable to contain her emotions. She thought of her mother, lying pale and wan in her bed, the familiar swell of her stomach deflated, the strength of her voice almost gone.

"My dear Jane," mother had whispered, cupping

the crown of Jane's head, stroking the silk of her hair. She could still feel the weight of that hand, the heat. "I had thought to bring you a baby brother for Chr-Christmas." Her mother's voice had caught, trembled. She had given Jane's hand a weak squeeze, her hand hot, so very hot. "But, life never unfolds as one expects, pet."

Jane had been frightened by her mother's tone, by the strangled noises of distress her father made from the doorway. She had not understood it was the last time she would have to speak to Mama. She had patted the feverish hand, then held it to her cheek and said, "Do not cry, Mother. If you have lost my little brother, Papa will buy you another for Christmas. Won't you, Papa?"

Her father had made choking noises and stumbled from the room.

"Jane!" Miss Godwin, her governess, had sounded cross as she snatched her up from the side of the bed.

But Jane had clung to her mother's fingers, the strength of her grasp lifting her mother's arm from the bed. Something was wrong, terribly wrong.

Her mother's clasp was as desperate as hers. "Cherish what is, my pet, not what you imagined," she said, the words urgent, the look in her eyes unforgettable. And as Miss Godwin had gently pried their hands apart, she had said with an even greater urgency, "Promise me, Jane, my love. Promise me you will not allow regret to swallow you whole."

Jane had nodded, not knowing what she promised, looking back over Miss Godwin's shoulder with a five-year-old's conviction, no comprehension of the words. Promising was easy. Honoring that promise was not.

"Look for the silver surprises, my love, in the plum pudding at Christmas, and know that I put them there for you." Her mother's words were almost drowned out by the muffled desperation of her father's cries.

He sat, bent over in the dressing room, a balled hand-kerchief stuffed in his mouth. His shoulders had shaken in a manner she had never before witnessed.

"Is Papa all right?" she had asked Miss Godwin, all concern.

Miss Godwin had made comforting noises and carried little Jane off to bed, her own cheeks wet with silent tears, her shoulders shaking like Papa's, as hard as Jane Nichol's shook now as she rocked back and forth, her fist pressed to her mouth.

The wet hem of her skirt had soaked her petticoats. Her legs were cold.

"Oh, Mother," she whispered as she stood to wring out the wet. "What silver surprise am I missing? 'Tis all soggy pudding, this."

The rack of clothes mocked her silently. They were dry, and perfect, a reminder of her past in so many ways, and yet she must remember they promised to throw her carefully constructed present into chaos.

Jane turned to the old mirror that had been tucked into the corner behind the door. Clouded at the edges, it had been removed from the dressing room, replaced by a newer, less timeworn cheval. The buxom, brightly dressed woman that stared back was still a stranger to her, not the picture of herself she carried in her head. Her frizzled brown wig was even more frizzled from exposure to the rain. Her oval spectacles were speckled with raindrops. The careful veneer of face powder and rouge was much besmeared by her tears.

Jane had to laugh, a tragic, pitiful gust of a laugh, as she took off the horn-rimmed spectacles that so completely dominated her face, and wiped at the streaked powder with the damp sleeve of her gown, exposing smooth, youthful flesh, complexion quite at odds with the sad horsehair wig and matronly mobcap.

A sight—a proper sight she was. She could not face customers looking like this. She needed a fresh powdering—dry clothes.

The wedding dress caught her eye, the ball gowns and walking dresses, morning and evening gowns, the capes, and pelisses, and negligees. Dry clothes. Beautiful dry clothes, so beautiful any young lady would be tempted to wear them.

The silver surprise of it made her smile as laughter filled her chest and shook the weight from her shoulders.

She rose to examine her choices with a devil-may-care tilt to her head, a daring idea taking hold—a silver surprise of an idea. She laughed again, and fingered the fall of satin flowers at the sleeve of the second ball gown.

A light rap came at the door, and Marie called out, "Madame, Mrs. Bower has gone. Shall I lock up?"

"*S'il vous plait.* Do not wait for me, Marie. I have a bit of work to do." Jane fell into the French accent she affected without blinking, without thinking. It came so naturally now, the pretense.

Time to stop pretending, if only for an evening. What a relief it would be. What a joy.

She needed joy. It was a Season of joy, was it not?

She peeled off the dreadful wig and undid the ties on her dress. The false bosom fell away, the padded hips. She felt lighter, smaller—herself again. A different silhouette looked back at her from the mirror—a tear-streaked face, and swollen eyes. She ruffled her fingers through flattened flaxen tresses, exhaled heavily, and straightened her back with a rising sense of resolution.

Lord Fowler had left her with good advice if nothing else. His words still rang in her ears.

"The duke must pay!"

And so he must. It was a necessary solution. She needed the money desperately, and she would not allow His Grace to leave Bath before he had given it to her.